Oni

– ANTHONY BEGBIE –

FASTPRINT PUBLISHING
PETERBOROUGH, ENGLAND

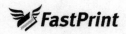

www.fast-print.net/store.php

ONI
Copyright © Anthony Begbie 2011

ISBN 978-184426-979-2

First published 2011 by
FASTPRINT PUBLISHING
Peterborough, England.

An environmentally friendly book printed and bound in England
by www.printondemand-worldwide.com

Mixed Sources
Product group from well-managed
forests, and other controlled sources
www.fsc.org Cert no. TT-COC-002641
© 1996 Forest Stewardship Council

PEFC Certified
This product is
from sustainably
managed forests
and controlled
sources
www.pefc.org
PEFC/16-33-415

This book is made entirely of chain-of-custody materials

Foreword – About the Author and Oni

This is the part where I need to tell you a little about myself and the book that you have lovingly bought for your personal entertainment. I'm not one for introductions or lengthy speeches so I'll try and keep this as short and sweet as possible.

Firstly, a little about myself. I was born in Hereford, UK to my dad who was a factory worker and my mum who was a housewife. My parents split up when I was just a baby (some could say that this was the early signs of a 'home-wrecker' but I beg to differ) and I was brought up solely by my dad with little to no contact from my mum. Although some may say that this was a disadvantage, I wouldn't agree as many fine people have come out alright despite similar circumstances.

Through my school years I emerged to be fairly academic across a broad range of subjects though I did tend to slack off slightly in my college years in pursuit of 'other interests'. Throughout these early years though, there were a couple of things that did bring themselves to light. I discovered I had a love for the Orient and the Far East, mainly anything that was linked with Japan. I loved the history, the culture, the cuisine and the philosophy that comes from the numerous and great cultures. I pursued my interests into these topics through many hours of personal study.

This then provided the entry into the Martial Arts and my secondary love for combat related sports of all descriptions and origins. At the age of seven I took up Karate, taking lessons at my local sports centre and from that moment on I was hooked! I received my junior black belt at the age of eleven and my first adult black belt at fifteen. Currently, at the time of publishing, I am at Sandan level (3rd Degree black belt) which I received from Master Yamada, head of the World Shukokai Union and I help teach at my Instructor's dojo's in and around the Herefordshire area.

Along the way I have had the fortune to be able to follow the sporting side of Karate and have competed in tournaments not only on the domestic circuit but on an international scale; representing my association at country level successfully in more foreign afield such as Australia and Japan.

When the concept of Oni first came to me I saw the entire project as a bit of a challenge. I was faced with an idea that came to me during a not so adventurous night out when I was in a 'quiet' nightclub back home, with not much background or experience into anything that would resemble writing in some length. Up to this moment I had written some short stories and a spot of poetry that I never would've dreamed about putting out into the public domain as they were just too personal to me. In the past, anything that I could consider as the early 'beginnings' of a full scale novel I had simply scrapped as they didn't meet my own personal standards or was perhaps on a subject matter that either didn't capture my full interest or was not covered extensively by my own personal repertoire of knowledge.

So what possessed me write Oni? Firstly, it was to see if I could accomplish it; for I am a great believer in the notion that every person out there has a novel buried somewhere in them. Secondly, I was going through an extremely difficult patch of my life during the writing stage that many people out there have also had the unfortunate displeasure of being faced with. I was suffering from extreme depression of the monetary fashion with lack of work accompanied with all the hardships and turmoil that come along with this. At the same time, I lost someone who I cared for very much and what made it worse was that it was mostly my own fault. With all the factors culminating together I was left in a bit of a rut when it came to life and if I didn't have as strong a character as what I have, I believe that I wouldn't have been able to muster the mental strength to fight through it.

So what did I do to see me through and pull me out of the downward spiral that I was heading in? I put all of my focus and energy into my writing to block out all the negatives that were bombarding me and when I put my mind into something it has the tendency to become more of an obsession. This I enjoyed and was a more preferable option than the worries that were waiting. I wrote solidly and paid little attention to anything else, drawing my influences from my study of my earlier years into everything that was Japanese. Oni and the sequel novels to come are the result.

For the reader, who may not have much prior knowledge in the ways of the Japanese, I will attempt to try and provide you here an insight prior to your continuation of this story.

The Japanese culture is almost unlike anything that you find in the Western world and so may appear quite strange to a Western reader. The Japanese are traditionally a warrior race, much like the Romans, Spartans or Mongols. Japan having perhaps the most conflict and war throughout history with little in the form of rests of peace dotted along the way. It is from this continual revolution of war and peace whereby the warrior class that we commonly recognise as the samurai, developed some of the most comprehensive and effective combative systems (that we refer to as Martial Arts).

The samurai are not warlords or mere 'soldiers' as is the common misconception amongst the West, more so, they are combative servants of the Lord that they served. The name samurai simply means 'to serve' but do not think of them as 'slaves'. Each samurai swears their life to their master and follows a code of warrior honour (Bushido) that ties their life in with the life of their Lord and governs the way that they act in society. There is such strength in this honour bond that if a samurai were to fail their Lord disastrously or if there is some questionability regarding their loyalty then they can be asked to commit seppuku. Sometimes even mere words, if damning enough, could condemn a man to conduct the ritual. Seppuku (also referred to as Hari Kiri) was the ritualistic suicide whereby the individual would disembowel themselves with their short sword or knife and before they would bleed to death a secondary would then slice off their head at the neck as the condemned began to fall upon the blade of their short sword. This may sound very gruesome and unnecessary in our eyes but for a samurai, a death by seppuku was just as honourable as a death on the battlefield. Such was the honour that was entailed in such a death that even the witnesses would find watching such a spectacle to be an awe enthralled sight and would feel quite humbled. There was nothing worse for a samurai than to receive death by some dishonourable means as it was seen that their soul would pass on into a world of purgatory (like the concept of hell in Western society).

Although the days of the sword wielding samurai are long gone, there are still aspects of this time that still remain vigilant in Japanese society. The notion of respect (sonkei) and etiquette (reishiki) are still as paramount now as they were back then. If you go to Japan and speak to a local you will find them to be very polite and respectful which is a quality that is unfortunately not so strong in Western society. You will also find that when a Japanese commit themselves to a task or the development of whatever they are doing then they present a display of discipline that is likened to a martial way.

When reading this story, do not think that everything about Japanese culture and mannerism are entailed here. This should be regarded more along the lines as an introduction so that you can research yourselves and I hope, are able to embrace yourself in the magic and wonders that the Japanese culture can teach; like I have discovered.

I also hope that Oni is able to inspire its readers, no matter what age or nationality, to look into the martial arts. The martial arts are a wonderful thing and if you are able to find a strong, reputable club to join, they are able to instil numerous benefits to the practitioner. The qualities of respect, discipline and teamwork are but a handful of benefits that a regular practitioner can receive through diligent study of the martial arts. I truly believe that if it wasn't for all the years I had in the martial arts and the good, life-long friends that I have met along the way that I would've stayed stuck in that endless rut. So you could say that this work is a homage to the martial arts and all the glorious challenges that they present.

When looking at Oni, to sum it up, it is a euphemism of the struggle of my own personal demons and my fight to overcome them.

So all that is left to say is that I hope that you enjoy this read and if you have your own personal demons to overcome then I hope that this is able to inspire you to take the first steps in order to do so.

Special Acknowledgments

In life, there are many good people that help you when you have to walk down its long and often difficult path. Sometimes, these people are often not acknowledged as well as they should by those they assist and their efforts are often overshadowed by other things that clouds an individuals mind.

It is these special people, of which everyone has their own, that you must sometimes step back from the world and take a moment to fully appreciate everything that they have done for you.

For it is these people who are the ones that contribute to moulding an individual into who they are and without them, sometimes even someone who is considered by everyone to be as solid as a mountain, can easily be broken down and washed away by the bombarding tide that life produces.

I would like to take a moment to thank the following people:

Sensei Paul Jones *4th Dan Shushokan Karate*
Sensei Louise Vaughan *3rd Dan Shushokan Karate*
Sensei Tom Beardsley *7th Dan Samurai Karate*

Thank you for your trusted guidance and support over the years both on and off the dojo floor. It is yourselves that in one way or another have helped shape me into the man that I am today.

I would also like to thank,

**All of my friends and family
In particular, my Dad**

Thank you for allowing me to become centred again when my world had become shattered by tragedy and turmoil.

"In a world of grief and pain, flowers bloom, even then"
- Issa

Oni

Chapter 1 – Training

*T*he sun beat down harshly on that memorable day, that day when a stranger visited and challenged the dojo. As I recall the blast of the summer heat was intense and the air was drier than it usually was as we worked out our swordplay in the time old manner, undeterred by the less than normal conditions that surrounded us. After all, we were Samurai and practitioners of Budo, the warrior way; our bodies were conditioned and strong as were our minds of steel. At least, that was the case in the senior students, the majority of the juniors who were fairly new and a little 'softer' did struggle slightly but most, I was glad to say, had the raw and undeniable spirit of a warrior to continue regardless of the harsh setting.

That day, two of the novice students had already collapsed through the intense heat and were being tended to in the corner of the dojo by a couple of the numerous servants of the house. They were unable to leave the dojo floor until classes had finished, this was one the rules of the dojo. They were deemed to not be critically hampered or inflicted enough to warrant being removed from their daily training ritual and once they had recovered they were expected to resume training.

Our dojo in Kakogawa on the edge of the Hyogo prefecture was the primary source of effective swordsmanship within the local area and has produced in its glorious history a long lineage of overly competent swordsmen. Some of which had achieved great fame known throughout the land, through many feats of daring combat and personal displays of their talents with the sword. Such is the quality of our system that our dojo had been elevated to the position of providing its skills to the members of the local Daimyo lord and his personal guard. The fief of our dojo was estimated to around five hundred koku, which was a highly respectable comparative figure of the time. At present it provided accommodation to around thirty or so full time students and around ten servants who tended to the daily running and maintenance of the dojo and its respective attached house.

The air hummed with the melodic and near hypnotic sound of cicadas as they played out their haunting song of high pitched clicks and whirrs. An insect orchestra that was crudely interjected with the hollow clashing of our bokken and the erratic thumping of our bare feet upon the hard wooden floor as we moved. It were as though we were trying to harmonise with their song but was failing easily.

The West wall of the dojo was filled with regimented sword racks filled by the swords of its students. Most were fairly plain, regular battlefield swords. These were owned by the novice students who had not yet shown the right levels of both skill or character attributes to warrant the commission of a highly prized sword made by the local master sword smith.

However, amongst the senior swords, that were positioned to the left hand side of the sword racks were a few weapons that were made by some of the finest sword smiths in all of Japan and were decorated as such to represent this fact; featuring intricately lacquered scabbards, fancy silk saya cords and intricately carved tsuba hand guards. They were not only beautiful pieces of art but were also extremely dangerous masterpieces with their razor sharp, curved edge having the ability to slice through limbs or even a thick torso in the hands of their skilled owners. Fatally beautiful works of art that the unlucky victim would only have the singular opportunity to experience their deadly craftsmanship and highly prized by their owners and almost coveted by men of lesser character.

Sensei Imamoto knelt at shomen, the front of the dojo, upon a raised section of the dojo floor where he had full observation of the proceedings going on in front of him. Sensei Imamoto was reaching his late eighties which was a very good age for any Japanese of this time, especially one who had seen as many instances of combat and war as he has.

His face was wrought with numerous wrinkles that came with his age, produced by years of studious hardship and near brutal training. He was master of the Imamoto style and head of the household, know also as Kaicho. His word was law within the walls of the grounds and even the simplest of tasks that came from his lips were met with the complete obedience of any of his followers who heard them; and all who heard them would be willing to lay down their lives if necessary to ensure that his will be done.

Although he was resplendent in his owagi and pure white hakama, his family crest emblazoned proudly upon his chest; his age gave an appearance of a man who was beyond effectiveness in battle and one would expect him to become slowed with the passing of time.

However, Sensei had a nasty habit of providing a false image of himself which allowed him an edge that he always exploited to its fullest extent.

Looking across at Sensei who sat so peacefully; tranquil and observant as if he were merely a statue of wind-weathered stone, it reminded me of the unwritten rite of passage that all new initiates must face when they are granted permission to join the school. A prime example of this method of deception that he has mastered.

Within the gardens of the house, there is a small cedar tree within an enclosed area of luscious grass that provides good shade when the sun is out in full force. On the hotter days, Sensei would take the time to relax and sleep in its cool shade; leaving his sword free beside him.

New initiates to the school would be goaded, mostly by the seniors, who would often wait around to revel in the hilarious spectacle that would arise from it; were made to try and steal the master's sword as he lay asleep. Over the years some would try to boldly walk up and take it, others would try to creep as silently as possible. There were some that would try to approach from behind the tree itself. Everyone who had tried had failed.

My own attempt at this was no more successful than those who had gone before me. Though I have been told that I was in fact one of the closest to actually achieving the prize of the sword. Upon creeping as silently as I could over the grass I was able to place myself in a position whereby I could grab the sword. I slowly reached down and as I touched the sheath with my fingertips, the master opened his eyes, grabbed and locked my arm before slamming me, head first, into the cedar tree behind him, knocking me unconscious.

I remember how I awoke minutes later to the sounds of my seniors laughing heartily as they helped me to my feet after my misfortunate attempt and the master was gone. All I could remember of the encounter was the surprising speed and fluidity of movement that Sensei demonstrated as he was able to move from total inertia to combative speed with impossible ease.

It can be seen as to be a strange ritual and its origins are shrouded with mystery and much confusion. The common explanation is that it came about from the Master in his youth, when he was a mere junior under the tutelage of his sensei. It is said that he had with him a highly coveted sword by his peers, a sword that was his own family sword, passed down through the generations. It's said that one of his peers tried to steal this sword for whatever reason, be it because of his desire to have it or perhaps simply in jest. With a similar situation as the ritual of today, the foolish thief met with a similar punishment and this is whereby the ritual received its origins. At least, that's what some would say.

Times have now changed, I have grown to become the senior now goading the unwary novices. Shihan of the dojo, outranked only by Sensei himself and Dai

Shihan Ryoko who was both a personal mentor and perhaps my closest friend. My predecessors from my initiation have practically all vanished through time, dispatched by whatever means over the years be it in battle, a terrible disease or just the timely passing of age. But the master is still breathing and still silently enjoying the unwritten ritual.

"Yamae!" called Sensei, the clashing sounds stopped abruptly and all eyes on the dojo turned to Sensei, in autonomous anticipation of the next command. He parted his arms in front of him which signalled his desire for a space to be made in the middle of the dojo floor. The room split in half, knelt in seiza position at the edges of the dojo, bokken placed at the side of each member of the class. It was Sensei wishing to see some individual bouts between the students. Free sparring, or randoree, was one of the more *authentic* methods of displaying an individual's skill with a sword by placing the student in a situation whereby it was not controlled by the rigorous parameters or choreographed outcomes of a mere training drill.

Beckoning one of the novice students, they acknowledged and made their way to the newly formed space. Sensei looked around the congregated, caught my eye and smiled warmly.

"Yoshida Shihan" he beckoned me with his hand to join the novice in the centre of the dojo of which I accepted.

Once in the centre we bowed to Sensei, bowing low and humbly before turning and bowing to each other. Respect for one another is primary in any dojo but we had it as one of the founding principals. *'Respect your opponent, your instructor and ones' self.'*

From here we produced our bokken, wooden counterparts of our real blades. The tips touching, we produced a reasonable combative distance between us. In swordsmanship, if the opportunity arises where the blades can touch before a strike is made, it is one of the first tells on whether your opponent is competent or not. When the bokken touched, there was a distinct feeling of rigidness in my opponent's stance. The novice was not relaxed at all. The look in his eyes revealed he was nervous, if not afraid; for him the battle was lost before a single blow had been conducted. I was surprised that his bokken wasn't shaking as he was tightened by his fear.

His open show of his nerves was to become his downfall and was pitiful for a man of my stature and experience to behold. However, despite this, there were some schools that used this 'show of nerves' as a means of luring an unknowing or overconfident swordsman into a sense of security for what would appear to be certain victory. Like the ensnaring nature of a sea snake when it plays wounded or even dead. When the overconfident swordsman would then initiate the attack, their opponent would simply move from their rigidness to a stage of complete relaxation and as such able to move and fight at such a level that it would overcome their foe. This variation of basic technique is referred to in some schools as the 'calming of the wave'.

An unearthly silence filled my body and soul, it was the trained focus of combat that centred my mind purely on my opponent in front of me. The tune of the cicadas vanished; I became aware of everyone in the room, knowing exactly where they were relative to my own position. Just as the silence hit its peak, the novice sprung into action, too soon was his attack, too rushed was his need to strike that he presented himself wide open and easy to counter. The novice raised his bokken high above his head preparing for a vertical strike that was intended to hit me squarely on top of my head, in the attempt to render me unconscious or worse. Such was the rashness of his movement that I was able to manipulate myself easily around his strike.

Leaping forward I covered my head with my bokken, his strike landing solidly upon it's edge with a tremendously dulled, wooden crack. Still moving, I grabbed hold of his wrist, turning fluidly inside his guard before pulling him forward and slamming my body into his; resulting in a dramatic flip over my hip, his body circled around mine and hit the floor with a loud thud. Before the novice could recover his surprised senses, I struck my bokken hard in a cutting motion into his ribs. The novice let loose a painful groan as pain shot into his body and I won the fight simply in a singular move.

Stepping back and away from him, my eyes remained transfixed upon the heap on the floor that was the novice student. Although I had clearly won the fight, I still maintained a constant eye on him; a real combative situation was never over until the threat was either dead or maimed beyond any effectiveness in combat. It was just the way that I was trained, the principle indoctrinated immovably in my mind.

Painfully, the novice attempted to rise to his feet. The lack of experience from the young student meant that he was getting to his feet in such a sloppy manner. His lack of regard for the awareness of combat meant that his slow, haphazard method of standing I found practically disrespectful to both me and the name of the dojo. It began to anger me.

Unable to stand such blatant disregard any longer, I dropped my bokken before leaping angrily at the novice. Grabbing hold of cloth and the topknot in his hair I slammed him hard into the floor with force. His head bounced dangerously off the hard surface, knocking him unconscious. The limp body lay motionless with blood beginning to slowly ebb from a newly formed cut that appeared on his forehead.

"Stop!" I shouted, raising a palm, as a servant immediately rushed over to tend to the body in the middle of the floor;

"No-one should touch him until he come to himself!" I commanded sternly. The aide moved away, instantly respecting my command due to my rank within the dojo's hierarchy.

Now satisfied that the contest was completely over I returned to my starting position, picking up the loose bokken from the floor and bowed towards Sensei, another smile formed broadly on his wrinkled face.

"Yoshida Shihan" said Sensei softly, "Why did you continue the contest after you had clearly bested him?"

"Sensei, his lack of awareness of the combat around him I found to be disrespectful to both myself and the name of this great house. A lesson had to be made, an example set to the others for the benefit of the future standing of the dojo" I responded as respectfully as I could be.

"Did you truly need to treat him in such a manner?" Sensei was still smiling, he was anticipating my next response.

"The pain that he receives now will benefit him, it will make him strong for I hope that he will remember what has occurred today and help develop the proper responses in order to stop the pain from reoccurring in the future." I returned a smile at Sensei as I bowed again, low and humble.

"Everyone!" Sensei declared loudly and with authority that caught the attention of everyone in the room. The novice who I had bested was beginning to come round, shaking his head to regain focus he was now being tended to by the house servants who rushed over to him as soon as they saw the first signs of movement.

"Yoshida Shihan has produced for you a valuable and very important lesson. Remember the teachings of this dojo…Always be ready. If you are still breathing, you are still able to fight. If your opponent is still breathing, they are still able to fight. Do not become complacent in your actions at any stage of any confrontation." Sensei turned to address the novices. "Novices especially, if you do not wish to be slammed disgracefully into the dojo floor by Yoshida Shihan…then please move quickly if you have to return to your feet. Show him as a senior and yourselves the proper respect that is deserved for practicing students of this dojo." The novices nodded in acknowledgement with stunned expressions at the spectacle that had been presented before them. Perhaps some of them believed it to be unnecessary, some maybe thought that it was an extreme way of providing a lesson; it did not matter to me. I gave them a lesson that they needed to learn in order to survive. They would all learn the Way, in one respect or another.

The entrance to the dojo was pulled open smoothly yet unexpectedly, bathing the hall in the naturally clear and unobstructed light of the outside. All eyes turned sharply to the figure that occupied the space as if they were insulted that the sanctity of their training had been disturbed before it had been finished.

It was one of the house servants who bowed respectfully as he found our eyes to be transfixed intently upon him. He was dressed in the regular colours of the household, a deep brown kimono with a grey obi belt holding it all together. "Sensei, I apologise for disturbing you and the students. There is a man who has entered the grounds, a samurai who has travelled across the country who wishes to speak with you."

"Please, beckon him in"

The servant moved to the edge of the doorway with a shuffle and bowed, his old space became occupied by the stranger. His hair was pristine in the application of his samurai top knot. His clothes however, were not so well kept and it was made apparent by the condition of his dulled kimono that he was well travelled and that he has not stopped in any given place for long periods of time. He carried with him a straw jingasa hat that he held temporarily down at his side in one hand. His obi was framed by a pair of swords, the daisho, a samurai's symbol of their status as the warrior servants of the country. They were pretty plain and ordinary, similar to those carried by the lower students of the school. The stranger obviously did not care for flamboyance or perhaps he was as lowly as the novice students of our dojo. It could've been a ruse to lure us into a complacent level of thought and security regarding the skill of the stranger. Further observation is required.

"My name is Fujibayashi, I am a student of the Toda school of swordplay under master Toda Nakamura. I am here on a holy pilgrimage of the sword, blessed by the Gods themselves in the attempt to improve my swordplay and study the techniques of other styles…if they are worthy…" the stranger's voice was hinted with an air of defiance as he spoke, I found such arrogance insulting and in truth, not in line with the spirit of Budo in its purest of forms that thrived upon modesty and the essence that was simply of combat, of life and death.

"My pilgrimage has led to me travelling all across Japan and I have yet to find a school who's students' skills were equal, if not better than that of my own. This dojo is famed for it's *superior* technique, said to be unrivalled and master style of this area and I hope to find the answer to my pilgrimage here. If you allow it Master Imamoto, I wish to challenge some of your students, or yourself if you prefer? I know that I would prefer to face the source of the style directly." The stranger was issuing an indirect challenge aimed at Sensei himself! Most unwise and foolhardy in my learned opinion. This stranger needed to watch both his manners and tongue, it would not be wise to insult a room of swordsmen when all he had was himself on his side.

The master spoke in response, politely and respectfully as he would naturally do, keeping in line with etiquette.

"I am honoured and gladdened that our dojo has the reputation of which you speak of. I have had the pleasure of meeting Master Toda once, during the Shogun's council of swordsmanship many years ago. He is a wise and skilful practitioner of Budo and I am honoured to have one of his senior students in my house."

The stranger bowed at the compliment, maintaining etiquette and perhaps attempting to make up for his slight lapse in respect that he rudely displayed earlier. Sensei was showing his higher character, for Sensei was a man of great moral fibre, disregarding the hidden insult in the stranger's earlier speech.

"I will allow the challenge to commence, it is encouraged by our dojo's tradition to spar with members of other styles and is considered part of all students' training. As you well know, this tradition is one that has become increasingly common through sword dojo's up and down the land; I believe Master Toda is a great patron and encourager of this form of practice. I would not like to disappoint both yourself and the teachings of your Master. Please spar with one of my seniors and if you are not satisfied with the technique they provide you, then I will spar with you to the best of my ability.

Please be aware that the rules of our dojo state that all challenge matches will be conducted with plain bokken and that the use of live blades in challenge matches are strictly prohibited. We see it as a waste of skill and a waste of life for only a challenge, as well as it being intrinsic with the laws of this great land; we also do not wish to dishonourably stain the hallowed grounds of this dojo with reckless and foolish disregard for life."

"Thank you Master Imamoto, that would be satisfactory." Fujibayashi removed his swords and placed them on the racks in a disciplined and well practiced manner. Placing his jingasa neatly on the floor near to his swords he picked up a spare wakizashi bokken; a wooden representative of the shorter of the pair of swords carried by the samurai. Upon checking his new weapon to ensure it was suitable for the challenge, Fujibayashi moved to the centre of the dojo to await the selection of his opponent.

Master Imamoto turned his head towards me and beckoned me once more to join Fujibayashi for the challenge of which I accepted gladly.

"I accept" I said softly. To not accept would show cowardice and would disgrace the name of both myself and worse, the school. A shameful act, especially in front of an outsider. I was a senior, this was what was expected of me.

The dojo fell silent. A deathly silence that was entirely ominous, with all eyes around the room focused upon us. Personally I would find the experience that I was to undergo to be quite enjoyable, for I had never fought against a practitioner of the Toda school and their technique was just as legendary as our own. But that enjoyment will come *after* the fight, I could not allow myself to be clouded by such thoughts as even though our blades were not real and razor sharp, death could still arise from a precise and deadly uncontrolled strike by the wooden counterparts.

We bowed to each other before adopting our kamae, or fighting postures. Fujibayshi turned sideways, his legs crossed over and bent, dropping his weight as he spread his weight evenly on both feet. His bokken, held in a singular hand was positioned horizontally over his head. An interesting position and one that I have not encountered before.

"Fujibayashi Shigeru, Toda short sword style" declared the challenger, as according to the official practices of challenge etiquette whereby the challengers were not of the same school. I responded by dropping my bokken down to my hip turning the sword so that the tip was facing away from him in a posture known as waki no kamae.

"Yoshida Kintaro, Imamaoto style" I said, positively as our eyes locked, postures unflinching. The stillness seemed to last an eternity before I initiated, my mind saw a path upwards that would strike my opponent under the chin and I allowed the images of the strike to play themselves in my mind as I anticipated his movement and within a split second I had considered several probable outcomes. From my mind's eye, my body followed and as I swung the bokken vertically I was sure of a connection with his body and a swift finish to the fight.

But as my bokken swung at high speed, Fujibayshi seemed to wait just until the last moment, before spinning and turning out of the path of the strike. His timing was impeccable as my bokken missed by a small fraction of a second. Again and again I struck out, circling my strikes to attempt to disorientate and confuse but with every strike, Fujibayashi just turned to avoid or parried each blow away. His fighting style was unorthodox, his bodily movements so fluid and close to a point of complete relaxation that he appeared to be like a shadow dancing and flickering around in the candlelight that was the edge of my weapon. He frustrated me so as I felt belittled by his highly capable defensive strategies. If there was one thing that really itched at my soul was the thought of being made to look amateurish by an outsider.

Then; we both moved to strike and counter simultaneously, our motions were the same and our strikes landed together. Hitting down upon each others collarbone, were it not be the fact that our weapons were made of wood, the blows would've cleaved us cleanly from shoulder to hip and killed instantly.

We stayed there motionless, neither one of us showed a flinch from pain as our collarbones felt the full impact and any harder, they would've snapped. Our deathly stares remained in total deadlock as we maintained our silent shows of strength and toughness. Neither one of us was going to admit defeat.

"Ikki waki" Sensei called. The contest was declared a draw and we broke from our positions back to a kamae position as neither one of us was able to achieve the upper hand.

"Yoshida Kintaro…" spoke Fujibayashi softly, "Your technique is strong and you have great precision and the strength of a mighty swordsman; but I believe that it is quite conventional and as such, I know all the methods of overcoming it. If you continue to fight me, then you will surely lose and I do not wish you to lose face in front of your students. For your sake, yield."

"Please Fujibayashi-san, I would like you to enlighten me on my weaknesses" How dare he speak to me in such a manner. His arrogance irritated me and it was difficult to maintain my neutral composure with him. I had to calm down, the bubbling rage would only hinder my future efforts to overcome him.

We adopted our fighting postures again, this time I was determined that I will not lose. We continued our combat, this time I opted to use a series of strikes that were taught only to students of Shihan rank and above, the strikes flowed effortlessly and the kata that these derived from was named as the 'Dragon's Dance'.

It was a kata created by Sensei's teacher and was said that he created it's highly complex and effective series of techniques upon reaching a stage of enlightenment where he was visited by the spirit of an ancient dragon who passed on the secret teachings. The truth that surrounds this is clouded with superstition but none of us would ever challenge or even attempt to dispute the details that were involved. Although I had learnt its series of movements, knowing the sequence of the kata without the need to think on it; I had yet to completely master it as it would require a life long study to truly understand it. To use it against Fujibayashi would be simply another step to understanding it. Though I was haunted by the niggling suspicion that I might be scolded by Sensei for showing the technique in the presence of the novices; but I would have to deal with that when I eventually receive it, for I was that focused on beating the stranger, I had to do so no matter the cost.

Blow after blow struck out at Fujibayashi, who's circular defensive technique seemed to withstand the seemingly endless onslaught. The clashing dull sounds of the bokken emanated from us over the calming silence until one well practiced strike managed to break through his defences and hit him squarely in the stomach, doubling him over with a painful groan that replaced the dull thuds and was quite pleasing to my ears as it signalled that I had struck him with the first blow. As his solid concentration on his defence vanished, replaced by the sudden introduction of pain, I took advantage of his disarray and did a final finish before he had chance to recover, where I plunged the tip of the bokken into his back sending him sprawling onto his hands and knees.

Fujibayashi stayed upon his knees, his eyes sunk down as if he had been struck by some terrible news. He exuded an impression of sadness and disbelief as this was possibly the first and only time that he had been defeated since he began his epic pilgrimage judging by the look on his face. His face became awash with surprise and pain. Sharply he turned and kneeled in seiza before Sensei.

"Sensei Imamoto, I have been bested by your student and your school's technique. It truly is a magnificent system. I have no need to challenge yourself as I believe that your technique is even more purer than that of your student and as such it would be futile to even believe that I could best you. Through all my journey I have not been beaten by anyone and for this to happen today it means that I am one step closer to achieving my pilgrimage. Please except me as a pupil here, I believe that here is where I will find answers to my quest to achieving enlightenment through the study of the sword."

Sensei stood up, before completing his way to the exit of the dojo he said, "It is not the practices of this dojo to accept just anyone who comes to our door, please rest in the confines of the house, the servants will tend to your needs and I will give you my answer in the morning....Shihan Ryoko...Shihan Yoshida...please come with me. Class is dismissed, please go about your duties"

We all left the dojo, the students bowing low until we had left. We left to decide that afternoon the future fate of Fujibayashi Shigeru.

Chapter 2 – Journey to Japan

The intercom sprang into life, with a tuneful ping before the captain spoke out clearly;

"Welcome to Emirates flight 723 departing from Dubai to Osaka. As captain I would like to welcome everyone aboard this flight and wish everyone a safe and pleasant voyage. In a moment our cabin crew will embark on a safety demonstration, please take time to familiarise yourself with these instruction and we will be departing shortly. Our estimated time of arrival will be roughly 10:38am local time. Thank you for flying with Emirates."

'Here we go again' I thought glumly, we were now on the second leg of our journey and it seemed like forever since we set out from London. It felt surreal, knowing that soon we will be touching down in Japan, a first time for me and most of my team mates.

We have been training now for the past eight or so months, hard and long practically everyday to prepare ourselves for what we were about to face. An international tournament, one bigger than any we have been in, set in the homeland of our art of Shitoryu Karate. The amount of hours that we shed sweat and blood, putting ourselves through the rigorous training regime that was put to together by our coach; it was unimaginable.

Thinking ahead, it was hard to imagine the scale of it all. There was at least eight different countries competing from what we've been informed with prior to our travels and we were representing the British contingent. But it was not only a competition, it was an exchange of cultures and nations for it was classed as a 'Goodwill' competition and designed to unite the practitioners together no matter what nationality.

Along with the tournament, our trip itinerary included training with our head instructor of our system worldwide, Sensei Takeo 9th Dan and direct senior student of the founder of the style. Also, there were numerous trips and excursions as we were following in '*The Footsteps of Musashi*', a trail of one of the greatest swordsman that has ever lived. He had killed his first man at the age of thirteen and during his lifetime had slain over sixty individuals in combat. His exploits are legendary and many different documentaries and films have been made about him and his life. Very exciting, or at least it was for a historical culture buff such as myself.

The cabin crew started off with their highly practised safety demonstration, pointing out the operation of the buckle seat belts and the important procedures of what to do in the 'unlikely' event of an emergency. I decided to drown them out and reached for the in-flight magazine and menu. I heard all of this before during the first leg of this ridiculously long journey and didn't want to waste the time listening to it again. I also found that most of the demonstration is pretty much common sense really. Like seriously, who out there doesn't know how to operate one of the seat belt buckles!

Andrew, one of my team mates who was my neighbour for this section of the flight, a tall and slim, blonde haired athlete with bright blue eyes and beaming smile; decided it was also a good idea to check out the in-flight entertainment which attracted his eyes with its overly bright and colourful front cover that depicted a collage of celebrity related icons and shortly after perusing on the cover, reached for his copy.

The contents of the magazine weren't overly thrilling, but contained the listings of the in-flight programs that were to be shown over the course of the journey, which I was sure to keep me busy for a few hours at least of the ten or so hour flight that was ahead of us.

Such was my gross interest in the magazine that I didn't notice the demonstration had finished and it was only when the engines had kick-started into life that took my attention away. We were now moving. Remembering from the first part of the trip I looked for Sarah, who I knew had a fear of flying; or more rather the fear of the 'crashing' part!

A quick glance around and I found her. She was situated at the end of our row. Unfortunately, due to the number of our group, it was hard for the travel agent to get everyone situated together when the flights were booked with the airline and most were scattered throughout the cabin. Again, her fear of flying was showing, her hands gripped the arms of the seat so hard for a moment you would think that they would get ripped off at any moment. Her knuckles were white as she gripped tightly. Her face was now dangerously pale, borderline ghostly white as she began to mouth some words to herself in the hope of calming her obvious nerves and we haven't even taken off yet!

Catching her attention, she looked across at me where I silently mouthed over 'It's ok'. A desperate attempt to try and keep her as relaxed as possible. She nodded briefly and laid her head back on the seat and closed her eyes to make things easier, if that were at all possible.

Once the plane had reached its final position prior to take off, the engines roared loudly into life, accelerating us forward until the speed reached the required speed for takeoff and we were propelled into the air. The land below quickly minimised until it was finally out of sight and we had hit the clouds.

"Argh, my ears!" moaned Andrew, as we reached the point where they needed popping with the change in pressure. His hand was rubbing his ears frantically, trying to help break the pressure.

"Yeah I know, it's annoying" I said, as mine had reached the same stage and my voice seemed as if it only echoed inside my head and was not being projected clearly enough. "It will go soon."

Now it was time to just sit back and relax, place the head phones on and let either the movies or the music pass the time.

After a couple of in flight movies and a few hours of regularly interrupted sleep, the captain pinged the intercom back into life to signal our descent.

"Ladies and Gentlemen, shortly we will be starting our descent to Kansai Airport, Osaka, please remain seated with seatbelts fastened. Thank You."

Peering out of the window, you can see the line in the distance that was the headland of Japan. The waves lapped and bobbed naturally beneath. The approach to Kansai airport is a strange one as the airport itself is a man made structure set into the ocean itself, one of the biggest in the world in fact. As the plane descended, our stomachs jumped and churned as the altitude dropped. The ocean was becoming ever so closer, almost to the point where you think you're actually going to land into the sea itself!

Suddenly, the view beneath changed from ocean to runway, there was hardly any medium between them. Soon, the scrape of the wheels and the jolt of the plane signalled our landing. We were now in Japan. The feeling of relief of finally ending our journey became stronger than the excitement of seeing Japan for the first time. It was too long a flight and as we had to economise in order to get to Japan, the seating arrangements were a bit too claustrophobic and sweaty for my liking and I was looking forward to a nice long shower and feeling clean once more. A part of me would feel disappointed at this inappropriate emotional sensation.

The tannoy crackled into life once more as the aircraft started to slow to a moderate pace prior to parking and our disembarkment.

"Ladies and Gentlemen, we have now landed safely and without complication in Kansai Airport, Osaka. Please remain seated until the aircraft comes to a final resting. We wish you well

with your stay in Osaka and thank you for flying with Emirates."

Within minutes the plane finally rested to a standstill and the seatbelt lights beeped off, at that moment the cabin erupted into motion with everyone bustling into life, moving to try and quickly slot into the queue to disembark or fumbling around with their hand luggage that had been kept safe in the over head compartments. There was a desire to stretch the legs, breath fresh air once more and just have the feel of terra firma again after such a lengthy flight.

"Right, everyone quickly get their gear and we'll all meet together on the other side, no wandering off, we're now in Japan and we need to know exactly where we're headed" came the familiar voice of Coach, who had his bag in hand in anticipation and ready to head off. He would scout on ahead and act as a living rendezvous point where we would congregate before continuing on through the airport as a unified group.

Everyone was wearing their squad tracksuits, a mixture of red, white and blue that really looked the part of a travelling, professional sports team. This was where the goose bumps started to appear, look out Japan, here come the British team!

On the bus to downtown Kobe, it was a trip through a foreign wonderland. Everything excited me; from just watching the people shopping or making their way to work to the simpler things like the road signs and the shop signs. Even though I knew I had no chance of picking up individual Japanese script, I tried to associate individual symbols with what each building was. A restaurant, a bank, a bar, clothes shop, but alas, still had no clue as to what they were! The signs were just passing by me too fast to make them distinguishable but still, everything was new and my focus was that like a child in a city of mysterious wonders.

It would be an hour or so from the airport to the bus stop at downtown Kobe and a ten minute walk from there to the hotel. We were warned beforehand that there would be a lot of travelling on our excursion and as such our luggage options were adapted and looked more like we were on a mountain expedition than a regular sporting holiday with plenty of backpacks and hold-all bags with regular, hard suitcases kept to a minimum due to the awkward unwieldiness that they presented especially in situations that involved the train services and subways.

The temperature was very hot and the air was moist with such rife humidity, everyone had began to sweat since stepping out of the airport. Again, we had been warned to expect these sort of conditions and plenty of fluids were recommended; in fact, they were more like essential!

As we were a team we travelled in unison, our team colours displayed our school name that was written in Japanese script across them and some of the locals noticed and some gave mixed looks of acceptance, others a slight peculiarity, either way our arrival was gaining some notice which felt good and uplifting. If only we could be greeted by a host of paparazzi but then again, we weren't movie stars.

"There's the hotel there on the corner." Pointed out Coach, and we peered ahead to see where our digs would be for the next few nights. The Casabella Inn appeared quite nice and acceptable from the outside, a tower block shaped building with a revolving door that was framed in a bright, well polished brass surround. Prior to the trip, frightening stories of hotel rooms with nothing more than a simple tatami mat and straw filled pillows, typical of a traditional Japanese setup were going round, spreading like vicious and demoralising wildfire. So despite the relatively modern and nice appearance of the exterior, there was still that lingering dread that we'll all be sleeping without proper mattresses! What sleeping on basically a hard floor would do to my back was not even worth thinking about!

Once inside the lobby, the modern look of the outside continued further, the lobby was a marbled tile with a plush, black leather sofa set over to one side and a payphone near the entrance. The reception area had the tiling intermingled with a dark rose wood style effect framing it. Behind the counter a short, smartly dressed Japanese man in around his mid twenties, dressed in white shirt and black tie, stood proudly at attention; awaiting us to settle as we piled into the lobby area, almost filling it and devoiding it of space. Coach approached and spoke with the concierge who pottered off briefly to a back room before returning to the desk with an armful of white envelopes which contained the room keys.

"Right…" cried out coach, "Listen up for your names"

"James and Sam…"

"Sarah and Emily…"

"Sensei Craig…"

He continued to rattle off the names and with every calling handed out the keys. Once he was finished, everyone appeared ready to dart off to check out the state of their rooms.

"Wait you lot!" he called, stopping everyone in their tracks and delaying the bustle for just a moment.

"Tonight you have a free night, so you can do what you want. But please, if you're thinking of leaving the hotel at all tonight let either myself or Sensei Craig know where it is you're going or doing. If you need to get hold of me my room is number 231. We meet for breakfast at 8.00am tomorrow. Sharp!" He paused briefly, sensing the anticipation from the group to dive into the elevators and head to their rooms.

"If no one has any questions, then you can go." With that signal, the activity rose as people dived without decorum into elevators, scrambling with bags and suitcases as they packed into the elevators like sardines in a tin. The cramped conditions were short of claustrophobic and I began wishing that I had waited for the next elevator run but the excitement of being someplace new was just too overwhelming.

"2nd floor" said someone within the cramped confines. My floor. As the doors opened I practically fell out, much to the delight and laughter of the rest of the elevator. Their chuckles died out as soon as the doors closed again. Straightening myself out, I saw the sharp, smiling features of Andrew as he stood waiting for me.

"Alright there?" he asked sarcastically, obviously witnessing me almost falling on my arse.

"Yes I'm fine!" I said, my ego slightly bruised and embarrassed.

"Let's find our room" he said, chuckling.

We turned into the main corridor on this level of the hotel. As we did so, we came close to bumping violently into another couple of residents of the hotel. But these visitors were more familiar and we were quick to familiarise ourselves as to who they actually were.

The pair we almost bumped into were dressed in the bright green and yellow tracksuits of the Australian team. The spiky blonde hair of the thin faced guy who stood before me was instantly recognisable.

Bruce Fenchurch.

Bruce Fenchurch, the Australian team captain and one competitor who I have had the 'pleasure', so to speak of facing before in Goodwill Championships of previous years. He was a very capable and strong competitor, one of the Australian team's finest and he had beaten me time and time again, much to my bitter frustration. To me, I considered him as an arch-rival of sorts and he had my secret contempt as such. He was the *Joker* to my *Batman*, the *Lex Luthor* to my *Superman*.

"Jason! Heya buddy how are ya?" his jovial, quirky accent was quite sickening, it was hard to detect if there was any ill intent or sarcasm. It tended to frustrate me even when I was in the best of moods. No doubt he was just simply being friendly, acting upon the *goodwill* part of the 'Goodwill Championships' and I was now just being rude.

"Bruce…I'm good thank you." I responded, slightly cold if anything, my words being difficult to utter from my lips as I was made extremely uncomfortable with being face to face with him this early before the competition.

"How was your flight? Hope it was all good?" he asked.

"Long…a bit too long perhaps" I said, making Bruce chuckle, though I couldn't tell beyond his sickeningly exuberant manner whether or not this was slightly false.

"Well I'll let you get to your room and drop your bags off. If I don't see you later, catch ya at the tournament buddy." With that we went our separate ways; the chance meeting with Bruce sparked something off inside of me; he had beaten me in finals year after year and although they're only meant to be the 'bad guys' until after the tournament, he always did manage to hit a nerve with me even once the thrill of the competition had passed. I couldn't help but hold some level of grudge for him. You could call it petty really, but I like to think of it as 'competitive spark'.

Coach knew that I held some degree of discontent for Bruce and when we were being 'beasted' as he called it, during our long and hard training sessions to get us ready for the competition, he was always the subject of Coach's shouting when they were being aimed directly at myself. Coach was good at that. Good at knowing exactly how to push each of our buttons so that he could receive that little bit extra from us during training. He wanted us to be at our best and the more we put into our training, the more we got out when we were on the competition mat.

Room 240, took me completely off guard and by surprise, as we entered my head was full to bursting of nightmarish thoughts of small confined spaces and beds that were nothing more than a hessian roll mat accompanied by an unequally uncomfortable pillow. Thankfully, the rooms were actually not that bad. Not conforming to the stereotype I had associated to it, it appeared much like a regular road side hotel from back home than the more traditional styled rooms that we were threatened or teased with. It contained all the usual amenities, beds, television, kettle, etc. The only part of the room that was a bit of a let down was the bath/shower combo which was very small and square! It reminded me more of a confined cubicle than a regular shower with a small step inside of it that you could sit in while you bathed.

"Phew!" cried Andrew, he too showed his relief at the surprising condition of the room. "At least this is something we can stay in reasonably comfortably. I thought we'd have to sleep on one of those bloody mats they have." Striding over to the far bed he dumped his bag down and dived onto the mattress to embrace it as if he hadn't seen a bed in over a month.

"That's better!" he said, spreading out over its surface. "This is what you need after that bloody long flight! Don't want to do that again!"

"Well, we are going to…" I said dryly, "we got to get home after all" Andrew picked up on the fact that my heckles were up from the previous surprise encounter with my nemesis.

"Hey man! Don't let Bruce get to you! I'm sure you'll kick his ass this time round"

"He hasn't gotten to me" I snapped, involuntarily as if covering up some form of hurt.

"Now, now, Jason how long have I known you? Now shut up, cheer up and see how good these mattresses are!"

Good old Andrew, he was right, he has known me a long time, we practically started training at the same time and I'd grown to trust his opinion. He also had the great knack of being able to sort my head out whenever I get annoyed and together we've both been through our shares of strife and adversity.

Diving onto my own bed I realised how right he was. Soothing myself contently into the mattress, it did feel good as it lightly moulded itself around the contours of my body. A noticeable contrast to the hardened airplane seats that we had to endure through for way too long.

"How do you feel about finally being in Japan?" I asked him, staring at the pearly white ceiling above us.

"Yeah, good I guess. I'm not too sure about the food though! I'm not a great lover of fish when it's cooked let alone when it's raw! Like what is THAT all about? Haven't they heard of deep frying a nice battered cod!"

"Yeah I know what you mean, never tried sushi, but surely they do more than just fish?" I asked, "Maybe something to do with chicken?"

"Well they better!" exclaimed Andrew, "Otherwise it's gonna be a Macd's each and every night. The 'food of kings!'" he joked, "So what we got planned for tonight then?"

"Hmm, good question. Well, we've got a free night tonight and I don't know about you but I don't really fancy staying in tonight, not on the first night, it's a bit boring" I said, trying to remember if I saw anything of great significance that was nearby. Not that if I did, I would understand what it would be as I couldn't read Japanese.

"Yeah, let's ask Emily and Sarah if they fancy going." Andrew sounded excited at the thought. As well as he knew me, I knew him just as well and his particular interest that he showed in Sarah.

"Well, we know why you want to ask Sarah to come…" I said teasingly.

"No, no! It's not like that, it's only 'cos I think she would like the idea of not staying in. You know if Emily goes anywhere Sarah has to go as well!" Andrew replied hastily, obviously slightly embarrassed at his feelings being exposed.

"Yeah, sure, whatever you say" I replied, still teasing "You know me, don't forget that I know YOU as well!" I couldn't blame him for how he felt, Sarah was beautiful and blonde. Any guy would think the same, there was a part of me that felt that way but I knew that I wouldn't have stood a chance when it came to getting with her.

"Well get on the phone and ask them, they're in room 332." I said pointing to the phone that was set between us in the gap between beds, upon a plain, standardised wooden bedside cabinet.

"Yeah, I will in a bit, I think I'm gonna get some shut eye for an hour or two." Andrew stretched back, touching the head board and yawned. "I'll set the alarm to go off in a couple of hours and we'll get ready then."

"Good idea" I replied, rolling over onto my side, closing my eyes ready to drift off into a little snooze, dreaming of the wonders that we would see and do while we were in this strange new country.

Chapter 3 – The Omi-no-Ken Ceremony

Myself, Ryoko and Sensei sat in the quiet confines of his small study. We have had presented before us an interesting situation. An outsider, a practitioner of another style of swordplay requested to join our dojo and become a student after losing a challenge to myself. In all my long years of study at Imamoto dojo, there has never been a case of accepting a student in this manner, in particular one who has come from another system. The practices of swordsmanship were generally kept secret and a school's techniques would just be kept for those who studied there.

Students that had the honour of training here were normally selected from the household of the Lord or had a link with the Lord himself whether it be from one of the powerful families that served the Lord, even from the personal retainers of the Lord himself. Ryoko sat with a puzzled expression as he pondered deeply over what was before us.

"Your thoughts, seniors…please" said Sensei as he broke the silence, his voice such as to not give away his personal feelings on the matter, he wanted our honest opinions on the subject and did not want to produce any bias towards influencing our own thoughts.

"It is an intriguing subject Sensei but one that I believe presents its answer very clearly" replied Ryoko, ever the pious one amongst us "It has not been heard of for this dojo to just simply take students in 'off the street' as it were, at least not during my days of study here. I fear this act may damage the reputation of our dojo and we'll have every down and out miserable Ronin knocking at our door. We will almost be considered as charity, a warming home for lost dogs." As Ryoko spoke, he let loose a tone of complete discontent at the thought of *scraps* at the door. In a way he was right and I would have to agree with him in that respect; the Imamoto dojo was a highly revered place of practice in swordplay and teacher of skill to the local lord.

It would be dishonourable to its name and to the ancestral students to just let anyone practice here. But, even saying this, there was something different about Fujibayashi; he was not just any old Ronin, he was here purely on the search of knowledge which was an admirable thing. I could only imagine what it would've been like to live on the road, all the hardships that would be involved; I could find respect for such a man.

"Yoshida Shihan?" asked Sensei, turning to look at me for my views as I sat quietly and patiently in the company of my seniors. Although I was a junior in front of these men, my opinion was still taken into account when we were called for meetings such as this. I knew, however, that I would have to be tactical when it came to expressing my thoughts.

"Ryoko Shihan is right, however…" I paused, taking a slight moment to gather my thoughts so I could phrase my response in the most appropriate way so as not to appear insulting to Ryoko's experience and wisdom. One always had to be careful with one's words, to speak out of turn and out of rank is not only rude but also unseemly for a samurai. In the wrong company, it could also lead to challenges or orders of suicide if the words were damning enough to warrant this level of response.

"There is something different about him that sets him apart from the rest of the lack lustred Ronin out there in the wilderness. He is highly skilled, even more so than the most promising novices of our school." When I finished my sentenced I froze out of fear that the latter half would be considered by those present as an insult against my own school. This was never a wise thing to do.

"True, he is a skilled swordsman" interjected Sensei, he too was pondering hard over the whole thing, the fact that he didn't say anything more was far more worrying for myself who may've damned my existence and position unintentionally with what I had just said.

"It's just never been done before, why change the practices of this dojo for this one man? What if the outside world misconceives our actions here. It is just not heard of!" Spouted Ryoko. I could see that Ryoko was beginning to get fired up by the whole thing. It was a rare thing for anything to eat away at Ryoko. His love for tradition and the methods and practices that this dojo has is showing itself here today, he was truly the zealot.

I quickly interjected before he had the chance to go off on a verbal rampage which Ryoko has been known to do, normally over a strong bottle of rice wine but this sort of subject would provide the same effect.

"I see potential in him, his short sword style is impressive and we can learn from it as much as he can learn from us. After all, I too have not lost in a challenge match, apart from against yourselves and this outsider managed to gain a draw out of me. Sensei, the practices of this dojo require us to fight those of other styles in an attempt to improve our technique. If we do not take these opportunities to learn, then why fight them in the first place? Other than to keep our reputation of being a formidable style.

By knowing his system, ours can grow so that we can beat that system comfortably in the future..." I stopped, dropping my head and realising that what I was saying was actually quite radical and almost near *blasphemous* to an extent, especially in the eyes of the pious Ryoko with his solid and unyielding traditional values. Raising my head expecting to be greeted with scornful looks from my seniors I was shocked to find both of them was smiling.

Sensei spoke quietly, "Both of you are right. Your opinions are both equally correct. Yoshida Shihan, you are certainly wise beyond your years and right in your opinion that we must learn from others to better ourselves, times are changing not just in the Ways of the Sword but with our country in general. We must adapt with the change in order for our school to survive. Ryoko Shihan, you too are correct in your love for maintaining tradition and your cautions on how this can damage our dojo's reputation are certainly valid. We must be careful in how we continue with this matter."

Sensei rose from his position and our eyes followed him as we awaited what was to be his final words on the matter, at least, for today.

"Fujibayashi will become a student at this dojo. I believe too that we can learn from him, but caution must follow with how we present ourselves to the outside world. I do not need to remind you both that our dojo is a hallowed ground and not a refuge for every lost swordsman without a home to call their own. We will accept him based only on his promising, superior skills and nothing more or less.

There will be no more talk on the matter now. Yoshida Shihan, as you were the man who bested him for the first time he will automatically have a personal connection with you. Please go to the quarters that we have given him temporarily and inform him on his acceptance into our dojo. Also, you must prepare him of our ways for the initiation ceremony. He will begin his training at the advanced stage and will be mostly in your charge Yoshida. Now Ryoko, please go and inform the servants to prepare for the Omi-no-ken ceremony. We will conduct the ceremony at the first light of the morning sun. I must now rest and prepare myself. Go about your business now, we will all meet for the ceremony at the designated time for such matters."

We bowed in respect and the acknowledgment of the Master's order and left to carry out the commands we had been set.

Fujibayashi was very excited when I gave him the news of his initiation, I instructed him that when it came to the initiation itself, he was to kneel before Sensei, not to move a muscle and to show the true spirit of a warrior throughout the proceedings. The ceremony is such that the slightest movement can result in injury to the initiate and in some rare instances can result in death. He took this news with the proper respect that should be shown which I found pleasing.

The time had come for the formal initiation of Fujibayashi into the Imamoto school of swordsmanship. It was a beautiful morning, one that could inspire a poet to write great verses or a bard to compose a pleasing song; which held good sway with the decision for Fujibayashi's initiation as the morning proved itself to not be considered as a bad omen by any of those who attended. Perhaps the gods themselves in their infinite wisdom have decided that it would be beneficial for Fujibayashi to join our school, I enjoyed thinking of it in this manner. No matter what the true nature of this morning was, there was definitely also the consensus amongst some of the more pious students that they didn't fully agree with the new bloods initiation. But they would never openly voice their opinion as it would show their disagreement with the official order that came from Sensei himself.

The ceremony was to take place in the courtyard which the servants had dutifully prepared in the official manner, with banners depicting the Imamoto family crest outlying the ceremonial area, fluttering lightly in the light morning breeze. Fujibayashi knelt silently and solemnly in the centre of the courtyard upon a small red dais. His swords have been removed and his kimono removed from his shoulders to expose his torso, similar to the manner of a man committing seppuku; ritual suicide. This comparison was symbolic of the students change in his path; as one life changed for another as a caterpillar changes into a beautiful butterfly.

This exposure showed that his body was very well conditioned, the muscles were sharp and defined, especially on his abdomen and his back where it appeared to be pure muscle without any show of fat; I wondered on what particular exercises he must've done in order to achieve this high definition and I was looking forward to eventually learning them from Fujibayashi.

Myself and Ryoko sat upon simple wood and fabricated stools off to one side of the initiation area. The rest of the students knelt in seiza on the ground behind us in regimented lines, it was part of the practice for all of the students to witness every ceremony if they were able, as the new initiate would soon join them as a disciple and become one of the ranks alongside them and in a way this allowed the first steps of an eternal bond between the initiate and those who had already been.

Ryoko had with him a small, decorative wooden box which had depicted on its lid images of dragons and bamboo laid in with the finest coloured lacquers. Within it held the omibushi plum that was to be used for the ceremony. I couldn't recall the number of times that I had set eyes on this tiny, decorative box for this purpose and as such I could instantly recognise it and know exactly what was to come.

The Omi-no-ken or 'Plum Sword' ceremony was a means of initiation that was developed by Master Imamoto's instructor, it is a show of the skill that can be achieved through diligent practice of our particular style. Conducted at the first light of a new day it symbolises the birth of a new path of training and a new life for the initiate involved. As the first rays of the new morning crested over the main house and flooded into the courtyard, Sensei entered into view from the main house.

Silence filled the area as Sensei walked fluidly towards the dais. He was dressed in full battlefield yoroi [armour], a dark crimson lined with a bluish trim and cords of dull orange that held the pieces together tightly yet were flexible on his body.

All eyes followed him eagerly as he approached. The ceremony itself was not without its dangers and in the past, individuals have left with permanent scars from cuts and in the rarest of circumstances have lost their lives through improper show of the true essence of Budo, the warrior way. It was important that Fujibayashi did not even flinch an eyelid for although Sensei still retained a great skill from his youth he was still aging and there was the minor fear that perhaps his eyesight was not as accurate as it once was in his youth. It would be disastrous for Fujibayashi if he moved.

"Fujibayashi Shigeru...You have been found worthy through your demonstration of skill and martial character to join the honoured ranks of the dedicated students of this dojo. As such, you will dedicate yourself to upholding the great name and status that this dojo holds and will conduct yourself in all manners of life with honour and the integrity of a samurai and a honorary member of this household. At all times you will provide the perfect example as to the nature of this great school to your teacher, your fellow students, those outside and most importantly, to yourself. Never will you speak ill of this household and be prepared for retribution from your seniors if you ever did so. You will single-mindedly devote yourself, mind, body and spirit to the practice and development of the teachings of this school."

Sensei paused "Fujibayashi Shigeru, you first started your journey under the scholarship and tutorage of Master Toda. He is a respected and skilled teacher but you are now a member of this household. Do not forget your beginnings and forever honour your first Master. But, you must face your path ahead with an open mind and allow yourself to empty your cup so you can fully learn the teachings that we have to offer you. You are the first outsider to be admitted in this manner for it is not traditionally our custom to do so. As such, always be mindful of the way you are perceived by others both within this school and those outside of it so as to not discredit this house."

As Sensei finished his speech and before Fujibayashi had any time to respond in acknowledgment of the words that Sensei had spoken, Ryoko sprang forth into life, rising off his chair and bounding to the dais with the grace and speed of a mountain cat. As if he were in a silent, battlefield charge where he was closing in on a helpless enemy. He opened the box he was carrying and drew out the plum from within.

Taking a moment, he balanced the plum carefully and precisely on the top of Fujibayashi's head where it remained still and unwavering. The atmosphere tensed ready for the next piece, this was the part where the ceremony could take an ugly turn. Ryoko moved away with the same grace and silence as he had entered so as to not distract Sensei. Once Ryoko was clear of the dais, Sensei placed his right leg forward and sunk his weight into a combative stance, his hand hovered over the grip of his sword. The suspense was almost unbearable, as if time had been ordered to come to a standstill as Sensei stood motionless in front of the vulnerable Fujibayashi until…

Swoosh! Swoosh!

In the time it took to simply blink an eye, Sensei had reached for and grabbed his sword and performed both vertical and horizontal cuts at the plum that rested upon Fujibayashi's head. It was so fast that after the first cut, the plum didn't have time to separate before it was cut again by the follow up cut. Sensei's sword was old but still as deadly as the day it had been first forged and sharpened, being an heirloom that was passed down through several generations of his family. It had been drawn by the skilled ancestors of his bloodline on countless occasions on battlefields beyond comprehension. It had slain opposing warlords and brought peace to the area on more than a singular occasion. Truly was it a blade of legend.

The metallic scrape of the sword as it was returned to its sheath was closely followed by the squelchy separation of the plum as it fell from Fujibayashi's head in four neatly segmented pieces. Juice, not blood, flowed down the forehead as Fujibayshi knelt motionless as if frozen by the near deathly ceremony; a slight sigh of relief was released by the congregation that no blood had been shed today in the honoured gardens of the dojo's household.

As the seniors of the dojo we approached Fujibayashi first and with solid warrior like pats upon his back and with the atmosphere and feeling that arises from a group of battlefield brothers we welcomed him in our own way. He was now our battlefield 'brother' as well as a fellow student. Like a band of warrior brothers we would protect and fight alongside him if the need arises and we were sure that he would do the same.

"Please follow me, Fujibayashi" said Sensei, turning and walking back towards the house. Fujibayashi followed, to continue to the signing in on the official documents of initiation. He was now a member of the Imamoto Dojo;

However, it would be left to fate that would decide the path that was to follow him and we all had the niggling worry that his path would not be as smooth as we would hope.

Chapter 4 – Warm Welcomes

O̲ur first night in Japan, a free night in the inventory and as the majority of us were new to Japan a few of us decided to band together and go take a wander, to take in the sights and just to get general bearings of what's around us. We have already bumped into some of the other nations that were also staying at the hotel. Mixed feelings of welcome and contempt were felt as we remembered what our coach had drummed into us...'They're only the enemy until after the competition!' The competitive drive that was indoctrinated into us as a measure of the 'sportsmanship' that surrounded the event. It was this psychological training that gave us that little extra drive to train harder and faster. It was an edge and we believed that it allowed us to train harder and more effectively than any of the other nations.

So, to get over this we went for our wander. The receptionist mentioned that one of the temples that were situated down the road was conducting the harvest festival and would be an interesting sight to witness. It would be our first taste, if you will, of traditional

Japanese culture and celebration. With lack of all other alternatives we decided to embrace this option and myself and four others left the hotel and went upon our way to the temple.

The temple was literally a couple of minutes down the road and as we approached we could hear the initial whoops and yells muddled with random synchronised clapping of the festival dancers who were already away in full swing of the celebrations; dancing joyously and harmoniously in the street at the entrance of the temple. There must've been about twenty dancers, dressed in short blue kimono's that depicted a wave pattern across their backs. They also wore scarlet red shorts that bagged around the knees and brightly coloured head bands of a multitude of colours and patterns. From the looks of the dance it must've been designed to celebrate a particular harvest of the fruits of the sea.

Our camera's clicked into life as we made an effort to capture what we could of our first real experience up close with the Japanese. The dancer's moved undeterred as they moved together in unison, some had situated themselves very close to the audience that had gathered to watch and as such meant we were able to get some good snapshots.

The spectacle was very interesting and the dancers carried on dancing down the street, allowing us opportunity to enter the gateway of the temple itself which was very large and ominous. The gatehouse itself was more like a castle gatehouse and was very sturdy and strong.

Walking inside, we were greeted with colourful stalls that lined the entrance path. Stalls of all different shapes and sizes, some offered little trinkets and souvenirs, others had hot food or what could be considered as food; from what we saw on display, we actually made a game of attempting to identify what it was. We passed through the stalls and entered an open area of the grounds. A stand decorated with bright slivers of paper stood proudly in its centre. Upon it stood the impressive visage of a large taiko drum. A traditional drum of Japanese origin that was one the central instruments of most traditional Japanese music.

"What on earth do we do?" piped Sarah inquisitively as she tugged on my arm.

"What do you mean?" I asked, unsure on what she meant.

"Well, we're foreigners in a Japanese temple! What do we do? After all, we don't want to cause offence to anyone. I forgot to look up how to act in a temple, I know it was in the handout we were given but it was something I was going to read later on. You know what the Japanese can get like, they're quite xenophobic as it is! I don't want to get kicked out, it'll be so embarrassing." I started to catch on with her point, of which it was a good one. We didn't want to cause offence or worse on our first night in Japan! Everyone knew, as foreigners we would be watched intently on the sidelines by the locals and judged by our performance with the correct etiquette and customs.

"I see, good point. Everyone..." I called, pulling together my teammates. "Try to be as respectful as you can, take a moment to watch the Japs and see what they do. Let's try and copy it to the letter shall we. I'm sure we don't want our first night in Japan to be a crap one by having ourselves escorted from a temple for doing something that they would find offensive. You know that if Coach found out, our asses would be on the line!"

With that I surveyed the scene, scanning for people who have just entered the grounds and following what they did. Luckily I caught sight of one particular local who, upon entering the temple ignored all of what was around him and went straight towards a small fountain that had in it two, long handled ladles. Of course! It triggered in me, I remembered reading a passage about this! Running water is a key feature in most temples, not only is it a spiritualistic centre with significant meaning but it is also used to purify and cleanse the body before prayer. With this I signalled the group's attention and we headed over to the fountain.

"Right…" I said, confidently, "I think this fountain is the first place we need to go. Use the ladles to wash your hands and arms. I'm sure that's what that guy did." Leading the way I took the ladle in my hand and slowly washed myself. The water looked very pure and was icy cold to the touch as it splashed and trickled off my arms into a small drainage system at the base of the fountain. The team followed suit.

Again, looking around, for the same Japanese man that was to become our unofficial 'guide', I clocked him as he made his way up the steps of the main temple front. At the top of the temple front, three huge ropes hung down, each rope was so thick they were probably thicker than a man's arm, similar to the type of rope used for making birth large ships at harbour. At the top of each of these ropes, partially hidden in shadow appeared to be what looked like a bell and in front of each was a large trough.

"Let's go up there." I said, indicating to the steps and we made way to the top. Our 'guide' had now reached the top and from his pocket he produced a small amount of change which he threw into the rustic trough. Grabbing onto the rope he proceeded to shake the rope calmly, the bell ringing out in clear tones. From here he stopped, clapped his hands twice in a fairly regimented fashion and then bowed.

"Follow my lead, everyone grab change from your pockets…oh, make sure its Japanese change if you've got it" I said as I scrambled almost excitedly in my pockets for some change.

"I haven't got any Japanese change!" exclaimed Andrew as he frantically searched for anything that resembled a Japanese coin.

Sarah piped in and handed over to Andrew a small collection of coin that he happily accepted "Here." She said "Use some of this, it's weighing my pockets down anyways" she added.

Proceeding the same way as the local did we threw our change into the collection trough. In my head I wished for luck and success for the tournament that was only a couple of days away, a good feeling came about me and made me smile.

"You!..." a short sharp voice rang out. We looked around, slightly panicked, finding its source to be from the Japanese man that was our 'guide'. He had his arm outstretched, his fingers drooped down and flicking quickly. Was he telling us to go? All of us froze, panicked as we struggled to consider what to do next. Did we offend him?

"Please...come here" he spoke again, it seems like his hand gesture is one to approach. Sheepishly we walked over to him.

"Where are you from?" he asked, his speech slightly broken as he attempted to speak English.

"E-E-England." Replied Sarah, a look of worry on her face. The Japanese man smiled.

"Ah, England...What are you doing here?" we offered no response. "Here in Japan?" he asked again.

"We're here...for Karate shiai" I offered. Hoping that he would understand our intentions. "We..." indicating to the group, "...are karate-ka."

"Oh..." The Japanese man had an impressed look across his face. "Karate-ka" he smiled and bowed, so we returned the gesture.

"What style you do?" he asked, his look changed, more inquisitive now as if he found some common ground and wanted to know more.

"Shito-ryu" I offered, I only hoped that what I was saying was making sense to him. I only assumed that I was even making the correct pronunciation! The stranger raised his eyebrows as the words were distinguishable enough for him.

"Ah! Shito-ryu! Well known here. What belt are you?"

"I'm Nidan" pointing to myself, Nidan being a second level black belt, pointing to the rest of the group, "Shodan" which meant first level. The Japanese man's eyes lit up, I only assumed he understood.

"Ah!" he exclaimed, "Nidan...shodan's...very good!" he produced a thumbs up which made us all smile and relaxed the tension significantly. He waved his arms towards the rest of the festivities behind him.

"You have good attitude...please...enjoy! You are most welcome!" he finished his flourish with a formal bow, bowing back we turned and returned to the festivities.

"I guess that means we did things right then!" joked James, chuckling softly.

"I thought, when he first called us that we messed up! He sounded very stern, I thought that he was going to ask us to leave." Said Sarah, now sounding very relieved that we were able to stay. "What do we do now?" she asked.

"Guess just enjoy what's happening" was my reply, "Just everyone be careful how they act. We could still be asked to leave if we do something wrong. Keep showing respect and there should be no trouble." With nods of understanding we split up to explore the grounds and activities that were on offer. As well as the food and souvenir stalls there was a small stand that had lantern making; a string of completed ones hung proudly above the stand, this attraction was intended more for the kids but we were on tour and keen to show support and do everything that we were able to do. There was also the main information kiosk that doubled up as another souvenir stall. This was the first point of call for Sarah who showed an interest in the history of the temple.

Despite all this, I walked through the stalls, there was something that was drawing me above the sounds and colours of the proceedings over to a small corner of the grounds where I went to almost instinctively. It was a small garden, very pretty and picturesque. At its centre was a small stone ornament, very Japanese and very in keeping with its surroundings. As I approached this area, my mind became awash with strange emotion. Standing at its edge I felt very humbled as I viewed its miniature beauty; it was a similar sort of feeling where you get déjà vu. It was as if I had known this spot before and this particular spot held a special meaning to me. I simply brushed this off as coincidental nonsense, after all, this was my first time in Japan; there was just something about it however, that made me subconsciously want to bow and so I did.

Motionless and silent, taking a pause to let the moment sink in, my moment of silent meditation was interrupted by a familiar voice. "I see you bow. Show respect. This very special spot…" Turning, I was greeted by the Japanese man that took us by surprise earlier. His voice had dropped in tone, he became very solemn as if in remembrance.

"This spot, famous warrior lies." He continued, his head held low in revered respect.

"It is a very beautiful garden. Who is it that is buried here?" I spoke slowly, still not quite sure the level of English that he spoke. "A Samurai?"

"Yes…a Samurai, great warrior."

"Miyamoto Musashi?" I enquired, offering to him the only Japanese warrior that I knew. Miyamoto Musashi was a very powerful swordsman who's written works are still alive even today.

"No, no, no, not Musashi!" smiled the man, "His name was Yoshida Kintaro. He was very good swordsman, though not well known as Musashi." The man took a deep breath, taking in the fragrance of the flowers in the garden which were producing sweet and strong fragrances in the night air.

"He was student of the sword. Fought in many great battles…especially with the Oni…"

"Oni?" I asked, the word unfamiliar to me. My Japanese was quite bad even at the best of times as I could only offer simple sentences at best.

"Yes…Oni…Demon" the man, looked me in the eye, he was very serious as he spoke with sinister tones. Surely this was just silly folk lore. I smiled at this.

"In Japan, there are many demons. Many different types, each with their own legend. Yoshida Kintaro, fought with many different demons. He was even victorious against one of the greatest demons of them all, a Dai-Oni."

"I see…" I tried to sound like I believed what I was hearing, trying not to appear rude.

"Ha!" the man burst into laughter. "You not believe!" He had clearly seen through my attempts to deny disbelief in his words. "Maybe one day you meet demon.

Then I think you believe" beaming with a broad smile, exposing a mouth that was not completely full of teeth he walked away, leaving me to stare once more at the garden. He continued to laugh and shortly turned and left me at the garden.

There was something about that man that was fundamentally creepy and although I didn't believe in his little stories of demons and typical folk lore, there was just something, a little something, that made the hairs on my neck stand as I departed from the garden.

I spied the rest of our group making one of the paper lanterns at the far end of the temple and so I thought it best to go and join them. As I got closer I could hear their loud chatter and it appeared as though they were having fun. A couple of them had already finished off their lanterns and they were stood proud on the table ready to be put up with the rest of the completed ones.

"Heya Jason" said Sarah excitedly "Come join us!" and soon I was sat down with them. On the tabletop were several plastic frames, a couple of piles of different printed sheets and a tub of pens of all different shapes and sizes.

"All you have to do is just write your well wishes on the pages and attach the sheets into the frames. One of the locals told us, so easy to do. We're only here 'cos we're not too keen on the food stands." Sarah pulled a disgusted face "They're selling all kinds of mulloch on there!"

I picked up one of the sheets and took hold of one of the pens and held myself over the sheet as I contemplated what to write.

"What you gonna wish for?" Asked Emily and I paused for a moment as I thought what to put down on the paper.

"I know, I wish for good luck at the tournament for all of us." I said and I wrote inside one of the printed squares on the paper. Smiles came on the faces of the rest of them as my wish struck a good chord with them.

I scribbled it down quickly and finished with a small drawing of the fist that was the emblem of our karate school. It felt warming to know that I now had some 'spiritual' help on the way for the tournament that was to come.

"Konbanwa!" cried out a voice on the loudspeaker as a female voice crackled over the practically antiquated speaker system. This was closely followed by sentence after sentence of Japanese that was nothing short of scrambled gibberish to my ears. Despite this, there was still a couple of words that I could pick out mostly 'gaigen' which meant foreigner and 'karate-ka' which meant students of karate. It became clear that we were being talked about and at this we were all ushered back to the central stand with the taiko drum looming predominately over us. Now the drum had a drummer, a short Japanese with a plump round face and squared glasses that could be compared to the classical wide-rimmed glasses back home. It was a friendly face and appeared very welcoming. Upon being gathered together like sheep we were approached by a woman carrying in her arms some colourful robes of bright blues and yellow, that she beckoned us to put on.

"Now, you dance with us" she said, smiling brightly.

The drum was put into action, accompanied by some local music that was being played over the loudspeaker. Joining us were some of the locals that worked at the temple, who began to act out a dance that circled the drum stand in the centre. Struggling with the movements we attempted to join in, looking highly uncoordinated we tried copying, until eventually we started to pick up the pattern.

It was like being new in a dance class; although we looked very silly, it was quite enjoyable. With little steps we soon became very fluid and we were turning and clapping and waving our arms in togetherness with the rest of the dancers. What a feeling! It gave us all a buzz and we were laughing and giggling with childish glee as the hospitality of the locals embraced us.

Dance after dance we moved on through the night, the dancers around us changed, most of the civilians that were watching had jumped into the circle and danced alongside us. It was a communal event and it was all very surreal. However, we stayed through the dances until the end as we were unofficially named as their guests of honour and felt privileged at being invited to dance with them. Such was the spectacle that was 'us', that the spectators were taking more photographs of *us* than that of the dancers who were officially meant to be there. I had never felt such hospitality and the great feeling of well being was practically overwhelming. In a sense, it was almost shameful and humbling when comparing how we treat outsiders back home.

The night pressed on as we danced into the darkness, the sweat was pouring off us from the humidity that was just as rife and noticeable as the twilight evening settled in, soaking into the bright kimono's that we were presented with but we didn't care, it was the time of our lives. Alas, however, all good things come to an end and the festival was coming to a close. Exhausted, we handed back the borrowed kimono's, thanking the locals with what broken Japanese we possessed, we left to return to the hotel and to rest from the fun and excitement that was our first evening in Japan.

We were now buzzing, our voices loud and full of life. Even as we returned to the sanctity of the hotel, our voices echoed in the corridors. There was a risk of waking people up but that didn't bother us, we've just come back from a pumping start to our Japan tour.

Slumping back down upon my bed I released a huge sigh as it became clear that with the combination of jet lag and the dropping of adrenaline my body was physically shattered beyond belief!

"Wow!" I said, "That was probably one of the best starts to a tour ever!"

"Yeah, you're telling me" replied Andrew, who showed an equal amount of exhaustion.

"How did things go with you and Sarah?" I enquired, too tired to turn it into a teasing and playful conversation piece and making it sound like a general, actual interest.

"I don't know man, we get on very well like, but I'm just worried that I might be in the dreaded 'friends zone' and if that's the case then I don't stand a chance. She's so beautiful, she's like…perfect for me!" He sounded a bit low when he spoke, I knew he liked her just didn't realise that it was this bad.

"Well have you told her how you felt?"

He scoffed, "Hell no man! I'm too scared to tell her. I've been hurt so many times before, I don't want to get like that again. Besides, we're in Japan, it would be too weird for the rest of the trip."

"Well, if you don't ask, then you wont know will you. Best not ask her before the competition, you know what she gets like beforehand." This was very true, she does get very 'focused' before a competition. If you tried to speak to her, especially on these sort of matters then you're more likely to get your head knocked off your shoulders than anything else. As soon as she finishes competing, then she's nice as anything.

"I guess you're right mate. But when should I ask her?" A good question, but there's only one place to let these matters loose.

"Well what about the after party? Best place for it, everyone's relaxed and chilled. She'll be better to speak to then."

"Yeah, good plan…can you speak to her for me?" It was quite comical how shy Andrew could be, it was strange as he was probably the better looking of the team.

"Good night Andrew!" I said, jokingly changing the subject as I rolled onto my side ready to nod off.

What an evening, only speculation and imagination could spark what we would have to come on this trip.

Chapter 5 – Strange dreams

The climb was indeed long but I had reached the end of my journey. The temple ahead was where the foul beast was hiding and so ended the long months of searching and extensive tracking. It had once been a thriving place of worship for the local community but that was many years ago, an unknown age and time, for it was now a place of desolation and desertion. No one spent the hours meditating or praying at this sacred ground, not unless they didn't fear death itself at the hands of a terrible monster like the one that was here. A monster that will claim your soul to fuel its despicable spirit and your body to feed its grotesque physical being.

It's once clean and sturdy entrance was now overgrown with vines and nature had resulted in the cracks and holes developing in the walls. Silence was the only sound present in this dark place, not even the calls of the birds or the cicadas could be heard. I felt alone in this place and the dread feeling of loneliness penetrated my hardened and steeled heart.

Walking steadfastly into the temple, dimly lit with the morning sun that shone through the open doorway and through tiny holes in the structure that had been created through the arduous wear and tear of age; picking out little pockets of beaming light, that were casting long shadows in their wake. The air was rife with the feeling of dread and the solemnest aroma of death and as I continued into the darkness my mouth became dry with the anticipation of what was to come and the hairs on my neck were alive with its own electricity as they stood proudly to attention. It was as if it were a warning, as all the hairs on my neck were screaming at me to leave this place as fast as possible. I put this down to the desperate urge to be alert in this dangerous surrounding and did not want to shame myself with the notion of fear creeping into my conditioned heart.

Continuing my way, my footing slipped slightly as I stepped upon what was wet ground, taking my balance that I easily recovered from. Peering down to see the cause of the upset, I turned my nose up in disgust as I saw that the cause was a sickening pool of blood laced with the grisly unidentifiable remains of human flesh, mingled with stray bone and gristle. This pool was obviously fresh, the blood had not yet dried into the tatami mats. It seems that the beast had recently fed and had perhaps returned to a state of rest or hiding.

Scanning briefly, similar pools festooned themselves around the room, most were old and the blood had turned into a coppery stain where it lay upon the mats and splashed wildly against the walls. The faded scenes of religious origins that once lined these holy walls were now ruined with the grisly defiling that had been committed. Some were soiled with the taint of blood, others had been clawed away to a state where they were unrecognisable by unappreciative talons that I assumed came from the beast itself. Such a scene was as horrifying as a slaughter that remains from a bloody battlefield and there was no doubt in my mind that such a scene would leave its own distinctive mark on my battle hardened mind.

Caution should follow my steps, as if this blood was as fresh as it indeed it was, it means that the beast that made it, still presided on these once respectful grounds. To proceed idly would mean that the next pool to be added to this grisly collection would be that of my own. Such a thought brought a knot up from my stomach into my throat that I had to quickly gulp back down. My thoughts were soon confirmed as the dark silence was disturbed; disturbed by a low, bestial growl that rumbled as a low thunder. Deep and feral it echoed around the contours of the room that provided good acoustics.

Instantly I reached for my sword, gently resting my hand on its hilt and steadying my thoughts as the touch upon my old companion tended to comfort me; allowing me to centre myself so I was not to become constricted by being riddled with fear. The beast would soon taste its cold steel like countless others of its vile kin before it.

From the corner of my eye I spied the next way point of my journey. A hole, larger than a man had been blasted away as if by some fiery explosion; exposing the bare rock of the mountain that the temple was situated upon. Rubble lay scattered and strewn haphazardly around the mouth of this rough entrance.

This must've been the way to the under catacombs, the inner sanctum, where the demon had once been imprisoned. So long ago that it was uncertain when it was originally detained.

Something had somehow disturbed its supposedly eternal slumber and as such it had broken free to feast on human flesh once more. It was up to me now to not just subdue it once more but to banish its soul back to the hell in which it had been born from.

I was hit with the question as to why would anyone build a temple on top of this beasts tomb? Was this temple originally built as a means of showing triumph over the imprisonment of this unholy monster? Or perhaps the architects and labourers of old were made unawares and naïve to the presence of the demon and this temple was erected many years after its imprisonment.

My sword was one of eight ancient blades that had the ability to send the spirit of the beast and its kin back to the otherworldly abyss from which they came. It helped provide some comfort along with my trained sword-arm. Steeling my nerves, I approached softly, with my footsteps producing only the slightest of noise, almost indistinguishable to the untrained ear. Closer and closer I approached, with every step, the smell of death became stronger and stronger until it reached the point where you could taste its bitter sting on the tongue. Such a stench was practically unbearable to the average human being with a weak stomach but still I managed to press on as I stepped inside the crude archway. Through my travels I had seen many instances of death and the stench was beginning to grow on me where it did not bother me.

The hole opened out into a deep stairway of tall, rough steps cut directly into the rock. The passage itself was lined with a slimy moss and water sporadically dripped from areas on the wet walls.

At the bottom of the stairway, a dull bluish-green light provided sufficient enough lighting so I could pick out where I was going; yet it was, at this point, where its source was not yet known as it flickered and pulsated like light as if off a pool somewhere in the dark. The light reflected sharply off the moss covered walls and was eerie and spooky to say the least.

Again, the growl made itself known only this time it was louder and I knew that soon I would be face to face with its owner. At this point my left thumb pushed against the hand guard of my sword unlocking it from its sheath, ready at any point to provide a lightning fast killing slash to anyone or indeed, anything, that wished to attack me.

"Weeelcome…" snarled a feral voice, its beastly tones went straight through me to my very core. It sent chilled shivers down by spine and I felt that all the warmth in my blood had been sucked away. My heart pounded heavily in my chest as the static in the air intensified brilliantly.

Approaching the bottom of the stairs my view suddenly became blurred as the world around me vanished out into simply nothingness only to be replaced by the grim visage of the demon, eyes yellow with ebony pupils that were mere slits that contrasted vividly against the yellow. Its thin snarling face outlined by a brilliant and wild mane of crimson hair. Its mouth opened, displaying row upon row of irregularly spaced, sharp, pointed teeth; presenting itself with mix of both drool and ichors of its countless victims.

"JASON!" the voice screamed out with a terrifyingly deep rumble of a beastly nature. The scream bounced around in my head with the harmonics of it making me feel that my head would explode at any point.

With a bolt I sprang up, to find I was just in the safe confines of my hotel room. Although still dark, my eyes were quick to adjust to the dark conditions. My body dripped with the heavy moisture of sweat and my muscles twitched slightly, uncontrollably, as I struggled to control my breathing which had become a shallow and erratic pant. Grabbing my heart with my one hand, its pulse was fast, as if fuelled by adrenaline as thought I had been fighting for my life.

But no, it was all nothing but a bad dream, a nightmare. The guy at the festival must've struck a chord, how silly of me. Looking across, Andrew lay fast asleep, lightly snoring, my nightmarish antics had not disturbed him from his peaceful slumber. That's good, at least I've not been embarrassed. But what a strange dream, throughout it I was sure that I had that same feeling of a 'connection' that I felt when I stood at that little temple garden; right before that strange Jap decided to try and freak me out with talk of demons. Well, I say try, it's obvious that he managed to succeed on a level. Scorning myself for succumbing to such idiocy it was time to head back to sleep.

Gently slipping out of bed so as not to disturb Andrew I made my way to the bathroom and switched on the light. The bright and sudden glare of the bulb strained my eyes as they attempted to refocus with the introduction of such a suddenly bright light.

Staring forth at the mirror above the white sink I looked dreadful! My pupils were wide and the bags that were underneath my eyes were almost as large as my luggage. Pouring myself a quick glass of cold water from the tap and moping my moistened face with a hand towel I returned to my bed a little more refreshed and calmer than before.

Lying back on the bed, taking a brief moment to stare at the ceiling before my eyes closed naturally by themselves.

It was only a bad dream, nothing more. Bloody Japanese and their outdated superstitious nonsense.

Chapter 6 – I don't speak Japanese!

Day two of our Japanese experience; on the trip itinerary it was the official welcome meal for all nations where we would be greeted by Sensei and begin to set ourselves mentally for the competition that was to commence on the following day. Although it was meant to be a case for the nations to begin mingling, the socialising and networking with each other that is implied with the welcome meal would not be the case before the tournament and everyone tended to keep themselves to themselves; banding together with others from their home country. It was all based around the principle of safety in numbers. There is a time for socialising and cultural exchange but this was not it and everyone wanted to maintain the tight bond and focus that they have developed as a team.

Our welcome meal we've been informed was to be a traditional Japanese meal and this did not bode well with most of my team mates. Most had never tasted Japanese cuisine before and the majority were put off with the thought of raw fish, a typical stereotype as to the regular 'Japanese' dish. That was the narrow minded impression that we had ingrained into us and we knew of nothing else that could constitute as 'Japanese'.

To be honest, I didn't quite stomach the idea of it either but I was willing to give it a try unlike the majority of my friends; I always lived by the motto *'try anything once, twice if you like it'*. Some of my team mates had already decided to sneak off to a burger bar a couple of hours beforehand and grab a quick bite, so as if they didn't agree with the food then they would not starve completely tonight. Unfortunately I didn't think of this tactical brainwave and so was preparing to hit the foreign food head on and do my best to disregard any bad tastes that might be encountered for the purposes of controlling my hunger.

The meal was being held at a large hotel that had one of Japan's finest restaurants and bars integrated into it. The hotel itself we were told was situated on Kobe's picturesque harbour front which offered some very fine views especially at night where everything around is lit up spectacularly, especially by the occasional cruise ship and floating restaurant that held dock in the harbour bay.

"How do I look?" asked Andrew as he stood in front of me, awaiting my approval. Dressed in smart blue jeans with a sleek black, short-sleeved shirt. His hair, immaculate, in its spiky yet stylish mixed up look. It was so perfect that you could probably figure out a mathematical formula for the angles and vectors that the individual spikes were subjected to.

"Yeah, you look good mate. Not my type, but good none the less!" I joked.

"Do you think Sarah will notice?" He asked, his mind still on *other* things.

"Yeah, she should, just remember though it is *before* the tournament. You know what her head is like now. Don't push it and she'll be alright. Also, coach will rip you a new one if she ends up getting too distracted before the competition." I turned to the mirror and went to straighten up my shirt that I was wearing. I was similar to Andrew with what I was wearing except that my shirt was a brilliant white with a small pattern on the chest. Silently I spoke to myself, reassuring myself that I look good.

"We better make a move on" I blurted, peering over and realising what time it was. Rushing out the door we both scrambled down to the reception where everyone was to be gathered. Arriving, coach's face was grim and grey.

"You're late!" He scorned, eyes transfixed on us as soon as we entered the lobby.

"Sorry coach" I replied sheepishly, unable to keep eye contact with him.

"Right everybody, the taxi's are waiting. Load up and let's get going." Coach's attention turned to the rest of the group who have all turned out smartly dressed for the meal. On his command the team piled out of the lobby and straight to the convoy of taxi's who were lined up ready and waiting; the drivers stood by their vehicles dressed in smart shirts and pristine white chauffeur styled gloves. They appeared more like limo drivers than taxi drivers; it seems they go that extra mile for first impressions in Japan. Another cool aspect of Japanese taxi's is the automatic rear doors; to some this is just more of a gimmick but I did have the nature of enjoying the little things in life.

In my taxi was myself, Andrew and Emily and as we got in we noticed how clean and immaculate even the insides were, mirroring perfectly the look of top quality professionalism that the drivers instilled. Very nice I thought. The air conditioning that blasted out regularly kept the taxi at an ambient temperature, very pleasing, as it was still quite humid and near intolerable outside.

"Ohiyo Gasaymasu" spoke the driver. I looked blankly at him, luckily Emily knew what he said and responded.

"Ohiyo Gasaymasu" she said quickly, "It means hello" as she turned and informed me.

"Yeah, yeah, I know that" blushing as I didn't like being corrected on small details that I should know about. The taxi's engine started up and the air conditioning kicked in, the blast of the cold air was refreshing and we set off.

"Everyone take your seats, we're table number three" said Coach as he pulled out a chair with a loud scrape. The restaurant was filling up as the other nations were quick to join us. Each country had been assigned their own table, each marked with flowery centrepieces in oddly shaped glass bowls that contained the flags of the respective nations. Flanking our table there were the Australians and Japanese. Beyond them lies the French,

Italians, Spanish, Germans and last the New Zealanders. At the head table were the national chiefs of all the respected countries and Sensei Takeo who sat upright with perfect posture.

The restaurant was lit very cosily, up lighters on the walls and down lighters on the ceiling complimented each other and provided a relaxing yet upper classed atmosphere. The high ceiling provided the perfect acoustics that amplified everyone's conversations so that it became a jumbled cacophony of mixed language. What I discovered was that this helped to loosen everyone up so that the first welcome meal was not rigid and completely formalised.

Our table settings were individually lined with crystal glasses and several pitchers of iced water, each place setting made up of the menu, a folded cotton napkin and a pair of ivory chopsticks resting upon little stands so that they were raised slightly off the table surface. Faces began to grimace all around me at the possible thought of the lack of knives and forks. Sitting down, a couple of my teammates went straight for their chopsticks and with focused, concentrated stares attempted to master the art and come to grips with how to use them. As Brits, we did tend as a whole to be not so knowledgeable and open minded when it comes to other cultures and their ways which would appear strange and alien to us. A weakness in our own culture if you wanted my opinion.

The next comical moment was when people decided to look at the menu and reeled back in shock and exhaust grunts of horror as it was all entirely in Japanese. There wasn't even a picture option to accompany the lines of unreadable scribble that they could rely upon as a back up so they can randomly point to and have some idea in what was coming.

Bracing myself, I picked up my menu and opened the hard backed cover, but as I stared at the menu, I didn't join my comrades with their orchestrated groans.

What luck! It seems as though my one was the only menu that was in English and I took a moment to scan the contents. "I think I'll be quite adventurous tonight." I thought to myself, doing my best to try and inspire me with confidence.

"What would you like sir?" asked the waiter who seemed to appear out of nowhere. Peering around, everyone else on the table looked blank and was waiting for someone to speak and start off. After a few moments of awkward silence and as no one else was seeming to take the initiative it was up to me to start.

"Can I have the mixed sashimi as the starter, followed by the soba noodle chicken with rice and miso soup on the side please?"

"Of course sir, can I get you something to drink?"

"Just a coke please, and a small serving of sake, lightly warmed through if possible" I was amazed at how well the waiter could speak English. We were indeed the luckier table as a quick inspection to our neighbouring tables revealed the language battle as the groups attempted to convey their wishes to the rest of the staff.

"Certainly sir, is the rest of the table ready to order or should I give you more time?" the waiter asked, speaking to me as if I was the head of the group. Smiling at this misinterpretation of the hierarchy I responded politely with,

"I think they'll need a few more minutes." With that the waiter bowed politely and left to attend to another table. Emily, who was sat opposite me was staring at me puzzled and confused.

"Lazarus?" asked Coach, his voice somewhat light and questionable, making me turn my head in acknowledgement to the calling of my name.

"Since when have you been able to speak Japanese?" he asked.

I raised an eyebrow, what a random question to ask! I don't speak Japanese and I haven't really spoken a word since arriving in Japan.

"Eh?" for some unknown reason, that was the only response I could muster to the question at that given moment.

"Well first of all, how are you able to know what's on the menu? The damn thing's in Japanese! And we all know that it's not as if anything on there looks anything that could resemble English." Coach pointed down to the open menu that lay in front of him, true enough; his menu was completely Japanese. I smiled wickedly.

"Oh. Well I've got an English copy here" as I picked up my copy of the menu and passed it over to him for his inspection.

"Good man! You should've bloody said before Lazarus" he said cheerfully as he eagerly took my menu from me. Eagle eyed he peered at it before saying with a dumbfounded tone accompanied by a raised eyebrow, similar to the one I showed him.

"Are you having a laugh boy? This isn't in English." He passed it back to me with irritated eyes and I opened it to look at it to confirm what he was saying. Surely Coach was having a laugh back at me. But I was greeted by page upon page of just Japanese script. It was completely unrecognisable and obviously not the menu I was looking at earlier.

"Has anyone else picked up the menu I was looking at? It was an English menu." Looking around I was hoping to obtain some support to my claim but everyone else just looked at me funny, no one had picked up my menu or was at least not claiming to have swiped my menu.

"Even so Jason, if you're *mystery menu* is around here somewhere. When did you learn to actually speak Japanese? I didn't know you were that fluent!" Coach seemed to have it instilled in him that I knew Japanese. "You could be elevated to our unofficial translator for the trip!"

"But Coach..." I stuttered, bewildered "I don't know how to speak Japanese, only karate related words and 'hello', 'goodbye' and 'thank you'. That's really about it. Just ask Emily, she saw how bad I was in the taxi. I wouldn't know where to begin in stringing a sentence together." Now even I was starting to get confused with everything.

"Nah, now you're just messing about!" he said, "You spoke with the waiter you muppet! You spoke perfect

Japanese and ordered something, we all heard you! What was it you ordered anyways?"

It then hit me, Coach had a knack of catching me off guard with whimsical little jokes, surely this was one of those times. "Coach, now *you're* just messing about. The waiter spoke English, very well I might add. I ordered some sashimi, chicken noodles, rice and some soup. Oh and a coke and some warmed sake, I heard somewhere it's what they drink over here." Again spying my team mates, hoping that one of them would be smiling to give the joke away; but no one was smiling. They still were transfixed by confusion. Emily spoke out again;

"The waiter didn't speak English. You were speaking fluent Japanese." There was an air of shock in her voice.

"Didn't you hear him? The guy speaks English!" I contested. Again, all faces looked confused, everyone was really working overtime on the joke to maintain its clarity. Quite admirable but I was beginning to become a tad bit frustrated at being the centre of yet another practical joke, which was considered to be the normal practice.

"Yeah, you'll see…" I snorted. "Wait until he comes back and I'll look like the *fool* when I ask him if he speaks English." I spoke very confidently, I'd caught onto their little prank but it's ok, someone had obviously switched menu's with me when I wasn't looking and they're all in on the 'lost in translation' gag. They played a similar one in Italy a few years ago, though it wasn't me who was at the centre of it. In fact, it was such a while back now that I totally forgot who it was.

"Here he is!" I called, spotting the waiter approaching the table again. It was definitely the same waiter as before, I was so sure of it that I would've bet money on it. This time he went straight over to coach who was trying his best to speak slowly and using his hands to try and get his message across as precisely as he could. He was really trying to sell this gag and I felt sorry for the poor waiter who probably didn't have a clue what was happening in regards to the joke. I began to feel embarrassed as it was sounding almost patronising.

"Can we…" Coach waved his hands to indicate the rest of the table. "…have what…he is having." He pointed to the waiter's little order book and then pointed to me. The waiter bowed his head repeatedly as if he understood.

"Coach, don't try and trick me, the waiter speaks perfect English" turning my attention to the waiter "Don't you?" I asked. My question was met with a puzzled look from the waiter, who appeared not too dissimilar as the looks from what my team mates gave.

"Surimasen. Wakanimasen" said the waiter, still puzzle faced.

"It means he doesn't understand" piped in Emily smugly. But how could that be? He was speaking English earlier on and there was no way that anyone could've taken him aside to let him in on the joke. After all, everyone was still at the table and no-one had left recently. Now it was my turn to appear properly dazed and confused and I could feel my face burning red.

"It's probably just a different waiter." I passed off, trying to find some rational form of explanation for what just occurred.

"No, I think it's the same one" said Emily, being pretty sure on the fact. Perhaps I was going mad? Ever since coming to Japan, things have been a little more stranger than they normally are. Perhaps I was still suffering from jet lag. Yeah, that must be it, I managed to convince myself. I was just jetlagged and tired from the seemingly endless flight here that everything is just one giant trick on the mind.

It wasn't long for the meal to come swiftly out to us, everyone laughed and joked with the earlier peculiarities that happened becoming now long forgotten. Or at least forgotten to everyone except myself as I struggled to provide a strong enough case to satisfy me on what had just occurred. None the less, apart from the small mystery, it was still an enjoyable and relaxing time.

Interrupting the noise, came the high pitching 'ching' of a tapped wine glass and attentions turned to face the head table. Once the din had settled, Sensei Takeo and another man who I guessed was his appointed translator stood to their feet. Sensei spoke, a strong accented Japanese closely followed by the interpreter. His speech went something like this;

"Good evening and greetings to everyone. I, as the head of the association in Japan, would like to welcome all practitioners from the many nations that are here today. You have all come at good time, to celebrate the art that we all practice, in its homeland. You are all students of Budo, the warrior way, and I look forward to the display of skills and the attitudes that a student of Budo should show during the following competition. May the competition be successful for all and enjoyable to all those who take part in it.

This journey that you are about to undertake should be to all more than just a sporting meeting and I hope that in your travels to come, you will enjoy the beauties that the Japanese culture and its people has to offer. Please enjoy everything that you come in contact with and please experience with an open mind. As things in Japan are much different to your home lands. Please enjoy and learn from other nations as we, as karate-ka should not become clouded with personal opinion and we as a people can learn from everyone we meet. Now enjoy the rest of your evening and enjoy the tournament tomorrow."

With the end of the speech came the rapturous applause as all nations joined in recognition of him and of each other as we stood together. It was almost deafening as the echoes crescendo all around. Then came the dawning thought, the tournament *was* tomorrow! Time had come around very fast and the pinnacle of our training over the last eight months was to come to fruition in the morning, it was always an electrifying thought to know that a tournament was practically upon you, it was the competitor in me coming out that revelled in the fact.

Once the applause ended, the room returned to the relaxed, yet noisy atmosphere that it had prior to the speech. Everyone was having a good time, the drink was flowing very well around certain areas of the congregated nationalities and some of the members of the other nations were beginning to become too much under the influence and some reached the realms of boisterous. This was especially true amongst some of the Italian team who's naturally relaxed 'party' characteristic was becoming amplified by the intoxicating liquor. Our team had been given strict orders not to reach that level of drunkenness until after the tournament, although the temptation was great, we knew that the wrath of our coach would be that severe that it was best not to.

Tomorrow we will be sharp and on the ball. Tomorrow is when we show the rest of the world what we can do. The British team was in the homeland of karate and were going to kick ass!

Chapter 7 – Kamaitachi

S ensei called for my presence of which I obliged. Kneeling outside of his study I requested to enter.

"Sensei, it is Yoshida, you called for me?"

"Please, Yoshida Shihan, enter." Sensei's tone was soft as he spoke fairly quietly. It was difficult to ascertain the general feeling as to the reason I was called for. On acceptance I pulled open the door and swiftly entered, crouched low and knelt before Sensei who was in the process of preparing some tea.

"Yoshida Shihan, thank you for coming so quickly. I have an important errand for you. Yesterday we had received a surprise visitor from the Imperial council arrive to our dojo. You were away, so you unfortunately did not have the pleasure of meeting him personally, as I wished that you could've. They have informed me of a tournament that is to be held in Himeji. This tournament is at the instruction of the almighty Shogun himself and its purpose is as a test of swordsman from all the provinces.

The prize of the competition is the commission of eight swords that they are calling the 'Eight Dragons'. These swords are said to be crafted of the highest standard and as such are rumoured to be granted with special abilities. The best of the eight is said to be so sharp that the blade itself can be cut through a pool of water and because of its sharpness will come out without a drop on its blade and be as dry as it first went in.

Now, I have been granted, because of the school's prestigious name, the opportunity to present two students for the competition. It is an honour to be allowed to present this number of participants as the majority of schools that have been asked to attend have only been allowed a singular place. As such, I have chosen both you and your charge, Fujibayashi, to represent us at the competition."

Sensei stopped just momentarily to pour some hot tea into a small cup that he had placed in front of him.

"This is a great honour for both yourselves and the name of the school. I have chosen you and Fujibayashi to be our representatives because I believe you will be able to show the true essence of our style in front of the Lord Shogun. For I am far too old now to present myself to such a gathering."

"Thank you Sensei, but may I suggest Ryoko as a more suitable representative to myself." Keeping in line with protocol I had to suggest my senior before presenting myself.

"Ryoko is a good choice, a grand choice, but I have a separate errand in store for him that is for him alone. No,

I am confident in my decision with you and Fujibayashi" Sensei sounded very sure of his decision and so I was obliged to accept.

"Now the errand that I have for you Yoshida, is to deliver the letters of acceptance to the Imperial representative who is staying at an inn just outside the provincial borders. Please inform Fujibayashi and then deliver the papers."

"Yes Sensei, it shall be done" I replied formally and bowed to him.

"The papers you will find over there." Said Sensei, as he pointed to a small wooden cabinet that was off to the left hand side of the room. I looked over to it and sure enough, even from here I could see that atop the small dark wood box was the papers; a scroll that was rolled up neatly, sitting motionless awaiting for me to receive them.

I sprung from my position over to the cabinet and grasped the scroll gently in my hand as I removed it from the cabinet. The parchment rustled in my hand and the wooden ends that helped keep the cylindrical shape had some form of gold filament pressed on the carved knob endings.

"I shall see to it at once Sensei. Do you require anything else from me?" I asked before taking my leave.

"No Yoshida Shihan. That will be all."

The journey to the inn would take just a little more than a day as I was taking the southern road, which was the quickest. I would pass through two of the outlying villages before coming to the bridge that crosses the river at Osuyama on the edge of the province. It is at this bridge where I would take a short rest period, the inn is situated around three hours walk from the bridge and it is a familiar place where I have been before on occasion.

It is a peaceful little place where the willows swayed gently in the spring breeze and nature was at its finest and purest, so it would be the perfect for a spot of light meditation to settle myself before meeting the official representative of the Shogunate. It would be the perfect preparation before a meeting with someone of such a high stature and whereby the subject matter was of this importance.

Reaching the bridge, everything was as it should be. The willows were unspoilt, the river flowed smoothly under the bridge, the sun bouncing tranquilly off the light ripples and waves of the sparkling clear waters. Within the water itself would be small fish and other forms of river life that existed in harmony with this spot of beauty.

Even still, there was just something not right, not with the surroundings but the feeling I got when approaching. It was as though I was being watched and I felt the bitter, metallic taste on the back of my throat that was a instinctual reaction to something being amiss. A warning sign of trouble.

Reaching slowly and smoothly with my left hand I held the scabbard of my sword for good measure and security as I walked, the tip of my thumb lightly touched the base of the hand guard. Perhaps I was just being too overly cautious. After all, there was no evident sign of anyone, no movement in the trees or the bushes. But there were also no noises that you would expect to be made by any birds or insects who would be undeterred about my being there. There was something wrong, something not natural.

Stepping onto the bridge, the wood creaking naturally and noticeably underfoot, this was nothing new, for it was an old bridge and I had heard this noise before. The wind picked up all around, rustling and howling through the multitude of surrounding trees. The sound of the sudden gush was both haunting and chilling. The sky clouded over almost instantly sending everything near black. It was as though the sun had been extinguished, a candle snubbed out by giant unseen fingers. It was the river however that became the most disturbing and told me that there was definitely something afoot. The once cool, clear waters had become tainted. They flowed a blood red, fish and other pond life replaced by bobbing and flowing skulls and other bones of defiled, long dead corpses. What manner of sorcery was this?

Across from me, materialised what appeared to be the image of a man. He was slightly taller and broader than the average man and he wore old armour of an earlier fashion that I had not seen in a long time, tarnished with the visible signs of age and neglect. This was completed with ripped and torn cloth underneath which one could only imagine was once a kimono. His face was partly hidden by a sort of scarf; similar to the ones worn by the Yamabushi or mountain warrior monks but not as clean and well presented as it should be like the ones worn by the mountain spirituals. From what I could see, his skin was as grey and pallid as ash and his eyes were as red as the river that flowed beneath us.

"Who goes there?" I called, not truly wishing to know what the response would be.

"I am the Kamaitachi Mitsuo, I have been waiting for you Yoshida-san from beyond the great void." the man spoke, his voice was gruff and distorted in a sense that he was hitting more than any singular note at any given time. But if he was what he said he was, then he was no man, he was Kamaitachi.

The Kamaitachi were demonic warriors, said of legend to be born from the souls of evil dead warriors of old, their hatred of mankind powerful enough to make them reborn from the world beyond in a different form.

If this was indeed the case, then this monster would be unlike any other warrior that I have faced before for they are powerful creatures of the darkness; fast and strong with the strength and ability to crush a man's skull with their bare hands. They were no longer men and the blood of the demon flowed through their blackened hearts. But this all must surely be some kind of trick, devised by an elaborate illusionist or a very well educated bandit, for Kamaitachi are only said to be merely legend. I will see if I can uncover this little ruse.

"How do you know my name Kamaitachi? If that's what you truly are!" I challenged, inquisitively but not dumbfounded in order to gauge the strangers reaction.

"I know a lot about you Yoshida, for I have seen into the depths of your very soul! I know what lies ahead for you and it is from this knowledge that my Master has ordered me to end your life this day."

Grabbing my sword hilt, I crouched my weight low, dropping my centre ready for the charge.

"We will see which of us dies today demon! But I can assure you it will not be me!" I cried out, locking into his eyes with my own we were ready to fight. The Kamaitachi raised his hand and chanted some archaic words. The language was not one that I understood, an obscure dialect that wasn't recognisable and as he chanted his hand glowed with an ominous, pulsating swirling yellow light. From this eerie, pale light materialised the demon's weapon of choice. A naginata. A halberd atop a long pole, the blade standing taller than the average man when the end of the staff was stood on the ground. This one was thicker and heavier than regular naginata that a samurai wielded and a single swing of its long curved blade would easily cut through the muscles and bones of a man's torso. As it was this beast that was wielding it, I could only hazard a guess that it may cleave through more than one body in a single swing! For this I must be careful.

The eyes of the Kamaitachi narrowed to thin, menacing slits as he swung the naginata into a fighting stance; the blade swooshing through the air, he pointed the long, cruel-looking blade towards my throat. With a martial roar I leapt at him, drawing my sword and parrying the blade aside in a singular smooth motion and then cutting downwards towards the demon. But my strike landed short as the beast moved with a supernatural speed, jumping back out of range and swinging the naginata in a deadly arc towards me as he glided in the air.

Ducking my head at the very last moment, the massive blade sailed over me and crashed mightily into the bridge, sending a multitude of splinters and wooden debris up into the air. Rushing in to strike, the beast pulled the naginata back and parried my blow against the thick staff before we both pulled back out of range of each other once more. Our initial engagement resulting in nothing more than a simple draw.

"Now it's my turn" said the demon, turning the blade as it pointed dangerously towards me. He jumped and swung, strike after strike he sent at me, whistling the blade that cut through the air without resistance and crashed through sections of the bridge, sending volleys of splintered shards wildly about. My only attempt against such brute strength was to dodge the blows as they came and I twisted and turned and jumped around them all, bar one. The final strike of his deadly combination caught me off balance as the skilled warrior became quickly accustomed to my methods of movement and my only hope rested in stopping it with my sword as I moved to block. But the naginata crashed into my comparatively small blade and the sheer strength forced my guard to collapse under its power as it cut into my arm. With a wince of pain I dropped to a singular knee and the Kamaitachi pulled back ready to deliver the final death blow.

Pain and anger filled me, the very thought of defeat at the hands of another warrior was shameful. My sword lay prone next to me, there was no time to grab it and strike. The demonic warrior stood defiant over me, his heavy naginata held strongly and unflinching.

"It is now time for you to die, Yoshida, Shihan of…" But before he could finish his sentence, I took advantage of the over confident pause to the fight as he began to monologue my demise. From here I had moved explosively from my kneeling position like a bolt of wild lightning. His decision to speak was to be the instrument of his downfall, a distraction that took his focus away for the briefest of moments, but long enough to make significant change to the situation; diving to my feet and moving inside the extended length of the naginata I had managed to move so fast that I was now face to face with the demon. My right hand had shot forward, the fingertips strong through years of diligent training and penetrating the demons fleshy throat through his makeshift scarf that fluttered with the breeze. The look of defiance and mountain like strength in the Kamaitachi's face soon changed to one of shock and the horror of its impending death.

"How?…" he asked, gargling a bloody noise from his throat. He tried to bring his naginata to a position to help him but my other hand held it locked in a vice like grip, he continued to jolt and struggle with the weapon but it was no use. With a rapid twist and pull I had ripped the beast's throat clean from his body as my fingers pierced its leathery skin; and he emanated a horrible, curdling death cry, a scream that was produced mysteriously without the requirements of a voice box and as the life flowed from him, his soon lifeless body fell onto the bridge with a hallowing thud followed by a light bounce.

Now he was dead at my feet and I stood over him, victorious.

From the dangerous pitfalls of combat came a new technique and one that I grew quickly accustomed to. With a short prayer to the gods I took some quick moments to reiterate in my mind the technique that I had just brought into the world. From the method that my body prepped itself to the final tear of the demon's skin. It felt very good. A mental note I took, to remind me to develop this technique further as it had just saved my life against what would've been one of the most dangerous of opponents. The sheer importance of this technique means that it will require a new name. This too requires some thought and later on today I would take the time and effort to meditate over this decision.

I looked at my fingertips, observing them with a brand new light as I gazed at them briefly as though I had never truly paid proper attention to them, before peering down at my fallen foe. His face scarf had removed itself from his face to reveal the truly disgusting sight that was his mouth. Most of the flesh had been removed but though not by my hand, more so as if it had been conducted at some point during what was his wretched life; before his resurrection as an ethereal warrior of the demonic; if indeed this was actually the nature of my foe. It revealed dirty, scorched bone that was the broken and jagged remains of his jaw and accompanying teeth. Bone that had been scorched by the numerous fires of hell. The sight almost turned my normally iron clad stomach.

With the Kamaitachi now dead, the scene and its surroundings changed back to how it was before our encounter. The sun returned in the sky and the winds had died down to the mild breeze that was present before. The river had also reverted back to the clear refreshing sight of water, the blood red torrent now crystal clear and peaceful. Everything was as it should as the illusionists spell had been swiftly removed with his passing.

Peering back to the demon, its body had vanished and I assume it returned to wherever the spirit of the beast had originated from. I was now left standing on the bridge that still bore the scars of the battle.

My arm was still wounded and with blood still ebbing from the open cut the need to seek a doctor became paramount. Although I have had the experience of seeing many different types of sword wounds I was by no means a learned expert in the field of treatment. Though I did understand enough to know that I wasn't going to be losing the arm which relieved me thoroughly. My light meditation could wait. I needed to get to the inn.

Chapter 8 – Tournament Day

"**W**here's my pads? I cant find my bloody foot pads!" said Andrew frantically, as he scurried back and forth in the cramped hotel room. Pacing quickly, lifting random items of scattered clothing, he panicked and was working himself up into a mild frenzy. "I've got everything apart from them! I'm sure I packed them. My lucky red foot pads! Where the hell are they!?"

"Have you looked in your kit bag?" I said, as I emerged out of the bathroom. Towel around my waist, steaming from a nice hot bath to warm and loosen up the muscles.

"Yes!" he said, snapping short "First place I looked!"

"Well, look again, I'm sure I saw them there earlier." I said, knowing that his frustrations would probably make him clumsy and careless.

"Alright!" he snapped angrily as he gave in to my suggestion, "I'll look again…" he picked up his kit bag and peered inside, digging his hands in and rummaged the contents he stopped in realisation as he grabbed hold of them as they laid hidden at the bottom.

"Ok smart arse!" he said scornfully. I've never seen him get so stressed before a competition. It was almost amusing to watch, in a cruel way mind you, but I resisted the urge to wind him up further and considered a more reassuring, calm approach would be more tactful at this time.

"Relax!" I said, as I started getting dressed. "It's just like any other competition mate, you don't normally get this worked up! Just chill."

"I know, I know" he said, trying his best to calm himself down. "I don't know why I'm on edge mate, guess it's because it's my first time against the Japs." He was right, it was the first time for most of us, we were already given the stories of tournaments past by Coach and Sensei. Stories of the Japanese's skill and their nature. Some stories revolved around how they fight their competitions without softened mats underfoot and that throws and take downs were made on the hard wooden floors. One even stretched to how one fight resulted in a competitor being thrown onto the floor and their Japanese opponent stamping on their head, knocking them out cold! This extreme variation of competition was completely alien to us and it made some of us slightly more on edge I guess.

"Chill mate, we've worked hard for this, just do what you do and you'll do alright. Doesn't care what bloody nationality they are, just kick ass and take names." Shrugging off the competition, I must've sounded cocky but if it lifts spirits…

"Yeah, you're right…" he said, "Now, where's my belt gone?" he continued. I let loose a slight sigh as I felt my attempts of cheering him up fell upon deaf ears. I carried on getting ready, unlike Andrew I always carried a separate bag which I knew had everything pre packed and ready to go. There were no last minute jitters in my mind when it came to equipment prep. The constant need to be prepared and the meticulous attention to details and planning was a part of my character that some say is a blessing, others more of an irritation. I know that some even went to referring to it more as Obsessive Compulsive Disorder!

Soon I had my trackie top zipped up, as I spied myself in the mirror. It's emblazoned badge and machine stitched 'UK team' stood out proudly. Every time I put it on it always filled me with a warm feeling, a good feeling that was proud and almost majestic. It's a feeling that I assume that all other athletes share no matter what their particular sport, it's the glory and honour of representing your country.

"Right" sighed Andrew "I think that's me set. Pads, gi, belts, gum shield. Yep that's me set" as he drummed off the mental checklist.

"You got plenty of water?" I asked, knowing how hot and humid this country is, he'll definitely need it.

"Ah!" he exclaimed worryingly "No, I haven't yet. I guess I'll get some later when I see one of those vending machines." With that I threw him one of my spare bottles, as I knew I had more than enough to see me through today.

"Cheers" he said as he pressed it in his bag that was close to overflowing and forcefully pulled the zip shut. "I'll buy you a drink or something at the afterparty."

"You should have a kit bag like mine, ready to go, then you don't have to worry about missing stuff." I said, boasting, smiling at being proud of my overly obsessive preparation.

"Are you kidding? You know me! I'm not that organised..." said Andrew "...cramps my style!" he laughed. "What time we at?"

"Got about ten minutes before we meet down in the lobby." I said, "You sure you're ready?" I asked, acting more like his bloody mother than a teammate.

"Yes, mate, all under control and good to go."

"Good, how are you feeling? You ready to rock?" I asked, doing my bit to build the sporting attitude up a notch.

"Yeah, I'll be fine. I guess it's because I just want to impress today that's all. You know what the Japs are like when it comes to people who do good at this sort of stuff. They like it" Through his voice, I knew there was a different hidden agenda, he was awful at lying.

"Yeah, I'm sure it's the *Japs* you want to impress!" I said sarcastically, knowing full well it was a certain blonde member of our team that he meant, at least subconsciously.

"Shut up!" he said, throwing a clumsy, playful punch at my arm. I moved out the way, causing him to miss easily.

"You're gonna have to move quicker than that if you want to win and impress Sarah and steal her heart!" I joked with a dramatic flourish, dodging another couple of playful punches until one landed on my chest.

"Enough of that!" he said, turning red with embarrassment "Let's get our stuff down to the lobby ready to go. Better not be late again" Remembering the scolding from Coach the other day we grabbed our bags and left the room, shutting the door behind us.

We arrived in the lobby with plenty of time, but soon the tiny space was filling up and we became cramped together like sardines. Practically shoulder to shoulder with the people next to us it was becoming increasingly claustrophobic. Groups within the mass were chatty, the scene was similar to that of a busy chicken coup, where each conversation was incoherent to the rest.

"It's getting quite busy in here!" I exclaimed, as I stood uncomfortably with Andrew, Sarah and James, maintaining a tight perimeter with them.

"Yeah, you're telling me" replied James, as he got bustled about by people around him.

"Let's head outside, there's more space" said Sarah, already turning and making her way to the exit. "I'm in need of some air" she added. We followed closely behind as we slowly slipped our way through and out the door.

The freshness of the outside air and the humidity was more refreshing than the stuffy conditions of the cramped lobby. Sarah took a deep breath in as if it were to be her last.

"That's better!" she said, stretching out now that she had more room. "Anyone nervous?" she asked.

"A little" said James, a tad quiet.

"Nah, not really." Said Andrew, trying his best to appear confident. I couldn't help but smile after the little fiasco earlier.

"*Really*?" I said, as if in disbelief and implying otherwise. Andrew gave me a funny look, willing me to shut up and not make him look bad as he made what he considered to be his first play on Sarah.

"What about you Sarah?" he asked, trying his best to change the focus off him.

"A little..." she said, unenthusiastically. I was gobsmacked! It was the first time I've heard Sarah say she was nervous. Normally she's off psyching herself on her own somewhere. It looks like this trip was bringing out differences in all of us. Maybe it was the long flight, or the different food, who knows! Maybe even the Japan air!

"That's not like you to say Sarah." I said, shocked at hearing her say she's nervous. I continued, there was an obvious need for spirits to be lifting and people needed to fill up with confidence. "Come on everyone, pull yourselves together. We're here to do a job, now lets get sorted and sort it out!" Everyone smiled, just as two great long buses pulled up outside the hotel.

Chatter came from behind me as the crowd in the lobby began to pour its way out onto the street. Not only was there the British contingent coming out but some of the other nations were joining us as well. Triggered by the prompt arrival of the buses.

"Ok Brits, bus one! Get your bags on and get on asap!" came Coach's voice, booming over the hustle and bustle of the crowd. Instinctively we grabbed hold of our gear and moved quickly over to the bus.

Coach wanted us to stick together; it was a tactical ploy that he always employed on all tournaments, be it foreign or domestic. Everywhere we travelled he always ensured that we were all kept together and that we were never to travel in separate buses or cars. This was to reinforce the team spirit as we bonded together prior to the action. It meant that we always were a strong team that looked after each other; even if the tournament organisers wanted the countries to mingle for the purposes of social interaction, Coach always found a way to go against this. Coach always did have his ways of getting around the so-called 'red tape'.

The journey to the competition venue was short, which was good as I felt it was too quiet a journey. It was very solemn on the bus, resembling more like a funeral procession than a hyped up bus of highly trained competitors. It was the way in which people on our team got themselves ready.

Or at least, that was evident of our end of the bus. Unfortunately, we were found to be sharing the bus with the Australians, who always seemed to be talkative and chatty no matter what the situation. A bunch of bloody canaries in the front end of the bus. It was one of their tactics, to try and *psyche* us out, make us annoyed or disgruntled so our heads couldn't think straight when it came down to performing the business on the mat.

Well, I wasn't going to fall for that as I put on my headphones and let the music on my phone drown it all out. Some hard rock was playing as I closed my eyes and nodded my head to the rhythm of the music. The world faded out of contention to the sound of heavy drums and a damn good guitar solo.

A nudge from Emily who sat next to me provided a distraction from my music as I opened my eyes and swiftly removed my headphones so I could hear what she's after.

"What ya listening to?" she asked, beaming an interested smile.

"Oh this?" I said, "Just some rock stuff, nothing major." I palmed off.

"Yeah? I can hear it from here!" she chuckled. "Can I have a listen?" she asked and I offered her one of the headphone's ear pieces. Placing it to her ear she nodded along trying to get into the music.

"Not my sort of stuff really." She said, as if she tasted something that didn't quite agree with her. "You got any R'n'B, or a spot of trance maybe?" Typical I thought. The sort of music that I didn't like!

"Erm…no sorry, this is the 'fight' mix!" I joked. "Gets me pumped up."

"OK, I'll leave you to it then" she said with a giggle, handing me back the headphone. With a smile I plugged back in and drifted back into an almost self induced hypnotic trance.

Another nudge later on signalled that we arrived at the venue and that it was time to depart from the bus. Putting the headphones away I reached for my bag in the overhead compartment before shuffling off single file down the gangway of the bus.

Stepping back out into the air we saw the venue that, for the next eight hours or so, would be the most important building of our lives. A simple little place, it was a sports complex attached onto one of the Japanese High Schools, who's name I had no chance of pronouncing! Students that were attending Saturday classes stood outside and peered through windows curiously as we all made our way into the centre.

We were shown where the changing rooms were and we were soon quick to go get ourselves changed. Myself especially, as I preferred plenty of time to get warm and loose and to just get a general feel for the competition hall. Like the lobby of the hotel, the changing room was small and we crammed in tight to get ready with the sheer overwhelming numbers that were here to compete. Too many bodies in the one changing room does tend to be a little uncomfortable in more ways than one.

Once changed, we entered the competition hall. Polished wooden floor, with seating that spanned two levels. There were spectators already taking their places overhanging the event. Some of them, helpers and parents and other karate related individuals that were not in Japan for the competition and more rather the training that was to come later on. Some of the onlookers were even students from the neighbouring school that was there for reasons unknown, dressed smartly in the schools uniform. Maybe they had a friend competing? Perhaps they were just passing the time. I wasn't going to dwell on it too much.

The competition floor was divided into three matted areas. The areas blue with red outlining mats to signal the out of bounds area. Each area had an officials table and five seats placed on the corners and the front of the area. Upon these seats were two flags, one red, one blue; used to signal the judges decisions on the match that they were judging.

"Hey! Jason! Over here!" Came a loud voice, attracting my attention. Looking round I saw Coach and the others gathering in the one corner making our 'base camp' for the day. Running over I was quick to join them.

"Right, everyone's here. Good. Right, listen up you lot, now is the time where we see where the past eight or so months training has been put to good use. All I can ask of you is to do your best and remember…the after tournament party is always much sweeter when you have a gold medal around your neck!" the old line that many of us have heard made us smile, we've heard that one so many times before and even now it is able to motivate us to do well. "Get yourselves ready. The fighting team stick behind for a moment. Good luck everyone!" Most of the team dispersed, leaving James, Emily, Sarah, Andrew and myself.

"I know it's a little premature but here's the order for the fight. We'll have Jason leading out first man, you'll be in charge of setting the tempo for the event. Emily in second. James, you're out mid man. Sarah out forth and

Andrew you're our safe man in fifth if we need the win. Lets win it all by fight three please guys, remember it's the Japs we've got to worry about today; we've beaten all these other nations before so they're not gonna prove to be much of a problem. The Japs, they're all line fighters, move off line as they come in and they're yours to play with. Now do your best out there and good luck guys!" Getting in the zone we left to do our own thing. As I was about to walk away, Coach touched me on the shoulder, holding me behind alone for a moment longer than the rest of my teammates and said "This is your tournament Jason, I can feel it. Show these other countries how we do it in the UK. Now off you go and give them your all."

The day had started well, Sarah got a silver medal in the ladies kata. Kata being the set prearranged forms of a series of punches, blocks and kicks in some martial arts they can often be referred to as 'patterns' but we preferred the Japanese name. Traditionally, kata was originally a tool for the masters of old to catalogue their particular techniques and combat methodology. These were then taught to their students who practiced them daily so that they can improve their own combative prowess. Nowadays, in the terms of karate competition, it was used as a means of showing the practitioners perfection of the basic technique and the aesthetics of the display that determined the winner of the event. Before the introduction of the flag system to show the judges preference, the display of points much like a gymnastics or diving competition was the preferred choice.

Sarah was unlucky enough to face the Japan teams top female kata competitor in the final, Momoko. We later found that she had also won the All Japan Cup earlier that year, so it wasn't a shameful loss. The female kata team won their division, beating the Australians narrowly in the final. I myself was having a good year of my own, winning the men's kata division, comfortably going through the rounds before a narrow win of 3-2 flags against the Japanese champion who had won the event the previous year.

After my victory in the kata I felt unstoppable and it fuelled my desire to beat Bruce even more. I knew positively that I would beat him this year. I just had to. My kata gold was enough to send my spirit soaring to new heights.

However, watching him in his fighting, it looked as though he was on his best form this year, even better than his performance in previous years. There was even one bout where he didn't conceive a single point to the opponent he was fighting! Perhaps my early boost of confidence was a little premature.

I also discovered that he was in a different weight category than me this year, so I couldn't face him in the individuals but I knew I would take him in the team event. He was their best fighter and they always put their best man out first. Was I too premature to get my hopes up? Or was this a gut feeling that I knew events would pan out the way I thought they would do.

That does not matter now, as my category was coming up. The 'individual male under 85kg fighting'. James was also in this category which was always welcoming to see. As a competitor it was always a good feeling to have one or two of your own team members around at the edge of the mat to gee you up and make sure you were ready.

Though if I had to face him in any of the rounds then I knew that neither of us would show the other any quarter on the mat. You could rely on the fact that we all wanted to win and the respect for each other was only marginally different to those we would show the other nations.

The referees took up their positions, one on the mat itself controlling the events, two sat on the far corners with flags in front of them. We bowed in.

"Jason Lazarus, UK, red! Kamihachi Asamu, Japan, blue!" signalled the referee on the mat. 'Great!' I thought, first fight of the category, doesn't give you any time to get a feel for any of the other fighters or the general standard of the category. Oh well, here goes nothing!

Putting on a red belt, making it easier for the sombre judges to distinguish my points I stepped out onto the mat. Before me was my opponent, a short Japanese athlete who had a chubby face with messy matted jet black hair and spiked up to unimaginable proportions. His face was expressionless as was typical of the Japanese fighters before a fight and it was beginning to be a little unnerving if I was completely honest.

"Hajime!" shouted the referee, and we began our fight. Bounding forward and backwards in our stance we squared off, testing each other to find a weakness in each others technique. With an unexpected quickness my Japanese opponent was upon me, before I could do anything about it; bang! He hit me in the face with a punch that dazed me slightly. The flags went out for a point from the corner judges which prompted the main referee to call 'yamae' to stop the fight.

"Blue, one point!" he called, and stepped back to restart the fight. That punch was the wake up call, I needed to get myself more alert and get my game head on. Although Coach had said to move off the line of attack when fighting the Japanese; that wasn't really my strong point, you could consider that I was more Japanese in my fighting than anything else. In fact, I was more Japanese in everything really! But that was another matter. In this fight I was going to adopt one of two strategies, either, stand firm and see if I hit first or I'd charge first, turn their fighting method on themselves and hoping that he would be uncomfortable as a defensive fighter.

My plans were working but it was a close run battle. Every time I ran up a lead, he caught up and vice versa. My favourite technique was a lead hand jab and it was working well for me as I used it to pick him off as soon as he moved. One point I had picked him off strongly, planting a solid hit on him with my jab and with a powerful kiai, or martial shout, I was in his face to show complete dominance.

"Yamae!" cried the referee. Damn! Another point to him, now the score was at 5-6 to my learned Japanese opponent. Standing on the start line I glanced at the clock. Fifteen seconds. There wasn't long left, I was cutting it fine! But I knew that the fight could still sway in my favour, I just needed to pull something special out of the bag.

"Hajime!" As soon as we stepped off our start lines I initiated an assault. Bounding forward I lifted my lead leg and committed to a lead leg roundhouse kick. It moved up with ease slipping inside his guard and tapped sweetly off his cheek. All the referees flags went up straight away, sharp with a satisfying crack as the cloth whipped its way up.

"Yamae!" cried the referee again, a cheer went up from my teammates who stood on the sidelines, watching with complete anticipation. Three points for the head kick. The referee called out the point, now the score was 8-6 to me. Ten seconds left on the clock.

"Hajime!" We restarted the bout, although there was little time on the clock and the victory of the bout was almost certainly in my grasp; many competitors have been short sighted enough to relax at this point and a single head kick or take down to him would mean he would win.

I moved around, making sure that if he went to hit me I would not be there. The time counted down. 4...3...2...1...The bell sounded and another cheer erupted from the crowd as I had secured the win.

I couldn't contain my excitement and shouted a little cheer of my own on the line. My Japanese opponent looked a little down hearted. But in this game one person has to lose.

The rest of the category went well for us Brits. James was doing well in his fights, beating his opponents easily and my fights were going just as smoothly. A Jap, German, Italian, all of them got out fought today no matter what the nationality. Eventually there came the final of the category; it was between James and myself.

Although I knew that I shouldn't, I always felt too much respect whenever I fight my fellow team mates. Don't know why I do, but it does sometime affect my judgement and my ability to score points. Its very frustrating for me as I always like to win.

Unfortunately for me, my mutual respect for James overtook my desire to win today and no matter how hard I tried, I just couldn't out fight him. The result ended 3-2 to James. A close final that had the entire rooms attention throughout.

Although I lost in the final, it didn't bother me as much as it should. My victory against the Japanese was what I was after. So far this tournament I haven't lost at all to a Japanese which I found more than satisfying. It was also James' first big win at an international tournament so I didn't mind losing and took the bite of the sting as I knew this had made his trip all the more special. When the bout finished a clasp of hands and a hug was made.

"Good fight James!" I said.

"You took it easy on me!" he said jokingly. "But hey, UK 1st and 2nd, Coach would like that."

As we stepped off the mat, Coach came over with a big beaming smile. He tapped us both on the shoulder. He was indeed pleased with the result.

"Well done lads! Good result!" he said, squeezing his grip appreciatively "Some more silverware for the UK clan. It looks like we've got a few more events and then the team event. Keep yourselves warm and get plenty of fluids in. I know we can take it this year!"

"OK Coach" we said in unison as we walked away. Both our faces now bright and full of life. It was a good result, and the confidence we got from this carried with us. We felt ready for the team event. The blue ribbon event of the day.

"You got some water?" asked James, beads of sweat over his brow. His normally matted hair soaked through.

"Yes mate, some in my bag. Help yourself, I'm gonna keep myself warm." As I moved off to keep stretching.

The team event is the *blue ribbon* event of any large karate competition that was worth its salt. The set out of the team often varies from competition to competition, usually either five men or three women dependant on the organisers preference or the number of competitors that have entered. In this one, it was a five person team of three men and two women. The women fight off in position two and four.

There were no weight divisions as such and fighters fight off in the order that their coaches or captains hand in to the head table before the event starts.

The winner of the event is the team that achieves the most individual match wins. If individual bouts draw then the draw stands for the final score. At the end of the five bouts, if the total scores are tied, then there is often a playoff bout where the team chooses their best fighter to decide the win.

Surprisingly there were only four teams entered for the team event this year. Australia, New Zealand, Japan and UK. Luckily, we were drawn with New Zealand and Australia got the strongest team that was Japan. We had the easy draw, as New Zealand weren't the most brilliant of competitors and we found that we had turned them over fairly easily in previous competitions.

Australia and Japan started off proceedings. True to form, Bruce was the first man out and he truly was on form, destroying his opponent effortlessly 8-2. The Ozzies lost their second and third fights and won the forth. It all rested on the final fight to determine whether or not we would face the Australians in the final.

It was a tough call but the Australians narrowly pulled it through in the closing seconds of the final bout, with a decisive body kick nabbing them two points and clinching the bout with a tight score of 8-7. They were through to the final if the event. We all stood with baited breath when the result was called as we expected the Japanese to win.

Our fights against the New Zealanders went as easy as we thought as we ended it all by fighter number four winning with a comfortable 3-0 score. We were joining the Australians for the final.

The hall was alive and the air was electric. The atmosphere fully charged by the anticipation of both the competitors and the crowd, ready for the final with the stands now almost at full capacity. Explosive displays of various kaleidoscopic colours filled the seating as fighters from the different nations grouped together in their multitude and diverse colourful tracksuits, providing a casual yet unified appearance in the various pockets of the stands that they occupied.

It was the final event of the day, all the other areas were packed away, leaving just the one area dedicated for us. 'Area two' slap bang in the centre of the hall. The rest of the refereeing officials that were not directly involved in the administration of the finals were gathered on a makeshift seating area of fold out seats on the south side of the combat area. They sat up tall, smartly dressed in their official blazers and ties. Takeo Sensei joined them and sat in the centre of the front row of the pack of officials.

We were called to the mat, Australia wore red belts and pads, we were uniformed in blue. The five fighters from each side lined up facing each other on opposite ends of the area. Staring across we could see each other's eyes. Each pair, filled with pure determination to win. Like two miniature armies on opposite ends of the battlefield.

"Shomen-ni rei!" said the chief referee as he indicated with his palms towards Takeo Sensei with his surrounding entourage of chief instructors and we bowed low and respectfully. "Tagare-ni rei!" followed as we faced the opposition and bowed again. It was time to begin.

"Darrell Chambers, Australia…Jason Lazarus, UK" asked the referee as we moved into our starting positions. Damn it! The Australians had changed the order. They did have a right to do so as we were classed as a separate round and it was part of the rules themselves that teams can change the order with subsequent rounds. Maybe it wasn't this tournament that I'll get the chance to beat my life long nemesis.

Cocking my head to the side I cracked my neck solidly and shrugged my shoulders to release the tension as I stood ready on the line. First man out is such an important position. A win or a loss here can often sway the mental approach that the rest of the team faces. The Australians were a top team this year after beating the Japanese, it was important that I got the first win.

Staring him down I gripped my toes tightly on the mats ready for the command to start so with a sudden release, I could beat him to the off. "Hajime!" came the call and I was quick to move forward into stance with a loud kiai or martial shout. In order to get the win I needed to dominate the fight from the get go both physically and mentally.

With a snap I launched a body kick that hit squarely in his ribs. Darrell groaned as he attempted to make his body strong for the impact, as I was a little over touch contact with the kick. Fight stopped. Back on the line I got my two points. Good start with an early lead. He looked strong and solid when we were on the line; he wasn't going to show minor injury or pain. Very good, very admirable! Something I liked to see in fighters, too many these days try to 'exaggerate' injury in order to achieve points and ultimately bouts. Modern day sport karate-ka can sometimes lose track of the spirits and traditions of the art that they practice, with the emphasis being too much on the win itself and not the acknowledgment of the art. I nodded slightly in the acknowledgement of his spirit.

Restarting, Darrell wasn't going to shy down, in fact he was the opposite as he became fired up at being behind on the points. Perhaps too fired up. It wasn't long before he returned the favour with the odd hard shot to the body to let me know he was still there. The score was now 2-1 to myself and my ribs were noting the score personally.

Feeling the same heat building in me with the last shot I returned to the fray, a hard knock with a back fist to the side of Darrell's head resulted in a contact warning.

"Cool it Jason. Don't get mad, get points." Said Coach from the sidelines, his trademark clipboard and baseball cap at the ready. Listening hard, I tried to get myself back on the right tracks and we were off again.

We battled on, very little points were clean and technically sound enough to count as we were equally determined to win the match and the score was kept very stable. Though we did end up with a couple of knocks which was all part of the *fun* and no doubt we would laugh and joke about them afterwards.

With thirty seconds left on the clock the score stood at 4-2 to me, the fight was pretty uneventful but that didn't matter because the victory was in sight and the mental edge was waiting. Darrell attempted a last minute surge in an act of desperation to try and regain some points but I was able to pick him off as he tried to score against me. The fight ended 5-2, a good start.

Emily's fight ended in a draw. She was hard pressed by her Australian counter part who despite her ferocity in her fighting was managed to be held at bay by Emily who really pulled it out of the bag to obtain the draw. She was fighting quite admirably as her opponent was of a higher class than she was used to.

James won his fight, always maintaining his distance and constantly kept circling and moving around his opponent. He didn't allow the Australian to settle into his own rhythm and this gave him the advantage.

Overall victory was in our sights, 2-0 up with one draw, if Sarah could win her fight then that would secure it for us. Unfortunately things didn't pan out and whether it was nerves or tiredness at this point, but Sarah lost it and got beat.

Two wins to one, one draw, we could still win it, it was down to Andrew, who was now up against Bruce Fenchurch because of the order change at the start of the event; which after all, they were entitled to do.

It wasn't looking good as Bruce was showing himself to be on top form all day, but then again, stranger things have happened on this trip so far and we still had a sliver of hope for outright victory. Each of us began our own silent prayers and other lucky rituals that surround athletes of all descriptions and backgrounds.

Nerves were on edge, Andrew bounced on the spot, trying to relax as he stepped up to the line.

"Hajime!" and the fight began, Andrew gained an early advantage as he shot a combination of blows from the line, the last one catching Bruce squarely in the gut. We cheered loudly, excited at the early lead we got. Hope flooded over us as we started to think that this could end up quite positively for us all. Perhaps we were thinking a bit prematurely?

Bruce responded with a snappy head kick that took us all by surprise! It was that quick that we didn't even see it move until we heard the light slap against Andrew's face. All of us stood gobsmacked by it. We've never seen anyone kick like that before! Now it was Bruce who held the lead after he woke up from the early blow that he took.

"Don't worry Andrew, you can pull it back mate, don't give him the room to use his legs." I shouted reassuringly, adding my chants and calls to those that Coach was making from his official chair, making sure that Andrew wasn't downhearted by it. "Keep going mate" I added.

Shaking it off, Andrew stood back on the line. Bruce stood opposite him smugly, bowing to the referee with appreciation as the score was awarded. When the fight restarted, Andrew tried to keep the fight within punching range trying his best to nullify the use of Bruce's fast legs. Even this didn't seem to work as Bruce pushed forward, smothering Andrew's range and pulling him tight, just before the referee could call 'Yamae' to break up the fighters, Bruce pushed him away and scored with another head kick while Andrew was just backpedalling. Things were not looking good for Andrew. The score now stood at 6-1 and it wasn't even a minute into the fight!

The rest of the team stood slightly horrified on the sidelines, it was looking pretty grim at this point for the outright win and our fears were confirmed when he scored another head kick. 9-1, and only after thirty eight seconds into the fight! With an eight point clear lead, the referee was forced to stop the bout and award Bruce as the winner as was dictated by the rules.

'Argh!' I thought, as the event was left down to a fight off. Now it was up to the coaches to decide who to send in for the final fight. It was pretty obvious to everyone that the Australians were going to send in Bruce. If they didn't, then the coach would need to get his head checked. This would've come from a solid slap round the back of the head by the Australian chief instructor who was part of the officials for the day, but was sat with the rest of the additional referees.

Who would coach send in for us? Now I was in mixed emotions; a part of me really wanted to go up and beat him, as I was desperate to get my own personal win against him. But after seeing the way he's fighting I didn't want to let the team down. Maybe James? He was fighting really well today and he did beat me in the individuals. He would've been a really good choice to make.

"Jason." Said Coach, disrupting my thoughts. "You ready to go?" he asked.

"You're sending me in?" I said, almost flabbergasted.

"Yes, now shut up, focus and get your arse out there. Remember what I said, it's your tournament this year"

Assuring cheers and good lucks came from the team as I replaced my gum shield in my mouth and stepped up to the line. As predicted, Bruce was the one facing me on the opposite side of the mat. I guess I will be facing him this year after all. 'Come on Jason' I spoke to myself, getting myself in the zone for the fight.

"Remember, it's your tournament!" cried Coach just as we were about to start.

"Hajime!" with confidence I made my stance, making my initial kiai as I was prone to do. Coach was right, this was my tournament this year. The past god knows how many months was preparing me for this moment.

Bang! I got caught suddenly and the flags went out. The fight was stopped.

"Come on Jason, pull it together" came a small voice in my head as I shook it off.

Bang! A head kick went up and a slap was heard. But it was not the slap of my face. I managed to surprise myself that I managed to get a hand to it and stop the kick and as he landed his foot I jabbed him with my lead hand. It hit true to his chest and it was a solid blow. After doing it, I thought that it was going to leave a hole in his chest!

A contact warning was issued after Bruce staggered back from the shot. That didn't phase me, because somehow I had managed to stop one of those lightning fast kicks of his and this gave me a small measure of hope.

We began once more. I sank into my stance, he came at me once more and I drove another punch into his stomach. I caught sight of the one flags flicking out for a point and the fight was stopped again.

1-1.

We continued fighting, point for point as the fight progressed, it was quite an epic confrontation that was unfolding. Everyone cheered and booed, congratulating points and scolding poor decisions from the judges as the atmosphere was becoming more electrifying. Karate was like any sport, if perhaps a little more civilised than perhaps your average footie match. It seemed to all that this year we were evenly matched.

My punches were met by his, his kicks were met by mine. When one of us achieved a lead, it was not held for long as the other was quick to retaliate and regain control and vice versa.

Thirty seconds remaining, the score held at 9-8 to myself. Could I just hold out a little while longer? Ten seconds to go, still the score 9-8. The win was there. Four…three…thud! I got caught with a last minute punch. The Australian side cheered with giant rapture, my teammates moaned slightly in response and I was forced to feel downhearted as I realised what this meant. The bell rung, as the referee awarded the final point. The fight finished 9-9. So close! I thought. It was time now for 'Encho-sen'.

'Encho-sen' or sudden death, is the term used if the deciding bout ends in a draw. It is where the first person to score will win the fight. A minute is set on the clock and the scores are wiped clean, save for the penalty warnings which are maintained the same. If at the end of this minute no one has been fortunate to score, then it is down to the referees to decide who is the best fighter. I didn't want it to go down to this point, as it could go either way and fighters have a fifty-fifty chance at this point.

Over the intense noise that was building from those around, I heard Sarah shout out, "Come on Jason! You can do this!" and I looked back to see my team egg me on with passion from the sidelines. The tension was unbelievable, if I wasn't first to hit, I was going to lose it not just for myself but for my teammates as well.

Turning back to face Bruce, I could see it clearly in his eyes that he was thinking along the same paths as I was. Two warriors we were, determined to beat the other by any means almost to the extent that life and death was on the line by the outcome of this match.

"Encho-sen...Hajime!"

For the final time we squared off, this was the last fight of the day and the one that all who was bearing witness was looking forward to watching. To the two teams directly involved, this fight bore the same level of meaning as a World Cup Final, the Ashes, the Superbowl! No quarter was to be given to the other and none was to be expected, this was it.

We circled, getting ourselves comfortable with each other. Neither of us was overly hasty to get involved from the word go, the slightest slip up or missed focus would result in the a loss for that individual.

The hall was still as alive as it was before, as a hundred eyes watched intently to every slight movement our bodies made. Nerves and anxiety culminated into an enjoyable spectacle to watch.

Testing each other with simple feints we continued our personal chess match, we looked for an obvious weakness where there was none.

Then something within me changed, instead of my usual fluid bounce I stopped. Maintaining my fighting posture I sunk low in my stance, my knees bending, loading my muscles ready for a quick release. I felt them tightening, the tension adding to the build up of a powerful sprung action that was compressed ready for the right moment.

Bruce continued his usual light bounce contrasting heavily against my sudden static approach. Around me, the almost deafening screams of the crowd faded out and my vision tunnelled until all that was still in focus was the familiar outline of Bruce. I've never felt this experience before in a fight.

Then Bruce initiated into a flurry of lightning fast moving techniques. He came at me with a lead punch aimed at my face, followed by the reverse hand targeting low to my abdomen. With ease I parried the front hand, and as the second one came in low I blocked it away and grabbed it. The contained spring in my legs allowed me to jump forward sharply as I took hold of his jacket with my other hand. Quickly I turned and threw my leg out so that it lay across both of his. With a quick pull and push of my hands I used his momentum to pull him over my leg. Tripping him he tumbled over, almost somersaulting over the leg until he landed cleanly upon his back.

As he lay there, staring up at me and the ceiling above, I delivered a couple of fast punches that struck him on the chest with a terrifying kiai uttered from my lips.

Sound returned to my ears as the rapture of the crowd returned. My team mates were jumping ecstatically on the sidelines. Even Coach leapt from his seat, throwing the clipboard to the ground in exaltation, as he was prone to do when good things in his favour come from tense moments. Though he also did something similar, perhaps less savoury, if things weren't going in our favour.

'I did it' I said to myself, in utter disbelief and shellshock. As I looked to see the flags from the judges on the edge of the area had been shot high into the air, with a defining snap of the fast moving cloth, signalling the three points scored. The referee was quick to stop the fight with a stern and excitable 'Yamae!'

"Blue…sanbon…blue…winner!" said the referee regimentally.

I dropped to my knees, the excitement running through me as my heart pumped ecstatically at victory. That was, until I quickly got hold of my senses as I remembered where I was, bowing to Bruce and going over to him to shake his hand and pat him on the back in a pleasant display of sportsmanship.

"Well done." He said sportingly, as I shook his hand. "You deserved that win"

"Thank you" I replied, soon turning to face my team, full of delight they ran onto the mat and swamped over me. Hugging and congratulating me, I felt like I was on top of the world. Like a football player scoring that match winning gold in the extra time of a cup final match. Bruce returned to his team to a chorus of hearty commiserations but it was all in good taste and good spirit.

"Oi! You lot" shouted Coach, disrupting the early celebrations. "They haven't announced the result yet! Get in line!" breaking up they sharply returned to the edge of the mat and stood ready to receive the final result of the team event.

The referee stood smartly on his line. Eyes front, he was like a statue or like a soldier standing to attention on a parade ground.

"Winners...Team UK!" he spoke loud and clear, his left arm rising to the side to indicate that we were the overall champions of the event. We ended like we started, with a bow to Takeo Sensei and then to our opponents. As soon as we could relax at ease, both teams approached each other on the mat and continued the atmosphere of good sportsmanship by congratulating each other. The coaches followed and did the same.

"Well done matey!" said Coach as he put his arm round me. "I thought you were going to throw the whole damn thing away in sudden death, luckily you didn't disappoint! The way you were fighting today, if you'd lost that one, you wouldn't have needed your return ticket...I would've kicked your ass back to Heathrow!" he joked, those around us laughed. Although he joked, I knew that Coach was just as passionate about the team winning the competition as we were. If you lost because your opponent was simply better than you then everything was alright, there's nothing you can do about that. But, if you were stupid enough to lose because you performed badly or didn't have your head in the game, then I've seen Coach give such 'rollockings' that you could never believe! We all knew though that this was just because he wanted us to do well and there was always no malice or discontent held against someone after the telling off had passed.

"Well done to all of you" he continued, addressing the team as a whole. "Great day at the office! Plenty of silverware coming back to the UK. But we'll get that all later."

He peeked down to his watch, its thick strap prominent on his thick wrist.

"This thing's overrun! Don't want to rush you lot, but we're behind schedule for the party tonight. So everyone, get your water on board and get your backsides changed. It's now six o'clock and the party starts at eight. I'm sure you ladies would like as much time as possible to pretty yourselves up, so get shifting!" He said frantically, as the rest of the team scattered like headless chickens to grab bags and rush into the changing rooms. All that was left was me and Coach.

"See Jason, I told you that this would be your tournament. Now shift your arse because I'd like to get a beer sometime this year! It's been just as stressful for me as it was for you!" As he simply swatted me round the head lightly and playfully, sending me victoriously on my way.

Chapter 9 – Sword Duel in the Presence of the Shogunate

The 8th day of the 9th month. In preparation of the first full moon of the harvest season twenty four skilled samurai swordsman from across the nation, including myself and Fujibayashi, had gathered at Himeji castle ready to present ourselves and display our talents to the Lord of the Province and from what rumours have begun spreading, the Shogun himself. The supreme military commander and divine ruler of all Japan.

For all of the other samurai that had gathered, an aide was brought with them to tend to their needs during their stay at the castle; these aides came from their respective houses or dojo's and displayed the family crest of those they represented. Myself and Fujibayashi did not call for this additional luxury which we saw as simple indulgence and we kept ourselves to ourselves during our stay.

The politics amongst samurai of other clans were more often than not very much double standard at the lowest of levels when it came to the discussion of politics. Especially at times where similar unstableness of the top of the pile, their masters, can result in the country coming to full scale nationwide war.

However, it can also be noted, that if there was one area of political interest that one could always be sure about; it was their individual loyalty to their Lord, for a samurai's life is not their own and their direct purpose in life is the sole servitude to their lord and master. After all, the word and title of 'samurai' simply means 'to serve'. It was because of this reason mostly, that we decided to not get involved with the other gathered warriors in the run up to the event. For politics had an awful habit of clouding the mind and when you have to go into combat, this was never a wise thing to do.

We were escorted to our room by a member of the official party of the castle. For a gathering such as this there were often many who worked behind the scenes from runners; who organised everyone to where they needed to be; to geisha's; who tended to the samurai's more earthly desires and *entertained* them at their whim. A *gift* as such from the Lord of the castle and the more beautiful and skilful the geisha shows the wealth of the hosts hospitality. We humbly choose not to have such entertainment prior to the official proceedings. As well as politics, women often had similar abilities to cloud the mind of a swordsman.

The room itself was large and decorative, the cream coloured walls lined with numerous intricate and highly detailed murals depicting scenes of the countryside and songbirds. Upon the floor either side of the large space were our beds that were neatly arranged upon the tatami mats, beside which were small pieces of furniture and a sword rack for each of us to rest our blades. These too were carved so delicately and extravagantly sickening to a warrior of modern means such as myself. However, despite the decadence even a modest samurai can take a moment to admire the work and time that the artist took to create little slices of beauty.

"All participants will meet in the North courtyard at the appearance of the full moon to be addressed by the Lord. I will send someone for you when the time is ready. Please attend the address in ceremonial attire, though I don't think I need to tell you that. Is there anything that I can get or arrange for you gentleman? Please state it now and I will see to it that the castle servants will see that it is done." The official spoke with such formal tones, befitting of his role and the image of the contest that is at hand.

"No thank you, that will be fine. We will not require any further assistance with our preparations" I replied, maintaining the formality and returning the hospitality that we were being shown.

"Then I will leave you to rest. Take your time to save your strengths, for the contest will be swiftly upon you." The official turned, sliding the door closed behind him. The light in the corridor highlighted his silhouette through the thin paper inserts in the door as he walked away.

"By my reckoning we will have around two hours before we will be called upon. Yoshida Shihan" Said Fujibayashi, pulling his katana free from his belt and resting it upon his sword rack that he had been provided with.

"Yes, that is true Fujibayashi, ready your mind. We must be like the unmovable rock and must not be easily read by any of these other samurai. I have a feeling that we will require all of our focus over the coming day for our competitors and enemy will be highly skilled from styles that we may not yet have encountered."

My thoughts went momentarily to Sensei. It was unfortunate that he had taken ill a couple of days before we left for the gathering. He was not well and was showing some very serious signs of his health deteriorating. I suggested to Sensei about myself and Fujibayashi staying and helping to attend to him and the duties of the house while he was in his ill state; but when I did so, Sensei was adamant that we attended the gathering as the name and reputation of the house was seen to him as more important than his health.

Such selfish thoughts to oneself can be conceived by some as improper attitude for the ways of Budo. He also stressed to me how this was a gathering made by the official request of the Shogun and he reminded me of the importance of maintaining respect and obedience for the Lord of Lords. By not attending at such of a request can be strewn by some as treason and in any case the House would suffer as a result. Sensei would be punished and this was not acceptable.

"Yoshida Kintaro, Fujibashi Shigeru. It is time." Came a small voice from outside our quarters. Leaving our seated positions of quiet meditation, we made way to the door. Now dressed in more formal attire of kimono and hakama, at our waists we held our wakizashi or short sword as was customary of official etiquette for visitors of such an important household; we followed the aide down the winding corridors of the castle. The air was mild, with sweet smelling herbs that provided the pleasant aroma that filled our lungs and stimulated our senses. At set intervals, a candle was lit, dimly illuminating the way ahead.

Eventually we turned into the Northern courtyard stepping out into the night air onto a wooden walkway that surrounded the pebbled square that was the courtyard. The other samurai were already present, kneeling in rows with their aides closely behind them. At the sound of our approach they turned their heads; almost in unison, staring at us intensely as we approached with eagle eyes. It was as if a single look from any of them would kill, such was the intensity of the atmosphere that surrounded the prestigious gathering. Stepping onto the gravel courtyard to join them, tiny stones crunching underfoot, the samurai soon returned their view to the front; eagerly and attentively awaiting the address that was still to come.

Adopting our positions, slotting neatly at the end of the rear row of warriors, we joined the samurai in complete silence.

Around half hour passed as we sat motionless, so silent was the courtyard that one could hear their own heartbeat from within; so tranquil in the twilight hour that it was practically the perfect place to meditate or to enlighten oneself. After this time had passed the door that everyone was observing slid slowly to one side. An aide of the Lord of the castle knelt to one side, in proper attire and wakizashi presented in their obi. He bowed low, hands pressed into the ground, forehead lowered until it lightly touched the floor. The Lord presented himself. At sight of someone of such high stature, signalled the ingrained response as we all bowed low in practiced unison. Reishiki or etiquette required us to do so.

With steady and formal tones the Lord spoke clearly, "Please raise your heads, skilled warriors of the nation." Obeying his command, we returned to our kneeling posture. As we returned our heads, we saw that the Lord was not alone. With him was a man dressed in extremely fine reds and gold, flowing seamlessly as if a stream, it was obvious to all that this man was the representative of the Shogun. This decorative stranger was allowed to step forward into full view as the Lord of the castle stepped aside, his head bowed slightly in show of respect and seniority.

"Welcome to all. You have all been chosen as representatives of your school, your Sensei, your provincial Lords and yourselves to present your skills for the Lord Shogunate Iyomitsu. Tomorrow you will face each other in battle and those whose skills are deemed worthy will be presented with one of the prestigious Eight Dragons of the Shogun as a suitable reward for your excellence and perfection in the art of the sword. Do not hesitate in the display of your technique and conduct yourselves accordingly.

The enemy of this country is not only man, there are more sinister foes amongst us that this country must face in order for it to prosper and blossom like a great flower. Those of you chosen with the carrying of the Eight Dragons must strive to affect those around them to make this country great and to maintain everlasting peace within the nation. You will be regarded by all as direct retainers of the Shogun himself! I thank you warriors of the nation."

The over extravagant stranger produced from his side a flat stick like object. With a sharp yet delicate flick of the wrist, the stick opened to reveal a beautiful war fan which he held proudly in front of us for all to view briefly upon its beautiful surface. The surface of the fan was decorated with the personal crest of the Shogun, atop a red circle vividly bright within its centre with gold Kanji across it bearing the Iyomitsu family name.

To be present in front of this fan is seen to be as if presented in front of the Shogun himself and this was equally as important as the representative who wielded it. You could perhaps compare it to be a 'spiritual' representation of the Shogun. All those who viewed it bowed again, keeping our heads low to the ground; failure to do so would be seen as an act of violation against the Shogun and to not show this proper respect will result in being punished by death. Only after the noise of the strangers footsteps echoed out of earshot and the door returned to its closed position did we raise our heads again. It was an honour for us to be present in front of this fan, it was a rare occasion for anyone.

Left before us now was the castle Lord, who smiled wickedly at us all. There was something about him that was unnerving but these concerns were not duly justified.

"Proceedings will begin at noon, a practice area will be set up for those who wish to use it before the tournament. Go now and rest." With a wave of his hands we stood and bowed politely once more before the gathering dispersed to go about their business. Rest was definitely required and we quickly made haste to our quarters.

Shortly after noon. The sun was high up in the cloudless sky, a slight breeze carried the electricity of the event through the air. Ourselves and the twenty other samurai had been gathered for the competition and we knelt in one straight line at one end of the vast expanse of the castle gardens upon a wooden platform that had been specially constructed for the event. The other side had the congregation of officials, noble dignitaries of the richer or more powerful families from the area and even some from the surrounding provinces. In the centre, hidden behind a fine silk screen sat from what I could distinguish as the Shogun's representative and the castle Lord.

So far a few matches have already taken place, some of the combatants were indeed highly skilled while others provided a spectacle that was entirely dubious and almost insulting to present in front of the high ranking dignitaries that had taken the time to witness these skills. It wasn't surprising to witness that those who were less than competent often found themselves quickly bloodied and bruised when they were made to compete in their matches.

On the left hand side of the congregation, at the end of each bout one can see the odd small purse of money passing back and forth, faces matched with a mixture of anguish and contented joy as the money was quick to change hands. The lower dignitaries were in the act of placing bets on the bouts.

The sheer thought of betting on these bouts was utterly distasteful in my eyes and sickened me as I watched every insulting transaction being made. How dare these people place bets, every combat that is made can result in the death of the combatant. Bokken can still kill and many have lost their lives in a 'friendly' match with these surprisingly deadly, 'safe' counterparts. To place a wager on someone's life in this manner is in my eyes is a dishonourable insult to the very nature of Budo and it was fortunate for them that with the ranks and positions they held that I was powerless to publicly voice my objections against their actions. To do so would be seen as extremely bad manners despite the fact that my opinion was just in this circumstance.

My annoyed mental ranting was broken off by the blood curdling battle cry of one of the pair of warriors who were up and fighting. This was closely followed by the gravelly thud of one of the exponents on the ground and the unified applause of all those who were present. Reactively I joined in the clapping, but with no real intent to do so and was completely uninterested in what had occurred on the small battleground.

The bested warrior shortly returned to his kneeling position beside me. His face screwed up tight with pain as he knelt. From his return I observed a fresh, irregular red cut that had been produced upon his cheek. From the abrasion came a tiny trickle of blood that the warrior wiped away with a sleeve, staining the cloth. He also held his one rib on his left side, trying to cradle it and support it as with every breath he took wracked him with pain. Clearly a tough match. Soon I will be called upon and those thoughts were shortly answered.

"Yoshida Kintaro...Sato Yamazaki...please come up and present your skills" cried out the official that was acting as the position of 'referee' for the contests. Bending forward slightly and peering down the line, I caught sight of my opponent.

Sato Yamazaki from what I remember was once a mountain warrior monk, his cleanly shaved head still representative of such backgrounds. Now out of his spiritual pursuits he has denounced his position as a spiritual monk and turned ronin, allowing him the opportunity to compete in this gathering. He hailed from one of the many mountainous regions in Japan where he spent his solitude working on both his spiritual position in the universe as well as his swordplay.

His physique was astonishing, his broad shoulders matching his immense trunk he towered high and mightily over me. Some have even dubbed him as an 'Oni' purely upon his brutal physical appearance. Luckily for myself I managed to observe his technique as he was foolish enough to practice beforehand. From what I could see, his main principle technique was called the Kabuto-wari; the helmet splitting technique.

This technique suited his gargantuan build as his body provides enough strength and sheer power so that his sword has the ability to cut and smash through tough plated armour, in particular, a thick heavy helmet and this is where the technique obtains its impressive name. Even with bokken, such raw power would kill if it were to be done without restraint and if I allowed him the opportunity to strike me with such a technique my skull would surely collapse under the intense pressure.

There is however, one advantage that I have; his technique is considerably slower than my own as his body would require every ounce of strength to be directed into one singular blow. Though, perhaps, was his pre-training routine merely a well planned bluff? A routine sent to put those watching under a false impression. There was only one sure way to know for certain. It was time to call his bluff with a gambit of my own.

Standing tall I turned to Fujibayashi sat next to me and presented to him my bokken. With stunned looks from those around, Fujibayashi accepted my surprising offering and stuttered "But… Yoshida Shihan…"

"Do not worry I shall be fine" I said, walking forward to take my position on the contest arena. Stunned silence and unbelieving eyes followed my every step until I was in position.

"Yoshida Kintaro, are you admitting defeat already? You are not carrying a bokken?!" asked the stunned referee, I believe even *he* was unable to fathom what he was witnessing with his own eyes. "This is a *sword* gathering for the Shogunate." He added, overstressing the use of the sword. I looked at him with dead eyes.

"I believe, that for my opponent I do not require a bokken to best him. Without insulting my learned opponents skills, I believe that my technique will overcome him. My body will be my sword" I answered, confident yet maintaining manners so as I did not appear arrogant.

Despite my attempts to be as polite and correct as I could, in Yamazaki's eyes, fire could be seen as he had taken what I said in the wrong light. Although not intended, this firing up of emotions could be played to my advantage. Such negative emotional content has resulted in many swordsmen losing matches. It was time to take advantage of this fortuitous incident.

The referee turned around to the head of proceedings to obtain confirmation that the match could continue. An inquisitive nod confirmed that we could begin and the referee turned back to face us.

"Begin!" he shouted and stepped away so as not to distract us and also to stay out of striking range.

Sato raised his bokken, which from the look of things was longer and thicker than the average bokken. This was made to match his abnormal physical makeup and was in proportion to his own monumental body. There was no doubt in my mind that the abnormally sized bokken also mirrored the dimensions of his own personal sword and briefly I felt the urge to wanting to see such an immense blade.

"Sato Yamazaki, Sato mountain style, Kabuto-wari!" he called, his voice riddled with strained anger. I responded by placing my right leg forward, arms out in a receiving posture with palms turned to the sky.

"Yoshida Kintaro, Imamoto style, muto-dori."

We stood motionless, I was waiting to anticipate his move. The anger bubbling up within Yamazaki caused his muscles to shake and spasm as adrenaline filled him. Now I know he was mine.

"Yaaaaaa!" cried Yamazaki, releasing his anger into a singular vertical blow that was aimed for the very centre of my skull. Twisting, I turned my body sidewards, so as the bokken sailed harmlessly past my face and in front of my body. It was a precision technique, as I allowed little gap between the bokken and myself. There was no doubt in anyone's mind that I had insulted Yamazaki that much that he was intending to kill me with that strike; to bludgeon me to death with the half a tree that he called a bokken.

Pushing off with my left foot I advanced quickly, rapidly closing the distance between myself and Yamazaki. Using the bokken as a guide for my advance I used my right hand to rise up and grab the bokken at its handle. My left hand gracefully rested on the back edge of the bokken. On a real blade, this particular area is not made razor sharp, the bokken counterparts mirrored this and had a similar flat, blunt edge in representation of this fact. In a flowing pull and push of my hands I pulled Yamazaki's bokken in a circular fashion, yanking it out of his grip. In the same motion, the tip of the bokken came up sharply and struck Yamazaki squarely underneath his chin.

With a grunt of pain he stumbled ungracefully backwards. When he recovered, before he had chance to observe me with his shocked and confused eyes or to check that he was not bleeding, I had thrust the bokken so that the tip was touching his pulsating throat. A technique that if I had allowed to strike fully would've been a killing blow. I always found that the killing of an opponent with a bokken to be distasteful to the spirit of the event and it was because of this that I pulled my thrust just short.

The contest area was frozen with surprise and it took them a brief moment before erupting loudly with an appreciative applause at my efforts. It was clear that I had won the contest and the necessary exchange of coin followed silently in the wings of the contest area.

Through the continued applause, the referee called the result. "Winner! Yoshida Kintaro" with the match result called, I returned the bokken to its owner who still remained amazed.

"How?..." spoke Fujibayashi as I returned to my seated position. "I have never seen such technique, it is truly marvellous!" His voice was mixed with shock and admiration.

"There are some techniques, that you have still to learn Fujibayashi-san. I understood from having the chance to observe him before hand that I my technique was faster and more reliable than his. It was from this prior knowledge that I was able to strategise the way that I did and the sudden change to the way in which the combat was to be fought threw his focus off. One day you will understand."

"Yes. Yoshida Shihan. I will remember that" he replied, bowing his head in enlightened awe.

Matches continued on, there was no set 'knockout' format. Matches were fought at the will of the Shogun's representative and today some of us will be required to endure more bouts than others, based upon the desire of the representative himself. Samurai were dropping off and narrowing down in numbers as the matches continued with the contestants becoming ever more increasingly zealous in their application of technique and their desire to win.

Fujibayashi had four contests that day, winning comfortably in them all and against some very competent swordsmen. Even from the first day that he had walked into the dojo and challenged the style, it was clear that he had plenty of potential and a lot of talent. He was proving himself today to be just as competent as any who was here and I was proud that he was here in the same capacity as me, representing the style perfectly and maintaining its good name in front of the seniority that was also present. Sensei would've been proud of his efforts if he was here today. It was truly a good omen to initiate Fujibayashi into the ranks of the Imamoto Dojo.

When it came to my own personal thoughts on my performance, I only had two matches up until now and this number included the one against Sato Yamazaki. I noticed all the other competitors had so much more opportunities to demonstrate their skill. A part of me thought that my unusual display in the first match had perhaps been construed by the Lord as too arrogant and that they may've believed that I was over exaggerating the need to impress and this was beginning to dwell into my mind.

My second match I had used a bokken and beaten my opponent easily as I was placed against one of the few 'deadwood' exponents that was called for the competition. Was this an act to try and humble me? Perhaps I had destroyed my chances unwillingly.

The day was passing almost too quickly and it was becoming apparent that it was almost close to the final end of the proceedings. The referee was called to the high dignitaries area and upon darting over to them, knelt quickly with lowered head to receive instruction. There was some talk, too far away for it to be distinguishable to our ears. A minute or so passed before he rose to his feet again and returned to his initial position.

"Itosu Anaki...Uoyama Wakai...Takeo Watakaze...please step forward" The three samurai promptly stepped up onto the contest area. "Yoshida Kintaro..." With the sound of my name being called, I moved promptly to my feet. The referee spoke out again. "You will not require your bokken." Intrigued by his request I passed my bokken back to Fujibayashi once more and entered the contest arena.

"The Lord Shogun's representative is impressed by your muto-dori skills Yoshida-san. As such, this next match is to satisfy his curiosity for the full nature and extent of your technique. You will face these three samurai alone and without the use of a bokken."

"Thank you, I understand" I said humbly, as I bowed in acceptance of the task given to me. The samurai were quick to adopt positions that would surround me as they made their stances ready to attack.

This was more than just a 'fun' match now, perhaps this was a way of the representative of secretly punishing me for what could've been interpreted as arrogance. Maybe that this was the easy way of giving me a beating to remind me to not be so cocky and playful with such a serious event and to provide me a 'simple' lesson in humility. Or, on the more positive side of things, it could be that he truly was impressed by my skills and wanted to know their full extent. For what purpose other than his own curiosity I did not know nor did I care to find out anytime soon.

Closing my eyes I took a moment to concentrate, allowing my other senses to take affect as I cleared my mind in that singular instant so as not to distract me. The samurai around me circled to try and achieve some advantage in their initial positioning, the fine stones on the ground gave away their position as my ears picked up the slightest of noise as they scraped and crunched underneath their feet. Two were positioned behind me, off at separate angles. One was positioned in front of me but not directly. I opened my eyes. I was now ready to receive them and hopefully, beat them.

Attempting to get the jump on me from out of my field of vision and to make this a quick match, the samurai that was to my left lunged forward, cutting and slicing and thrusting the bokken in order to achieve a successful blow that would connect with me and impair me. These strikes I dodged with efficient, well practiced footwork and flowing turns of my body, this was called taisabaki. I parried myself away until the foolish samurai got within the range that I needed to counter him.

Ducking underneath one of his strikes I intercepted his blow and grabbed hold of his arms tightly, wrapping them in tight with our bodies close and pressing against each other. Now I was behind the wooden blade where it was safer. Kicking out at the side of his knee I took his balance and the stability of his stance crumbled easily as his knee crunched with the solid hit. Slamming my body into his I took his weight and went to throw him over my hip. At mid throw, the corner of my eye spied the second samurai coming in to hit me while my attention was taken with the first.

Twisting my body and completing the throw in the same motion, I used the first samurai's body to crash down heavily into the second as he rushed in, sending them both sprawling to the ground.

Looking over to the third he remained stood at distance, his bokken pointed at my throat in a posture called chudan-no-kamae. Now it was just one on one between him and myself as the second samurai was still struggling to return to his feet as he tried to clear the first one off of him. Sweat was dripping from his brow from the different contests that he had been subjugated to prior to this one. It was hot and no doubt he was not as fresh as I was with my limited exposure to the contest area. I had the advantage.

He rose his bokken to the side of his head in hasso-no-kamae and stood still as he awaited me to get into his range. He wasn't as foolish as the others who considered me as an easy target as I was both outnumbered and unarmed, he waited for me to make the first move. I approached, arms close to and in front of my body, hands were opened in a defensive posture.

With a diagonal swing he faked the first strike, hoping that I would fall for it and react prematurely. It didn't work as I felt the intention of the feint. His tactical intentions were there but his execution was easy to read.

From pulling the bokken in close to his body at the end of the strike he flowed into his true intention, a direct thrust aimed at my throat. The effort and intent that he put behind the thrust meant that he was after more than just a simple win from this match. Twisting like the first bout I dodged the thrust with ease. This time diving forward I took hold of his hands with both of mine own and pivoted on my feet.

The force of the turn spun him wildly around me like a spinning top as my foot acted as the central point from which he arced round. When it felt as though he was close to achieving a full circle around me I quickly changed direction, twisting sharply I twisted his wrists sending his body somersaulting through the air to land at my feet. With a quick thrust of my palm I slammed it into his forehead, driving it into the ground with a disgusting crack and I let cry with a martial scream as I defined the finishing blow to the encounter.

Stepping away from the body before me I saw that the other two samurai did not wish to pursue me any longer and knelt in acknowledgment of their defeat with their bokken by their sides. They knew that deep down in their hearts they would not defeat me and to continue this bout would be a waste of time.

Leaving the still squirming, pain ridden body of my third opponent, I turned and bowed low and polite to the screen of covered dignitaries and returned gracefully to my seat.

Chapter 10 – The Dragons Acquire New Owners

That night we were called, myself and Fujibayashi, to attend an official ceremony in the inner heart of the castle, in a specially selected audience hall right in the very centre of it. We left our live katana in our quarters as is customary when being within the castle confines of a Lord who was not your own.

It was late in the evening, roughly similar to the time that we attended the first audience, however, the air was different and we felt this in our hearts. The entire day had been filled with the wooden cracking of bokken serenading with the echoing sounds of clapping. The sounds still echoed in a haunting fashion in my head as I replayed events. A habit of mine and one that I did not out of the fear factor or the rush that comes from such an event but as a means of self progression, as I analysed every slightest movement that I and my opponents made.

One samurai had already lost his life from an uncontrolled strike that connected with his throat. It was a sight that I had seen before many a time. An accidental, though sometimes purposeful, strike that crushes the windpipe. The unfortunate victim is left gagging and spluttering as they struggle to get air past the blood that replaces the pathway through the rupturing of the windpipe itself. They essentially drown in a sea of their own blood as it flows into their lungs. There was a time whereby I was worried that I might've been the body being carted off the area. The way that I had angered Yamazaki meant that anything could've happened as the heat of his blood replacing rational thought.

In any case it was most distressing for the individual involved who would know that their demise and have nothing that they could do to prevent it. Also, it was disheartening to those who have to witness it, as this was meant to be a simple display of swordsmanship and a death at an event like this was always tragic. The samurai who commited the blow had the standard of his technique scorned by the representative as a man who is distasteful in the eyes of Budo, a damning insult and if the samurai who committed such an act was indeed a true warrior; he would be forced to commit the act of seppuku.

Seppuku is the art of ritual suicide for a samurai warrior. It is used in instances of defeat on the battlefield or in the case of a great shame if they have disgraced themselves or their Lord in the eyes of a superior. It involved the one who was committing the act to disembowel themselves with their wakizashi or tanto. When the committed are about to fall forward on the rest of the blade a second samurai armed with a katana would cut off their head. It is both a spiritual and skilful ritual and those conducted the kaishaku (the severing of the head) had to be very skilled so that they produced a clean cut. Certain skilled exponents could even slice cleanly through the neck but leave a small flap of skin untouched at the front of the throat so that when the body fell, the head would remain tidy and controlled in the lap of the individual committing seppuku. A rolling head that rolls far away from the body can sometimes be interpreted as a means of dishonouring the spirit of the warrior who is taking their life.

From what we have been told by members of the house, the candidates who have failed had already been sent away, to develop their swordplay further. I doubt however that they would ever receive the same honour of presenting their skills again in front of dignitaries of such high regard.

Now we sat within the audience chamber, the Shogun's representative sat at head of the circle of the successful samurai that were joined with us. It was a display of equality as normally such a high ranking individual would be sat at the head facing a tidied group of rank and filed warriors where there would be a distinctive display of rank. Although this was quite pleasing to be a part of, I did feel slightly uncomfortable by it as I didn't regard myself in equal standing with the representative in my own eyes.

Behind the representative stood four other samurai retainers, each bearing the emblem of the Shogun himself. These retainers would've been from the Shogun's personal guard and for the representative to have them accompany him meant that he was on a very important mission.

Each of these retainers held long boxes, wooden and lacquered a deep blood red. They shone beautifully in the bright light of the candles that lit the room and glimmered almost mysteriously. Other than the beautiful sheen of the lacquer, they were quite plain and didn't have the intricate carvings as I have seen on some higher quality cases. My guess would place them as the caskets for the Eight Dragons.

"Warriors of the nation. Today you displayed your skills for your Lord Shogun and you did so magnificently. As honoured representative of the Shogun I salute your skills of the sword in the name of the Lord of Lords. All of you are masterful and your diligence and training in your arts have paid you well.

This country has had in its history much strife and confrontation from both within and from foreign shores. Much of its history has been written in the blood of the fallen hero's of which there are too many to fathom in our long and turbulent history.

However, it is not the threat of invasion of the foreign barbarians or the twisted ambitions of a provincial Lord that should be feared the most. No, it is from something far worse. For we as a nation and a people are under the hidden bombardment from creatures of spiritual existence. Creatures born of the evil and malice that man possesses and exist in our lands.

All the 'fairy' tales and stories of the common folk that you may have heard throughout your lives are not just made up by old women to scare children or by the talented story telling traveller to provide entertainment around an evenings camp fire. Behind these stories of the dark lies a true darkness as some of these creatures are made into reality.

Long ago, long before the ruling of the Shoguns, where man was in his infancy and naïve to the world, there were three main species to walk these lands. Man, Dragon and worst of all, Demon. Long ago, Dragon and Demon fought one another while Demon fed upon mankind for its existence and sustenance. In an attempt to overthrow the Demons, the Dragons of old united with man. They taught man the skills to survive and gave them new ways to help fight off the Demon world. This included the art of the forging of swords and other weapons of arms.

Together, the Demons were driven away into hiding, weakened by the combined strength of the allied Man and Dragon. Man rode the back of their heavenly allies wielding swords of great power and the blood of Demons soiled the land until they had all but vanished, cast back into the shadows where they would remain in constant hiding. Once more there was peace in the nation.

However, Mankind in their arrogance got greedy and required more power and independence for themselves. They hunted the Dragon with their newly gained weapons and skills until the Dragon had been totally removed from the land. A terrible shame and displays one of the many weaknesses of man.

The beasts of the night feed upon the fears and desires of man and with every passing day they are thriving in number and slowly emerging and making themselves more known to the world once more. They are becoming stronger day after day." As the representative spoke, the words he said would've been shrugged aside as silly superstition by the more radical warrior, but after my near fatal encounter with the Kamaitachi I was inclined to think a little differently.

"Now, you have all proven yourselves worthy to carry the Eight Dragons. These swords have been in the Shogun's possession for centuries beyond count and were forged in manners that that have been long forgotten. These are the last of the sacred blades carried by the dragon riders. Each of these blades have the special ability to kill those creatures of the other world where your ordinary blades will not.

You warriors, carrying these blades, are now representatives of the Shogun himself. Those who lay their eyes upon you with these blades will know you are directly associated with the Shogun and answerable only to the Lord of Lords himself.

As the owners of these swords, your task, your sacred mission is to inspire those around you both commoner and those of status, to take away the negative feeling that is flourishing in the hearts of man so that we as a country can become great beyond measure."

With a delicate raise of his hand, the four warriors stepped forward and opened the lids of the boxes. Inside the caskets were lined with fine purple silks that surrounded the main contents. Swords of different shapes and sizes greeted us and the audience room emanated both awe and wonder as they were shown the light of day for the first time in what must've been an age.

The representative pulled out the first sword from the collection of boxes. It was a long sword, a tachi, gilded with gold and the handle encrusted with delicately beautiful slivers of ocean pearls.

"Kenjiro Santoku", with the calling of his name one of the samurai bowed forward before crouching over to receive his sword.

Next came a short white coloured sword, a wakizashi.

"Fujibayashi Shigeru"

When his name was called, a warm feeling flourished itself inside of me. I considered Fujibayashi as a personal disciple of mine as master had charged me with the majority of his training in our style. It is a great feeling for any teacher no matter what area of expertise they specialise in, to see their students achieve a level of recognised greatness, especially as it was an experience of this magnitude. Despite the formality, I couldn't help a pleasing smile forming on my otherwise emotionless face. Today was certainly a good day for myself, Fujibayashi and Sensei.

Sword after sword was presented to the victorious few. All were a kaleidoscope of colour, beauty and superior craftsmanship the likes of which I have not had the fortune to witness before now. Mine was last to be given and it was simply building up an irritation that a child gets when they are forced to wait for a gift. As the representative picked it up, he took his time to admire the sword. From the way he was studying it, looking at it deeply as he held it aloft in his hands under the candlelight, there was something different about it.

"Yoshida Kintaro. Step forward if you please."

As I moved to kneel before him, he kept his eyes on the beautiful sword as he marvelled at its beauty. "Your skills today were extraordinary. In all my years, never before have I seen such skill, not even from the Shogun's personal guard." This was a compliment of epic proportions and if there were no special swords being handed out, this compliment alone would've been worth a hundred swords.

He continued, "Please forgive me for having to test its competency in the manner that I asked of you today, it was necessary. That is why I present to you this very special sword. This sword has been given the name of 'The Emperor Dragon.' Of the eight, this sword was cast first and special care was taken in its creation. As such, it is the father sword from which all the others were forged. Such is the power that this sword holds that it has the ability to slice through rock and stone without dulling its edge. I cannot give this sword away to just any skilled samurai, but you; you have shown me that you possess the right level of the warrior way to warrant you the right to carry it and be its next owner.

The purpose of the Emperor Dragon is to empower the bearer with great power, strength and honour. The bearer of the Emperor Dragon, one day, will attain such a level that even he would not have to use it. The sheer essence of the bearer will overpower the darkness.

Please take this sword and use it with honour and integrity. You are the master of the Shogun's Eight Dragons. As such all other Dragons will look upon you for spiritual and technical guidance and leadership." The representative turned to address the remaining Dragons who were present. "Other than the Lord Shogun, the word of the Emperor Dragon is law to all other Dragons."

With that he handed over the sword and as I touched it, I felt very humble and honoured at being granted this auspicious honour.

Then I looked upon my sword. Its length was perfect for me, the scabbard was of a deep red lacquer with carvings of dragons and other mythical beasts flowing down its length. As I stared at them, they seemed to almost glide across its surface. Transfixed with it my eyes widened as I took it all in. The temptation to remove it from its sheath and admire the length of its blade was almost overwhelming. But then I remembered where I was. To remove the live blade in front of the representative would result in his four retainers cutting me down very swiftly where I knelt.

"Thank you for this honour" I managed to stutter out, practically overwhelmed with what was happening. Before returning to my place. Returning to become the Emperor Dragon of the Shogun's Eight Dragons.

Chapter 11 – The After Party

Heading back from the competition, as we crammed ourselves back onto the cool air conditioned buses; it was a completely different atmosphere from the morning. Us Brits, at the back of the bus were now full of the energies of life, pumping through the adrenaline of victory that still flowed in our veins. Laughing and joking, it was a cracking result for us as a team and especially for myself. The back end of the bus was alive with noise in comparison with the Australians who were a little more modestly subdued than their earlier antics at the start of the day.

"Well done today" said Emily as she sat next to me. "I've never seen you fight the way you did" she was smiling with her perfect smile. "You were amazing."

"Thank you" I said, more modest than what I could be at this given moment "Guess it was just being on the mat I suppose. It was a shame I couldn't get the hat trick…" I indicated over to James who was knelt tall on his seat, happy and content he was leaning over and messing around with the person sat behind him. He was laughing heartily as he fooled around with what seemed as though he didn't possess a single care in the world. "…But I think it made his trip, so its all cool." As I spoke, I realised what it was I was saying and realised how sportsman like and 'big' of me it was to accept the result as it stood.

Normally I would've been livid if I lost to someone on my team who I *knew* I have beaten time and time again. Perhaps it was the modesty of this very country that was beginning to rub itself off on me.

Emily looked back to see how happy James was and returned to face me, eyes sparkling. "Yeah, that it did. He was saying it was his first ever gold in one of these, he's going to ring home as soon as he gets back to the hotel and spread the news. Well that is if the time difference allows it!" I couldn't resist letting loose a happy little chuckle. I remembered what it felt like to win my first gold at a competition like this one, I imagine that he was going through similar feelings that I went through once.

"That's cool, he earned it. He fought very well; he definitely pulled it out of the bag today" I said. Looking round, I saw that Andrew had managed to slide his way so that he was sat with Sarah. They were chatting away in a world of their own. Andrew looked as though he was a tad bit nervous however.

"I see that Andrew is getting quite cosy there. Sneaky little slinker" I said, making Emily curious to investigate, ever the one who was interested in a bit of team gossip.

"No!…You don't think?" she said, in excited gossipy revelation of what I was implying to her. "Does Andrew like Sarah?" she asked mischievously and I saw her face turn to match the mischievous tones that she was uttering.

I raised an eyebrow in disbelief at her reaction "Emily, don't tell me you didn't notice? I was sure it was quite obvious." I said. Although Emily was quite bright, there were times, those odd little moments when she was not quite the sharpest cookie in the jar.

"He's liked her for a long time. But he's too shy to ask her out. I would've thought that someone like Andrew would've been able to do it by now."

"Do you want me to have a *word* with Sarah? We're rooming together, it would be perfect!" she uttered a little girlish giggle at her match making schemes.

"Oh no! I don't think he'll appreciate that!" I said, laughing nervously, beginning to regret letting her in on it. "You're not really supposed to know."

"Well…I'll be as discreet as possible." She said reassuringly, but if there's one thing that I knew Emily was not the best at, it was being discreet. Oh well, if its going to happen it's going to happen I guess, I'm sure Emily will mention something even if I said to her not to anyways. So I thought it best to just let Emily run with the idea.

"Well, try not to make it all uncomfortable. Andrew would kill me if he finds out I've told someone. Especially one of the team!" Asking wholeheartedly, I didn't want to be put in a sticky situation with Andrew that could make the rest of the trip difficult; particularly as I was rooming with him for most of the trip.

"Ok, I'll try not to get you involved." She joked "I'll make it sound like I just...noticed. Because I am naturally quite observant!"

As of yet, we haven't been presented with our medals and trophies that we had won. A little strange we thought, as we normally have them presented either after the individual event had finished or at a special ceremony at the venue at the end of the competition. But as we later found out from Coach, they would be presented at the after party which we were told was going to be held at the same hotel-restaurant that we were in for the welcome party. A fitting and touching finish of style and class to a successful competition.

Another party, I thought, this was going to be quite a trip and this party would be most rewarding of all of them. Coach was always right in what he said. 'It's always sweeter when you have that gold dangling around your neck.'

Back at the hotel, there was a mad scramble by everyone to get ready. The tournament had overrun therefore our window of opportunity to get ready was shortened significantly. Some of the girls were complaining on the bus back that there wasn't enough time. But then again, is there ever enough time?

"Right, first shout on the shower!" called Andrew as we scurried into the room, the door swinging wildly behind us to shut loudly.

"Ok, don't be too long! We don't have much time" I replied, as Andrew burst into the shower room and locked the door, knocking me aside in the process.

Slinging my bag down with a clunk I opened the wardrobe, to see what was available for me to wear for tonight's festivities. Thankfully I packed a couple of different shirts just in case there was more than one official party occasion. Grabbing two out of the wardrobe, holding them gingerly by the hangers I placed them up against me. My choice lay with blue or black. Blue or black, I repeated in my head. Blue! I thought, throwing it on the bed and replacing the other one back into the wardrobe.

With a quick selection of light blue jeans with my brown shoes, my outfit for tonight was ready.

"Hurry up in there!" I shouted, not realising that he'd only been in for roughly a minute.

"Alright! Calm it down mate, I've barely got in!" he said a little annoyed.

"Sorry" I said, apologetically.

Andrew remained in the shower room for around about another ten minutes. Unable to do much else until he had finished I resorted to switching on some Japanese TV. Flicking through the channels, there was not much on. A couple of Japanese talk show style programs, a cookery show and an old samurai film; all of which I had no chance of fully comprehending or understanding as it was completely in Japanese. Then I suddenly hit one channel which was showing an old, old version of Dr. Dolittle; in English as well! It had Japanese subtitles, but this was not overly that distracting. It was an adaptation that I didn't recognise, possibly from the 70's perhaps early 80's at a push. It was quite ironic that I had to fly halfway around the world to find me an English film that I've never seen before back home. Some would probably find this irony quite amusing.

"Hey Andrew! I've actually found something in English on the tele!" I called as I sat back to engross myself in the film while I waited.

"Yeah? Cool beans. I wont be too long mate, then you can have the shower." He replied, slightly muffled and seemingly uninterested through the door.

Soon Andrew emerged from the shower room, towel around his waist, another small yellow hand towel in his hands that he used to dry his hair. As he emerged, steam poured out of the doorway, rolling lightly into the small tunnelled area from the doorway of the bathroom.

"Ah good!" I said, quick to take over from him. The steam in the bathroom was really smothering and lingered in the tiny confines. "Jesus mate! How hot did you have the shower! It's more of a steam room than shower room in here." He didn't reply and I continued with getting washed. Quick to switch the shower back on and hop underneath it.

"I see you were getting pretty close to Sarah on the bus earlier." I teased as the hot water pelted itself off my body.

"Wha…what?" He said, stammering slightly at the mention of him and Sarah.

"On the bus…it didn't take you long to slide in and start laying the foundations. You little slinker you!"

"Oh...erm...no, nothing like that...we were just chatting. Talking more about the tournament than anything and the party tonight."

"Yeah...did you tell her what you'd like to do with her *after* the party?" I joked.

"Shut up Jason!" he muffled but was clear enough through the door. I laughed at his defensive response to my insinuation.

"Anyways, enough mucking about. You making your move tonight? Or are you just gonna bottle it as usual" I asked.

"Well, I don't know mate, I don't know what to say to her. I don't even know if she likes me like that." He sounded slightly downhearted.

"Don't be stupid! Of course you should have a crack tonight mate! Just think about it, everyone's in good spirits because we kicked ass. Sarah will be in good spirits, it'll be the perfect atmosphere for your unrelenting love to blossom." As I said it, I changed the style of my voice into a highly dramatic flourish, flourishingly my hands as I washed.

"You think?" he said "But I don't know what to say? How do I know if she likes me more than just a mate like?" He was starting to frustrate me a little.

"Look, just be yourself mate, find out more about her; laugh at her little jokes, you'll do fine." It was silly little pieces of advice, because we had grown close as a team anyways so we almost knew everything about each other anyway.

I opened the door to the shower room and rushed round with my towel to begin to get ready. "And to know whether or not she likes you…well that will just present itself."

Drying my hair with a secondary towel I added.

"Or you could get her absolutely steaming." I laughed. "I did hear you liked your women like old buildings…" Andrew looked at me strangely and I gave a brief moment before delivering the punch line "…close to collapse!"

"Cheeky bugger!" he cried, as he was now fully dressed up for the occasion; currently in the process of preening his hair, slapping in it his trademark excessive amount of hair gel and spiking it to unfathomable heights in a choppy fashion.

"All you got to do is relax and I'm sure she'll come round to your charms." I joked.

Entering the restaurant again for the second time, the place was dressed up for glitz and glamour with the layout changed for the occasion. The one side had the bar open and already there was a small crowd flocking around it for a bit of 'light' liquid refreshment before proceedings got under way.

The stage at the front had long banners flown proudly upon it, the central one displaying the fist emblem and the kanji of our style and was the emblem that was recognised worldwide in karate circles. Either side of this one hung the flags of each of the nations that were here in attendance. I felt proud to have the British flag right next to the central one. An important place, I thought, just how it should be.

At the back of the stage stood two long tables joined together, upon this table, the medals and trophies were lined up smartly, they stood brilliantly underneath the many spotlights, sparkling magnificently they appeared most beautiful. It was warming to know that a couple of those would soon be in my possession and quite a few in the possession of the British team.

All the tables had been moved aside, creating an empty space where groups were congregating and chatting casually. Before, it was a case of sticking with your own country, now, it was an unaffiliated mix. All nations were now mixing up and networking and socialising as was the intention of the trip. It was always nice to see when the atmosphere and competitiveness between nations broke down to a more relaxed, more 'human' nature. To continue with the rest of this trip with the highly strung 'competitive' nature would've been simply unbearable, not to mention completely unsociable!

After getting a quick drink at the bar I saw Andrew already having a go with Sarah. Doing his best to relax, he subconsciously couldn't help striking an attempted 'cool' pose. Almost comical to watch as I saw him going through the first stages of floundering.

"Hey Jason!" said Emily as she quickly darted over me. She was wearing a sleek black dress that clung to her body tightly, her hair was straightened and glistened slightly due to some special form of hair product. She looked quite stunning, in fact she was pretty breathtaking. "You'll never guess!" she said shrieking with excitement, the simple sign that she had some gossip to report back to me.

"No...what is it?" I said, shocked at the sudden intrusion.

"Well...I was speaking to *someone* earlier" her implications towards Sarah was obvious to behold.

"Oh!" I said, catching on to what she was implying. "Would this particular someone be a certain blonde on our team by any chance?"

"Yes! Sarah!" she exclaimed excitedly "Well, when we got back to the hotel. Well, you know what us girls are like, gossiping and all..." From the positive sound of it, I guess that Andrew is going to have his *highlight* of the trip at some point tonight.

"And did this little piece of gossip have anything to do with a certain male member of this team as well." Trying to usher her into getting more to the point.

"Yep." She said

"I guess that Andrew is going to have a *good* party then" I winked continuing the insinuation.

"No, not Andrew!" she said excitedly, taking me back somewhat by surprise. I took a quick sip of my drink.

"What? Then who? Not Bruce is it? That would really tick him off"

"Well, when we got back to the hotel, she kept going on about tonight, and she kept talking about one person in particular."

"Yes…WHO?" I exclaimed, as I was beginning to get quite involved in the gossip. Normally something that I wasn't in the habit of doing. Gossip often turned to rumours and rumours did tend to produce either awkward situations or ruin good ones. But there was something telling me that I needed to know who Sarah wanted to 'get' to know this trip. Emily's knack of building the suspense was infuriating. Emily paused, smiling wickedly.

"YOU!" she said, placing her index finger on my chest. 'Oh no', I thought as the thought of upsetting Andrew became apparent. I feared that this revelation might effect our friendship while we were on tour. It would definitely provide some form of sourness and friction to the practically perfect start of the trip

"Are you sure?" I asked, hoping that she was just messing about. "You've got to be joking right?"

"Yep, its true" she replied, confirming it. Her eyes giving away that she was in fact telling the truth. "You know what's she's like with winners! And well, to be honest, I think she's fancied you for quite a while now…Do you like her?"

"Well, yeah, she is hot, but…" my sentence got cut off mid way.

"Excellent! Ah so exciting!" she returned to her giggly, happy scream stage. She went to turn away, probably to go report to Sarah who was still around Andrew so I needed to stop her.

"Emily, wait!" I cried, she stopped and turned.

"If you'd let me finish, I was going to say yes, I think she's hot. But…" I sounded more uncomfortable "Andrew really likes her. You should listen to him talking about her all the time. I'm just worried that this might really hurt him you know?" I hoped, in fact prayed that she understood. To be honest with myself, if it were anyone else other than Andrew that liked her, I wouldn't have hesitated at the chance. There was a heavy feeling that I was going to regret this.

"Ah…I see your point" said Emily, her voice dropping in the tones of hyperactivity. "That's not good. What are you going to do? It's quite a sticky one this."

"I don't know, I don't really want to tell Andrew because I think he'll take it the wrong way. It's not that I don't want to, bloody hell, she is really, really beautiful; I just don't want to hurt Andrew in the process. He'll probably think that I had this planned, that I *stole* her from him."

I stood there pondering on what to do, sipping my Japanese lager methodically hoping that the answer to the situation will present itself and enlighten me. Do I allow things to happen with Sarah? She was after all, amazing! And I never found 'love' on tour before although I have tried with several failed attempts. Well, it was colloquially known as 'love' but in reality was more so down the lines of lust and a bit of a mess about and very rarely did it turn into anything serious once the trip had ended.

But that would upset Andrew and from my experience, it's never a good thing for two mates to fall out over a girl. Normally very messy and was often made worse by the fact that it was between two karate-ka and we would have to share the same room for the rest of the tour.

Or do I do what the rational side of my brain is telling me is the sensible option. Resist the temptation and miss out on finding 'love' this trip with perhaps the fittest looking girl here. Although there was a part of me that was purely *screaming* at me to go for it; there was the obvious outcome that comes with that. The other option of resistance would be one that everyone would be more happy with and that no hard feelings or grudges would be born on this trip.

If I decide to not get with Sarah, then I would needed to find someone else to target my normally failing attempts at. Though there was one girl who has caught my eye already...perhaps I should try her?

"Attention everyone!" came the call from the stage, "Can I have your attention please?" Takeo Sensei's translator stood with Takeo Sensei on the centre stage. Eyes turned and within mere moments, the mass of people quietened down.

Sensei spoke like he always has done at the welcome meal with his translator providing the English explanation.

"Welcome to all competitors, coaches and instructors. Today we witnessed a true display of the spirit of Budo set within modern application of sport karate. All athletes today, both young and old should feel proud of their performance and great thanks should be shown to their instructors and sport coaches for providing them the skills for their performance today.

You young athletes are now the future of our art. In the years to come, some of you may leave to follow other pursuits, some, most I hope, will stay. Those that stay with training will have the chance to one day pass their skills onto the next generation.

We now come to the end of the tournament proceedings. After this night of celebratory presentations of medals you will embark on a journey that will open your eyes to the splendour that is Japan." Sensei spoke with such pride for his homeland, a characteristic that was common amongst the Japanese who until recent years were relatively xenophobic when it came to foreigners in their homeland.

"Your journey will take you on the footsteps of Japan's greatest and most well known warrior, Miyamoto Musashi. I hope that by following this warrior of olds' footsteps that you will develop yourselves as modern warriors and be inspired to greater yourselves."

He nodded to his translator who went over to the medal table and picked up the first batch. The shiny medals dangled and jangled upon sky blue ribbons.

"Ladies Individual kata, under eighteen years old." Called out the translator. Emily's category. She won a bronze in this event, getting beaten by the eventual winner in the semi finals.

"Joint 3rd...Emily Parton, UK...Sandra Francis, Australia. 2nd place..."

The called names walked proudly up to the stage, following up a small set of steps that were situated just off to one side of the massive stage.

There they stood, side by side upon the stage it was a sight to see. Emily smiled wide and broadly as she stood in front of Sensei, hands straight down at her sides.

Sensei presented them with their medals and as he did so everyone cheered, the hall echoed with their claps and their appreciative whistles. Despite being from nations all over the world, of different nationalities, colour, religions; there was no animosity here now. We stood in recognition of the successes of our peers.

Into the night the presentation of the medals continued, each category being read out loudly and the names of the victorious made their triumphant way to the stage to sound of the rapturous applause. From looking from the main floor you felt proud of the achievements of those names that were called even if it was made by those from another nation, but especially for those on your own team.

Though when you're up there personally, it's as if you are on top of the world. That was the feeling I got when I got presented my first gold in Japan. The medal was heavy and diamond shaped. Embossed into the metal was the fist emblem and kanji, which I ran my fingers over inquisitively, feeling every bump and ridge. It was unlike any other medal or trophy I had ever received; it was not the most flamboyant but it was indeed one of the most special and memorable that I possessed.

"Well done mate!" shouted Andrew as I exited the stage. The UK team was still clapping harmoniously as I walked down the steps. As a team we supported each other through everything, both victory and defeat.

"Let's take a look at that metal ware." He said cheerfully as I approached. My medal began swinging in synch with each step, catching the light at various angles. When I reached him he peered at it and picked it up in his hands.

"Nice!" he said in admiration. "Looking forward to getting mine!"

"Yep, soon enough matey, soon enough" with that, Sarah walked over and placed her hand on my arm as she got close.

"Well done Jason." She said, "You kicked ass today." She spoke slightly saucy, with seductive undertones that I was managing to pick up, it was a little uneasy given the circumstances with Andrew stood right in front of me.

"Thanks" I managed, uncomfortably seeing Andrew's face drop with a detectable hint of jealously. It had begun. The downward spiral that would ultimately lead to a very sticky situation that could affect the rest of the trip. I needed to get out of this.

"I fancy another drink." I offered uneasily, as I turned hastily to make my way to the bar.

"No you cant go!" said Sarah grabbing onto my hand. "The team presentation is about to start in a minute"

And she was right, as soon as she finished speaking, the event was called by the translator and we quickly grabbed James and Emily so we could ascend onto the stage together, as one.

"In 3rd place, New Zealand and Japan!" clapping proceeded as the two nations went up together and received their medals. Once the stage had been cleared the announcement continued

"In 2nd place, Australia!" bubbling within me was the anticipation for our turn. It shivered through me wildly.

"And in 1st place, and this years team champions…" the announcer paused, infuriatingly to me. "…UK!"

The five of us marched our way to the stage, heads and spirits held high in the air for we were the champions of the blue ribbon event this year. Our pathway cleared as if we were celebrities and we walked through a gangway of appreciative clapping.

We received our medals with special grace and humility and exited to the continued rapture from the crowd.

"Now it's time to party!" said James as the music crackled into life. Loudspeakers dotted around the hall blared the uplifting music; a set list combination of Japanese pop and western pop music that was more recognisable to us. Throw in a little bit of rock and roll and you have quite a musical cooking pot that resulted in an above average party. People started dancing in the centre of the open floor making in an impromptu dance floor and the party began to liven up.

I spent most of the time just trying to keep my distance from Sarah who tried to hound me to dance whenever she caught me in my sights. I dared to think what she was thinking in regards to me and what she will be thinking after tonight. Perhaps she thought I was playing hard to get? Playing some form of *cat and moose* game with her.

As the night grew on, Andrew caught wind of Sarah's actions and attentions and he too began to avoid me. Or I got the feeling that this was the case. I could see from here that it was beginning to become a bit of a disastrous evening for us all.

But then, just before I thought things would get worse, they suddenly turned around for the better. As I stood at the bar, attempting a conversation with one of the German competitors, which was no easy task as he spoke little English and I spoke no German at all. The corner of my eye caught sight of a small, slim female figure approach me.

Turning my head, it was Momoko, the number one Japanese competitor today, who had beaten Sarah in her category. The one who I had noticed since the first meal when we arrived.

"Hello Jason-san." She said politely, I couldn't believe that she remembered my name. It took me somewhat by surprise. All be it, a very pleasing surprise.

"Hello...Momoko-san" I began to turn quite shy. She was looking amazing, her fit, athletic body was framed nicely with a spotless white blouse and a tight three quarter length pencil skirt and tights. Her hair was done up nicely and the way it hung brought out her eyes which themselves were highlighted by a subtle application of eyeliner and mascara. Casting my eyes on her she was just pure beauty personified and there was something about her, that she was beginning to affect me in ways that no one else has ever done. Could it be the cliché condition that inflicts some lucky few, namely called 'love at first sight'?

Before tonight, I would've fought to prove that this way of thinking was merely a stupid way of thinking; preferring to think that love could never blossom until you truly get to know someone. Though, my stomach was bounding and leaping in its own manner and I could feel myself tensing up through nerves. My cheeks felt as though they were turning red and I dare look in a mirror to clarify that. Could it be that this encounter might be contradicting my previous viewpoints to life?

"I saw you fight today. Your karate is very good."

"Thank you, so is yours" I offered genuinely, I was in shock that she was actually watching me compete, not only that, she remembered me. It felt really good.

"Are you enjoying your stay in Japan?" she asked, still in her welcome host mode. A typical trademark of the Japanese people, their desire to ensure that foreigners and guests are treated royally. It is seen as an honour to them to make sure that we were looked after properly. It is a shame that this wasn't the case of the majority of people back home.

"Oh yes, very much so. Such an interesting and beautiful country. I feel that I will experience more of the beauty it has to offer as this trip progresses." I tried to put in a hidden agenda to my last sentence. This made her smile, if there's one thing I've learnt while being in Japan is that if you compliment the country and its traditions you can get on with the locals. Though I don't know whether or not she understand my secret implications due to language barrier.

"You speak very good English Momoko-san, how long have you been studying?"

"Thank you, I am still learning. I learn in school." She said, her English starting to break down just ever so slightly as I engaged her in more general conversation.

"Are you going to be joining us on the Musashi Tour?" I was hoping for a positive answer, I wasn't hoping for a swift trip that involved Momoko. She smiled again.

"Yes Jason-san, I am acting like translator for you. I too am interested in Musashi Tour. Studying history in school."

She shared the same interest in Japanese history as I did which I found very refreshing. I had a feeling that I could enjoy traversing back and forth and learning about Japanese history from her. Jumping ahead of myself I gave a quiet 'yes' inside as I thought of it as a great positive that we had something in common other than karate.

"That's good, can I get…" before I could finish offering her a drink, Sarah latched herself onto my arm from nowhere, like a limpet on the rocks.

"There you are! Come on! Get yourself on the dance floor champ." She said, pulling on my and yanking me away from Momoko.

"Excuse me…" I said politely to Momoko, looking back to her as I was being dragged discourteously away to the dance floor. Momoko just smiled and bowed her head graciously. I groaned to myself with every step as I got closer to the dance floor. I could punch, I could kick,

I could even perform some of the more technical kata, at quite a good standard might I add; but there was just one simple thing that I couldn't do well and that was dancing! You would think with my years of martial arts training and expertise that I would have the footwork, the coordination…nope, I was awful at dancing.

I also groaned to myself for the fact that my conversation and ultimately my act of trying to pull Momoko had been cut prematurely. Perhaps I'll get the opportunity to pick up where I got off from later on tonight, at worse, later on this trip.

Finding a space among the crowd, the dance floor beginning to fill up with different groups and couples; I tried to loosen up, swaying to what I thought was the beat. I kept my hands in tight and low in front of my hips. I blushed with embarrassment for I knew I had no rhythm whatsoever. Sarah was dancing in front of me, slightly provocatively.

"No, no, no!" she said playfully "You got to loosen up your hips" as she said that she placed her hands on my hips and moved her body closer to me. She ran her hands up my back as she pressed herself sassily against me. Her eyes looking up into mine seductively, she opened her mouth slightly, wetting her soft moistened lips in a sultry fashion. So tempting, she was definitely a major tease but there were the voices in my head that shouted at me, in such a way that I had to consider Andrew's feelings.

"That's more like it" she said slowly "Now you're beginning to loosen up" she teased as she continued her raunchy dance. In fact, I thought she was revelling in the sight of my awkwardness when it came to dancing and having a quiet joke to herself. I was certainly a fish out of water.

"You think?" I joked, trying my best to hide the nervousness contained within my voice.

"Yeah" she purred as the song changed to something more slow, she pressed her head into my chest. I placed my arms around her, not quite sure where the best place was to put them.

"What do you think of Andrew?" I asked, hoping to spoil the moment slightly and shift attentions.

"He's alright, a cool mate." She replied, a little unsure of what I was asking.

"Just a mate?"

"Yeah, just a mate" she said bluntly "he's cool and all, but that's all." She picked her head up and looked me in the eye in a quizzed fashion. "Why you asking about Andrew anyways?"

"Well, it's just that he really likes you. REALLY likes you! And I am slightly uncomfortable dancing like this because I don't want to hurt his feelings."

Sarah sounded shocked, as this was news to her. "Oh" she exclaimed "I see, well he cant be *that* much in love with me."

"What do you mean?" I became just as shocked as she was. She looked over to her right with a little nod and my eyes followed. Before my eyes was Andrew, standing tall and dancing close with Emily; lips locked and there was no sign that they were coming up for air anytime soon. I had to chuckle silently, bloody dog on heat!

"Ah, I see he is quite fickle." I said with a dramatic Shakespearean flair as if I was quoting from a legendary play. Rolling my eyes, there was me thinking that I was going to hurt his feelings with Sarah and he moves on as if it didn't even bother him, always thought of the little bugger as a bit of a player. He was fortunate enough to have the looks and when he isn't acting all nervous and shell shocked, he has the patter to go with it.

I should've suspected that he would be quick to set his sights on another *victim*. Or maybe the sly fox had me fooled from the very start? He could've had his eyes on Emily from the very beginning and he said Sarah as a means of covering it up for whatever reason. Maybe he thought that I wouldn't approve of him and Emily as a match, but that would be silly as Emily was actually very good looking herself and I didn't have any personal feelings for her anyways that would've gotten in the way of things.

Before I had time to laugh loud, Sarah had placed her hands on my face and planted me with a deep kiss. Her lips were soft and moist and I closed my eyes and enjoyed the experience. She was wearing some form of flavoured lip balm and as embraced me I could taste sweet fruity, exotic flavours. Her kiss was really sensational as my body warmed with the thought of being lip locked with a beautiful blonde like her. There was a part of me however, that wished that the girl I was kissing was Momoko.

Chapter 12 – Death of a Great Man

Victorious and now gifted with two of the Dragon Swords we made for our long journey on foot back to the dojo and our home. We were quiet with each other, as was befitting the relationship between teacher and student and little words were said throughout the long journey on foot back to Kakogawa.

On the way we would stop in various taverns and have the occasional drink together and a light meal, usually of local fish and sweet rice balls. A relatively quiet means of celebration, we were after all, samurai who followed the code of Bushido very close to the letter. Boisterous and extravagant actions were done by the more vulgar and somewhat uncouth of our class and of that of the commoner, something which I always seen as distasteful and unbefitting of swordsmen on their way to spiritual enlightenment. It was unfortunately a negative quality that a higher proportion of our class were beginning to display as I noticed more ronin, master less samurai, that roamed the countryside and populated the cities.

I could understand why battle brothers may converse openly with one another with the bond of warriors whereby they were on the knife edge of death with battle looming upon them. Where tomorrow could be their last and during long campaigns, the strong brotherhood of a close group of warriors would dwindle in number as sometimes not everyone comes back alive; but this was mostly during wartime and was a general fact of war that everyone accepted. At present our country was at peace, or at least, it was from each other and from the threat of foreign invaders.

It was only when we were in such establishments as taverns and the like, that we would become more talkative and open with one another; as when we ate, we ate more along the lines as equals and the strict etiquette governing teacher and student relaxed slightly, but only slightly; it would've been a bad example from myself if I allowed Fujibayashi to raise himself above his position when speaking to me; even at meal times for it would slowly break down the proper structure that the relationship between teacher and student and once broken down, it would never be able to be fixed.

The subject matter of our conversations didn't evolve around anything that we considered too trivial, the state of country scale politics or the affairs of others were normally a taboo subject whenever we ate as we cared not for these things; and Fujibayashi often governed the purpose of the conversation around improving his swordsmanship to a higher standard. He would often discuss the fundamental principles of techniques and the means of developing it further and I would often ask him about the Toda style which was his foundation style. It was really refreshing for me to see a student with such a curiosity for improvement, many these days don't tend to share the same zealous passion and commitment as I possessed, as such they generally tended to develop at a slower but gradual pace. Fujibayashi was unlike these lowly students and his obvious natural skill is the result from his extensive curiosity that meant his technique was excelling at a phenomenal rate. I was always obliged to help pass on my knowledge.

Sometimes I would ask him a couple of small questions in regards to his past and background. I would aim my questions with an air of allowing him to tell me whatever he wanted to say. Some people's past were often best kept to themselves, but I realised that through all my time working and mentoring him I actually knew very little about him.

He told me that his past was shrouded with an element of mystery with a lot of information that he did not possess. He could not tell me the full extent of his infant years. Orphaned when he was just a baby by means that he didn't know, he was left at the doorstep of Master Toda's household during the period of the harvest on the eve of the harvest moon; no note, nothing but the swaddling that he was wrapped in. It was his cries that alerted one of the servants of his presence at the doorstep who took him straight to the master. Because of this lack of accompanying information that it was uncertain as to his true age and even the subject of his natural birthday. Master Toda decided that he adopt the harvest moon festival as his birthday for this was the day that he was discovered; the 'birth' of his new path with Master Toda's household.

Master Toda passed him on to one of the female servants of the house who raised him as her own and it was this woman that Fujibayashi always considered as his mother. As he was the adopted son of the servant, he initially was forbidden to partake in sword lessons as it was considered unethical for someone of non samurai birth to be taught the ways of the sword.

However, with Fujibayashi's own incessant curiosity for the quest of knowledge and the natural affiliation of swordsmanship, it didn't stop him from secretly observing classes whenever he could; as he would peer through cracks in the walls or look through windows. He joked with how he would receive beatings from Master Toda personally whenever he was caught but still this didn't phase him.

It was after he had celebrated what he considered to be his 'twelfth' birthday that he was put in a situation whereby his natural ability with the sword came to light. Recalling a situation where he was consistently teased and taunted by one of young students who was at least three or four years his elder. This bully took advantage of his social position as being the son of one of the more wealthier retainers to constantly insult Fujibayashi and his unknown heritage. The bully often referred to him as a lost dog and how he was simply a pet of Master Toda who had him around to take care of the scraps that were left at the Master's table. This insult had enraged the young Fujibayashi who spat in the young samurai's face and so he challenged him to a duel.

Meeting on a small open hillside in the local area that was often one of the more popular areas for the partaking of sword duels of all manners and descriptions, the two fought it out with wooden swords at the request of Fujibayashi and the displeasure of his opponent who was looking forward to testing out the sharpness of his blade. They were watched by three other students of the school who acted as the witnesses for the challenge and to ensure that the fight would be fair.

Fujibayashi won hands down on all attempts of the young samurai to best him and his opponent received quite a beating in the process. Things however, got more serious and nearly out of hand when the young samurai reached for his own live blade that was being held safely by one of his witnesses, out of the frustration brought about by someone of his standing being embarrassed by his perceived junior. Fujibayashi recalled how he was forced to act quickly and bludgeon the young samurai quite forcefully about the head using his make shift sword as he managed to draw the live sword out of its sheath with the intent of using it on Fujibayashi.

Although he didn't kill the young braggart and merely incapacitated his ability to fight by knocking him out, he did fear the worst for actions, that he would receive the wrath of Master Toda upon returning to the household on the recommendation of the students wealthy patronage. For an instance like this did require retribution in some form.

To his surprise, when Master Toda heard of what had occurred at the duel and the run up of events, he merely scolded the other samurai for his lack of manners and from this point recognised Fujibayashi's natural ability. It was also believed that the family of the young samurai shared the same beliefs as Master Toda and they too punished the samurai. Then began Fujibayashi's official indoctrination and instruction into the Toda style of swordplay where he received personal tuition from Master Toda himself.

His above average skill and the strange, unusual circumstances of how he was accepted into the school was met with a fair amount of both jealousy and contempt by some of the other students who felt insulted by the presence of Fujibayashi on the dojo floor. They were displeased by the mystery that surrounded Fujibayashi's history; though none would ever dare to speak out to Master Toda and those who were caught displaying their distaste at the situation received punishment and scolding accordingly by the Master. The fact that Master Toda took charge of Fujibayashi's tuition personally and not from one of his senior students meant that his position within the school was secured. It seems that Fujibayashi does tend to become enrolled in schools in out of the ordinary circumstances and did tend to change the protocols surrounding the enrolment procedures.

As Fujibayashi presented the story of his past and some of the hardships he had occurred when following the path of a warrior, it made me smile with reverence to both his character and the superior attitude that he displayed. It became clear that his desire to learn is possibly a need to define himself in life and to show to the world that he was born to become a traveller on the path of the sword. He had the ambition and the drive that every legendary swordsmen requires.

Though there was a part of him that, although he didn't openly say so, he longed to know more about his past and that this quest of swordsmanship that he was undertaking would always be overshadowed by the fact that he did not know himself fully. It was as though he was incomplete without it. For him I considered an element of empathy towards him that I believed will help strengthen the bond between us as I could only imagine the emotions and outlooks that he had to life.

Two days of travel with little time for rest and we were soon back on the edge of Kakogawa. Entering the town, the sun was not as harsh as it usually was this time of year and the breeze was light and cooling. Although the weather was definitely pleasant, there was something different about the town. The streets were fairly quiet considering this was supposed to be a market day. A strange veil had descended on the town, it was harrowing and disturbing.

"Something's not right" I said grimly

"I agree Shihan, I feel it too." Replied Fujibayashi as we continued our march down the streets, now with added pace and desire to reach our final destination.

The sight of the dojo was uplifting in its splendour and it filled my heart as it came into view. But this warming sensation would not last long as from its great gates hung two banners of pure black silk. They fluttered lightly in the breeze and this did not present a good sign.

The flying of the black banners and flags from the dojo gates was a sign to all who viewed them that a senior member of the household had passed. With myself here, that would mean it would either be Ryoko or worse, Master Imamoto and with Sensei not well before we left on our travels I feared that the worst had happened and that this was a symbol of Sensei's passing.

With vexation in my heart I burst into a sprint, taking Fujibayashi by surprise and ran to the dojo gates. Once Fujibayashi had come to realise what was happening he was close to follow.

A crash through the gates and I was surrounded by the students of the dojo who turned their heads in reaction to the sudden burst through the doors. My fears continued to be confirmed as the students were dressed in formal attire, there was no classes being conducted today.

They dressed smartly with a navy blue Yukata; a formal form of the typical kimono with extended sleeves. They wore navy blue hakama over their legs as was befitting the lower status of the student themselves, if Master had passed, then Ryoko would be dressed similarly except all in white. On their foreheads they wore white hachimaki and all of them were carrying their swords.

I stood in the doorway, Fujibayashi caught up and stood behind me, skidding himself to a halt. The students, recognising who the sudden intruder was bowed low and graciously. I ran over to the one.

"Kohai! Who has passed?" I said, my face furrowed.

"Yoshida Shihan...Sensei has...passed." He said humbly.

"When? How?" I asked, I needed more information and I barked my commands at him like an angered dog.

"Yesterday, at the rise of the full moon. He died in his sleep, he passed away quietly. We were hoping you would return for the funeral. Please if you would make yourselves ready and we will begin the proceedings." He bowed again but when he raised his head, I struck him with the back of my hand with an almighty slap, powerful was the blow that it felled him to the floor.

"Mind your tongue! Do not presume to order me about in such a manner, remember your place!" I shouted at him, vexation and grief overtaking my normal sense of decorum. It was the wrong thing to say at the best of times, especially now in the mindset that I was in.

"Where is Ryoko Shihan?" I asked, barking at him further as the student squirmed on the floor fearfully.

"He...He is with Sensei's body, preparing him for the final procession."

I walked away from the student who I floored, making with added pace to Sensei's room, this is where the preparations would've taken place.

Rushing on the veranda that encircled the building, my footsteps echoed on the wood. Another student was stood guard outside Sensei's domicile.

"Yoshida Shihan, I am gladdened that you've returned." He spoke formally, bowing low as I approached.

"May I pass. I need to see Sensei" I asked.

183

"Of course Shihan" he said and pulled the door to as I entered.

The room was solemn, the air ripe with sorrow and grief. In front of me was Sensei's body, laid out, fully dressed in white. His hands placed upon his chest, his sword by his side. In front of the body, with his back to me was the familiar outline of Ryoko who knelt silently.

I knelt beside him, to join him in prayer at Sensei's passing. Together we stayed there in complete silence.

Ryoko broke the silence "Welcome home Yoshida Shihan"

"Good day Ryoko Shihan…"

" How well did you succeed at the sword duel?" he asked

"Yes Ryoko Shihan, our style reigned victorious at the duel." I said, our conversations were being kept short and sweet.

"That is good news, Sensei would be pleased. We kept him here in anticipation for your arrival."

I pulled the Emperor Dragon from my obi and presented it in front of Sensei, holding it up horizontally in front of him, the carvings on the scabbard picking out the light casting loose shadows on its surface.

"Sensei, I have returned from Himeji and with me I hold the Emperor Dragon, the chief sword of the Eight Dragon Swords. Our style outclassed over the rest of the swordsman and as such I was presented this sword by the representative of the Shogun himself. Fujibayashi-san also performed honourably and he too was presented with a Dragon Sword. Our style has now two of the Dragon swords under its name. A feat that no other style present at the duel achieved." With respect I bowed forward with the sword in hand.

"Yoshida Shihan. I think its time to put Sensei to rest. Please prepare yourself for the procession." Ryoko placed a comforting hand upon my shoulder, indicating it was time for me to go.

"Please Ryoko Shihan. Allow me a few moments more with Sensei. So I can say my goodbyes properly." I asked

"Of course, excuse me, please take your time" he said softly, as he rose and exited the room.

I spent a while in silent meditation, collecting my thoughts on the time I had spent with Sensei. Remembering the important lessons that he had shared with me. Now that he had passed, the validity of the style would have to be continued through myself and Ryoko. Even if a singular lesson is to be forgotten or misinterpreted, then the style would not be as pure.

In my meditation I made sure that I commended Sensei's memory, for with my new task that I was given by the Shogun, there was little doubt in my mind that it would have meant I would've had to leave the dojo anyways.

When I follow my new path, it will be in Sensei's name as well as my own.

It came time for me to leave to prepare myself, dressing myself in a bright white yukata and hakama, I finished my formal dress with the tying of my hachimaki around my forehead, this was white to match the rest of my clothing.

When preparing for a funeral procession, my mind goes into the same format as if I was preparing for combat. The world fades out of view, thought on what my task is to be is the only process that runs through my mind. Everything that I do at this moment has the same emphasis as an official ceremony or ritual and every movement, now matter how small reflects this realisation.

Once I was ready, the Emperor Dragon showing proudly in my belt, it was already attracting attention as some of the more observant students had already picked up on the fact that I was carrying a different sword from my usual. I left to join the rest of the members of the house who were gathered in the courtyard gardens.

Sensei had been placed inside a formal processional box of dark woods and paper, a hallow palanquin held aloft by two of the students; it resembled a little mobile house or hovel. Ryoko and myself, being the senior disciples of the dojo led the procession, walking side by side as we began the slow march to Sensei's final resting place. Behind Sensei's final carriage stood the rest of the students, walking in two columns in regimented fashion. The head of this group held a small brass bell that he chimed rhythmically as we conducted our morbid march. This acted as a signal to those around that a funeral procession was passing them as well as a signal to the gods to let them know that Sensei's spirit was soon travelling to them.

Many people, villagers of the town, had gathered in the streets and they lined the edges of the street in solemn remembrance. The news of Sensei's death had obviously spread quickly through the town and it was enlightening and pleasing to see how many people came to show one last sign of respect to a great man. Sensei was indeed a loved man among the local population, even though he was quite ruthless in the realm of the dojo and it was obvious that his death touched the hearts of many more people other than ourselves.

As we passed them they bowed their heads humbly, some had dropped to their knees and performed a respectful kneeling bow as they recognised Sensei's status. They did not raise their heads until we had passed them in a show of respect.

One of Sensei's last wishes, more so, his instructions for his funeral arrangements; was to be buried close to a small stream that ran on the edge of the village. It was a beautiful spot and one which held a special place in Sensei's heart. The spot had been prepared prior in readiness for Sensei's final rest. Two tombstones had been readied. One showing the family crest and the details about Sensei himself, the other, a symbol based around the Imamoto school itself and the two stood together harmoniously near the edge of the stream, underneath a willow tree.

Behind that was a tall funeral pyre that had been stacked neatly and the processional box with Sensei's body was placed on its peak as if on top of a great mountain. Sensei had opted for his body to be cremated, his ashes to be placed in an urn and buried at the base of the tombstones. A method of burial that some of the population deemed to be wrong, though most preferred this method. We were not in any position to object to how Sensei wishes to be buried.

Ryoko and myself were handed a lit torch and we positioned ourselves either end of the pyre. With a synchronised placing of the torches on the dry stack of wood we waited until it had caught alight. Throwing the torches onto the fire we stepped away as the stack began to smoke and burn.

We surrounded the fire, motionless, silent, waiting. The fire burnt into the night, smoking into the air, the wood crackling as it burnt. It was an emotional sight to behold, but none of us flinched as we did not want Sensei to pass on with the wailing of a weak willed swordsman. Such an event would be very insulting to his memory.

It was dark when the fire had finished, the smoking charred remains of the pyre and Sensei remained in front of us. Ryoko beckoned all the other students to leave as he and myelf approached the cremated remains. It was still quite hot, but together we brushed Sensei's ashes into a copper urn.

It was Ryoko who buried the urn into the ground. I stood to one side and watched him as he did so and with a small offering of a cup of rice wine and the burning of a few sticks of fragrant incense; I rang the death bell three times and we commended Sensei's spirit onto the afterlife.

When we returned to the dojo, Ryoko had beckoned me to his quarters. It was the reading of Sensei's last wishes, his last commands for the students of the dojo that I was going to hear as I was one of the higher ranking seniors.

We sat down facing one another. The atmosphere was as sombre as the whole day had been. Ryoko pulled from a drawer next to him a rolled piece of parchment tied up with a piece of hemp string.

With the rustle of the parchment as he untied it from its bond he rolled it out and held it in front of him.

"Sensei knew that his time was close. This last wishes were made before your departure to Himeji." He looked down at the script upon the parchment and read aloud.

"I, Sensei Imamoto, on knowing that my time on this earth is close to passing and that my spirit is to be commended to another plane, have written the last commands for this dojo as it has been done for generations.

I have left no immediate blood heir on this earth to carry on my family name and the name of this household and its teachings. As such I leave the property and grounds of this sacred place in the hands and care of my Lord, who I have served with grace and pride throughout my many years. The monetary wealth from my estate will be divided equally between Ryoko Shihan and Yoshida Shihan to use it however they see necessary for their path.

To Ryoko Shihan, I have already instructed you on the task that I require you to do. There is nothing more that I have to command and I know you will conduct this to the best of your ability.

To Yoshida Shihan, you have been an outstanding pupil and your skill with the sword is a rare gift that not even I have seen in many students throughout my years. I am sure beyond any manner of doubt that you would have brought back with you one of the eight gifts from the Shogun, as such, you will have been given a set of commands of your own. I am not one to overrule the wishes of the Shogun and his greater wisdom so my last words to you is to continue to carry yourself with grace and dignity as a former pupil of mine.

The Imamoto Dojo is now no more and the students are to be disbanded to follow whatever paths they deem suitable to them. I trust that you will pass on this news to them.

The path ahead of you will be both mysterious and wondrous. The path behind you is now all in the past. Remember your teachings and the path ahead will be made easier to you.

These are the last words of Imamoto Gozaemon of Kakugawa."

As Ryoko finished, the sheer implication of Sensei's words hit home. The Imamoto Dojo was to be disbanded and passed on to the Lord of the province. My only hope is that he keeps it on as a place for the development of swordsmanship in memory of Sensei. It would be truly regrettable if it was to be made into something else.

Sensei, in all his wisdom knew full well that I had presented to me my own path to follow by the Shogun, his words would make the initial transition into this new path much more easier to endure.

"Ryoko Shihan, I will speak to Fujibayashi on the manner of the disbanding of the Dojo. He too is one of the Eight Dragons of the Shogun and as such he may wish to travel with me. Will you be the one to pass on the news to the students?" I asked

"Yes Yoshida Shihan. I will do so." He said deeply.

"Until we meet again Ryoko Shihan." I said, as I stood to my feet and bowed. Ryoko sat and smiled.

"Yes Yoshida, until we meet again."

There was something in my heart that spoke to me, its words were humbling for it spoke to me saying that this was probably going to be the last time that I would both see and speak to Ryoko Shihan; my life mentor, my friend.

"Goodbye Ryoko" I said softly and with an informal bow shared by comrades in arms, quietly I exited his room.

It was that evening, when the gravity of the events of the day had settled fully that I took conference with Fujibayashi. It was the task given to me to speak to him to inform him of the last wishes of Sensei. It was a sad time for all of the students of the dojo and I wondered what feelings Fujibayashi had on the matter; for he wasn't a student here from the very beginning of his training. But Sensei was a kind and generous man who allowed him the opportunity to stay and learn from the great teachings that the dojo had to offer; so perhaps he did recognise this fact and was also feeling some degree of sadness for Sensei's passing. I hoped so, as I believed him to be of a high moral standard and it would anger me more than anything else if he didn't show some level of remorse.

When I saw him he was within his room, knelt on the tatami in its centre and he was in the process of cleaning his sword.

A sword, whether it be a katana, wakizashi or tachi; was a samurai's primary source of arms along with the yari and also in some cases, the archers bow. It was his battlefield weapon that he trained with rigorously on a daily basis. With it, a samurai puts his mind, body and spirit into its stunningly beautiful yet deadly blade. A samurai's sword was a spiritual symbol that is his life and it was just as natural a part of him as his own arms and legs.

As such, it was a daily task of the samurai to make sure his weapon was clean and razor sharp and everyday they tended to their sword; as they did not know and could not predict when the next time they will require its edge.

I often used the process of sword cleaning as a way to focus my mind as a means of light meditation. Especially if I had a bit of a bad day or if I was frustrating myself with the learning of a new technique.

He was already part way through the cleaning process when I joined him. A small cedar wood box with a clear polished lacquer was neatly opened by the side of him and some of the tools for cleaning where laid out neatly. Tapping along the length of the blade with an *uchiko* , a small fabricated ball on a wooden stick. Within the ball was a fine, coarse sand that jumped onto the blade with every tap of the stick. This was used to help purify the surface of the blade, taking away all the negative particles of dirt and blood that may have rested upon it. If these are not removed then they may tarnish the surface of the blade and can even lead to rust which will ultimately ruin the blade beyond use. When the blade is wiped clean, the sand cleans the surface as it is wiped off with a light abrasion that will remove any particles that have dried on hard to the surface.

"I'm sorry if I've disturbed you" I offered, knowing how this cleaning process is often a cleansing of one's soul as well as one's sword.

"Oh no, you are most welcome Shihan" replied Fujibayashi as he continued the process, undeterred by my presence in the room.

"There is something I have to have conference with you about. Something important." I said, kneeling in front of him. "I have just listened to Sensei's last wishes. Because Sensei has no blood heir, he is passing on the estate to the local Lord and is not passing on the scrolls of succession to anyone, not even the seniors. He is officially disbanding the school and its students…"

Fujibayashi stopped suddenly, looking up at me and taking the attention off his sword as this news were indeed important to his ears. Slowly, he placed the sword down upon the mat between us and looked me in the eye, displaying that he was giving me his full attention.

"…He also spoke, about my arriving back with one of the Dragon Swords; he knows of the commands and wishes of the Shogun for those who carry the swords and he has granted me permission to carry on this path as is the will of the Shogun. I come to you now, because you are also an owner of a Dragon Sword. You too are free to follow the path that the Shogun has laid before you. It is your choice whether you wish…"

"…wish to join you on our journey" he interrupted.

"Yes Fujibayashi-san"

"It would be my honour to join you. I am still, after all on my own personal quest to develop my swordsmanship to levels of legendary competency and as you are one of the surviving senior disciples of the Imamoto style, I would be most gladdened and honoured to be able to walk at your side. For I believe the road ahead is to be long." He replaced the sword in its sheath, finishing the process prematurely and bowed before me. Before raising his head, he spoke again.

"You are now my principle teacher as I have recognised from the very beginning of my training and I feel that by following you on our journey I will be given the opportunity to develop my skills further as your disciple."

This news was good to hear. Although myself and Fujibayashi rarely spoke casually with each other, I have already been quite an influence in his development and as such there was still a bond that was there and it would make sense for this to continue.

"No, Fujibayashi-san" I said, bowing back in respect for him. "It is I who shall feel honoured to have you walk by my side."

Our new path had now begun, as the sun rose to signal in the start of a new day, it signalled with us our new beginnings. We did not know what lay ahead on the road but we knew that whatever it is that was thrown at us, we would see head on and overcome with our bodies, our minds and most importantly, our swords.

We were no longer the two swordsmen from Imamoto Dojo in Kakugawa. We were now elevated in rank and status as two of the Shogun's Eight Dragons. Two of eight skilled swordsmen presented with the task of reinstalling honour, glory and pride back into the hearts of man and to ensure that peace and order reigned over the people of Japan.

Chapter 13 – The Budokan

"**Y**ou're late" said Coach sternly as I caught up with him out of breath. Late I was, we had to catch a train to reach training today and I was stupid enough to get the times wrong by around fifteen minutes. A simple mistake I thought, a schoolboy error some would call it, but even then it wasn't good to be the one who holds the entire group up. If it hadn't have been for Emily who came back to get me, I would've missed out on the opportunity and would have to wait until everyone had come back from training before doing the next thing on the trip's itinerary. We had both ran as fast as we could through the streets to reach the train station with our bags bouncing away on our backs. Luckily enough, we made it in the nick of time.

"Sorry Coach" I offered, panting the words out and with a swift slap on the back of the head I was ushered to join the rest of the group as we all stood on the platform.

The platform was packed out, mostly by our group that was quite large, but we were also joined by numerous locals who silently ignored our being there. I took a quick moment to thank how lucky our timing was as the train pulled into view and slowed itself as it came to a stop at our platform.

The Japanese train systems were marvellously efficient compared to our ones back home. The Shinkanzen bullet train is late on average by only two seconds! Amazing when you compare that to the late times of around two hours back home! Although we weren't on the bullet train today, the regular rail network was still quite precise.

On the platform were marked in neat lines where it was that we should stand as it was at these points that the doors always stopped at; this is the efficiency of the Japanese railway and we all crammed into double ranks in anticipation of the train stopping.

"Right! Everyone on!" Cried out one of the instructors as the doors opened and once we allowed the previous passengers to disembark, we scurried on quickly.

I was quick to nab me a group of four seats with a table for myself and some of my other team mates. I slumped on the soft, plush seating and sunk into the fabric.

The train kicked off into life and we were soon speeding off to our destination.

"Lazarus!" came the raised voice of the Australian Chief Instructor, Sensei John Mansell. I poked my head out into the central aisle of the carriage and saw that his face had done the same. I could feel his normally jovial eyes, hidden behind a set of sunglasses.

"Yes Sensei." I said politely.

"Buddy. Would you mind explaining why on earth you would be late for the meeting this morning and cause me so much stress?" he said lightly "I wouldn't want to leave for the Budokan without you."

I gulped. I knew that this wasn't going to be good "I'm sorry Sensei, I mistook what the time of the meeting was this morning Sensei." I said honestly, stuttering my words as I was put under an unofficial questioning.

He hummed "I see, well I think you need to make sure you double check all meetings times now in the future. I don't want this to happen again."

"Yes Sensei" I said sheepishly. He removed his head from the central aisle and I did the same. I breathed a heavy sigh at the thought of that being the end of the matter. I had gotten away with it quite lightly.

"Oh…Mr Lazarus" his voice rang out once more. My heart sunk.

"Yes Sensei?" I asked. I knew that it wouldn't have ended that easily. I was in for some form of punishment, maybe a small fine for being late? This was a practice that our squad did for actions that meant that the trip didn't go as smoothly as it should; this included situations where complaints against individuals by hotels, etc as well as severe lateness.

"Just as a reminder to double check all times, can you just do fifty push ups for me." He said wickedly.

"Of course Sensei." I replied smartly.

"Erm...Buddy...I need you to do them for me now" he said, followed by a small chuckle. I could also hear the muffled chuckling from some of the others and I could see that even my team mates couldn't force back the smiles that broadened across their faces.

"What?...Here?" I said in disbelief. He didn't give a response, he didn't need to as I glanced at Coach who gave the singular raised eyebrow look to say 'do it now Lazarus!'

"Yes Sensei." I said reluctantly and left my seat to adopt a push up position down the central aisle of the train. Heads from all the nationalities glared on at me as they revelled in the embarrassing spectacle that I had to go through. I felt myself go red as I started the exercises.

Halfway through I was distracted by a quick flash of light. I glanced up to see Emily with her camera out.

"Emily, please" I pleaded and she chuckled mischievously.

"Sorry, I couldn't resist." She said and she put her camera away. I was greeted by a couple more flashes as some of the others followed in her example. With a slight growl I continued with my punishment.

Coach piped in when I was two thirds of the way through "You're lucky Jason. Last time someone was late, Sensei Mansell got the poor sod to carry his bags...and the other chief instructors, for the entire week! I guess he's going a bit soft in his old age." The last bit Coach said softly so as not to be heard by Sensei Mansell. Although Coach was pretty high up in the food chain he was still outranked by Sensei Mansell and didn't want to fall foul to a similar embarrassing display as the one I was forced to do!

"Everyone stick to a two column convoy!" Ordered Coach, prompting us to converge quickly into regimented rank and file columns as we squeezed onto the narrow pavement that bordered the main road. Not only was the tiny pavement making our journey slightly hampered, everyone was doing their best to not knock their neighbours aside with their kit bags which came in all manner of shapes and sizes ranging from small day bags to the largest of holdalls which seemed completely unnecessary.

"Coach! How far we got left to walk?" called out a random voice, it seemed like forever since we began walking from the train station and the journey to training was beginning to resemble more of a trek.

"Not far, it's probably another five minutes or so" replied Coach. It was only another 'five minutes or so' about twenty minutes ago! His reply was met with scattered moans and groans.

"Ah! What's the matter with you lot! Harden up, it's not that far away, there's nothing better than a nice fresh evening walk" Coach chuckled under his breath as he returned his attention back to the path ahead. "Anyone would think you lot were a little soft!" he said boldly.

The Budokan, one of the major centres for the study, progression and development of martial arts in both body and spirit was truly a spectacular building to behold. The sheer scale and size of it even from the outside would rival even a castle keep or major temple complex. Built as a culmination of traditional and new it featured the traditional clay slates mixed with the flat faced walls of a modern building; it had with it a quiet brook that flowed alongside and across the front entrance with a small bridge allowing passage into the Budokan itself. It was amazing.

As well as being a centre for martial arts training and a principal venue for high classed competition, it also contained a small museum honouring parts of Japan's turbulent military history and some of the early developments of the combative arts. It was a shame that the tournament wasn't able to be held here; that would've rounded off the experience quite nicely. I guess training here would have to suffice and I was looking forward to it intently.

The entrance opened up into a vast expansive lobby and reception area that was a brilliant white, so clean that you would think it had been built only yesterday; with everything bright and shiny. On the right hand side was the museum section, a simple open planned display of cabinet exhibits. From what I could see there were a few suits of armour and swords to match. Couldn't wait to get a closer view as this was the sort of stuff that fascinated me.

Coach went over to the reception desk and spoke with the receptionist out of earshot of everyone else. He was only over there for a few moments before he returned to address our group.

"Ok everybody, we've arrived early, chill out and take in the sights. The museum bit over there is free and open to everybody. Once it's time to get ready the changing rooms are just over there, training is in the West wing in hall B. If there is any questions I'll be loitering around here in the lobby. Right...go! Enjoy! But don't be late for training! If you are then expect a slap from me!"

Our group dropped our bags down together off to one side of the lobby so as not to get in anybody's way, then we scattered to experience the Budokan. I took the opportunity to check out the museum as I wandered over to the exhibits.

Before me was armour of a multitude of colours, set in such a way as if it was being worn by someone and sat smartly upon a pedestal. Beside each set there contained a neatly presented plaque displaying dates and brief nuggets of information about each exhibit. Where it was made, who it belonged to; all very interesting stuff.

Then came the swords. Each and every one of them an individual work of sinister art that could only be likened to that of a famous painting. All the swords were displayed out of their scabbards so that the light can fully show the patterns that flow across the surface of each blade, some appeared almost like a crashing wave. These patterns are created in the firing process when the sword was first forged and such is the method of firing that each sword is unique with its own distinguishable mark.

But there was one sword in particular that really caught my eye. It was a short sword, a wakizashi, just by looking at it, it emanated a feel a pure craftsmanship. Its shortened blade was as bright and polished as the day it was first made. A bone white silk covered handle and ebony scabbard accompanied it and even this was finely made. Its surface covered with carvings of ugly looking demons which was out of character with normal swords whose scabbards were often plain and not so intricately decorated. My eyes widened as a studied it. Reading the plaque that lay next to it, it read:

'The Lightning Dragon Wakizashi, One of the Eight Dragon swords presented by Shogun Iyomitsu during the sword festival in Himeji. Carried by the legendary swordsman Fujibayashi Shigeru, personal disciple of Yoshida Kintaro.'

"Oh, what's that?" asked an inquisitive voice that interrupted my reading. Turning I saw Andrew, so engrossed was I with the sword that I was unaware that he had crept up next to me.

"Oh!" I said, startled, "It's just a sword." I palmed off.

"The carvings are cool. Reckon it's still sharp?"

"Yeah, well it looks it!" I joked, returning my attention back to the sword that just kept my attention mesmerised.

"Hey, I'm gonna go get ready, it's early but I fancy a bit of a warm up before training starts. You coming?" Andrew asked, touching my shoulder.

"Yeah, yeah, I'll be there now" It was hard, almost painful in fact to tear me away from the sight of the sword but I managed to release myself from its hypnotic grasp and went with Andrew to grab my bag.

The Budokan had two main wings, the East and the West. Each Wing had in it a self contained changing facility and three halls that were sectioned off with a removable floor-to-ceiling partition that could be removed to create one singular gigantic sized hall. This was the normal practice for large scale competitions and other events where the requirement of an expansive floor space was a necessity. Our training session today was made up with the competitors and other representatives of three of the main groups that had travelled for the competition. The Germans, Australians and of course us Brits.

The other nations were being treated to other attractions elsewhere in Japan and will have their training sessions some time later on in the tour. This was only because there are just so many people that are linked with the tournament that Japan's national transport systems would not be able to cope with transporting both the local population and all of our nations. It would just end up a logistical nightmare!

Hall B opened out into a long, corridor like feel with a wooden floor that was sanded down into a smooth surface with a sprung feeling as you walked over it. At one end was a sea of lime green seating set in cascading rows that towered over the floor. The other end had a series of sliding panel doors that hid specialist equipment and the one door had been slid open to reveal a large taiko drum, similar to the one we saw at the temple festival the first night we arrived in Japan.

It was now a bustle of activity as the training area slowly began to fill up. White suited karate-ka were everywhere, disarranged and scurrying like ants as they began prepping themselves for training with Sensei. Some were up in the stands of seating, setting down bags and shoes so they are tidy, out of the way. Most however were already upon the dojo floor; swinging arms and stretching legs to begin the process of warming up. Some were working through their individual kata.

Kata is the prearranged sequence of movements that are found in almost every traditional martial art. Originally created for the masters of old as a tool to teach their students the combative techniques and strategies of that particular system or the secret techniques developed by the Masters themselves. Nowadays, most practicing karate-ka only see these kata as a display piece for competition purposes and in some schools that focus purely on the development of competition the entire concept of the combative meaning that is entwined deep in its creation are totally forgotten for preference of competition performance.

Luckily, our style keeps in mind the old ways, the study and in depth look of the application of kata being an intricate part of the training regime and the grading syllabus.

Across the hall I spied Bruce as he was chatting to Sarah. After beating him at the tournament for the first time ever, there was now a new found respect that was developed between us. It was a respect for each other's ability combined with just the pure basic thrill that comes from winning against an old time foe. Catching his eye, he nodded his head in acknowledgement before returning back to his own conversation.

"You better be careful of that one! Smug little git!" Andrew whispered bitterly to me as he caught me again by surprise. An annoying habit that he has acquired!

"What's that?" I asked, dropping down into a position to stretch my calves.

"Him! Bruce! Better be careful he doesn't steal your bird off you" he said suspiciously

"Nah, it's ok, Sarah's just being friendly, the tournament's over now and so we're on to the 'Goodwill' side of things" I joked, trying my best to ease Andrew's misguided worries, offering him a reassuring smile as I raised my head up from my stretching position.

"Yeah, well as long as that's all that happens!" snapped Andrew, as he relaxed slightly and joined me with his own stretching routine.

The doors opened and from the corner of my eye I spotted Sensei followed by an entourage of instructors and a couple of the Japanese students who accompanied him, including Momoko who I was now completely convinced was the true love of my life!

"Andrew" I said quietly, attracting his attention. Nodding my head over to the newly entered group I added.

"Although I like Sarah, that's the one that I would love to get from this trip!" I said confidently

"What? The Jap girl!" he exclaimed. "Nah I don't think you've got a chance there pal"

"And why not?" I asked, adamant to get a decent explanation to his lack of faith.

"Well, first off, she's Japanese. Secondly, I don't really think she speaks enough English to first understand what you're saying and to even comprehend what you're implying when you start reeling off some of your 'special lines'" chortling away, he shook his head as he altered his stretching position.

"We were speaking fine enough at the after party" I added, trying to make my case stronger.

"Yeah, I just don't think she'll go for the likes of you"

"Cheeky bugger!" I said, feelings slightly bruised, throwing a playful punch that hit him on the chest. "Just you wait and see mate"

Within minutes of Sensei's congregation of country chiefs entering the dojo, we were ordered to make lines ready to start the class. I stood to the left in the front line, hands by my sides and heels together in strict military fashion I made myself ready for training. Sensei stood on his own out in front facing the massed group of students.

"Seiza!" shouted one of the seniors. The command to make the kneeling position. As if orchestrated, everyone led with their left knee dropping to the floor followed by their right as we adopted the seiza position, sitting on our heels. The class moved in perfect synchronisation with Sensei as he led the movement.

"Mokso" came the next shout. The command to enter silent meditation. For this we cupped our hands together and placed them comfortably on our laps, close to our navel. Our eyes closing we used the next few moments to clear our heads of all outside distractions so full focus can be made towards the lesson and the content of that lesson. Whenever I enter this state, all that can be heard is the rhythmic beating of my heart that almost echoes inside my head. Its beat, like a metronome, allowed me to become one with my own personal rhythm and helped in throwing out all the unnecessary thoughts that would only result in clouding my judgement and my own ability to absorb the knowledge that I was about to receive.

"Yamae" this was our command to cease the meditation and now fully centred we became ready to train.

"Kaicho-ni-rei!" a bow to Sensei, the congregation placed hands upon the floor and lowered all heads until the forehead almost touched the ground. The term 'kaicho' simply refers to the 'Head of House' and is a respectable term given to the chief instructor of the association worldwide.

"OSU!" was our response. Acknowledging both Sensei and those who have come today to train. Sensei returned to his feet.

"Karitz" Again in unison, all students returned to standing and with another bow we began the lesson.

Sensei had started off, with the help of the translator, to explain the origins of a kata known as Neiseshi. An old and very traditional Karate kata and one that I have been fortunate enough to have some prior knowledge when it came to the actual sequence of the techniques. The way in which Sensei performed the kata was slightly different to how I originally learnt it. Each change shown was both challenging and interesting as I adapted to the altered version being taught. It was not uncommon for slight changes to be made when it comes to kata; especially if you're working with more than one Japanese instructor as each will apply their own personal experience or twist to the kata. The personal interpretation or artistic licence if you will is both refreshing and frustrating.

As we learnt the movements of the kata, we also were shown the bunkai, or the combative application of each segment of the sequence. This was the part of learning any kata that I enjoyed the most. Squaring off with Andrew, we acted out the one sequence that we had been shown.

Staring each other with complete focus and concentration, we both made our fighting postures. Pausing for a moment before Andrew sprang forth, stepping forward briskly and delivering a fast punch that was aimed for my chin.

Before the punch had the opportunity to connect with my chin my feet moved, almost mimicking his movement and I intercepted the strike using the technique of the kata. Slipping the punch with my one arm where my fist stopped short of his face and delivering a point perfect uppercut style punch with the other to his stomach. From here he delivered another punch aimed at my chest. Sitting my weight back into a cat stance, I rode back the force of his punch and blocked it aside before striking hard into his chest. Finishing off the encounter with a controlled throw over my hip, he laid before me. Confrontation now over.

"Whoa! Take it easy! Watch the control there" Andrew joked, rubbing his chest vigorously where I hit him.

"The pain you got now will benefit you. It will make you strong and develop the proper responses so that you don't feel the pain again..." Listening to the strange string of words coming from my mouth, I confused even myself with where that statement actually came from.

"Ok Confucius...Now help me up" he groaned, offering me his hand which I used to pull him up briskly back onto his feet.

BANG! BANG! BANG!

Earthly thuds that seemed to be followed by what sounded like the crashing of crumbling masonry. The sudden noise turned our attention back to the door. We stood with interest for a few moments. The interruption resounding from further down the building out of our view as the sound carried itself down the corridor.

"Aaarrggghh!" panicked guttural screaming from the lobby echoed down the corridor to the hallway. What was going on here? Puzzled and worried looks of equal number filled the room and prompted one of the German junior instructors to break from his training to go and investigate the rude disturbance to our practice.

He disappeared out of sight as he cornered round into the corridor outside. Further shouting erupted before suddenly his body was sent flying through the air, several feet off the ground, passing into view as he flew past the doorway to crash down heavily further down the corridor. Confused and scared chatter emanated through the group. The sight of the German being thrown through the air made one of the female students scream with fear and shock.

What had thrown him like that? Whatever it was had such amazing strength. What on Earth is going on! The class backed away from the door, as pounding elephant like footsteps resounded down the corridor. They grew louder and louder as they got closer to the doorway. The country chief representatives had already produced a protective circle around Sensei as they ushered him as far back from the door as possible. The thuds grew louder and louder until the source of the panic came into view and it was something that I had never seen before…

Chapter 14 – Kappa

Crashing through the door, breaking the frame with their tremendous bulk so that they could squeeze in, three large creatures burst into view as they flooded haphazardly into the training hall with an inelegant shambling of their giant, thick, legs. These creatures were large, twice the size of a man with sinuous arms that ended in large hands. Each finger sported a pointed claw that was cruel looking. A couple on the one creature were dripping with sticky crimson blood, probably from the poor soul who provided the guttural scream that we had heard from the lobby. The bodies of these unknown beasts were a sickly moss green, parts of their skin were covered in weeds and other watery plant life. Their pot bellies dripped with water and other slimy ichors indicating that they had freshly come from a watery source.

With their strange colourings and shape came their equally hideous faces. Each creature had a long, thin face, with wide, bulbous jade green eyes and a mouth filled with flat capped teeth roughly spaced in their mouths. But the strangest part of them were the bowl like cavity that was on the top of their heads. Within this bowl sloshed and waved a viscous, silvery substance. What were these things?

"Yaaaa!" with a martial scream, one of the students raced towards the lead creature without fear but his advance was swiftly swatted aside, his body lifted effortlessly into the air only to be stopped by the hard impact with the wall. Now rendered unconscious, perhaps dead, he lay like a thrown rag doll upon the floor. A monstrous strength came the creatures abnormal size it seems.

Peering around, I tried to look for another way out but there was none. The only way in and out was through the main door, the space now occupied by the beasts. The lead two charged towards us, ploughing through the masses like a ship cutting through the waves of the sea. Although they shambled as they moved, they were able to produce a speed that was powered by the weight and mass of the creature.

"The sword! Get the sword!" came a strange voice. One that I had not heard before that seemed to just echo inside my head. I looked around to see who had shouted it, but all I was met with were the wide-eyed panic stricken faces of those around me. Whoever it was, it was as if it was commanding me and my subconscious agreed with what it was saying and from that my body reacted.

Taking a deep breath in to calm my nerves, I pushed through the crowds towards the exit, jutting them aside with meaningful pushes. People were going about in all directions, scared and confused, unable to decide where they needed to go to reach somewhere that was considered safe, but I knew. My focus was set upon the door that was blocked by the bulk of one of the creatures. Barging and weaving through the panicked floor that was filled with the frightened flock that were my fellow karateka I made my way closer.

Ducking my head, dodging the lead creature as his arms swung wildly as it pressed forwards. Sending body after body up into the air in its wake as if he were ploughing his way through a field, harvesting grown crops. I didn't let it bother me as I pressed on towards the door. The creature on guard spied me and my attention that was focused upon the exit and stood alert, ready to receive me. Breaking from the main pack of people, my pace moved into an uninterrupted sprint as I was allowed more freedom of movement. The creature moved out to meet me and as it rose its grisly claws ready to strike me I dived forward, feet first, sliding upon the smooth wooden floor as I cleared past the creature through its legs. His swipe missing me completely and clumsily as it was left in disbelief that I had vanished out of his line of sight.

Returning to my feet in a fluid motion, sprinting through the corridors back to the lobby and over to the museum section. Several bodies lay scattered in the main lobby, blood splashed against walls and seating or providing gruesome trails on the ground as bodies had been dragged disrespectfully.

The lobby was deathly quiet, save from the occasional groan from a seemingly lifeless body that had not quite given up the will to live. The screams of those still under attack from the monstrous beasts returned my attention to my task at hand. I had to be careful, as I didn't know if there were any more of these creatures lurking about.

There it was, the white sheath and sword, now all I needed was to get at it. Turning my head to shield my eyes I slammed my elbow into the glass. It cracked and gave way easily under the pressure; the glassy ring of the pieces ringing out as they hit the floor. It broke so easily, I was glad that it wasn't toughened or safety glass as I think I would've been worse off.

Snatching the sword I sharply turned and ran back to the dojo. Passing through the lucky survivors, both scratch free and those that were bloodied alike, who had managed to make their way out from the slaughter. I moved swiftly and with purpose until Hall B had returned into view.

As I burst back into the hallowed training grounds, in those brief moments that I was away from the dojo floor, it had changed completely. Now before me was a disgusting and disturbing view of a bloodbath, similar to that of the lobby.

All three creatures had joined together in creating the carnage that had unfolded and they were at present, wading through the students with ease as they made way with bloody swathes. Instantly, I spied that one of the foul monstrosities had cornered Momoko who had somehow been separated from the rest of the group like a stray sheep from its flock. The beast that had cornered her growled deeply, narrowing his eyes as if ready to pounce on her and turn her into his next meal. Her face was filled with pure pale terror and she was frozen on the spot. I needed to act quickly. The other two creatures

215

continued to harass the others with clumsy slashes and swipes of their monstrously thick, muscular arms.

Running through the crowds, bumping and pushing the confused and frightened students that were frantically searching for an escape; the sword I carried held behind me poised to strike. Charging behind the one beast I swung the razor sharp blade that partially sliced cleanly through its knee. Green coloured blood splashed from the open wound as the beast roared loudly with pain, attracting the attentions of the other two who were previously focused on the rest of my group. The creature fell onto his one knee as it was now unable to hold the tremendous weight offered by its bulk, compromised by my deep cut. In a fluid motion, I swung the sword again in a back handed motion at the second beast, cleanly slicing open its stomach before bringing the sword back down to cut down diagonally in front of it.

The third creature, now aware of the pain that was being inflicting upon its companions, turned to face me and roared as if challenging me with sheer want and desire for my blood. Its arms fanned out low and wide as if goading me to close the distance and fight with him. He spread his gargantuan fingers apart, flexing the webbed claws open. More than happy to oblige him I jumped up at him and cut open the beasts throat before it had chance to swipe at me.

Its guttering death cry was queasy to say the least, I've never heard anything that came close to the noise it made. But as I stood triumphant over the supposed to be dying beast, I was stunned to observe the cut that I had just made miraculously heal itself. It sealed itself up as the skin reformed itself together and kept the life force from escaping from it.

The beast's face turned from anguish to desperation for retribution and anger as he recovered from my cut that should've killed him. A quick glance confirmed that the other creatures had also recovered. Now I was surrounded.

'Damn, the sword is a fake!' said the echoing voice. Didn't know what was meant by that, though I knew it couldn't have been good, but now I was more concerned by the three monsters that were still very much alive and now closing in around me with an enclosing circle.

Further cuts and slashes were simply futile as they healed almost instantly, as I continued to cut and circle as the ring of monsters enveloped around me. It occurred to me that if I stayed as piggy in the middle it would end swiftly and not in a good way for myself. The need to break free became apparent.

Without thinking, I turned my body into a makeshift battering ram and barged head on into one of them to try and make an opening for me to escape. Jumping up and into its bulk, sending my full weight through him. We toppled over together and collapsed in a heap on the floor, the momentum of us crashing allowed me to roll away gracefully and smoothly so that the creature could not grab and ensnare me. But this surprisingly, was not a priority on its mind.

Looking back, the silvery liquid that occupied the bowl like feature on its head spilt out onto the floor. Now the beast was thrashing, snarling wildly and frantically as if it were a fish out of water. It gasped and gagged as though struggling for air. The once full bowl was now steaming with a deep hiss and the smell of burning flesh filled the immediate area.

The other two looked on terrified, it seems that their weakness had been discovered and they turned and were quick to bolt towards the door. Their frightened shambling resulted in a few slips and falls crashing through the doorway; serenaded with a chorus of frightened screams from those who thought they had escaped or had returned to investigate the scenes of devastation to find themselves taken unawares by the escaping beasts.

Attention returned to the thrashing beast on the ground; it was changing, its body seemed to dry up as if it was wet clay left in the baking sun, shrivelling up until it became a mere dried up husk. Deep cracks appeared on its flesh like those of drought covered mud flats and had changed its colour to a light stone like grey.

My surroundings started to fade out to blackness. Without warning my head started spinning and with it my body began to sway uncontrollably. As I staggered on my feet, trying to keep my balance I had trouble keeping my eyes open and bright specks appeared all over my vision. It was as if I had been struck hard on the right spot by a thunderous fist. Though I knew that I hadn't been hit.

"Jason!" reverberated an unknown voice, bouncing around uncontrollably in my head, then the world went dark as I hit the deck.

When I eventually came to, my eyes opened to the pleasing sight of Momoko who was stood over me. Her dark eyes looked heavenly as she smiled when she realised I was finally coming around. She spoke in Japanese and soon she was joined by a Japanese man dressed in a brightly coloured orange and red suit. A paramedic. He took hold of my arm of which I was quick to shrug away his attentions.

"Please, I'm fine" softly I spoke, groaning myself upright, yet he remained over me. He readied himself to do some tests, fiddling around inside a small bag that he had at his side.

"I said I'm fine!" my tone raised sharply, I needed some space and I waved my one arm around wildly, signalling him to go and attend to those who needed his help for I did not require it. Thankfully, the message was understood clearly as he rose up and wandered off to help some other poor soul that was suffering. Momoko began to rise also as if to leave, she must've thought I was referring to her as well.

"Momoko, please, stay with me" I said, stopping her in her tracks, quickly latching onto her arm to steady her and keep her from going.

She knelt herself back down on the floor next to me. "How are you feeling?" she asked taking hold of my arm and joining me at my side.

"I'm ok, a bit dizzy" I replied, raising my one hand to my head that was pounding away as if I were suffering from a migraine. "What happened?" I asked groggily.

"You should let a doctor look at you" she spoke with such gentle tones, her voice was soothing, practically angelic; in my ideal world, it was the only treatment that I required.

"Please I'll be fine, just stay with me for a moment, I'll be fine." I was never a fan of doctors no matter what nationality they were. I don't know why that is, the thought of requiring a doctor made me feel uneasy. Maybe it was my own insecurities that I associated doctors with the feeling of being weak. Perhaps it was a case that I associated doctors with very bad things or the giving of bad news. A similar feeling that I get with visits to the dentists.

"You were very brave. Where did you learn how to use Japanese sword like that? You are very skilful." She said, her question was somewhat puzzling to me, maybe because I was not able to give a straight answer at the moment that even I managed to believe in.

"Erm…must've picked up a few things here and there…watch quite a few samurai films I guess." I struggled with the answer, since arriving in this country there were so many things that were completely unexplainable.

To try and think on what happened would only result in my headache worsening and it was clear that I was in no clear state of mind to even begin to fathom or comprehend anything. Though I did have to ask, "What were those things?"

"I…I don't know" was her reply, her face dropping in disbelief though there was a feeling that she wasn't telling me everything. "Thank you…for saving me."

Chapter 15 – Meeting Between Warriors

F rom the carnage of the Budokan, we were constantly hounded by the medics and soon the police and some reporters came to question us on what had occurred. The once peaceful grounds were now a scene of utter madness as the aftermath unfolded. Officials were dotted all over the place, the paramedics were carting off the final few bodies of the dead and injured to be either treated or put to a state of rest.

Luckily, I was ushered away by some of the guys, not fully recovered from events either mentally or physically. I was in no way fit and in any correct state of mind to undergo rigorous questioning from the police or anyone for that matter. Soon I was whisked away from the nightmare, hoping that it was all just a horrible dream like before and that I was going to simply wake up at any given moment. To find myself snug comfortably in bed, to stare at the lovely ceiling of the hotel room and laughing at myself for believing in this silly little dream.

But it was no dream, no horrible nightmarish concoction my head thought up during a deep sleep that could be cast aside by just opening my eyes and finding myself safe in the comfort of the hotel room or better still my own bed back home!

It was real, those creatures I battled with were real, everyone who lost their lives were real. Throbbing, the headache continued as it was all being replayed in my mind. What was that voice that resounded in my head? How was it that I was able to wield a sword in such a trained and dangerous manner? I had never touched a sword before in my life, my karate career concentrated on fighting without swords and whatnot but it felt so comfortable and dare I say it, natural; as if I had trained with it for years.

Could it have been that I have watched too many movies? No! Of course not! Even through there were countless hours spent on watching old and new Japanese films there was no possible, conceivable way of training my body to wield it so fluidly just by watching an actor do it. Even down to the comforting feeling that I felt when I held it the first time; surely there should've been some degree of unnatural thought in regards to holding it. It felt so right, as if it were second nature.

Was it that I was actually going mad? So many questions! I could just easily scream!

Andrew accompanied me back to our hotel room and straight away I rushed into the bathroom, giving no second thought to doing anything else. Running the cold tap, splashing my face repeatedly in an attempt to either freshen up or wake up. My body was bombarding me with such a uncontrollable mix of feelings that I wasn't sure what I was meant to feel; first I was dizzy, then I would feel like I was separated from reality in a haze and then I would be hit by nausea and desperately wanted to throw up.

All I wanted to happen was for me to get out of this nightmare, almost certain that any moment now that I would simply wake up and laugh at the idiotic dream that I was positive I was living. Andrew placed a comforting hand on my shoulder.

"You gonna be ok?" he asked sympathetically. "You've had one hell of an afternoon. Well, we all have. But you more than some I guess." he continued.

"Why is everyone asking me that? I'll be fine!" I snapped, growling angrily at everyone's overly cautious sympathy and sickening concern that was becoming a niggling nuisance, especially when it was hard for me to even understand what was happening to me properly. Andrew jumped back slightly at my sudden outburst, raising his hand from my shoulder as if he had wounded me unexpectedly or had accidently touched something hot. Suddenly I realised that perhaps I was biting untoward at the wrong people, especially as all he was trying to do was to help make me feel better.

"Sorry mate" I offered apologetically for the sudden outburst. "I didn't mean to snap at you, it's just that I'm just not sure how I'm feeling right now. There's just so much happening that's just so difficult to comprehend. Even since I landed in this god forsaken country that things have gotten strange and unexplainable."

"It's ok mate, I understand." He said softly

"It's like…take the restaurant for example…apparently I was reading and speaking Japanese! Now what is that about? I only know a couple of phrases at best to speak let alone try understanding all these complex symbols! It's not even a bloody alphabet!" I paced past him out of the bathroom and sat on the edge of my bed. He joined me by sitting on his, hunched over ready to receive what I was about to say next and there was plenty on my mind that I needed to say. Plenty that I prayed Andrew could suddenly give me a clear and infallible explanation for that I could just say 'Yes! That's it' and write it off my mind.

"And the Budokan! What exactly were those…*things* that attacked us? And tell me how on earth I knew how to swing a sword like I did! Unless I'm mistaken, we didn't exactly do anything like that in training!"

"I don't know mate. Honestly I don't. Those things were not like anything I've ever seen, let alone heard of! All I can remember is looking back, seeing you push through everyone and charge towards the door. I thought for a moment one of them was going to get you but the way you moved was just incredible. Never seen you dodge anything like the way you did. Then when you came back with that sword…" Andrew started to get excited as he recalled the exciting spectacle what he had seen, his arms became animated as he re-enacted everything. "…You…just…kicked ass man! Cutting and slashing, it looked out of this world! You couldn't choreograph that in a film or something! It was just so…real! " I gave him a look of complete unimpressed interest as I didn't care for his passionate iteration of the events. Where he saw it as something impressive, I thought that it was not the correct way to look at it when people died together and that I would probably be emotionally scarred for life by it. This soon made him dull his animation and enthusiasm down to an acceptable level.

"Sorry" he said sheepishly, realising his mistake "Got a tiny bit carried away there."

"Tell me…" I asked seriously "What do you make of what's happening with me? If there's anything I need now is something that is rational to explain to me…well, everything!"

Andrew asked, "Well, have you never had a sword lesson in your life?"

"Never" I replied honestly.

"What I know is…is that you're a martial artist. Man, you've been doing karate a fair bit longer than even I have! Just adding a sword in should be easy enough for someone like you. Especially as they say that a sword is just an *extension* of the body, or some crap like that." He paused and looked me in the eye with that compassionate twinkle that I has. "And all this means is that when you were under major pressure…which you were mind, you're brave enough to stand up and face it. As you know, when you're under stress, you can do many different things, sometimes even the impossible! You just rose up to it mate. I know I wouldn't have done! I was too busy trying to get the hell out of there, trying to save my own skin!"

That was one the best things about Andrew, he was naturally a good listener and if anything, he had the ability to make you just open up and just talk, offering a worthwhile conclusion that always helped. He was one of those people who always had the right answers to give no matter what the situation was. I always thought that everyone has a friend who they could rely on in that manner. If they didn't, then it was a part of life that they missed out on.

He smiled, "If there was anything good that is to come out of this; at least you made an impression on that Jap bird you like. If ever there was an old school romantic way of getting a girl to fall for you it is saving them from total peril; like a knight in shining armour! Just don't tell Sarah! You know how jealous she can get sometimes and she believes you've got your camp firmly set in hers." It did sound good to think this, like Andrew said, at least *some* good came out of it.

"Can I tell you something?" I asked, quietly. Without even waiting for Andrew to respond I carried on.

"It's not just today and the thing with the restaurant. There have been other...strange things that have been going on."

"Oh?" Andrew said inquisitively, raising an eyebrow at the possibility of being privy to new information. "You do know you are meant to grow hair there." He joked, but before he could continue to try and lighten the mood he was stopped by the disproving look that I sent his way. "Go on" he added, now more seriously.

"Well, when we were at the temple the other night, where that festival was going on. That was when the first of the strangeness was going on. While we were all exploring the different sights, I came across this little garden that was tucked away in the corner. As I got close to it, it felt really weird. As if this spot meant something to me, as if I have seen it before or even been there before…"

"Like déjà vu you mean?" Andrew interrupted.

"Yeah! Exactly like that! It turned out that what I was standing in front of was a grave, dedicated to some samurai who's name I cant remember. Yoshi…Yanshi…something along those likes. Anyways, while I was there, that weird Jap who we thought was getting angry at us. Do you remember?"

"Yep, I know who you mean, well, I think I do anyways." He replied

"Well, he came over and spoke to me. He starting saying stuff, something about demons, I casually brushed it off but I guess it must've affected me somehow 'cos that night I had the weirdest dream."

"I see, well déjà vu is a common phenomenon I guess, but I wouldn't spend too much time on that. It's probably just nothing, you might've seen the picture in some article or magazine somewhere and it triggered something. That's all that is, just coincidence." He paused as he shifted back onto his bed in a more blasé pose. "About that weird Jap, well, he was kinda freaky to be fair. It was probably just coincidence with what he was saying to you and what happened today. Don't let him freak you out man, you're not going to see him again anyways except by some strange, bizarre twist of fate." Although his words made sense, I did have to ask for his opinion on the creatures we saw.

"What about those monsters? Do you think the freaky Jap was right? What if they were demons?" Question after question rolled off my tongue as I barraged Andrew with them all.

"Mate, I couldn't say. Hey, now there's no such thing as demons; even you believe that right?"

"But if you don't know what they are, how can you rule out that they're not demons? After all, there's always the possibility right?" I asked, again trying desperately to seek closure.

"True, though its all over now Jason. Try to focus yourself elsewhere; you kicked ass today. You're a hero, everyone is gonna see that and no doubt talk about it. Let that fill you up mate, you should be feeling big and badass more than anything else. You are the *man*!"

It was harder than he says though, everything still bounced back and forth inside my head and every time I thought I was close to a definite answer there was nothing to back it up and make it confirmed. It just needed something solid to ease the questions. I also didn't fancy the thought of being the 'hero' of the trip, all I wanted was to be left alone and receive no further special attention. Hopefully, that might make the trip more normal.

"Jason, I'm going down to the store next door to get some much needed supplies. We need some snacks and stuff for here, to try and take your mind off things. Nothing like a good, old fashioned pig out on random munchies to do the trick! Do you want anything in particular?" Andrew stood up ready to make his way to the door.

"Nah, I'm easy, get whatever you think we need. I'll leave it up to you."

"You gonna be ok here on your own? I'll only be five or so minutes." He asked

"Yeah, I'll be fine."

When Andrew was satisfied that nothing bad was going to happen to me in his short absence, he left the room, sending it back into silence. Nervous and twitchy I was, pacing myself up and down the room with my head full of strange and bizarre questions with no real answers.

Suddenly, my head turned to the mirror on the wall. Startled by what I saw, I stumbled back, tripping myself clumsily over my bag and falling over; banging against the wall and the cabinet beside my bed.

The reflection in the mirror was not my own! Instead of my face and body that I would expect to be there, it had been replaced. Before me, within the confines of the mirror itself was a pleasant faced Japanese, dressed head to toe in some form of old outfit who stared at me through welcoming eyes. What on earth! Was I dreaming?

"Hello Jason" he said.

That voice; I have heard it before somewhere.

"Am I dreaming?" It was so hard during these recent days to distinguish what was reality and I rubbed my eyes hard to try and make the apparition disappear. But as I looked a second time, the Japanese man was still there.

"No Jason-san. You are not dreaming, you are very much awake. I am sorry if I had startled you." Within the mirror the apparition performed a courteous bow.

"Who?...Who are you?...Where are you?" I asked in shocked tones.

"My name, is Yoshida Kintaro and I am speaking from inside of you. Using the mirror so that you have some way of being able to see me for the first time we formally meet each other. I would prefer to greet you in person but my body is now long dead. Thank you for showing courtesy and respect at my grave. You were most kind."

"Wha...what?" I offered pitifully, then I remembered, the garden at the temple. I think that Yoshida was the name that the weird Japanese man spoke of. It was just so much to take in.

"This can't be real. How can you be *inside* me? How come I haven't noticed you until now?" my voice quickened as I got scared of what I didn't understand, my hands scrambled over my clothing as if I were frantically batting off an unwanted insect. This was just another crazy messed up occurrence that is here to make my coming to terms with all the weird questions ever more difficult.

"It is real Jason-san. I am inside of you because of an unexplainable force that affects us all named karma; and I have been brought back by the gods through the act of reincarnation, so that I can reside inside of you in order for us to perform some kind of deed together. With you being my vassal to act or myself to be your guide. Now, I had no idea what that deed could've been until your encounter with the Kappa."

"The what?" Yet another word that I didn't know, such unfamiliar words only sought to confuse further an already mind boggling situation.

"Kappa, Jason-san. They were the creatures that you fought, or rather *we* fought today at the Budokan. They are a form of demon, a particular breed that is often found near or in water. They are rarely seen but for some reason three of them decided to make themselves known to the world again. Because of what they are, it meant that I called upon you to obtain that sword so as to quickly dispatch them." Thinking back it hit me. The Budokan, it was the same voice that told me to go for the sword.

"Well it didn't work well" I interjected sarcastically.

"Most unfortunate. I believed that that sword was one of eight swords ever made that was such that it could kill demons when they are cut with it and send them back to the demon world. However, the sword that was on display was not Fujibayashi's sword and was a fake."

"Fuji...Fujibaya...shi?" struggling with the pronunciation of the name, it prompted Yoshida to provide me with an explanation.

"Excuse me, I forget that you do are yet to share the same memories that I have. Fujibayashi was once a pupil of mine. A very skilled swordsman. But that is another matter, there are more important things to discuss."

So much to take in. This was it, I was actually going crazy! It seems that I'm now channelling my madness into some imaginary vision that is showing itself to me through a mirror.

"I must imagine that all this is hard to understand so I shall do my best to explain it to you as simply as I can for we do not have long to talk. A long time ago I was once a samurai, a swordsman of the Imamoto dojo of swordsmanship. One day during my lifetime, I was awarded with a very special sword, one of eight made by the most masterful sword smiths in all of Japan from an age long shrouded in legend. Fujibayashi, my student, was also awarded one. These eight were made specifically to fight against demons and all of their kind. The existence of such monsters I once shrugged away as mere superstition like you are trying to do; however, throughout the rest of my life I met and fought with these dark creatures on more than one occasion.

You see, your world, once my world; is one of many and such is the relationship between these worlds that there are many places where they can cross over into each other. This is where the demons from one of the other words become born into our reality and live among us.

There is much talk and prophecy in the dark underbelly of the world of the possibility whereby demons of great power can pass through the otherwise weak links and become born into your world. If this were to happen, the connectional barrier that keeps out the more powerful demons between worlds would quickly collapse, weakening the barrier significantly and the cross over would be complete and the two worlds will merge into one. The thought of the carnage that would ensue is beyond reckoning and it would mean mankind's extinction."

"What has this got to do with me?" I asked. All this talk of the next apocalypse is not the news you want to hear and especially don't want to have a direct link with.

"As one of the original eight who carried the Eight Dragons my own spirit had reached a level of spiritual development beyond that of any ordinary person. This meant that my soul has been drifting in the mainstream of time and space until being reborn in you."

What on earth was he going on about? I thought, still trying to reason with the idea of apocalyptic endings. Now was he trying to make it even more difficult for me by throwing in the concepts of reincarnation of some description. It was beginning to overwhelm me.

"But why me? Surely there are more suitable people out there who you could've decided to flip their lives upside down."

"That is the mystery of karma. However, everything happens for a reason and the greater powers that be have decided that you shall become the vassal that will carry my spirit and continue the work that I started over five hundred years ago. The fact that it is now that I have been reborn in you means that everything is not as it seems. Those Kappa reappearing confirmed those suspicions." Yoshida's face was unflinching, everything that he was talking about he meant with the gravest of sincerity.

Denial however, still crept into my mind, at present he was merely some mysterious vision that has been brought about by the traumatic stress of everything; a stress induced fantasy. Yeah, that's it, he is just a figment of my imagination and as soon as this trip is over I'm going to need to make a few appointments with a professional.

"You aren't real!" I challenged, realising that I was still on the floor I rose to my feet, defiant of the psychologically induced mirage. "What's happening is that those creatures were actually some rare species that for some reason haven't been seen before. You are nothing more than just a mentally induced nightmare caused about from the trauma I've gone through."

"Oh no, Jason-san, I definitely am a part of you. After all, since when have you spoken Japanese? And when did you have the time to learn how to use a Japanese sword so skilfully? It was myself acting subconsciously through you so you could achieve these results." he cocked his head to one side, enforcing the fact.

The turning of the key in the door broke the ambient back noise, Yoshida turned to look at the door. "It seems we are not alone to further our discussion, we will speak again." With that his vision vanished from view, shimmering out so that it left me staring back at my own familiar face. The door swung open as Andrew returned, now carrying a couple of plastic shopping bags of supplies that he had bought.

"Here you go Jason!" he called cheerfully, "There's a possibility that I might've overspent a bit on junk but I'm sure we'll get through it all." Brushing past, he placed the bags down gingerly on his bed before inspecting the contents.

"Ok, well on the menu of our extensive and upper class buffet we have some crisps, chocolate, some local pot noodle like things…" looking up at me, his cheerful face switched to one of concern as he saw that I was in a state. My face stuck in an unflinching stare of surprise and disbelief.

"You alright mate? You look real pale! Like you've just seen a ghost." His voice was apparently full or concern.

"I think I have…" I slowly struggled to say. Plonking myself heavily on my bed.

"Here!" called Andrew as he threw over a small bag from inside his bag of goodies. I caught the brightly coloured package against my chest and looked at it. From the image on the front, it was a bag of crisps.

"Get some grub in ya, it'll make you feel better." Pulling out a similar package he joined me in the little feast.

"Now…tell me more about this ghost you saw"

Chapter 16 – Reuniting Old Friends

"Hello again Jason" spoke Yoshida, his voice like the harrowing of madness in my head. His story from before was almost unbelievable and I was trying to choose not to believe.

"What now?" I said quietly, trying not to catch the attention of any of the other passengers on the bus as it bumped along on the road. As a group, it was considered to be best for us to continue regardless with our tour, as planned. The events of the Budokan had been officially recorded as a tragic animal related incident and the Sensei's believed that the rest of the trip would be the best way to get our minds off what happened. For those who had died, the seniors were going through the arrangements of sending the bodies back to their homes and a couple of the country chiefs from those areas were organising flying back with the bodies to see to the grieving families that would be tragically awaiting on the other end. The events were already plastered on the news in Japan and I believe that they will also receive some coverage on the global theatre.

"I am sensing that you require further proof of my identity. More so, proof that you are not going crazy, perhaps?" Yoshida spoke quite softly.

"Yeah, that would help, but I still think I'm going crazy" I said trying to humour my mad voices. Sarah looked round at me funny.

"Did you say something?" she asked, placing her hand on my arm and moving her head forward to try and catch my eye.

"Oh erm…me…no, I said nothing important. Just going through some stuff out loud, sorry if I disturbed you." I struggled to try and make up a decent excuse. She raised an eyebrow, as if slightly worried about me.

"Well, anything you want to talk about? There's something not quite right with you today. You feeling a bit homesick perhaps? Or is what happened troubling you?" she offered.

"Yeah, maybe a little, I'll be alright I guess." I tried to reassure her the best I could with a smile, hoping she would put the subject to rest.

"Ok babe, I'm just gonna snuggle up to you if that's ok, might make you feel better. I'll chill with some music, if you wanna talk, I'm here." She continued to smooch up to my arm, the music on her headphones muffled out and was just recognisable as it sounded within the close confines of the bus seats.

Yoshida spoke again. "Jason-san, I understand that you may not be able to speak loudly, for you apparently talking to yourself might appear somewhat...strange to others." He chuckled within my head, much to my annoyance. "All you have to do is talk in your head as if reading to yourself and I will listen. It's something which you'll get used to with time. Think of it as if you are reading something quietly in your head. Let your inner voice speak."

I focused and tried, listening to my own voice as I spoke in my head. "Can you hear me?" I asked, not knowing whether it was working.

"Yes Jason-san" came the answer.

Great! Now I was talking to myself within the confines of my own skull. As if things couldn't get weirder. Perhaps I was actually going down the lines of being schizophrenic? Some studies have shown that these conditions can make themselves known after certain events of stress or life threatening incidents. If there is one thing for certain that the attack at the Budokan was very much a life threatening situation and stressful!

"Karma Jason, is a very interesting and ironic process. For you wish to require more proof on my existence and it is just helpful that the time in which I awaken myself to you in your mind, you just so happen to be on a journey whereby you are going to places that not only prove my existence but also will benefit us on our quest to come."

"Whoa! What quest? I'm not here for a quest! I'm here for a damn holiday!" I spoke passionately within my mind. "You're filling my head with this crazy talk of demons and whatnot, I don't believe in all that!" I needed to make a stand to my strange voice, the first step in trying to overcome them I guess.

"How can you say that Jason-san? You've already fought and beaten one of the denizens of the dark. You know of their existence and they know of you now. Karma has chosen you to be the vassal in which I reside. Together we must carry on the quest against the dark powers. You'll see. I have not been summoned into this world once more by the gods for nothing. There is a darkness brooding and soon we will get to the bottom of it."

"No! Enough of this! When I get back home I'm going to go and speak to someone about this. You're just a figment of my imagination, instilled by me being homesick or perhaps it's the local grub. You are just a self induced method of trying to cope with almost being killed by some unknown creature. You'll see, they have drugs and therapy for this sort of thing; to drown out the voices." I spoke with an air of certainty. Certainty that I knew what was happening and certainty that soon I can train myself to silence him. All it needed was time to condition myself against this detached element of my psyche.

"Wait and see Jason-san, you are going to the cave of meditation where the Kensai Musashi wrote his book 'Go-Rin-No-Sho', a masterpiece on the Way of the Sword. Here we will find an old friend of mine and you will begin to believe that I am not just a mirage in your mind."

"Why? We meeting some other figment of imagination that's been created in some other mad person's head?" sarcasm accompanied my inner voice as I felt compelled to fight against my insanity.

"Not exactly...no...I will leave you be until the time comes. Goodbye for now Jason-san" said Yoshida as my mind went quiet once more.

Returning to Sarah who had her head still comfortably snug into my arm, I lifted it up slowly and put it round her, the music still pounding from her headphones.

Our day trip was to the cave of meditation where many samurai and philosophers have sat upon the great stone that resides at its heart and meditated upon reaching enlightenment or developing some other technique or aspect of their lives.

With the recent tragedy at the Budokan, we needed to do something to lighten spirits or to just simply keep our minds on the right track. There was a lot of hushed talk around the subject of the Budokan, the Japanese authorities have assured us that it was simply a lost species of animal that came out of hibernation and went on a rampage. It was a very reasonable explanation, I thought and one that I would've probably come up with if asked to provide a statement about it. The problem was that I had some annoying little voice inside my head which is trying to say different.

I nudged Sarah awake and she looked up at me, she had started to fall asleep and her eyes had that innocent 'just woken up' look.

"Yes?" she asked, coming to her senses.

"Sarah…what do you think of what happened at the Budokan the other day?" I felt shy to ask her. I wasn't sure whether she was still quite sensitive about it all.

"Oh…" she said, looking down "…I think it was quite tragic, very scary! I thought I wasn't going to make it out of there alive" then she looked up at me.

"But you were very brave! The way you went at those things with that sword! Speaking of which, where did you learn to use a sword like that?" She asked

"I…don't know" I said "Think it's what I saw in a film or something like that."

"You're too modest Jason. I'm glad I'm with you though, I'm sure you'll keep me safe from any monsters that go bump in the night!"

"Yeah…what did you think they were?" I asked, eager to find out her opinion, requiring closure for my own personal thoughts on the matter.

"What? Those things that attacked us? I don't know, from what I've heard they were some kind of animal that hasn't been seen in a long time and that for some reason they went all crazy and attacked us." She said, thinking hard about what they were.

"What if they were something more? Not just some undiscovered animal." I threw the idea out there, trying to get some clarification of what was going on in my head.

"Like what?"

"I don't know, perhaps something more spiritual or otherworldly than just animals?"

"What?! Otherworldly? Like aliens!" she exclaimed.

"Well, I don't think that…" I became a bit sheepish, the way she said it made it embarrassing, I peeked around to make sure that no one else had been attracted to our conversation. If people heard what was going on then more rumours would be added to those that I was almost sure were already going around.

"Oh you do make me laugh" she chuckled. "What do you think they were?"

"Oh…erm…maybe something like a demon?" I said, doubtful as to whether or not to say it.

"You can be quite silly sometimes!" she said patronisingly, she paused and returned to her place on my chest. "Whether it be animal…alien…or demon…as long as you're here with me, I don't care what they are."

'Yeah' I thought, 'whatever they are.'

Pulling up in the makeshift car park, we were greeted by a giant sized alabaster white statue of Buddha. This was framed under a large arch of alabaster. The view was very spectacular and the sheer size of the statue was awe inspiring as it towered over the regular features of the landscape.

"Wow!" I said, already pulling out my camera and taking a quick couple of snaps. The bus came to a complete halt.

"Right everybody. Stay where you are" said Coach. Stopping all those who were already on their feet. "When we get off the bus, everyone stick together. I don't want anyone getting lost."

We soon made our way off the bus and crowded in the car park under the bright sun. Sheppard together our flock was ushered together. One of the Japanese instructors went over to a small information hut to register us in.

He came back, an armful of bright green bands dangling from it. He issued them out to the coaches of the nations that was here.

"Ozzie's over here!" cried their instructor "Brits on me!" cried Coach and soon we were segregating to our respective instructors who issued us with the armbands that clicked satisfyingly into place.

"Everyone got their bands? Right, follow me" said one of the other instructors, I couldn't see which one but soon we were converging on the information hut and squeezing through a small rudimentary turn-stile that rattled and clicked with every rotation of its silvery metal arms, bottle necking the group into a single file.

The way up to the cave consisted of a natural, small dirt path that was flanked on the one side by a lovely little tree line. More cicadas hummed and chirped within these trees. Their song becoming very irritating after a while, as we have heard them repeatedly every day so far and they weren't the quietest of insects. At this moment I would settle for a bunch of grasshoppers than these things, as the cicadas were at least four or five times the volume.

Before turning a corner, there was a mighty oak that stood strong. The guide stopped us and pointed to the tree.

"This tree, a mighty oak tree, has stood on these grounds for many hundreds of years. If you notice on its massive trunk this interesting cut." He indicated to a deep clean cut in the trunk, it was under a centimetre thick that cut through at least a third of its diameter. "This cut is believed to have been made around five hundred years ago by a great swordsman named Yoshida Kintaro..." as soon as he said the name, I went white with unholy realisation. Merely a coincidence I thought. "...it is believed that he made this cut with a special sword that he had in his possession. A sword that was presented to him by the Shogun himself."

"Well, not exactly the Shogun personally" added Yoshida, the first time he spoke since earlier on the bus.

"This swordsman came to this sacred place and upon meditation on the rock of meditation that you will see later on, he perfected a special technique and through that technique he made this cut." The cut itself was almost unnoticeable if you didn't know it was there, even still it looked quite impressive.

"But we know from sword masters of today that it is truly impossible for a sword to cut this cleanly through an oak of this age and size." The guide laughed heartily

"It is probably a hoax but we do like to think of it deep inside as the product of this legendary story."

"Ha! How blind to the realities of what can be achieved, the legend is actually true. I made that cut all those years ago and that with the years of peace so much has been lost when it comes to the possibilities of what a sword can do. My old friend that we spoke about is buried at its base, underneath where the cut is. You need to retrieve it for me."

"Shut up!" I said, a little too loud that turned annoyed heads to look in my direction.

"Jason! Shush!" giggled Sarah, who was attached to my arm. She looked around sheepishly, her face turning red with embarrassment hoping that no one was looking round to us but one or two heads did turn.

"If you follow me, we will make our way to the cave, seeing some of the other sights on the way."

The group shuffled forward, the track was quite small and it needed to be about another four or so metres wider to make it easier to accommodate the group more. I assumed that the area didn't get groups as large us ours on a regular basis. We turned the corner, following the path that was slightly shaded by the surrounding trees and provided some shelter from the sweltering heat.

On the right hand side was an embankment, slightly overgrown with grasses and the fallen leaves of trees that topped the embankment itself. On here was a variety of little statues, like miniature Buddha's. Some of these were in better condition than others, worn by the elements and time itself.

"These little statues, are representatives of those spiritual followers, priests and samurai, that have managed to reach the state of enlightenment. They are put as a reminder to those who gaze upon them that it is possible to reach this stage. They stand the test of time so that those who follow in their path will stay their course and reach it through time."

People stopped to take pictures with camera's, the clicks and whirring of the tiny machines overtook the noise of the cicadas in the trees.

Ahead of us, about two hundred metres or so was the entrance to the cave. The cave itself was not on ground level and leading up to it was a set of steps, cut away from the rock itself. A metal rail, a recent addition in the means of health and safety ran alongside. On the ground level, off to one side at the edge of the rock base was a small workman's shack, a tool shed as such, unlocked and unattended. Guess the Japanese didn't expect anyone to steal at such a sacred place. A level of trust that you couldn't really count upon back home.

"If everyone's ready, follow me and we'll make our way to the cave."

Again we shuffled in unison, walking past the eerie little Buddha's and hitting the clearing before the cave itself. The heat of the sun shone down upon us warmly, a contrast to the previously sheltered path we've been following.

"The cave itself is not large enough for all of us to fit in. It wasn't made for large armies to meditate at the same time!" joked the guide. "If you can organise yourselves into small groups. We can probably fit about fifteen at a time up there."

We quickly sorted ourselves out into groups, ready to ascend the steps. I slotted into the second group and we waited patiently at the bottom of the steps.

"What do you think is up there?" asked Sarah, looking up to the ominous entrance of the cave.

"I don't know, a big stone I think." I said, blasé in tone. I was more focused on the weird stuff going on in my head to take in or appreciate the relevance of our being here.

"Alright moody! You sure there's not something wrong?" said Sarah.

"No, there's nothing up. Honest!" I was hasty to palm off, producing an unconvincing smile.

We waited in the scorching heat for around twenty minutes, sweat forming as the air was quite humid and sticky. Some of the other groups had taken the sensible option and retreated to the shade. Then the first group emerged, descending down the steps, we got ourselves ready to swiftly take their place.

"What was it like?" Asked James, speaking to one of the Ozzie's who was descending the steps.

"A lot cooler than out here mate!" he said, smiling, concentrating on holding onto the rail so he didn't fall. "Careful with the steps, they're not the best."

Momoko was with the first group and as they came down I couldn't help but stare at her as she descended from the cave. Watching each step I was transfixed by her. She was wearing more of a casual outfit today which was nice to see. Dressed in denim shorts and baggy white t-shirt with a colourful design of splashes of vivid yellows and green with sharp angled lines of black and gold. Very contemporary. It provided another angle to her beauty as so far all I've witnessed is Momoko in formal wear which was always going to be appealing.

However, there was one thing that I did notice about her is that she appeared strange. Not different from the obvious down dressing, but the aura that she produces. So far, whenever I've had chance to see her she always looked fresh and happy. She provided warmth in me whenever she is nearby. Looking at her now, it is as though life had been stolen from her. Her previous warmth extinguished. Her hair was more rugged and not as well kept as it has been and her eyes were iced over. There was no doubt in my mind that the Budokan had taken its toll on her more than most. After all, there was a single point during it all where she was on her own with one of the lumbering monsters ready to turn her into a quick meal. I made a mental note to somehow have a chat with her at some point. To try and make things easier for her.

Sarah punched my arm "Are you looking at the Jap girl?" she asked jealously.

I looked down in shock "Erm, no I wasn't" I said, trying my best to lie through my teeth.

"Yes you were! I saw you! You couldn't take your eyes of her. What's she got that I haven't?" Sarah looked at me unimpressed.

"Nothing. I just thought she looks a little bit more disturbed by what's happened than most. Just like to know if she's alright, that's all."

Sarah frowned. "Well as long as that's all it is. You're *my* hero remember! Not some little Japanese girl's fantasy" She still sounded unimpressed, but was lightening up by a fraction. No doubt I'll feel more of the brunt of it later on if I did something else to displease her.

Momoko passed us as we prepared to make our way to the cave. I couldn't resist the temptation to look at her from the corner of my eye. My heart skipped when she made a quick glance at me, but her head was quick to drop her gaze to the ground as she saw that I was with Sarah..

"I'm warning you mister" snapped Sarah, pointing an angered finger in my direction.

"Right, group two. Come on up!" called the guide from the top of the steps and we made the slightly precarious climb up. The Ozzie was right, the steps up weren't in the best condition.

As we topped the steps, the cave opened out. It wasn't overly large, but it was quite cool. In its centre was a mammoth stone, its top flat and sloping down towards the exit of the cave. Behind it was a small shrine. Like a tiny temple for miniature people. On it was tiny offerings and a sand filled pot where remains of incense sticks, an essential element of Buddhist and Shinto practices, remained. A fresh one at the centre of the sand pot had been placed and lit, producing a small funnel of grey smoke that rose up and disappeared into the air. As well as the tiny bit of smoke it emanated a light fragrance of spices that helped overcome the general musty smell of the cave. It seems that the cave is still an essential part of people's lives even today.

We shifted ourselves around the outside of the stone in the middle. In the centre of the circle of tourists, stood the guide.

"Can everyone hear me?" he asked and with a series of nods from around the group he continued his speech. "Here before you lies the sacred rock of meditation. Upon this rock many swordsmen and philosophers alike have come in pilgrimage, in hope that the Gods will grant them with wisdom or give them well being or even luck in battle. Whenever they sat on this special stone they would focus on their particular problem and with time and deep meditation they strive to achieve their answers that they require.

Miyamoto Musashi, the most famous of all our warriors of old, who I understand you are conducting the tour of his life and famous battles; spent days, perhaps months upon this rock in constant meditation. Breaking only for food and water and one day as the sun crested this great entrance and shone upon his face did he become enlightened and wrote his most famous book. 'Go-Rin-No-Sho' which I believe many of you will understand as the 'Book of Five Rings' and is a comprehensive treatise to the Way of the Sword."

Many understanding nods and verbal noises of recognition came sporadically from the group. Especially from myself as I have a copy of the book back home which I found to be a very interesting read, even if parts of it I found difficult to understand.

"This place is still a sacred place of worship and meditation to those who will travel here. As such, it is still acceptable for people to sit upon this rock and meditate or pray. Please, sit upon this rock, one at a time. Close your eyes and concentrate on a problem at hand. Perhaps you too will achieve some form of enlightenment like the great warriors before you. Also, please feel free to take pictures." He beckoned with an outstretched hand to the rock before us.

One by one we sat upon the rock, some were taking the experience more seriously than others, closing their eyes and contemplating on their problems for brief moments. Sarah sat and tried to be serious, but ended up she couldn't resist the urge to giggle.

Then came my moment upon the giant rocky slab. Climbing on the rock, I sat at its peak, crossed legged. Before closing my eyes I stared at the open view that was from the cave entrance. I wondered what it would be like as the sun crests it, I'm sure it would've been beautiful and for the smallest of moments I could understand how Musashi became enlightened by its vision.

Then I closed my eyes, focusing on the problem of the little voices in my head and hoped that I would become sane once more.

But what I found was definitely not what I had bargained for.

Images flooded into my mind, flashes of light and sound. It was like a slideshow of someone's life, sped up, it was incoherent at first, so much information crammed into such a small space of time. But some were repeated again and again, images of nightmarish creatures and quick flashes of swords. Images of temples and other places, some more holy than others. A castle under siege and warriors locked in single combat. Then came the images of this cave and the sun rising. Following this was the image of the great tree around the corner and a long brown case buried at its roots. A coffin maybe? It was hard to distinguish as the images flashed too fast to gain a clear definition.

I opened my eyes and gasped loudly, as if my head had surfaced from being forced underwater. What the hell was that! I thought.

Looking around, all the faces in the room looked at me with equally puzzled expressions.

"You alright mate?" said James, worried as he cocked his head to one side.

"Yeah I'm fine…" I said, as I made my way off the rock. "I just need some water." Yes, water was the way to go.

James rushed over to me with a bottle of still mineral water. Taking a few swigs of the cool liquid, it felt refreshing down my throat. Sarah too rushed over to me.

"Are you ok babe?" she asked, brushing a kind hand across my cheek.

"Yes, I'm ok, I think I'm just a little dehydrated I guess." My face was white and the experience made me slightly dizzy.

It wasn't long before the guide too joined us. "Are you ok? I've never seen anyone act like that on the meditation stone." I nodded a quick nod to signal I was fine. I didn't want any more fuss, the situation was embarrassing enough. "Most interesting."

"He's just a bit dehydrated" offered James.

"Or perhaps he hit a moment of enlightenment?" the guide spoke with an uplifted face. Was this actually possible? He turned as one of the other members of the group asked him a question about Musashi and his attention went to answering.

"Let's get you out of here." Said James, patting me on the back, guiding me to the exit. As a trio we walked to the exit, we didn't realise that the rest of the group followed suit and soon as a group we were back at the base of the cave. I was quickly rushed into some shade by James and Sarah who sat me down on the soft grass.

The remaining groups went about their tours of the cave. Our group sat upon the shaded grass out of the harsh sun. It seemed that it had grown in its potency as the day grew on and this I used to try and corroborate my episode up in the cave. I rewound the images that bombarded me when I was up in the cave, picking out the ones that stuck true. It was as through I was looking through the eyes of somebody else and the actions that were being shown were like my own actions yet were not. It's a hard sensation to experience, let alone explain. It was like, the classic experience of your life flashing before your eyes when you are near death. The only difference was it wasn't *my* life that was flashing!

James allowed me to keep hold of the water he gave me up in the cave. It was the common belief that I was in need to get plenty of fluids in, that perhaps my episode was nothing else but a dose of dehydration or perhaps heat stroke. But with the images through my head, even I, who doubted the whole thing before, was starting to believe that this was no simple thing as a strange voice in my head.

Perhaps it was as if I was being instructed by some higher power; like a holy missionary maybe, being given the way to a spiritual quest. Like what Yoshida was implying. Normally I would look upon these sort of people who actively announce these 'experiences' as religious fanatical fruitcakes. But when you're the one that is being shown visions then the scepticism that one usually feels does tend to become clouded with an element of doubt.

There was only one way to prove it, the end vision, the one of the long brown box buried at the base of the tree. If the box was there, then that would confirm it and show me that these visions and voices are more than just mad ramblings or lucky images running through my head.

Although, there was still a part of me that thought strongly that perhaps this was all just strange and coincidental happenings; desperately holding on to what could be considered as rational reasoning. That I was really going mad.

But how was I going to get the box? After all, if I just went over to the tree now and dug it up, then it would be very strange to everyone the fact that I suddenly started digging a the base of a tree; especially if I was to find something! I needed to get it when no one was looking. But when?

Maybe it was best to not bother getting it? Then I could just put this all down to stupid twists of the mind. If I didn't search for it, then there was no hard prove that my head is currently occupied by a 16th Century dead legendary samurai. It's sure to help ease the therapy that I was sure to receive once I get back home go a lot more smoother.

"No! You must get the box!" cried Yoshida in my head and I placed my head in my hands, stroking my hands through my hair as if trying to clear a groggy head. This cannot be happening.

We waited and waited, breaking into small worthless conversations as we became bored of sitting around aimlessly, the episode in the cave almost forgotten. It was only because we had so many people in our group. Eventually, after what felt like forever, the final group emerged from the cave and returned to join us.

"If everyone would like to make their way back to the entrance, you have time to visit the gift shop before you are scheduled to get back onto the bus. Please follow me" said the guide as he mowed his way through us all.

As the masses made their way like sheep behind the Sheppard, I thought now was my chance. But I needed an excuse to break away from the group. Especially as I had Sarah holding onto my hand.

"Hey Sarah, I'm just going to go to the loo, all that bloody water I drank, going right through me. I'm sure I saw a portaloo or something back by the cave." We were at the back of the pack anyways, so I wouldn't have come to many people's attention by slipping off. "I wont be long hun, I'll catch up with you at the gift shop."

"Ok babe, see you in a bit" she said, giving me a quick kiss before departing with the group. I ran over to the unattended shed as the group turned the corner out of sight. The dirty, rustic blue shed was indeed unlocked, the door creaking open easily upon rust coloured hinges. Inside was a treasure trove of tools and tool boxes. The deeper corners and recesses that have been untouched were covered in silvery, delicate cobwebs.

Eyes scanned frantically, until I saw what I needed. A small, green handled spade that was almost hidden behind rake and leaf blower. With a restricted scramble I climbed over the obstacles that lay before me; grabbing the spade I pulled it free from the rest of the tools.

Triumphant with my new found tool I ran back to the great oak. Directly underneath the supposed impossible cut through the trunk I found a spot between a couple of its strong roots. This was the spot that was shown to me in my vision on the rock.

Sending the spade into the ground it sunk easily into the soft top soil. I had to move fast, if I was here too long, someone would come looking for me and it would be extremely hard to provide an explainable reason for my actions. I already knew of the whispered rumours regarding me and to be found doing something like this would not help quench them. Quickly removing the soil I threw it to one side. I was wondering to myself how deep I would have to go, until…Clunk. I hit something hard.

A pirate with lost treasure I dropped to the small hole, brushing the stray dirt aside, I had indeed hit something hard. From the shape it was a box of some description and I pulled it out of the ground sending dirt and soil aside. My vision was right, it was a box, long and thin it must've been about around a metre or so in length. It was wrapped in a tough burlap, to prevent it from getting soiled I guess.

"Quickly Jason, open the sack, I need to see the contents of the box." Yoshida spoke with urgency and I was quick to respond. Pulling the box out of its protective bag. It appeared rather plain, it's surface held little in the way of markings or other decorative fashioning. The lid held shut by a pair of brass hinges and a small brass fastening.

"Now Jason, open the box" commanded Yoshida.

Flicking open the small catch as delicately as I could I slowly pushed open the lid, unsure what I was going to find inside. Yoshida had mentioned earlier about 'an old friend' I just hoped there was no bones or other remains inside.

The lid opened, slightly stiff were the hinges that were obviously of some age, but it opened none the less. Inside the box, the lid had a deep regal blue felt lining, the main contents being a bright purple silk cloth that was wrapped around something; an object that was almost as long as the box. Carefully pulling the cloth back, it revealed something truly amazing. It was a sword. Yoshida released a sigh of relief.

"This Jason-san, is the Emperor Dragon Katana. One of the finest and most beautifully deadly swords that have ever been created. This is my old sword, my old friend. You see, a sword is the samurai's soul. It was our main weapon of choice and we trained long and hard with them daily, we cleaned and maintained our own swords, it became a part of us. If a samurai were to misplace their sword, it was often a shame that was unbearable for them and many who did have the misfortune, often committed seppuku. I buried this sword long ago, near the end of my life, for this sword is very powerful and in the wrong hands, it would become a weapon used to bring devastation about the world of man.

You Jason, are the first person to witness it with your eyes for other five hundred years. Congratulations."

I peered in awe at it, it looked perfect, it was as beautiful as Yoshida made it out to be as if it was just freshly forged and finished only yesterday. It truly was a magnificent piece and it released a heavy burden from me for it informed me that I wasn't going mad.

"Now quickly Jason, we need to get back to the group before we are discovered here."

With that I ran, the long clumsy box held at my chest.

Returning to the car park, the buses were already full, everyone staring at me through the windows, multiple faces that were full of annoyance that I was the one that was holding them up. Coach stood at the door to the bus, his face like thunder, frustrated that one of his team was the cause for the delay. He screwed his face with sheer annoyance.

"Jason! Hurry up! I know you kicked ass the other day, but if you don't shift yourself, I'M going to kick your ass! Now get on the bus" he shouted as I approached the bus. "What on earth is that!" he said, spying the long box that was in my hands. He stared intently at it, studying the contours and the form of the long container.

"Erm…this is just something from the gift shop, for the old man. That's why I was late, sorry Coach" I pleaded, hoping that he'll go easy on me and I prayed that he didn't wish to look inside!

"Right…how on Earth are you going to get that back on the plane? Ach, just get on the bus, we'll talk about this later. Now move!" I passed him, keeping my head sheepishly low, trying to be as humble as possible to avoid the wrath of Coach. Walking down the aisle of the bus, I was flanked by both sides of equally unimpressed stares. Quickly I moved through to my seat. Walking down the gauntlet of the aisle being assailed by vicious eyes. Though, I did manage to see Momoko, who was the only one of the busload of people that was still smiling.

Taking my place next to Sarah, who had occupied the window seat, which was normally my favourite position in any vehicle but I couldn't complain as I was late after all and kept everyone from going. She smiled at me. "Hey, what took you so long? I didn't see you in the gift shop."

"Oh, I *really* needed the loo!" I said, a little shy. She smiled, I think that she bought it.

"What's that you got there?" she asked, pointing to the box that I tried to position in a comfortable position between my legs but it was awkward to move.

"Just a little souvenir for my dad." I said, she continued to look at the box.

"Cool" she said, "That must've cost a bit! I just got these little banners" she added as she pulled some small hand banners from a plastic bag that rustled at her feet.

"What's that!" came an excited voice, a hand shot from out of view and touched the cedar box in my possession. Without even thinking, with one free hand I grabbed the wrist, a sharp twist locked the unseen arm and slammed the owner head first into the seat in front of them. Something told me that it was Yoshida who provided the overprotective reaction.

My head whipped round sharp to see James' face pressed hard into the seat. The one side of his face squished uncomfortably.

"You can let me go now." He said slightly muffled and I was quick to release the tension. He returned promptly to his upright position. "What the hell is wrong with you man!" he exclaimed painfully.

"Sorry, good reactions." I joked, at least I tried to chuckle along nervously. James didn't look too amused however and I don't thin that he managed to see the funny side.

"Don't worry about it" he spat as he turned back round and focused on something else.

"You are a little tense." Spoke Sarah, somewhat shocked. "Perhaps tonight, you can come round to my room and I'll work out that stress for you. You have been through a lot this trip. Maybe a little massage would loosen up the kinks." She spoke slyly and seductive as she ran her fingers up my back, sending pleasurable shivers down my spine and gently stroked and rubbed my shoulders. It felt nice, very soothing and although she has ulterior motives behind me coming to her room tonight, I'm sure that it definitely would make me relax.

Chapter 17 – Momoko

We had left the horror of the Budokan behind us. Our tour of Japan was taking us all over the place but our main 'base camp' from which all the other trips will stem from this point on is from a city called Himeji.

Not as compact and cosmopolitan as Kobe or Tokyo, it did however provide a relatively balanced mix of old and new Japan. It was more refreshing as so far a lot of what I saw was new built up Japan that had been heavily influenced and Westernised.

At the centre of the city was the castle, which had stood the test of both time and many different periods of war. It was an impressive figurehead for the city and loomed over it as if it were a giant guardian watching over its people.

As part of our trip we had visited this mighty monument of old Japan, walked the beautiful grounds and climbed up the vast tower keep at its centre. The view from this tower was phenomenal, where the eye could see for miles around.

"Excuse me?" said Andrew, trying to attract the attention of the man behind the reception desk. "Can you tell me where we can find a karaoke bar?"

The receptionist look puzzled. "Karaoke bar?" he repeated, slowly to try and make the receptionist understand. After several moments and poorer attempts to translate, the receptionist smiled excitedly.

"Ah! Karaoke-desu!" he said. And wrote down on a small piece of note paper some directions for the nearest karaoke bar.

"Ok guys here we go!" he says, waving the makeshift map in the air.

"Let's get going then!" said Coach who stood at the back of the group. We were going to have a night of winding down and sheer relax by going to one of the better things to come from Japan, a night of singing out of tune and somehow having fun doing it. The wonderful act of Karaoke!

Our group that was heading out consisted of myself, Sarah, Emily, James, Coach and one or two of the Ozzie's who were becoming increasingly bored of official meals and wanted a bit of a laugh. They accompanied us as we held the reputation of having the biggest *fun factor* of all the other nations. Coach was great at being one of the leaders of the playing up crew and out of the regulated structure of the karate dojo he considered himself as one of us and we did the same.

Although it was night time, the sun had long since set and outside was dark, it was still comparatively quite warm, more pleasant and tolerable than the daytime. So warm was it that we could still wear shorts and t-shirts without feeling so much as a chill. We walked through the streets without a care, as though the Budokan nightmare never happened. There's nothing like a good karaoke session and plenty of beer to really lift the spirits!

The bar itself we saw easily from a distance. It was part of a tower block, each level being dedicated to becoming a particular shop or restaurant. At the top, a bright neon sign read 'Rap Star Karaoke Bar'. It was that easy to find that I guessed we probably would've stumbled upon it eventually if left to our own devices without the need of asking for directions beforehand. It seems that this sort of Karaoke Bar was a national chain, as I noticed one when we were in Kobe but with the busy schedule where we didn't get much opportunity to have what you could call 'down time', we didn't get chance to go there.

The ground floor lobby looked very smart and well presented, the walls and floors lined with shiny marble slabs. The ceiling was like one giant mirror overhead, broken only by the fluorescent tube lights that lit the lobby adequately with its artificial light.

On the left were two elevators with brass coloured doors. The rest of the lobby was pretty empty apart from a random couple of potted plants and some posters that were in tidy frames on the walls.

"Ok guys, in the elevators. Top floor" ordered Coach as he pressed the button to call it down to us. With a ping, it opened and we crammed inside.

"What happens if the elevator goes out of order? Like there's no stairs!" said James, pointing out an almost obvious flaw that we could see in the building design. Emily gasped with horrific realisation.

"Shut up James!" said Coach bitterly, "Let's just hope that they shut down *while* we're up there singing. That way we don't have to go back too soon!" he laughed, turning the potentially tricky situation around. He was quite passionate about karaoke, almost as much as the karate.

The doors opened up at the top floor and we piled out as one group. The karaoke bar was not quite like what I'd expected. Normally, when one thinks of karaoke bars you think nice open pub space with a karaoke machine at one end and a stage if its quite upmarket. This wasn't like that, there were no open spaces and bar seating with drunken punters that you didn't know, listening to you sing off tune. I normally found that sort of environment quite off putting and embarrassing.

Before us, past the desk with a smartly dressed worker, was a snaking corridor and along its length were many different doors that lined the way, each one were identical, dark green and numbered with bright brass numbers.

On the left was a giant display board, illuminated from behind, it displayed what appears to be the insides of each of the numbered doors. We marvelled at them, each room different to the next, of varying colours, sizes and décor styles.

"Would you like room sir?" said the man behind the desk to Coach

"Yes please, there's…seven of us." He said counting us out.

"Yes sir. You are in room eight, down the corridor" said the man behind the desk, pointing down the corridor before us.

"How much?" asked Coach.

"You pay after, its ok"

Slightly sceptical, we went into room eight, there were fears that with paying after with no clear indication on how much this *experience* was going to cost, we would be charged an extortionate amount! Oh well, we'll have to deal with that when the time comes. A small, cosy room with a large semicircular couch that was pretty stylishly made to look like zebra skin. A coffee table with several thick, song catalogues and a remote that operated the machine that was in the corner sat in the middle of the room.

"Right who's up first?" asked Coach as he dimmed down the lights with a dimmer switch that was by the door.

"Me! Me!" cried Emily, rushing to the catalogues, if there's one thing we knew, it was that Emily enjoyed her singing and she wasn't too bad at it as well.

Long and hard we sang through the night. Oblivious to the time that passed we continued our songs. Coach preferred to do the rock classics and ballads of *Bon Jovi* as he was himself, a self confessed nut. I on the other hand just murdered the classics with a little bit of crooner style music; favouring a spot of Sinatra and the Rat Pack or other soft music from that genre. On some songs, particularly as the evening progressed, we would choose the song for the next person to sing which was quite entertaining with some of the weird and wonderful selections that were being made. This did bring about a notion of who your friends are and if you gave an embarrassing song, then you were expected to receive one when it was your turn!

We were kept refreshed by a simple telephone on the wall that went straight through to the reception desk. An easy phone call to the reception with our order of beers and it was quick to be delivered to us. The beer was flowing very well tonight.

The Ozzie's with us were a little shy at first, they have been brought up through a rigorous indoctrination of other enforced etiquette. But it was ok, I was sure we would have them *corrupted* by the end of the evening so they would be able to loosen up and have some fun! We considered it a challenge.

"Right. Last song." Said Coach, looking at his watch and having the shock of knowing how late it was. "Let's see…I know…how about everyone sing '*We Are the Champions*'!" he said, small gasps went out as we knew we had the Ozzies with us; thinking that this choice might not have been politically correct. But Coach just turned to them and said softly, staring them both in the eye. "Tonight…you two are honorary Brits…so you better damn well sing like it with the rest of us!" With initially shocked eyes turning to pleasant acceptance we all sung the last song. We sung it loud and proud, raising the roof and bringing down the house.

With us all finally finished for the night, we paid up at the main desk and left for the short stagger back to the hotel. Both myself and James secured Sarah who was swaying all over the shop and still singing although slightly slurred and drunkenly down the street. Normally we'd be trying to shut her up, but hey, its our holiday now and people needed a well required tension release, so we allowed her to sing her heart out until we got back to the hotel that is.

Staggering up the stairs after crashing through the lobby, I was left by my so-called teammates to carry Sarah who stopped me every third or fourth step to plant me with a kiss and a quick grope with wandering hands. It took practically forever before we reached our floor. She was a few doors down from my room and I thought it best to drop her off first before heading back to my room.

"Good night baby" she said drunkenly as she kissed me once more. Slamming me against the wall as she did so. Running her hands up and down me she became quite frisky, something I wasn't really used to, but I couldn't help but like it. Eventually she stopped. "See you tomorrow handsome." As she fumbled with the key in the lock, before almost falling face first into the room.

I turned and made my way to my room, my head looking down at my feet in happy recollection. Then someone up ahead caught my eye as I picked out approaching feet ahead and made me look up. The person who joined me in the corridor was female and as I squinted in the dim light of the low wattage bulbs that lit the corridor, its familiar outline revealed it as Momoko.

For her to be returning this late meant that the dinner must've really ran over time. Karate events, from what I could gather, particularly with our group, did have the sometimes annoying tendency to become dragged out or made longer than intended on a regular occurrence. Despite the military discipline that is connected and often drilled into the practitioner with the art of Karate, timekeeping with our Association was always an issue.

"Good evening Momoko-san" I said quietly so as not to wake anyone up.

"Good evening Jason-san" she replied with a soft smile. When she reached a comfortable speaking distance I saw that she was looking slightly run down. It was an observation that I've made over the last few days; it was clearly apparent at the cave. Since the end of the tournament and certainly after the Budokan. The late night that she just had to endure with the meal wouldn't have helped matters much either and she wasn't the sort of person to say that she was becoming run down. She would be best to have a night of rest.

"Are you ok?" I asked, making it a slightly obvious that I've noticed her in a less than perfect state; a look of awkwardness shot across me as I realised that this might not have been the best thing to do. There was a risk that I might've caused some level of embarrassment for Yoshimi; something that the Japanese do not take well to.

"Yes, I'm fine" she said, trying her best to cover it up. "Just tired. Not been sleeping well. Thank you for your concern."

She was quick to her door, which I noticed was next to mine. "Oh, this is your room?" I asked, realising that it's a bit of a stupid question really. "I'm just next door, number 237. If you need anything, just knock." I said chuckling nervously, as I ran a nervous hand through my hair to rest behind my head. "I often find that a glass of hot water and honey often helps me sleep if I'm having difficulty sleeping." It was a poor excuse to try and keep conversation going and I shied away a bit when I thought how lame I must've been sounding. She nodded and darted inside.

Fumbling with my key in my door, I was soon to walk into my own room. Andrew was awake, the light of the small bedside lamp on and the TV was on with the volume down low, almost to the point where it was inaudible. He was on his bed, under the covers with a pillow propping up his head. The reason he didn't join us for our enjoyable sing song was he was suffering from some form of ailment. We put it down to a simple bout of food poisoning he had picked up somewhere; probably from eating all that junk we bought back in Kobe and as a result he had his head down the toilet for most of the day. 'Praying to God on the Great White Phone' as we called it.

"How ya feeling?" I asked, sympathetically, noticing the sorry state that he was still in.

"If I was a horse, you'd have to put me down" he said, struggling to speak with groans and moans.

"Well you already look like one so you're well on your way." I joked, bounding on my bed with a huge released sigh.

"Have a good time?"

"Yeah, it was a good laugh! Emily missed you tonight." I said, offering some emotional comfort.

He sighed deeply, "I wouldn't have been much fun. Hopefully it should shift by tomorrow. I'll try and sleep it off" As he rolled over and turned off the light beside him. "Good night" he said.

I woke up once more. My body was sweating and my bed sheets were soaked with the salty fluid. Andrew still remained fast asleep, snoring loud like a pig with a cold.

Bloody nightmares! It was that same dream as before, except this time I saw more of it. After descending down the moistened stone steps from that unrecognisable temple of horrors and blood I saw more of the internals of the cave that I entered. Flashing images of faded faces, adorned in what appeared to be armoured helmets and clearing away to reveal a robed figure.

He stood in front of a stone alter and raised a massive knife of some description. When he plunged it down there was a sharp, piercing scream that echoed wildly. When that scream erupted, that was the trigger that woke me up as it rang inside my head and forced me to snap back into reality.

"Arrrghh!" came another scream, was I still dreaming? Was my mind playing tricks with me and making me hear things that weren't there? No; this one was definitely real. A women's scream, high pitched as if the owner of its ghastly noise was being hurt painfully or surprised by something truly terrifying. Again it sounded. Where was it coming from? It sounded as if it were near by if not quite immediate. I glanced outside the window but there was nothing that would connect itself to the scream. It was next door. Momoko!

Quickly I pounced off my bed, moving deliberately as if I were feline, throwing the covers off me wildly and without care. Slipping on one of the complimentary robes over my shorts I headed out my door and straight to next door, bumping clumsily into the small stool that was obstructing my way in the dark. My toe throbbed with pain and with a slight grunt of annoyance it was quickly shaken off as more pressing matters required my attention.

Rap! Rap! Rap! Came the hurried sounding of my knock upon the door. No answer. Again I knocked, but now with more urgency producing louder bangs; this time I could hear the sounds of movement coming from beyond the door so I waited for further response.

With the metallic sliding of the internal bolt the door opened slowly, only opening just a bit. Momoko's head poked round the door, riddled white with an overcoming fear, she had sweat pouring off her as like I did.

"Momoko-san! Are you alright? I heard screaming." I asked, whispering worryingly, trying to peer past her into the dark room behind her to see if there was anyone or anything else that was perhaps lurking within. She panted, when she returned to a normal breathing rhythm she spoke.

"I'm fine Jason-san." But from the look of her face I could see that she was obviously not.

I look her in the eye with a gaze of comfort "May I come in?" I desperately wanted to make sure she was fine and safe and nothing further was lurking in the shadows. With a little reluctance she nodded and opened the door fully, allowing me to walk briskly inside. She closed the door behind me.

Switching one of the lights on she returned to her bed. She was dressed in a see through dark negligee that revealed a set of black undergarments underneath. I turned my head away, purely out of politeness although inside I secretly applauded the sight that was utterly fantastic!

"Oh I'm sorry Jason-san. I did not mean to embarrass you." She said as she reached for something to pull over and cover herself more to maintain her modesty.

"Oh no, it's fine Momoko." I said, turning my head when I knew it was considered decent in her eyes to look directly at her. Now she had a small grey top, a hoodie pulled over. "What happened?"

"I...I...had a bad dream." She stuttered, the thought of it making her uneasy.

"I see, like the ones you've been having over the last few days?" she dropped her eyes with unease "I've had similar bad dreams since I've arrived here too." I said, I tried to make her feel more comfortable about it, so she didn't think she was alone. Though I didn't know how much I should tell her about mine.

"Really?" she asked, trying to scrounge some connectivity and thus perhaps some closure.

"What was your dream about?" I asked, she went quiet and I was worried that she might hide within herself and not open up to me.

"Oh it...its silly." She said, the fear of the dream changing to embarrassment but she continued regardless. "It was of an...Oni. Superstitious demon...Its just a silly story, of a monster that we get told about when we are children. I should be fine now."

Now this little spot of information sparked my curiosity further, was it perhaps the same dream as what I was having? After all, the creature in my nightmares could be easily described as 'demon like'. I've heard stories of more than one people having the same dream, I always thought it was silly coincidence. But curiosity had gotten the better of me and I went over to the desk and grabbed a piece of paper, ripping it clean from a small notepad that hotels often leave on their desks for clients. With pen in hand I returned to Momoko and offered it over to her.

"Can you draw what you see in your dream?" I asked, receiving a strange look from her. One that was slightly confused and perhaps a little uncomfortable.

"Erm...yes, I guess so." As she slowly took the writing equipment from me and began to draw.

Her artistic skills were not the greatest, but then again, I didn't need it to be an accurate masterpiece. Crudely she drew, I remained silent so that she could concentrate fully. Observing it from time to time, the shape was beginning to come clear as it materialised on the paper. She only drew the head, but despite the limited picture, I could clearly see what it is.

The horns, curved and natural. The long and flowing mane that surrounded its face. It's teeth, jagged and animalistic. But it was its eyes; she spent time drawing the eyes, deep and piercing, as scary as they were plucked directly from my dream.

It was indeed the same creature that I saw in my dreams, it was quite shocking to see that we were both seeing the same things. Do I tell her that it was the same one that I saw? Or do I keep quiet?

In the end, I opted for truth being the best option.

"That creature…I've seen it before." I stammered, she looked up in surprise, or perhaps she just thought I was trying to humour her.

"You…have?" she said inquisitively, becoming unsure as to what to make of my revelation.

"Yes, I too have seen this in my dreams as well." Now it was time for me to decide whether I tell her more. "I also see what is a mountain, I've climbed stone steps up the mountain and at its peak is a temple." I thought I'd share that much with her thinking that it would be more tactful to leave out the parts of the surrounding blood and gore as I entered the temple. It was clear that she had some ordeal in her dreams already. Her face dropped and so did the pen and paper that was still in her hands.

"That…is similar to my dream…But I am not climbing. I am flown there, in the talons of a giant black bird, a large crow. Dark clouds and a high wind at the mountain as well. Inside the temple is where I see the demon. He calls to me and it is like I become joined with it." Her face went cold, she hasn't heard of anyone she knows sharing the same dream but apparently it is a special sign in her culture.

"To share a dream with someone shows that the two people have a special connection with each other. Karma and the Gods in Heaven have allowed them the same vision for whatever purpose it holds. Each dream contains a special message for the people who dream it. I am honoured to have the same dream as you Jason-san, I just wished it was a better dream to share."

A thought that I too also shared, though I dare not tell her what I hoped to be dreaming. I wasn't too sure what to do now, do I stay with her and make sure she is calmed down and alright, or do I go and keep her from further embarrassment? She looked like she was completely shattered, so I guess the best option would be to leave her be and let her get some sleep.

"Well, I see that you're ok now, I think it's best that I leave you to get some sleep." I said, standing to stand to my feet.

"No! Don't go!" worryingly she cried out and she grabbed my hand tightly. Her skin was smooth, it felt nice and at the point in which she touched me for the first time I felt a warm and 'fuzzy' feeling inside, despite the thin layer of sweat that was forming on her palms. She released her hold as she realised what she was doing, embarrassment was taking over once again.

"I'm sorry, please stay a little while longer" she said, her head down "Just so I can be calm enough to return to sleep."

"Ok" I said, as I returned to my sitting position. I decided that I would stay until she managed to drift off to sleep again and then I would leave quietly. She removed the top she had on to cover herself and turned round to get into bed. I noticed in the light that on her back she had a birth mark, like an oversized group of moles it resembled the shape of a fire burning. Smaller pieces of the birth mark were situated above it as if flames dancing from the main blaze of the fire. It was certainly different, very interesting.

Slipping delicately in the covers she laid her innocent head on the pillow and closed her eyes. It wasn't long before she was drifting fully in the land of nod and I stayed a little while longer, just watching her compassionately as she gently laid still.

Even though I was officially 'with' Sarah this trip in the eyes of everyone, the fact that she hung off my arm as if we were inseparable every waking moment that we were together definitely supported that analysis; there was a strong part of me that felt passionately for Momoko. She was beautiful and sweet and from the first moment that I saw her, it was like 'love at first sight' if there was such a thing. Perhaps it was because she was someone that I think I would never be able to get with and this only helped to strengthen the desire I had for her.

Normally I don't believe in such cliché notions but there was just something about her that made her different from most girls I know. The fact we were sharing the same dreams only served to support this case.

When it was time for me to leave and I was sure that Momoko was fast asleep, her breathing becoming more shallow and regular as she drifted off to the land of nod; I went over to her peaceful body and couldn't resist temptation as I stroked her soft flowing hair, a gentle kiss upon her forehead and I left the room to return to my own slumber. As I left the room, I could hear the soft happy moan of Momoko as if she was enjoying a pleasant dream and as I closed her door shut I couldn't help but smile. It was nothing short than a cheeky smile.

Chapter 18 – Gamblers Paradise

Komatsu. A provincial trading town, one of many that were beginning to appear and grow as the country was beginning its evolutionary phase of expansion and prosperity. It provided essential and often vital trade routes for both goods and services as well as an important connection between the other coastal towns in and around Japan to help develop and expand trade and the commercialism that is associated with it. As the country was changing, the methods of travel as well as the regularity of travel and commerce was increasing. Now goods, including sake can be shipped across country. This was completely contradictory from how things once were, whereby the only times that people would travel out of their village was if they were called to war against a neighbouring warlord.

Once a simple fishing village long ago, it's citizens simply worked out their lives with regular work and daily chore caring only for their own survival and providing their portion of offerings to the local Lord who resided over the area like a landlord.

It was now no longer so, it had grown to around four if not five times its original size in a fairly short time frame. A busy port in an essential area, which attracted merchants and other less savoury characters who now resided there. This included a local Yakuza syndicate that grew to such power and infamy within this once tight knit community that the local magistrates are forced to turn a blind eye to their gambling dens and protection rackets which funded the rest of their underhanded organisation.

It was one of these characters that myself and Fujibayashi were here searching for. The head of the syndicate, Boss Kuchinawa.

Boss Kuchinawa was a ruthless mobster, who ruled over the community with an iron fist; those who stood against him ended up dead and often in peculiar and horrific circumstances, often with the bodies skinned of any trace of flesh and the organs removed and sometimes scattered in horrific visions among the streets to be found later by innocent villagers, sometimes children. It was meant as a warning to those who would also consider the possibility of standing up to them to regain justice.

These vicious scare tactics have proved very effective in allowing them to keep a close reign on the denizens of Komatsu. They have also produced many legendary stories and dark, grisly tales about the true identity of Boss Kuchinawa and what happens in his secluded household. Such tales have provided him with a demonic image that we were forced to investigate.

Our mission here was to sever the head of the criminal organisation and to provide peace again to this once tranquil community; to hand back control to the local government officials and if Kuchinawa was truly a demon in human disguise, then it will be all the more worthwhile to our cause to take his life.

We entered the outskirts of the village on foot, myself and Fujibayashi walking side by side along the makeshift dirt road that had been created through the constant wear of travellers and merchant caravans walking along it. Local peasant villagers bowed politely to us as we passed them on the road. This was customary as a sign of respect due to our samurai status and we returned the polite courtesy will small nods of acknowledgment of our own.

"What do you think we will find in Komatsu?" Asked Fujibayashi

"I think that Boss Kuchinawa is simply a ruthless killer. These terrifying stories of him being more than just a man are simply misconceived stories coming from frightened heimen. Nothing more. However, we still must investigate and perform our duties in the name of the almighty Shogun. If it turns out that Boss Kuchinawa is indeed a demon, then we would have excelled in our duty of tracking him down and ending his existence." Inside I knew that Boss Kuchinawa was nothing more than what I had declared, but in our travels we have both encountered creatures and beasts that would haunt a man's dreams or cause them to go mad with the overpowering feeling of fear. Perhaps the stories were true; in either case, we would have to go into the heart of the Yakuza syndicate and we would need to be ready for all eventualities.

Approaching the edge of the village, our first port of call was to find a place of shelter for our stay, which would not be too hard as this was now a thriving port and plenty of inns and taverns existed that would offer us a bed for the night. This would also act as the heart, from which our mission will take place once we were established in Komatsu.

With some pacing of the streets we came across a small tavern that had space for us. It wasn't grand or luxurious which was perfect for us as we did not want to make our presence known too early to those who we were here for and being on the road for as long as we had, we were used to not having the finest luxuries; no one told us that being warriors of the Shogun would necessarily be a grand, elaborate affair.

Parting the cloth banner that covered the entrance we entered the quaint little building. Behind a small makeshift bar was the owner. A portly fellow with unkempt hair, dressed in a dirty grey uniform. Behind him were giant urns and smaller white porcelain bottles with the makers script plastered across the front of them, filled with delicious smooth sake and other wines and spirits.

Looking around, the room was relatively empty save for a local who was drowning some sorrows in a large bottle of sake. He was sat at an old table with his head held sorrowful in his hands as he hunched his shoulders over the bottle that seemingly gave him some measure of comfort. Whatever the poor wretch had on his mind, it was definitely serious.

The landlord smiled as we approached, it seemed like he didn't get much trade these days and was gladdened instantly when he saw us. "Welcome! Welcome! What can I do for you fine gentlemen?" He bowed politely as and when he noticed our pair of swords at our waist.

"We would like a room please, we do not know how long we are staying at the moment." I said, politely returning the bow. The innkeeper's eyes lit up at the prospect of some patronage.

"Certainly! Our rooms are small and I am afraid that they will not have the amenities befitting samurai of your class. I'm afraid we don't get as many distinguished visitors as yourselves." He sounded as if apologetic that he was unable to provide us with decent rooms. "But they are comfortable! Some of the best beds in Komatsu." He added, chirping up slightly so as not to scare away a sale. He took delight in being able to present to us the standard of the individual beds themselves.

"That would be fine." Said Fujibayashi softly.

"My name is Ishigo. Would you like me to show you to your rooms now? Or would you perhaps prefer a drink first to quench your thirst?" he asked, his voice was very friendly and welcoming.

"A bottle of sake would be most appreciated. A local one if possible." Said Fujibayashi. I had noticed that on our travels he did like to support the local makers when it came to the soothing liquid. A habit that I'm sure he picked up somewhere on his arduous travels when he first set about his pilgrimage before coming to the Imamoto dojo.

"Of course sir, please take a seat and I will bring it over to you."

We moved over to another table on the far side of the room, with the sorrowful man sat with his back to his across the way.

"Yet another hole we are forced to stay in. I never knew being a swordsman of the Shogun is such a grand life!" joked Fujibayashi as he took his seat.

"Be careful when choosing the words you speak. Remember, as practitioners of Budo we are humble in life. This little tavern is perfect for our quest."

"I am sorry Yoshida Shihan. Please excuse me." He said as he saw that his joke did not hit the required tones with me. By making light of his newly found position in life as a specialist warrior of the Shogun made him appear as though he was speaking out against the Shogun himself. If it were a commoner that did this, I would've been forced to execute him where he stood as this could sometimes be conceived by some as treason. I excused him with a simple verbal scolding as he was like I, in the sense that he was a Shogun's Dragon. Also, he was my student and thus, I considered him as still young and still in learning of the Way.

The innkeeper came across with a slight shambling motion. In his hands was the bright white sake bottle and two wooden cups. He plonked them down on the table, arranging them correctly so it was easy to acquire a drink without too much fussing around.

"There you go gentlemen, please enjoy!" spoke Ishigo.

"Excuse me, Ishigo. That man sat over there, what is the matter with him?" asked Fujibayashi, curious as to why he was in such a bad condition and seeking refuge in his tavern. The lonely man was now sobbing lightly into his hands, he was unawares of our presence in the tavern as he remained locked in a mental battle with whatever it was that ailed him.

"Him? Oh he is a local man, once a big fisherman, had good business once. Then the Yakuza and their gambling dens came to town. He went there tempted by the chance to win it big, did very well to start with too; but over time he simply lost and lost. He's just got back from his last session of gambling and now..." Ishigo paused as he felt sorry for the poor man "...Now all he has is the ragged clothes that he is wearing. He is old friend of mine, known him for many years so I gave him his drink for free. Poor troubled soul."

"Who is the Boss around here?" I asked, just to confirm that we were indeed after the right person.

"The Boss?...That's Boss Kuchinawa. But you gentlemen don't want to get to know him. He's not the sort of character that people of your class would wish themselves to be associated with." Ishigo hushed his voice at the mention of Boss Kuchinawa.

"And why is that?" asked Fujibayashi curiously staring up at the innkeeper. Ishigo leant forward and whispered softly. As if there were anyone around who could actually hear him! It appears that Boss Kuchinawa had a terrifying reputation that went with his name and it was at the extent that even the innkeeper had to be careful what he said about him in an empty room.

"Well, you see, he is evil man. Very brutal! He runs the syndicate around here, in fact, he is the one that controls this damned town. Anyone who stands up to him dies; very badly! In such a way that not even their ancestors will recognise them in the afterlife! Some say he is a demon! I'm almost inclined to agree! I've seen what he does to those who stand up to him!" Ishigo's eyes were wide, as if he was damning himself for telling us this information. It seems that Boss Kuchinawa does have this town locked in a web of fear.

"So you see gentlemen, you don't want to look for him. He's nothing but trouble for distinguished gentlemen like yourselves." He added.

"Where can we find these gambling dens? In case we fancy our luck?" I asked, trying to change the subject and get as much information as I can out of the nervous barkeep.

"Oh...the most popular one for upstanding samurai such as yourselves can be found up on the north side of the town. Next door to the tea house."

"Is Boss Kuchinawa there?" I asked,

"Rarely does he go to his gambling houses, allowing his many minions to look after things. He keeps himself locked away inside the grounds of his house. He sits there like a king, the place is more like a fortress than a household, guarded night and day. I heard that a group of fishermen once even hired a ninja to break in and kill him, but he is still alive and there's no word of the ninja! The gambling den is run by his second in command, Sasaki is how he is known. He is the physical presence of

Boss Kuchinawa within this town. He is just as cruel and ruthless as his Boss."

"Thank you Ishigo." I said and he turned away to return to his position behind the bar.

"So what's your plan Yoshida Shihan?" asked Fujibayashi as soon as Ishigo was too far away to hear.

"We need to make ourselves known to him sooner or later. Tomorrow we will go to the gambling den and apply to work. Sneaking into the house is out of the question if it is as secure as what Ishigo says, and a direct assault may prove to be futile, so other means of entry are required. We will pretend to be ronin seeking employment as bodyguards in the hope that Boss Kuchinawa will employ us and that is how we will gain entry to his house." I said, I already had the plan worked out on the road to here.

"Yes Shihan, I understand."

The morning came and we followed Ishigo's directions to where the gambling den is said to be. On the north side of the town, the area seemed to be more built up and of a higher class than the area we have just come from.

It was just where Ishigo said it was. Next to the tea house, which had beautiful gardens and was the picturesque surroundings for conducting the tea ceremony to be one with nature. There was no doubt in my mind that Boss Kuchinawa also owned this particular slice of harmony as well.

Like a complete contradiction to the peaceful atmosphere of the tea garden was the gambling den.

From its entrance, excited voices and the hollow sounds of the game being played emanated predominately into the surrounding street.

We got closer to the gambling den as a disgruntled samurai emerged from its entrance. He looked down at the ground angrily, it was obvious that he had just lost and probably a fair amount by the level of anger that boiled up to his face. With frustration he kicked at a scrunched piece of paper that was on the ground, cursing loudly, cursing the gambling den and the mobsters as he walked with a fast pace away. For a moment, I thought that he might've possibility went for his sword and took his frustrations out on some unsuspecting victim.

"Be on your guard" I said softly to Fujibayashi as we went through the door.

Passing through the entrance, the gambling den was an open expanse. On the left hand side sat what I would assume was the banker for the den. A wizened old man with a short tufty beard and a receding hairline that was an ashen grey. Behind him stood two bodyguards, each armed with a katana held at their hip.

On the right hand side there was the main action of the den. A long table barely off the ground, with around twelve different samurai sat on the one side. Each of them had in their hands long wooden sticks, representative of money that they were using to place their bets.

Opposite them were three burly Yakuza. Each of them had their jackets removed so that they showed their muscular chests. This was a masculine show of control over the locals, a display of who they were associated with. Their bodies, as befitting of a member of the Yakuza were covered with an array of tattoos of all manners of descriptions. Images of dragons, demons, koi carp, great waves and warriors of legend covered their backs, chest and arms; save for a strip of clear flesh that ran down the centre of the body. It was quite distasteful for a samurai to have tattoos in this day and age and as such they have gone underground with the Yakuza being the ones to adopt them.

The central Yakuza was the man in charge with the individual rounds of betting. In front of him were two bone dice and a small wooden bowl placed upon a rectangular platform of dark silks. I spotted that the little finger of his left hand has had the majority of it removed from the first knuckle. This was from the practices of the Yakuza; whereby an individual member of the organisation who has committed an act that was deemed insulting or a complete lapse in their duties by the boss, would offer the end of their little finger as penance for their mistake. If they did another similar act then they would cut off the little finger at the next knuckle before moving onto the ring finger and so forth. It was a practice that insured that the members of the organisation were extremely careful of their actions as they valued their digits!

This practice was the Way of the Yakuza and not the Way of the Samurai; The Yakuza were disdained by samurai of higher standards. I know I certainly didn't care much for them and wouldn't be in their company unless I needed to be, like now.

The game of choice in this gambling den is a dice game that is popular in these type of dens across the country. What happens is the two dice go into the bowl and are shook up by the dealer. The bowl and its contents are slammed onto the table and those betting have to decide whether the total number on the dice is either odd or even. A correct guess doubles their winnings.

"Can I help you?" said the banker, his eyes looking at us with suspicion. It seems that strangers in this particular den were viewed with an air of mistrust.

"We wish to take part in the betting." I said

"How much do you wish to bet?" said the banker rolling his eyes as if we were mere cheap ronin who constituted the majority of travelling patrons that gambled here. I pulled out a small prepared purse of coin from my obi and placed it confidently on the counter.

"The amount there, if you please." The banker opened the purse and saw the gold coinage that was shining up at him. With a surprised glee he passed it to one of the guards behind him and he produced a bundle of betting sticks from underneath the counter.

"Thank you sirs! Please take your seats!" His voice became much more chirpier than the rude stereotypical noise he made earlier. He indicated to one of the guards who went to the betters and cleared the central seats that were in front of the main dealer. The best seats in the house for 'honoured guests'.

"Your swords please." He asked, indicating our weapons that we still kept in our possession. I was reluctant to relinquish my swords to him. "Please sir, they will be kept quite safe. Otherwise I cannot allow you to take your seats." Still with heavy reluctance I pulled my blades from my obi and handed them over, Fujibayashi did the same. As he quickly glanced at the blades as they were in transit, I could see that his eyes lifted at the marvellous craftsmanship of the weapons.

Taking our seats we began the process of betting. The dealer lifted up the two dice, crudely made of the bone of some poor animal, the numbers carved into each edge. He held them between his fingers as he presented them to the gathering of gamblers.

"Objections?" he asked, seeing if anyone was going to challenge the validity of the dice. This was the standard procedures of play before he rolls. No one responded. So with a quick flick he tossed them into the bowl and shook them about in small, circular horizontal motion. Then with a flash he slammed the bowl onto the table. The dice still hidden from view.

"Bets." He said

"Odd!...Even!" came the scattered calls of the betters. "Even" I said positively, placing a small number of the bundle on the table.

The dealer lifted the bowl. "2...4...total 6...even" he called as the two Yakuza either side of him pulled away unsuccessful bets at the unhappy groans of the losers and rewarded the lucky ones. My small bundle doubled and was returned to me.

I gambled on, being cautious and conservative with my bets, my luck fluctuated good and bad, though I managed to eventually increase my pot five fold. The majority of the other gamblers had either left with disgust of losing or been replaced with new lucky hopefuls as the time passed. The banker was looking cautiously over to me, my winning streak must've been very rare in this particular den and he watched me thinking that I was perhaps cheating in some way. Most gamblers would probably take this as a signal to get the hell out before trouble kicks off. But we were here for a different purpose and I remained in order to achieve the goal that we had come here for.

Then all of a sudden, walked into the gambling den, a man that exuberated raw power with every step. Tall and broad he had a stony face which sported a jagged facial scar upon its left cheek. Slung upon his broad back was a Nodachi, a long battlefield sword that had to be wielded with both hands. Larger than a regular katana the blade stood almost as tall as he did, with the handle being twice even three times the length of one on a regular sword. It was a terrible looking sword and hard to fight against because of its size, the owner probably picked it for its deadly and fearful impressions adding to the scare tactics that this mob had thrived upon.

He walked over to the banker who in conference with this stranger kept looking over to myself and Fujibayashi, clearly indicating us to him. It seemed that our presence here made some impression. This was exactly how I had planned this.

"Yoshida Shihan." whispered Fujibayashi trying to make me aware of the stranger of whom I already knew was there.

"Yes Fujibayashi, I know." I said softly, it seems that Sasaki has arrived. He would be our way in to see Boss Kuchinawa.

The stranger walked over to the table, and sat down upon a chair behind the main croupier. Allowing the flow of the events to continue undeterred he continued to inspect myself and my companion. He removed his sword from his back and placed it in front of him on his lap.

Without looking up from my winning stack I spoke formally. "Are you the one they call Sasaki?"

"Aye, that is me" he said in a gruff and harsh voice. His speech was rough and I assumed he was originally from a seafaring background and not a samurai from birth. "Who is it that wants to know?"

"My name is Yoshida Kintaro and this is my friend and ally Fujibayashi Shigeru. We wish to seek employment with your master, Boss Kuchinawa."

Sasaki laughed openly with a deep rumbling laugh. "Employment you say! I'm sure the master is in need of some *maids* for the household." An insult, foolish and big headed, one that is born of ignorance or the abuse of power. If I didn't have a higher agenda to fulfil or if he were a simple peasant, then I would've taken the opportunity to cut off his head where he was.

"We wish to be employed as bodyguards for the Boss. I hear from many of the locals that his current bodyguard is nothing more than a big headed braggart who knows nothing but how to blow hot air, let alone wield a sword in protection of his master...Aren't you one of his bodyguards?" I returned his insult with one of my own. I observed the room becoming more tense and even the Yakuza sat in front of me were becoming twitchy and on edge as they were fearful of the rage that Sasaki was famous for. The play had stopped as the attention turned to the verbal exchange that we gave each other. Sasaki's face turned red with a rage that he was struggling to control and ultimately was becoming overcome by.

"I'll teach you to shoot your mouth to me! You impudent dog!" he screamed, pulling the massive blade from its sheath, throwing the unnecessary scabbard aside on the floor with a rattle. With an almighty swing he brought the blade quickly to over his head, narrowly missing the croupier in front of him and with a scream he brought it down as if to split my body in half.

With a sudden clap I brought my hands together with a hearty slap, trapping the blade solidly between my palms and tightening my muscles in my arms and back to create a solid and unmoveable object. A gasp went up from the room as both gambler and Yakuza alike scrambled backwards to avoid getting in the way of such a large, dangerous blade.

Fujibayashi went to leap forward. "Stop Fujibayashi-san!" I cried, halting him before he could deliver a death blow on Sasaki. His index finger protruding from his fist stopping just millimetres from Sasaki's throat.

"It's very rude to pull a blade on an unarmed man. You must obviously be the uncouth man I've heard about" I said, soft yet intended, as I finally raised my head to look Sasaki in the eye, his blade still gripped within my palms.

Sasaki grunted with effort as he tried to pull the blade free from my grip. When he realised that it was useless to pull it free he laughed again with that deep rumbling laugh of his.

"I like your style Yoshida-san! You have a lot of guts and talent I see. Something that I admire. I shall pass my recommendations onto the Boss. If he is interested then we'll send for you...Don't worry, we'll find you when we need to. There is nothing in this town that the Boss doesn't know about. In fact he probably already knows you've arrived." He laughed again and I released my grip. Sasaki pulled his sword away and Fujibayashi returned at my side.

"Thank you Sasaki, that is most helpful" I said as I rose to my feet and went over to the door.

"Our swords please." I said to the shaking banker who scurried off and collected our blades. With them securely returned to our belts we left the den, the sounds of proceedings returning to life as we exited.

When we were clear of the establishment and insured that we were out of earshot of anyone Fujibayashi spoke "Why did you stop me Yoshida san?"

I looked at him with a sly smile "Because Fujibayashi, although Sasaki is a rough and uneducated brute, we need him. Remember the purpose of our mission is for Boss Kuchinawa. We need him in order to get allow ourselves conference with the Boss. All I needed was to make a lasting impression with Sasaki. The rest will fall into place in time."

Fujibayashi laughed "Yes Yoshida-san. An impression I think was made today." He continued to laugh, now died down to a small personal laugh. "What is our next step?" he asked.

"We wait." Was my reply "And hope that the Boss wishes to see us. Or we may have to resort to other means to get a meeting."

Chapter 19 – Boss Kuchinawa

The following morning we sat in the main room of our tavern. We were now awaiting the personal request for audience with Boss Kuchinawa. I was hoping deep down that the request would come from the Boss himself and that he would come out of hiding and see us here at Ishigo's. At the table we were presented with a simple breakfast of fresh fish, rice balls and a bottle of sake to wash the basic, yet filling, meal down.

Ishigo walked over with a fresh bottle as we ate silently. "You gentlemen have only been here a day and you've made a name for yourself!" he said, interrupting our silent ritual of breakfast. "Everyone is talking about what you did up at the gambling den the other day." His hand was shaking as he was unable to maintain control his excitement as he placed the fresh bottle on the table.

"No one has ever stood up to Sasaki and his sword, and especially with just their *bare hands*!" He exclaimed in shocked awe. He was almost forgetting the difference in class and status. An important attribute to some samurai who sometimes did not hesitate in the killing of peasantry if they did not show the proper courtesy or the understanding of the social hierarchy of the world. Luckily for Ishigo, we weren't that sort of samurai and respected the common man, not as the understanding of equal in the sense of status, more so as the understanding that we are all just human. It was also too early in the day for shedding blood.

"We do not wish to talk about it Ishigo, please excuse my rudeness when addressing on the matter." I said

"Oh no…of course not! My apologies, I'm sorry for intruding." He replied. "Please…enjoy your meal."

We waited patiently, midday had passed and we remained alone in the tavern. At first I thought we were going to wait all day for a response from the Boss as the time rolled on far slower than it normally does; I accepted the possibility that maybe we wouldn't hear from him today, until, just after the sun had passed over into the stages of early afternoon the sound of a raucous and rowdy group of men approached from down the street. Their bawdy tones that drifted on the air signalled to us in advance that our request was soon to be answered one way or another.

The rabble's noise grew louder and louder until it came to the doorway of the tavern itself. Through the curtained doorway came the source of the noise as Sasaki, along with a following of four other Yakuza came through the entrance. They were all armed but with their swords still sheathed and at their sides. I could feel Fujibayashi observing them intently as they shambled their way through the door and there was no doubt in my mind he was mentally planning strategies on how to kill them if necessary, should the need arise. The five of them instantly made the place look relatively busier than its usual sporadic occupancy as they entered.

If it were a group other than this uncouth lot then Ishigo would've favoured their custom in his tavern, but as it stands, he would probably have preferred not to have their money and have them leave. I believe that if the town wasn't so dead locked in fear of this gang, then he would've done so immediately without hesitation.

The four lesser Yakuza went straight over to Ishigo to get a drink and to generally be a nuisance for him as they harassed him for some rice wine at the bar, trying their best to avoid paying the full asking price.

Sasaki on the other hand, walked straight over to us. He indicated to the empty space and I beckoned him to join us with an offering of one hand. Sitting down to join us, he spoke with his gruff uncivilised tone "Yoshida, Fujibayashi, I trust you both slept well in this...*lovely* establishment"

"We did indeed, thank you" I said. Bowing my head slightly to acknowledge his arrival.

"I spoke to the Boss and did my best to describe how good your skills are. I hope I was able to do them justice" He paused, to create dramatic tension, or at least attempt to "He seems very interested in your offer. As such, I am here to take you to him so he may speak to you himself." He called over to Ishigo who was trying his best to both deal with the other Yakuza and not insult them. "Innkeeper! Sake for me and my friends here!"

"Coming right up sir!" he said uncomfortably. Ishigo was definitely unsettled by his Yakuza customers. I had to control myself, the thought that this low down ruffian of a simple ronin was referring to us as 'friends' was both sickening and insulting. I bit my tongue bitterly as to speak out against this would be damaging to our quest to see the Boss.

Ishigo rushed over with the sake, sweat from nerves formed tiny droplets on his brow.

"What took you so long!?" spat Sasaki as he displayed the grip of fear he had on him, making Ishigo jump at the thought of possible reprisals.

"Sorry sir…sorry" replied Ishigo who returned back to the bar as quickly as he could.

"Come! Friends! Have a drink with me!" said Sasaki who poured the cool liquid into the little cups.

"Kampai" I said, slightly maliciously as I raised the cup to my lips and sipped on the contents.

The house and grounds of Boss Kuchinawa was a grand affair as was befitting someone of his social stature, though somewhat gained through an infamous nature. Its cream coloured bordering walls were topped by the blackest of slate. The entrance doors to the estate were like that of a castles. Big and thick oak they had the studded hinges of solid iron holding them securely in place. They looked as though they could take on the pounding of a hundred soldiers before giving in.

Our group stood and waited silently outside this formidable entrance and we watched as the doors opened, creaking loudly as they were pulled apart. Ishigo was once more correct in his description, this place was surely a personal fortress as we saw guards and impromptu checkpoints throughout the household. If we didn't have chance to receive a personal audience with him, it would be difficult to get close to him without an army of soldiers behind us.

"Please, follow me" said Sasaki, the first time I've seen him be properly and genuinely polite. I could only hope that this came from some level of new founded respect or his acknowledgment of our status. We stepped into the frontal gardens of the house.

"The Boss will see you in his study. It is just up ahead." Waving a hand he showed the way and a servant opened the door that was ahead.

Myself and Fujibayashi went where we were shown and entered into the Boss' study where he sat waiting behind a small wooden writing table, with pen in hand he was focused on writing something on a sheet of paper in front of him with a bamboo pen. Many decorative scriptures depicting sayings of great philosophical meaning were placed periodically around the walls. Two dull cushions were set in front of the writing desk as if ready for our arrival.

As we stepped into the study, the Boss raised his head. "Welcome Yoshida Kintaro, Fuibayashi Shigeru. Both of you are most welcome here, please be seated." He said courteously. We obliged and sat in seiza in front of him but maintained official rigidness and posture as we did so.

The Boss was surely getting on in years, with a head that was shaved and cleared of any hair, much like that of a priest. Unlike most Yakuza who prefer to keep the tattoos just on their body where they can keep them hidden if needs be, the Boss had the majority of his scalp tattooed and had no thoughts of keeping the picturesque body art hidden from us. The poor light making the smaller details hard to pick out. His eyes were lifeless and appeared black in the light.

The Boss put down his pen tidily so he could give us his undivided attention.

"Sasaki tells me that you two are looking to seek employment in my house. He tells me that you have great martial skill, the likes of which he has never had the opportunity to see before. For Sasaki to say such words it is both an honour and compliment that you should accept humbly. Despite his ruggedness in his mannerisms he is quite the skilled warrior and one of my most loyal of servants."

"Please thank your man for recommending us so highly and thank you for the hospitality of your house." I said politely. Though the thought of someone of Sasaki's stature complimenting my skill didn't exactly excite nor humble me, not even in the slightest.

"I shall. Now, you are here for work as bodyguards for me and my household? Is this true?"

"Yes Boss Kuchinawa" said Fujibayashi.

"Honoured am I that both of you thought to seek me out as your employer. Its good to see that some people are strong enough in both body and mind to be not afraid of the stories that hail about me. At least, from outsiders like yourselves anyway. I hear that my name has become quite infamous among certain circles."

"I'm sure that you like the locals to believe them, helps maintain order and...compliance." I added. The Boss smiled evilly, showing pleasure at the way in which I worded my sentence.

"Yes, that is true. Without the order I maintain in these parts, this town would not have grown to the size that it has and chaos would've reigned instead of prosperity" Kuchinawa spoke with a vigour that is likened to any man who is consumed with great ambition. "It's funny to think that people regard me as a *demon*, just by the way in which I maintain order. It is quite a powerful image to have."

I couldn't quite tell, but there was a part of what he said that made me think he was merely testing us. Was he an actual demon? Or was this an elaborate ruse in an attempt to make us think so, to continue to instil the idea into the minds of outsiders. Then he slipped a malevolent smile and alarm bells began to ring in my head.

"But let's be honest with each other. You two haven't come here in order to become my bodyguards, have you."

Myself and Fujibayashi looked at one another out of the corners of our eyes as the atmosphere tensed slightly. It seems our charade had been uncovered somehow.

"Yoshida Kintaro, Fujibayashi Shigeru, two of the skilled swordsman of the once legendary Imamoto Dojo of Kakogawa. Winning swordsmen of the Shogunate's duel of the Dragons at Himeji. Two of the Shogun's Eight Dragons now sat before me." He sounded as if he were impressed by our resume, though I knew he was being double standard with his words

"In fact, Yoshida, you are said to be the leader of the eight warriors and carry with you the Emperor Dragon sword, the mightiest sword ever produced for combating demons, do you not? Do you not think that I don't know who you truly are? For it is my business to know everything and everyone who comes into my town" He narrowed his eyes angrily at us.

"You two charlatans have not come here for work. You two have come here in order to rid this miserable town of me, to relinquish my control over these peasants, these mere fodder."

Fujibayashi slowly reached down to unlock the sword from its neutral position by pushing the guard forward with his thumb. The boss continued.

"I know all about you. The Master has spoken to me, saying that you will come for me. He has given me the task of killing you wretched samurai. I shall end your lives and put my Master's thoughts at rest." With such smoothness he pulled his arms inside his kimono and removed the top half from his body with a confident throw of his hands and arms. Now he sat, his body exposed to the world. His skin, like those in the gambling den, was covered in tattoos. These tattoos took the form of giant snakes with gaping maws that encircled around his body.

As we watched, the detailed body art began to move on the surface of the Boss's skin, the snakes writhed slickly around his body. They began to hiss as they became alive by some unearthly power. This was no trick of the light in our mind's eye, the snakes were materialising themselves into the real world.

With lightning fast reaction as I touched the hilt of my sword, one of the snakes took physical form and snapped out from its owner's body. Flying across the room it was ready to snap its viciously sharp and poisonous teeth into my neck.

Rolling out of the path of the unearthly snake it snapped its jaw shut catching merely thin air. Raising onto my knee and pulling out my sword from its sheath I sliced up through the body of the snake, the head hit the floor and writhed in a deathly spasm. Green blood of a vile, corrupt nature gushed from the severed body, spurting and squirting out uncontrollably.

Fujibayashi went to draw his sword but more and more of the snakes came out of the body of Boss Kuchinawa. One had managed to wrap itself tightly around Fujibayashi's body, its muscled body constricting him with a mysterious strength as it tightened its grip to near bone crunching levels. Fujibayashi was now fighting for his life with the head of the serpent, holding its fang filled, snapping mouth away from him desperately with his hand. He grunted with effort as the unholy snake was slowly winning the battle.

Diving forward, I slashed out at the mass of snakes that were almost held suspended in mid-air, trying my best to cut a safe path through the entangled wall of snakes. Section after section of serpentine bodies and heads hit the ground as I continued to mow my way through them. Just as I reached what I thought was the base of all them, I plunged my sword with a thrust of desperation deep into the mass. Green blood quickly became mixed with crimson red and a scream of pain came of human origin from the writhing mass.

My sword had struck home and penetrated the heart of the demon within them. The mass of snakes shortly fell to the ground, lifeless, before vanishing like a wisp of smoke and Boss Kuchinawa returned into view. His chest had my sword protruding out of it and a trickle of blood flowed out from the base of the wound, flowing down his body like a stream that was winding its way through a valley.

"Noooo!" he screamed, his voice shrieking with the pain produced by my blade. "This cannot be! I am not meant to die this way! The Master said that I would kill you. He was going to reward me handsomely with your death!"

"Your Master seems to have gotten his information wrong." I said triumphantly as I pushed my weight onto the handle and plunged the razor sharp sword deeper through him, the blade slicing through his body with consummate ease and breaking free out of his back on the other side. Kuchinawa screamed bloodily before dropping his head lifelessly and with a quick twist I pulled my sword clean from his body once I was satisfied that the demon had ceased breathing.

"Fujibayashi, we must get out of here! Quickly!" I said with haste, realising that we were still in the heart of the

Yakuza household. Whether or not the minions knew of the true nature of their Boss was irrelevant, they would no doubt seek revenge for his demise. "It will not be long before this place is swarming with guards and our escape will be made difficult."

"I agree Yoshida Shihan" said Fujibayashi with a sharp nod of acceptance and we burst out through the door with swords drawn at the ready.

The guards of the house were already alerted that their Boss had been killed and were amassing in the courtyard outside the study. They waited there for our emergence from the house and blocked the only exit off the grounds. There were at least over a dozen of them and at their head, in way of the exit, was Sasaki with his monstrously large blade drawn and held out in front of them.

"Kill them! Kill them both!" cried Sasaki and the mob burst into a battle cry before they began their charge.

Three tried to rush us down, they were not like well trained warriors of a military household, more so along the lines of money motivated mercenaries who had been given arms in the form of cheap, mass produced blades and were quickly cut down with relative ease. Their blood was the first to stain the gardens of their unholy employer.

We advanced, two more came at us but they met the same fate as those before them. My one cut had sliced through one of them and sliced clean through one of the stone statues that laid behind him. The stone roughly ground its way apart, the top section falling with a mighty crash on the ground as it followed the diagonal line of my cut.

Still we advanced, cutting through the enemy who died worthlessly by our blades. Two that were left ran away, feeling the need to preserve their own lives. After all, they were not samurai and did not have the same honour when it comes to dying in battle. For them, running away from a superior enemy was an acceptable decision. As they tried to pass Sasaki at the entrance, he cut one them down in a display of displeasure of his cowardice. The lucky one managed to break free as Sasaki was unable to kill the two at the same time.

Now all that was left was ourselves and Sasaki who stood steadfast at the entrance.

"Sasaki, you do not have to die today. Now stand aside and live" shouted Fujibayashi, attempting to take authority of the situation, now tired of spilling worthless blood today.

"You will have to pass through me." He shouted in response as he adopted a stance of his own with the sword held above his head. I went to step forward and except the challenge but Fujibayashi cut me off.

"Your master was not what you thought he was Sasaki! He was not a man like yourself and I!" I said, trying my best to make the loyal but stubborn Sasaki see reason. It did not have the desired effect.

"That may be, but he was still my master and as his servant I am obliged to avenge his death or my soul will not pass on peacefully into the next life." Sasaki was adamant in his reasoning and it was clear to all that he was not going to budge from our path. I stopped to think that perhaps Sasaki had no other master before Kuchinawa. His loyalty to him was paramount and it clouded his mind.

"Please Yoshida Shihan, allow me. This will be...fun." Said Fujibayashi; I stepped back to give him some room as I detected a touch of sadistic pleasure in his voice. It would be interesting to see how he would combat a man who had the advantage with both positioning and weaponry.

The two warriors stood apart. There was at least ten or so metres between them, but with that massive blade, Sasaki could easily cover that distance and strike him down with just a couple of bounding steps. Fujibayashi was at quite at a disadvantage with the minuscule length of his wakazashi in comparison with the nodachi.

Fujibayashi turned sideways, his short sword held horizontal behind his head. His empty hand was free and held daintily by his chest. It was similar to the stance he made when I first met faced him at the dojo. But there was something different, his swordplay was much more unreadable than before. I assumed this was from the culmination of his previous teachings from the Toda school and the fusion of our own technique. I couldn't help but be completely embroiled in this confrontation and it took my attention away from the fact that there might still be guards lurking about.

Sasaki roared loudly like an angered lion, building himself up into a combative fury so that he would banish all fear from his spirit. As he went to make his strike but before he could move a single step from his spot

Fujibayashi had spun to face him square on. His sword arm making a wide circle and with a quick flick of his wrist he sent the short sword flying out of his hands and towards Sasaki. It flew gracefully in the air, spinning once, twice, then it hit. The blade had sunk kissaki [tip] first into the chest of Sasaki.

Full of surprise, Sasaki dropped his enormous blade which rattled and bounced upon the stone floor. In utter disbelief he peered down to see the ancient sword sticking out of his chest. It was amazing that he was still able to keep on his feet despite the terrible pain that must be shooting through his muscular body. He was indeed a strong and powerful man.

He looked back up, to eye Fujibayashi, for a man not initially born a samurai or a warrior in the military capacity, his eyes glinted with admiration for Fujibayashi's skill; it was a technique that he did not expect to be conducted by Fujibayashi. To be honest, I didn't even expect it from him. They say that it is the unexpected techniques that are the hardest to counter, even by the most skilful of swordsmen.

His loyalty to his master too was admirable also, for many would've ran when faced with two such skilful opponents, especially after their master had been killed. In another life, he could've well been a samurai, perhaps even one of legendary proportions.

As he looked up, Fujibayashi had ran and jumped, his arm pulled back ready to deliver that final blow, as if his sword had not done enough damage to the powerful Sasaki already. He landed strong, his body tensed as the muscles in his body connected and he fired his protruding knuckle punch that hit Sasaki in the throat. The same technique I had stopped him from finishing the day before in the gambling den. Now I allowed him to carry on with his finishing blow, more out of pity for Sasaki as he needed to be put out of his misery.

With a sickening gargle of blood as his body began the process of haemorrhaging from the inside, Sasaki fell hard on the stony earth. Blood drained out into a grisly pool that enveloped his body. Onlookers that were in the streets beyond the gates were looking on with horror and shock as we tore our way through the household of the Boss. Some let out panicked screams as we cut down those who opposed us in a whirlwind of death.

With a squelch, Fujibayashi retained his weapon, shaking the blood of the blade in the time old manner of the first steps to cleaning the blade, splattering red droplets against the doors. Perhaps it was his symbolic way of defiance to the name of the demon's house, and returned it to its sheath.

Walking over to him boldly, once I had snapped out of the hypnotic state I had put myself in, I asked "Where did you learn that technique?" As I stood impressed at the different technique he had displayed, I ran through my mind the different applications that could be done with it. I had absorbed the technique in its entirety, memorizing all the intricate details of the starting position and the method in which it was thrown.

"Toda style, secret short sword technique" he said confidently with a sly smile, pleased that his technique was both successful and produced some interest from myself. "Do you like it Yoshida Shihan?"

"An interesting technique, I've never seen a sacrifice technique like that. At least not from that distance. Most impressive Fujibayashi-san. It would be one that would've taken me by surprise if I had to come across it for the first time. Now lets leave this awful place."

Another reference of the sinister Master. It was a disturbing revelation that we were being targeted by the head of the demon underworld, a beast that commands such power and control that his followers will willingly go to their deaths for him. The feeling that one day we will have to face such a creature dawned on me. I will have to make myself ready for when that day comes.

Chapter 20 – Typhoon

We watched the weather forecast on the television intently, even though it was entirely in Japanese, it wasn't looking too hopeful for us. Tomorrow was supposed to be our trip to Kunimoto castle and some of its various major temples. It was looking like that was going to be postponed or even cancelled due to the upcoming typhoon warning.

The high winds and torrential rains would result in the Shinkanzen bullet train being kept off the track for safety reasons. We were essentially marooned in Himeji until the storm had passed.

The TV showed the typhoon area, a giant red spot, representing the epicentre that was shown to move across the land, around this spot were concentric white rings showing the outer affected regions of the typhoon. Luckily enough we were not in the inner epicentre but we were placed on the outsides of its effected area. Although this meant we weren't directly in the worst of it, it would still be a pretty bad storm.

It came early evening and the winds were already picking up and the rain lashed down without any show of mercy. We were forced to shut and fasten the windows in the hotel room as the catches were forced out of position by the high winds and the windows began to bang and rattle noisily. So far a couple of brief blackouts of power had occurred sending us into complete darkness with the longest time being around a minute or so.

Our room became the centre of the bored marooned team mates and James had brought round a deck of cards which we used for small gambling games of brag and poker, using the smaller pocket change that we had all began collating in order to increase our stacks enough to change back into notes at some point.

The girls had joined us and although their general knowledge of poker was not as *extensive* as ours, at least to begin with, a little coaching and some hastily written reference sheets of the order of winning hands and they were soon becoming professional at the game; sometimes employing strategies that we had not even discussed like different betting methods and timings of bluffing. The lads whispered rumours among us that they were actually sharking us from the very beginning! At the end of today I promised myself to never play cards against women again, as they have their own womanly wiles that affect my game and I didn't take losing money well!

"Does anyone know what's actually happening tonight?" asked Sarah as she began dealing cards for another round.

Andrew paused for a moment while he secretly peeked at the cards he was dealt "I heard that there's meant to be a meal tonight. Some local restaurant I think, nothing special, its an optional one because of the weather." Sarah continued her deal.

"What time does that start?" she asked.

"Meeting at the lobby at 8.30pm" replied Andrew as he now picked up his cards and looked at them more closely, covering them so their faces were secret to everyone but himself. The corner of his lip turned up in a tell of a good hand. Andrew didn't possess the best poker face.

Emily butted into the conversation. "Is anyone here going? I might go, beats staying in tonight."

"Probably, if anyone else goes. I don't want to be the only one here that's there though." Piped James.

"I'm not!" said Sarah defiantly. "Have you not seen the rain out there! I haven't got a jacket or an umbrella, my hair will get ruined!"

James sniggered slightly, thinking that whole statement was quite absurd and funny. If there's something that I've learnt is never argue with a girl and her hair.

Andrew looked up at Sarah and smiled. "You have your squad jacket don't ya?" Sarah looked at him unsure.

"Yeah, but it doesn't look good for a night out does it! Even if it is just another bloody meal." We all laughed, Sarah's obsession for her own personal vanity was quite amusing and when you are as bored as we were right now, then finding the little things to have a giggle at really helped to whittle away the endless hours.

The report on the television switched over from the typhoon to another broadcast. From what we could tell it appeared to be a massive fire at some warehouse or factory style building. The flames of the burning building were scarily high and looked as though it would be uncontrollable. Fire fighters scurried in camera shot to try and put out the flames. The report was all in Japanese and it was difficult to know whereabouts it was.

"Oh, that doesn't look pleasant." Said James, pointing out the action on the television "It looks like they could do with some of our rain!" he joked.

Time passed quickly, the rain and wind still battered against the window, it seems that it wasn't going to let up any time soon. Emily and James had already left, deciding that braving the elements beats staying in all night. It was just the three of us left now, chatting away about random things, though I was quite quiet. I was still confused with what was happening both around me and what was in my head.

I took the time to run through everything, from the strange happenings at the welcome meal. The Budokan, and the finding of the ancient sword. Amongst all this, there was the voice of a 16th Century samurai haunting my every step. At least, I classed it as haunting, he was trying to make me something that I thought in my heart I could never have been. Something that I didn't want to be.

"Excuse me, just going to the loo." I said, slowly bringing myself to my feet.

Walking in the bathroom, I locked the door behind me. Turning my attention to the sink I ran my hands under the cold tap, looking at myself in the mirror, I thought I was looking awful.

Cupping some of the cool liquid in my hands I splashed my face, doing my best to bring an element of refreshment back into it. Looking back up at the mirror I was shocked to see that my face had been replaced by Yoshida's. The surprise took me some what and I jumped back.

Dropping my face with embarrassed frustration. "I wish you would stop doing that" I whispered with added annoyance. The image of Yoshida smiled mischievously as if a schoolboy who had played out some comical prank.

"I'm sorry Jason-san. We need to talk…privately."

"What? What is there you need to say to me? Why are you haunting me now!" I said, again frustration was building.

"I am not haunting you Jason-san. You need to realise how important you are." He said, softly, slightly apologetically.

"I'm not that important, I'm just Jason. I do karate, I'm here to compete, which I have done to the best of my ability and now I just want to relax and enjoy my trip." It was annoying me that I was not able to convince him to just leave me alone. My voice had raised without me realising.

A quick knock on the toilet door turned my attention "Are you ok Jason? Who are you talking to?" came Sarah's voice from the other side.

"Yea...Yeah...I'm fine, sorry, just talking to myself." I panicked.

"Ok, do you need anything?" she asked.

"No, I'm fine, cheers" I said.

Turning my head back to Yoshida, who's image still remained in the mirror. "See! You're making me appear crazy in front of everyone!"

"Then let's go somewhere quiet. I fancy a drink anyways" he laughed.

"Go somewhere? In this?! Have you not seen the rain? You must be mad!"

Yoshida smiled once more, a twinkle in his eye "Well, you're the one that's trying to convince yourself that you're going mad. Might as well follow that reasoning. Bring my sword, in its wrap it should be fine and not so conspicuous."

Trying to reason myself, I thought 'fine, if it helps get rid of him then I'll play along'.

"Ok...lets go for a drink" I said reluctantly.

Unlocking the door, I scurried around, pulling out the sword still in its wrapping from out of the wardrobe where I kept it hidden. I quickly put on a jacket over the top of the sword, trying my best to conceal it but the purple wrap poked out from underneath.

"Where you going now?" asked a stunned Andrew, noticing I had picked up a jacket, ready to head out.

"Just need to go for a walk. Just a few moments to myself." I said hurryingly.

"But its still raining heavy out there!" added Sarah, who sprung to her feet ready to come with me.

"It's ok, it's just a bit of rain. I'll be fine, see you guys later." I said, making my way out of the door.

Through the rain that lashed hard against me, I wandered through the streets, the wind blowing the rain wildly down the winding streets and made it difficult to see. I was the only one in the street, the locals deciding it best to stay indoors; maybe I should've taken the hint from the locals wisdom. Not even a car moved on the emptied roads.

Turning down corners and hitting the back streets where I hoped the wind was not forcing its way down I came across an old temple. Its big red doors shut tight underneath a flowing archway at the top of a small set of steps.

Flanking either side of the doorway was a giant stone dog. These were common at certain temples and were initially a Chinese influence that came over during the time that Japan and China started trading. The purpose of these dogs acted much like the gargoyles of European churches, meant to scare away evil spirits from its sacred grounds, some were even worshipped as deities themselves by some. Through the dense rain, they looked very foreboding and scary. The great mouths of the stone beasts open slightly displaying a couple of rounded teeth.

Bowing my head in a sign of respect I continued my path through the rain. Turning a couple more corners, a light from a window beckoned me. It was a lighthouse in this dense storm and as I got closer to its brilliant light, I thanked the gods that it was a bar!

It was a small, modest place, like most bars in Japan it was not a big and spacious affair. It appeared like an Irish pub, or at least, the Japanese equivalent and understanding to an Irish pub. The bar itself being made of a deep mahogany style wood, constructed with the same trimmings and décor as that of an old bar back home. A Union Jack was stuck proud and predominant in its window and with a push of the door and a welcoming chime of a small bell above the door, I stumbled into the warm and dry surroundings of the bar.

I was there on my own, the front of the pub completely deserted of customers. Seems that not many people come out in this degree of weather, they were probably more sane that I was.

As the bell finished its chime, a door opened from behind the bar and emerging from a back room was an overly happy barman. Middle aged, he shambled over pleasantly before stopping just in front of me.

He spoke in Japanese, I didn't understand what he was saying. Yoshida spoke in my mind. "He's saying hello. Please allow me." Yoshida almost took over my speech as he returned the welcome in Japanese.

"What would you like sir?" asked the barman, picking up a glass and cleaning it with a cloth that hung from his black apron.

"Sake, please" I said, watching the eyes of the barman light up.

"Ah! Sake! Excellent choice sir! Let me get you something special." As he shambled back through to the back room, before I had chance to speak again.

Within a few moments, he returned with a small black urn shaped bottle. On its face was some Japanese script picked out in gold. The contrast of the colours make it look very impressive and it appeared to be a high quality bottle and thus, expensive.

Pulling out a tumbler glass from underneath the bar he began to pour the clear liquid into it. He continued the pour until it filled almost to the top. My eyes went back in surprise, my limited knowledge of sake expected a small cup full, not the size of a tumbler!

"This sake, very good!" said the excited barman as he placed the urn on the back end of the bar.

"How much?" I enquired.

"Say three hundred Yen" he replied, raising his hand up showing three fingers to me. I pursed my lips with surprise, three hundred Yen was very cheap and with a quick mental calculation I worked out that it was around about two pound sterling, perhaps slightly less.

With an impressed nod of my head I handed over the amount from change that I'd obtained from the poker earlier which the barman rung in a small cash till behind him.

Taking a sip, the sake tasted quite sweet, but had a little after burn that warmed the back of the throat. A small unexpected cough came from me as I was not expecting the sudden kick. The barman laughed in appreciation.

"See! Very good sake! I give you good price, you my only customer tonight"

"Yes…" I said, recovering from the initial sip "Very good sake."

The barman bowed repeatedly with short, sharp bows of his upper body before retreating to his back room once again and out of sight.

"That's better" said Yoshida, as I continued the drink. "It feels like an eternity since I experienced such delights. It truly is a good bottle."

"What is it you need to speak to me about?" I asked, wanting to get down to business and get this whole mess sorted out as quickly as possible.

"I detect from yourself that you are not happy with my returning in you." Spoke Yoshida uneasily.

"Really? You think?" I responded sarcastically, scoffing slightly. I didn't bother with my inner voice which was lucky for me as the barman was not in sight.

"I'm sorry that you are not happy with this. I think its time that I told you more about my life, tell you more about what I've done and the importance of the task that

I had to perform. The same task which I believe that you have been chosen to perform with my guidance."

He began to reel off his story, from his beginnings as a swordsman of great repute, the duel for the Shogun and the story that the Shogun's representative told him once long ago. He continued with countless stories of the demons he killed and the possible consequences that would've happened to the world if he hadn't.

All the while I just drank at the bar, to anyone looking in at me they would just see me as someone drinking in complete silence, not realising that in reality I was involved in full blown conversation. I took time contemplating his recollections with the fullest of intent. Some of them were very interesting and he had me enthralled at his tales of heroism. Fame and recognition in such a fashion is actually more enticing than it sounds and it didn't take long before such tales struck a chord with my own personal ego and dare I say it, made me want to emulate something similar.

It's similar to what you feel as a child, listening to stories of pirates, cowboys, great warriors and the like. When you hear them, you want to become them. It would've been a lie to say that I wasn't feeling the attraction to become a *hero* like this.

"...so you see, that is why it is important that my work in life carries on through you. It is the way of Japanese culture to pass on a trade through the generations, from father to son. Although we are not blood related, I believe that is the reason why I've been summoned back from the divine void by the gods. As such, I feel it right to become your mentor and guide you down the same path that I walked down." Yoshida finished his stories, I had remained silent throughout his last blast to persuade me to come round to the idea of becoming a hunter of dark creatures and he expected me to say something.

"But why me though? Why pick me for this?"

"Karma works in mysterious ways that we are not meant to understand completely. Though, there is one thing that I do know about Karma, its that it tends to reveal itself eventually to everyone. No doubt that we will find out the reason and there's a feeling within me that we will find out sooner than we think." Said Yoshida, as I was actually coming round to the idea.

"Why have you asked me to the bring the sword?" I said, realising that I had the ancient weapon propped against the bulk of the bar.

"This weapon is my old friend, an old ally, I spoke to you before that it is regarded as the *soul* of a samurai. I want you to have the same feeling and connection with this sword as I once did. This sword is one of your greatest weapons that you possess when combating the demon world. Carry this sword with you everywhere and the demons will not have the chance to catch you unarmed. With this sword and a good arm you will become unstoppable against any demon foe." Great pride emanated from Yoshida as he spoke about his sword. Its not surprising, for this was a kingly gift, presented to him for his personal skill by the Shogun himself. It made me feel obligated to continue the same level of personal worship of the sword.

"But I don't know how to use this sword in the same way as you do." I said. Yoshida laughed heartily

"Do not fret Jason-san. For when this sword is drawn in your hands, I can easily take control of your motor functions and wield it in the way that I know best. True, the way your body is built and developed is somewhat different from my own, this I feel I can adapt to easily with time."

I was glad he was feeling confident, happy that at least one of us did.

I allowed Yoshida to continue his stories of the olden days. It was mostly refreshing to hear what it was like in that time, it was after all, one of the reasons why I came to Japan. I wanted to experience the culture and how it developed. Didn't imagine it would be in such strange and unbelievable circumstances.

In the end I accepted that perhaps it was my destiny to continue this role and it was sinking in home as I drunk more. The concept of me being a 'superhero' slayer of foul beasts and monsters did sound exciting.

Eventually finishing off I bought the barman a drink before picking up the sword and setting back out into the rain. In Japan, the locals see it as almost an insult to just 'tip' them in the way that Westerners do. It is customary instead when celebrating the works of an individual in this profession and also of chefs, to buy them a drink in order to toast to their health.

The rain had not eased in the slightest, in fact, it was probably worse than it was beforehand as the wind howled down the narrow streets like a dog. Picking up the pace I needed to get back to the hotel as quickly as possible.

Turning down the little streets I retraced my steps, my hand pulling my jacket as close together as possible as I battled the elements. The wind was becoming so strong that as I turned the odd corner into the main street, it practically lifted me off my feet. I felt lucky there was no one around to see it.

Approaching down the street with the temple, I kept close to the edge of the buildings. Through the howl of the winds and the lashings of the rain I heard something else. It was a sound that seemed to be carrying itself over the surrounding sound. What was it? It was light and musical, it wasn't like the noises made by the extreme weather.

Looking around as I rushed through the streets, I expected to see perhaps an open window with the sound coming from a CD or other music player. But no, as I listened further, it was more fresh, not as dull and impure as the sound made by a recording.

Louder and louder it grew until it became apparent where it was sourced. It was hypnotic and it was coming from the front of the temple.

Chapter 21 – Shishi

In front of the temple doors there sat a man, crossed legged and seemingly uncaring about the inhospitable weather that lashed around him. In his hands was a long bamboo flute which played the harmonious noise over the deafening chaos of the blustery winds and the hard lashing rain. His face was covered by his enormous straw hat that, with his head bent forward, had the rim coming over and obscuring his face from my view.

I don't know what possessed me, but I had stopped, the rain continued to batter down upon me as I listened to this strange musical interlude.

"Something is not right." Said Yoshida, who observed through my eyes this strange scene that lay before us. I was inclined to believe him.

The music played for a few moments further and then it stopped abruptly. Now all that remained was the pounding of the rain.

"Hello Jason" said the stranger, his voice light yet said with sinister intent.

"Who are you? How do you know my name?" I shouted, making myself heard over the pounding of the rain.

"My name is not important. I know a lot about you Jason, in fact, I even know who it is that resides within you. How is old Yoshida-san? I hope his stay with you has been pleasant enough as it will not be lasting much longer. For it is I who is going to kill you and send both of your souls to the abyss. It is the Master's will."

"The Master...that cannot be" said Yoshida, shocked by this old, strange reference that was evidently recognisable to him and held some meaning that I wasn't sure of.

The stranger lifted his head, his eyes overshadowed by his straw hat. He lifted the flute again to his lips and played another light tune. As he played it his eyes glowed yellow with the light of two miniature burning suns. He continued playing and I spied the eyes of the dog statues either side of him glowing with the same bright yellow hue.

Shortly after the statues began to move with a ghostly creak, their once lifeless paws becoming filled with some otherworldly power, they lifted slowly with a ghostly crumble as the loose masonry around them fell away. Their heads did the same, rocking and swaying as they became ever more free from their previous bond. They growled eerily, feeling the first breaths of life.

"This isn't good" I said silently. "Get the sword ready Jason-san" said Yoshida as I unwrapped the sword from its cloth. Holding it and its sheath, the cloth floated on the wind to get snagged on a shop sign. My fingers circled the grip and gripped it naturally and loosely so I could draw it easily.

The demon dogs made their first steps, slamming their heavy stone paws as they moved, they had seen me and they looked hungry. As they descended the steps, it was smooth, more like a tiger stalking; growling intently.

Suddenly one of them picked up the pace and charged. Leaping with its massive bulk its mouth turned, ready to sink its gaping maw into me. With a dive of my own I dived underneath the diving demon. He sailed over me, trying to turn itself in mid air he crashed, side on, into a parked red car. It caved the side of the metallic chassis, breaking the glass in the window and buckling the metal shell effortlessly as its bulky mass hit it like a battering ram.

Rolling to a better position, the other demon dog attempted to charge me. Its intent on biting me just like that of the first. Another dive and the draw and cut of my sword caught the main bulk of its body. The sword cut into the stone, not deep enough to destroy the beast, but it sliced through the stony side of the beast nonetheless.

With a painful roar it hit the road and slid, a wounded dog. The first dog had rejoined the fray, this time it stalked close to the ground, seeing the mistake of its first charge he had opted to go toe to toe with me. A short bound he lashed out with his paws, Two sharp slices of my sword and it severed its front legs that fell and broke apart.

Dodging aside the forward momentum of the now two legged beast, I executed a final slice through its neck, decapitating the beast and causing his body to shatter as the demonic power that was instilled within him was driven from its being.

One down, one to go. But I spent too long making sure the first one was dead. Before I knew it the other one had charged me down, smashing into me with its weighty mass. He steam rolled over me and continued his charge way past me as my body was brought to roll on the ground, dragged underneath the dog momentarily.

Spitting out blood that came from one of its hefty paws cracking me in the face, I came to my feet. Using my sword as a means of helping me up. The demon dog howled victoriously before charging at me once more. This time, I left it right to the last moment, a matador against the rampaging bull. With a timed leap I jumped straight up, landing on the back of the dog as it continued its charge. It kept on going, trying to turn his head backwards and bite up at me but this was simply futile. Just as I got my balance strong I took my sword in both hands and pushed straight down in the back of the dogs neck.

As it penetrated and ground through the stone substance of the dog, it let out a painful high pitched whine that was close to ear piercing before crashing his head first into the road, stopping itself suddenly and launching me clear off its back to roll haphazardly along the road.

Now both of the beasts had fallen. It was time to face the mysterious demonic flutist.

My head whipped round sharply to see that he was still at the temple gates. Now he was standing and laughing.

"Very good Yoshida!" he shrilled joyously. "I like a challenge. I would've been disappointed if I killed you when you weren't at your best." He walked down the steps to join me at the same level on the road.

"Please, show me what skill you have boy" he said excitedly, stepping forward to meet me. His bamboo flute held in his one hand out to the one side. I accepted the challenge and made a stance of my own, sword held high.

With a quick slash I cut through him; but where I would expect to see the splash of escaping blood, it simply passed through him and his image shimmered. Like the disturbed surface of a once resting pond. He appeared again, slightly off to my side as he struck me hard across the back of the head with his flute. The sharp rack of the flute was painful and I reacted with a slash again to where he was. Again, I was met with the disappointment of him shimmering out of view.

This process repeated several times, every time that I thought I had caught him he was infuriatingly not meeting the edge or point of my razor sharp sword. Every time I missed him he had struck me with his blunt wooden instrument. He had struck my stomach, my neck, my face. Each time he hit it was worse than any punch that I had felt and white hot pain followed every one.

Argh! I thought to myself, I could feel that he had split the skin on the back of my skull and that my blood was trickling down because of it, mixing with the rain, diluting its thick and viscous nature into a reddened watery mess.

His voice rung through the air as if he was behind me. "You are pitiful Yoshida-san! Picking such a boy to be your host. He doesn't have the requirements to fit such a legendary swordsman such as yourself." I turned at the sound of his voice, slicing futile at him. He was indeed behind me and now had a bit of distance between us, my slash missing miserably. "Your poor judgement will be your down fall on this night. I will show you your errors with glee!" He cackled, charging and leaping, his flute high in the air, ready to come down upon me. I pulled back my sword and thrust to meet him, to skewer his body as he would fall upon its tip, but it went through the same mirage outline. A sharp thrust to my kidney dropped me to my knees as pain fired through me like wildfire. I let loose a scream of pain.

"Focus Jason-san" said Yoshida, trying to fill me with hope that I would escape this ordeal alive.

"Truly Jason, I am actually beginning to feel sorry for putting you through this. But your spirit is commendable! You shouldn't have come to Japan." Said the demon musician who appeared in front of me. My eyes met his burning suns.

"I will send you back to hell!" I shouted defiantly, almost spitting at him with pure hatred for him. The demon just laughed vilely, shrilling like an exciting child at the anger and pain he was inflicting upon me.

With one last final burst of rage and energy I swung my sword at him. He evaded it in the manner as he had done throughout the fight. This time however, as I was about to finish the act of the strike I spun the sword round and thrust it behind me, passing it underneath my armpit. This time, I was met with the satisfying feeling of piercing tissue and flesh.

Without even looking behind me I remained from my kneeling position. The rain belted down around us and then the rattle of the bamboo hitting the ground. With the squelch of sliced skin and organs I pulled my sword from his body and he dropped like a doll to the ground.

Standing and turning I faced him as he lay in pain on the ground. My sword had passed just underneath where his sternum would've been. He looked at me, his eyes dying from the spooky yellow that they once were to reveal two black orbs.

"I have failed my Master" he spluttered, his words stung with regret. "How could I lose to such a boy!" he spat.

"Who is your Master?" I shouted, almost barking the question at him "Tell me now and I will end your pain" as I moved the blade to touch the side of his neck.

"I will be dead soon enough samurai! You will meet the Master soon, he is looking forward to meeting an old acquaintance such as you." The demon cackled wickedly as he addressed Yoshida, sporadically coughing with the pain it was causing his lungs.

Then the demon passed, his eyes remained open wide with pain. Slowly his body began to blow away piece by piece as his flesh and substance turned to grey stricken ash. The wind carried his essence and scattered him, the flute being the only remaining presence of the demon's very existence as it rocked itself in the wind; that and the blood that remained on the edge of my blade. The wild winds blew over the holes in the instrument causing it to sing the odd weak note; the only musical sound that signalled the demon's passing.

"Now do you see why we must do what the gods have intended us to do. We cannot stand by and let beasts like him roam free on this earth. Mankind will not be at peace for we are the only ones left on this world that possess the weapons needed to send him and his evil kind back to their beastly world. Are you ready to take hold of the gods responsibility that they have sent you?" said Yoshida, quietly hoping for a positive answer from me. The task itself and the importance of completing the task dawned upon me and in a quick realisation, I understood what was required of me. The fact that I was made a target, the fact that this strange demon knew my name and knew about Yoshida enforced this importance. There was no way of being able to simply slip away from this.

"Yes Yoshida, I understand and I accept the task given to me" I spoke with dignity and providence, knowing that this news will please Yoshida and that it did.

"Excellent Jason-san. I am proud that the gods have chosen you to be my host." He replied and this lifted my spirits.

Moving to regain the cloth wrap for my sword, I wondered what the demon meant by the 'Master' and why Yoshida was so shocked to hear him being talked about once more. "Who is this 'Master' that the demon spoke of?"

Yoshida went silent, it seems that this was a bit of a touchy subject.

"The Master is the head of the demon household on Earth. When I was alive, we were plagued by the Master's demonic minions. In the end we tracked him down and killed him. But he is dead, I made sure of it!"

"Perhaps you didn't kill him?" I offered. I didn't want him to misconceive the question as him being incompetent.

"No...I'm sure of it" he replied. "Though, if the demons are stirring as much as I think they are, then something is not right. There is one source we can see to find out what is happening..." he paused, "...We need to see Genki."

On returning to the hotel, Andrew was who was left in the room, Sarah had left to go do other things shortly after I left for my outing. I was completely soaked through and water dripped from my clothing with every step I took.

"Oh my god! You're soaked!" exclaimed Andrew, inspecting my drowned rat state.

"Yeah, its slightly wet out there" I attempted to joke, as Andrew's face changed as he inspected the blood that was also dripping down my face, diluted with the intense rainfall.

"You're...bleeding. What the hell happened to you!?"

"Oh…wind blew me off my feet. Banged my head off a curb, it's ok, I'm alright." Hopefully, this would throw him off any more questions he would badger me with. After the night I had experienced, I didn't need persistent questions. Even if he did ask many questions, I don't think he would be able to receive my answers without thinking I was crazy. It would probably be best if he didn't ask, for his sake more than mine.

Placing the sword carefully away into the wardrobe out of sight I retreated to the bathroom where I stripped out of my wet clothes and padded myself down. The blood being highlighted against the bright yellow towels.

"What time did Sarah leave?" I asked through the door of the bathroom, still doing my best to change the subject at hand.

"Shortly after you left mate." He replied "She's a bit worried about you mate, you've been a bit distant recently." His voice was hinted with worry. I imagine he too was also concerned about me.

I needed to try and instil some confidence so he would back off "I'm fine, trust me! Just in a different country, taking in all the culture around me. I'm a bloke, cant do more than one thing at a time" I joked, continuing to dry myself roughly.

Andrew went quiet as I stayed in the bathroom to make myself more presentable. Then all of a sudden he erupted out with a amazed horror.

"Hey! What's this?...What on earth!" he cried out. As soon as he said it, I knew what the source of his outburst was and quickly burst out of the bathroom.

Horrified, Andrew held before him the sword. His eyes locked with it's deadly beauty as the scabbard lay on the bed. Tiny specks of the demons blood still splattered upon its surface.

"Let go of that" I shouted, rushing over to him and snatching it from his grip. Picking up the scabbard I returned the blade to rest within it.

"There…there was blood on it!" stammered Andrew, shaking his hand as he pointed to the sword.

"That is not your concern…I cant tell you more, you wouldn't believe me if I did." I said, wrapping the sword back up.

Andrew stood motionless, he wasn't sure on how to be, he was very much lost for words.

"Andrew, listen to me." I grabbed him by the arms, he shrieked as if afraid of me, that saddened me slightly that he would react that way around me but it was one way he could react. "How long have you known me? Listen to me. I haven't done anything bad. What you saw on the blade was not *someone's* blood. I cant tell you more, if I could, I would. You've got to promise me that you wont say anything about what you saw."

Andrew was white, stuttering. "Promise me!" I shouted, forcing him to comply and answer me.

"O…Ok…I…Promise" he said, I released my hold on him and he managed to relax himself a little bit as he shook some of the tension out that had riddled him.

"Good. Now, tomorrow, the storm would've passed, I have got to go somewhere so I wont be around for the trip. Now, you've got to cover for me, make up some excuse why I cant go, say I'm ill or something. Can I rely on you for that?"

"Yes…I'll say you had what I had." He said, still shaking in disbelief.

"Good. I knew I can count on you." I said somewhat relieved, looking him in the eye with a soft welcoming stare. Andrew tried his best to return the same but it was still quite hard for him to come to grips with seeing a blood stained sword in my possession.

"Where are you going?" he asked sheepishly. "What if Coach comes and checks up to see how you are? What am I going to say?"

"I cant say where I've got to go, I would really love to tell you but it's actually best that you don't know…for…your safety." I took time to pick my words to say; after managing to lower the tempo of the subject I didn't want to make Andrew return to the scared, overly excitable state that he was in earlier. "If Coach comes and checks up when you get back, just make up some stuff that I've probably gone out or something to get some air. Or something like that, I'm sure you can think of something."

I placed a reassuring hand on his shoulder. Placing the sword underneath my bed, somewhere where I could have easy access to it. Now I was a target for the demon's, I didn't want to stay around my friends, for I did not want them to get targeted also because of me.

Chapter 22 – Genki

"**W**e wont require much for the climb" said Yoshida as I took a moment to stare up at the foreboding journey ahead of us. All I had on my personal possession at this moment in time was a simple small bag with a few provisions, enough for a couple of light meals and the sword, wrapped in its purple cloth with golden geometric circular designs, secured closed at both ends.

This was where climbers had gone missing over the years, the large hill with its stretch of woodlands along the hillside made the landscape picturesque and hid the fact that it held something evil upon its surface. Myself and Yoshida knew the reason of the disappearances, but we were unable to go to the police for fear of being laughed at. Genki. He was also a valuable piece of the unfolding puzzle and soon we will know more of the reason behind the return of the demons.

"That's fine, lets begin, the quicker we get this done, the further forward we are to ending the whole mess. Where about is Genki's domain?" I asked silently, it was such a blessing now knowing the method to talk silently to Yoshida, as I mastered the technique of being able to keep my personal thoughts personal yet able to communicate with him without having to speak out loud. The embarrassment of this was starting to take its toll and it attracted too much attention to me.

"He is up on the North face of the hillside. Do not worry, I remember the way. Be on your guard Jason-san, for Genki is mischievous and cunning. Let your guard down at least once, and it may be the last time you ever do." Yoshida was stern, although he has faced Genki before. He knew the perils that came with demons and was not going to allow me to make any mistakes that would jeopardise our quest.

A tug on my shoulder attracted my attention as I had suddenly before me an old Japanese merchant. His hunched back and wispy beard was like something out of a film, very stereotypical. With him he had an arm full of straw jingasa. With a smile of broken and missing discoloured teeth he pointed to the hill top before us;

"Hello there! Are you thinking of travelling up the hill? Care to buy a hat? Keep the sun off your face, very cooling!" the merchant spoke with a quirky but croaked beat.

"Yes, I am thinking of going up the hill. How much for a jingasa?"

"Ah! You know jingasa! Very good! For you sir, I offer for five thousand yen. Cheapest and best hand made jingasa around."

Fumbling around in my pockets I produced the handful of change equal to his asking price. Presenting to

341

the merchant who was now wide eyed and excited at the prospect of a sale. It seems that business has been slow for him recently.

"Thank you! Thank you! Be careful up there young sir."

"And why is that?" I asked.

"That hill, cursed it is! Many people disappear when they go there. Hopefully sir, when you go up there, you come back down, yes?" his bouncy tone quickened as I handed the money over to him. Receiving my newly bought jingasa I placed it on my head, tightening the thick cotton cord underneath my chin. It felt snug and true enough blocked out the harsh rays of the sun off my face with its wide circular rim.

"Ah! Yes sir! It looks very good on you. Thank you, thank you, have a safe journey!"

"Thank you" I replied politely and turned to start the ascent.

The scenery was breath taking on the climb, or rather, more of a gentle hike as the slope of the hill was not as treacherous or as steep as it appeared to be from its base. Yoshida was guiding me along a natural path that ran up and snaked through the forest surroundings. It was amazing that the path remained the same and recognisable for him after so many years. The trees swayed naturally, their leaves intertwining and letting through little pockets of light that illuminated the colours of the leaves and other foliage of the forest floor. Birds chirped and cicadas chanted, it would've been a walk that would've carried more of a special liking if it wasn't for the fact that I knew the reason why I was here in the first place; and the creature that I was here to see.

Up and up we travelled, the conversation between me and Yoshida was minimal, as I was sure he was enjoying the views as well. I broke the silence between us by asking the question.

"Can you tell me more about Genki?"

"Of course Jason-san. Perhaps I should've said more before. What is it you would like to know?"

"Well, how did you meet him in the first place? And just whatever you can about him."

Yoshida paused, gathering his thoughts together before proceeding with his story.

"Genki is a creature which you as a foreigner might know more as a troll or goblin; an ugly and foul little beast. I first met him through the same reason how I know he still exists today. He has an insatiable appetite for human flesh and from his hobble he would entice and kill travellers on the road up the hillside…"

I interrupted "How is it that he is able to entice people to him then? If he is obviously something as horrible as a troll?"

"…You see, he has the been blessed with the ability to transform his image so he appears to be like a man. He often turns himself into an old hermit and appears to the not knowing, harmless enough. Though do not be fooled, for when he is his goblin form, his mouth can open wide and swallow a man whole in one bite. That is why there is no trace of the walkers who go missing."

"If there is no trace, then how is it that he was found out the first time?" a valid question, I thought.

"Well, long ago, he was unfortunate enough to have one of his victims escape. They gave him a nasty facial scar with a knife that they had hidden on their possession, before making good their escape. At the time I was staying in the village that was at the foot of the hillside. The same one that we just came from in fact, though you must realise its very different from when I was last here. The locals made me aware of the incident and the local magistrate ordered me to go kill him."

"Why is it that you let him go?"

"You see, it was him who told me of my own destiny. Foretold me as a legendary slayer of demons with the sword that I was presented with by the Shogun. He told me the way to kill the most terrible of beasts, even the likes of a Dai-Oni. Perhaps he should've been slain by my hand the first time round, as is the will of the Shogun and for the good of mankind. But when my sword was above him, ready to deliver the final death blow. He pleaded for his life and for some unknown reason I allowed the pitiful creature to live, something within me made me grant him mercy. It was against my oath to the Shogun that I stayed my hand and allowed the vile little creature to live. With my sword poised at his neck he swore to stop the killing and eating of men. It seems that five hundred years later, he has decided that its now time to break his promise."

With a further understanding for Yoshida's compassion, I silently applauded him. Though perhaps it could've been conceived as pure naivety on his part that he let him go, for who can really trust a demon to keep their word. Maybe there was some other reason why Genki has returned to the feasting of human flesh after so long.

"We must leave the road now Jason-san and go into the forest, we are not far from Genki's hobble, if indeed he still resides there and night will soon to be upon us" Yoshida spoke with a small urgency in his voice. True enough the twilight of night was approaching and before it would become too dark to see, we must reach Genki.

Turning off the road, quickening my step from Yoshida's sudden tone of urgency we pressed on through the thick of the forest. Pushing aside bush and branch, weaving through the trees we made good time. The light was fading fast and when I thought we would have to stop and rest for the night, the smoke and smell of a wood burning fire entered my senses. Finally we stumbled across Genki's home.

Before us lay a small cottage like structure, made in the old fashion of wood and paper windows, most of the small square compartments of the windows had holes in the paper slats. It was not the quaintest of places, in fact it was more run down than anything. Outside, a man scurried around, back bent with age, fumbling with pieces of firewood that were stacked neatly in a pile at the side of the house,

"That's Genki" spoke Yoshida.

Taking a cautious step forward, I winced at the sound of a twig snapping loudly underfoot. There goes the element of surprise. The man turned his head sharply at the sudden noise.

"Who...who goes there?" his voice was broken and strained harshly as he spoke.

"I'm sorry to have startled you" I called out "I think I have lost my way, do you know a way off the hillside?" deciding that now I wasn't able to use surprise it was probably best to employ a more subtle approach.

"Yes...I do traveller. But night will soon be upon us and this hill can be pretty dangerous when night time is here. You never know what might happen, you might trip or fall in the darkness and if you do yourself injury it wouldn't be pleasant trying to continue down the hillside. Please, wont you come inside. There's soup being made on the fire and you can rest here until morning." Good, I thought, he has taken the bait.

Now that Genki was showing a little trust, or was believing he was enticing an easy meal I walked boldly towards the house. Genki walked in first and as I followed him he ushered me over to a small pillow to sit upon. The room was very small, everything was self contained in this little hobble; on one side there was a small stove and true enough, a pot was boiling away; the smell of its gloopy, soupy contents wafted pleasantly in the air. On the other side was a small roll mat bed and a tiny mahogany bedside cabinet.

"My name is Fukihawa. What is yours?" asked the man, wandering over to the pot with a strained shuffle like an old cripple to check on the status of its contents.

"My name is Jason."

"It's a pleasure to meet you Jason. You must be tired from your walking. Please rest and have some soup with me, it will warm you right up and give to strength for when you are back on your way." Fukihawa spoke so pleasantly, it was easy to see how so many were trapped by him before with his honey like tones. Luckily for me I knew who and what he was beforehand.

"Nice to have some company these days, I don't get much chance to see people regularly. Many don't climb this hill anymore." He turned back to the contents of the pot and stirred it gently with a spoon so it wouldn't bubble over. So as not to be connected with all the niceties that were being shown it was time to play Genki's hand.

"I've heard from some of the locals that there's stories of a Genki killing all the travellers that come up here." This I said slowly, judging Genki's response. Genki paused over the pot at the sound of his true name. Stunned almost, that someone of foreign shores would know of Genki, before returning to stirring the soup so that it wouldn't boil over. Peeking over to the pot, the broth steamed invitingly, as Genki stirred, the vegetables bobbed and swam in it. There was also something else in there, red meats that flowed with the vegetables, completing the soup. My stomach dropped as it dawned on me that the delicious looking meats in the soup were probably not originally beef or pork.

Slowly and as silently as I could I undid the top fastening of the sword wrapping ready to show it at a moments notice. Genki let loose a chuckle.

"A Genki you say? This is merely a fairy story told to children." He chuckled again, "After all, this has been my home all my life. Surely by now if this Genki was here, I would've either seen it or worse! Been eaten by it! You don't believe in fairy stories do you young man?"

"Perhaps you haven't been seen or eaten by it, because *you* are the Genki" I responded confidently. Looking to draw him out of his false façade as I did not wish to carry on the charade much longer. There were more important matters at hand and I couldn't be left here for too long, carrying on this monster's little game.

I could, through his clothing, see the muscles in his back tightening up. The colour of his skin was slowly changing. He was transforming into his true form. His identity now exposed.

"Jason..." he spoke slowly and bitterly, "...Unfortunately, I am now forced to not give you any food or shelter for the night, for what happens next I am truly sorry for I..." Quickly he spun and prepared to pounce upon me as he revealed what he really was. But stopped with horror in his tracks as he turned to find the edge of my sword had already greeted him close to his neck. The feral eyes soon turned sour as he realised that he was the one who was trapped.

"Do you not remember this sword Genki? Please take your time in looking, I believe you were familiar with it once before" Genki looked on in horror, eyes flickering up and down the sword before narrowing as he became more suspicious. From his flared nostrils, Genki sniffed and sniffed again. A somewhat familiar scent had hit his nose and it was obvious that he was attempting to place it.

"That smell…where have I?…" dropping his face in complete surprise he became increasingly aware to my own unique identity.

"No…it cant be! Is that *you* Yoshida, you son of a diseased whore!" Inspecting me he became enlightened to the fact. "YES! Yes it is you! I know that rancid smell of honesty and integrity anywhere. But how can this be? After so long?…Ha! You have been brought back from the spirit world." His eyes sparkled almost gleefully. "The gods have you reincarnated in this…boy. A foreigner to say the least, how shameful for you! How truly shameful. The gods do have their warped sense of humour after all" he cackled loud, frustrating me further as he continued to blatantly insult me.

"That will do Genki!" I spat, fire building up inside me. "Sit down!" I commanded, forcing him down to the ground.

"What do you want from me Yoshida?" growled Genki with annoyance.

"Information." I said bluntly, no hint of niceties in my voice "I'm sure you are still a reliable source for that. It's in your nature to know everything that goes on in both worlds. There has been an intense increase in demon activity of late. As you can see, I have come back from the dead at this time. You yourself haven't been completely quiet, hence the reason why I'm here now. I require answers from you."

"Ah! I see. There's me thinking it's because you missed old Genki." He cackled mischievously "The greater powers do have their mysterious ways. Let me tell you a little story...Now if you please." He coughed, indicating and highlighting my blade that was still precariously close to his neck. With reluctance I lowered the tip so that the edge of it rested more sociable upon my lap.

"That's better" he said "Now...Let's begin on why the demon world has been becoming more...*active* as you put it..." he paused, shifting himself back into his human form.

"Go on" I pressed, not interested in his theatrics or his incessant need to turn into the storyteller.

"Impatient, I see! Well, the talk amongst my people is that the demons have been preparing for the arrival of the Dai Oni Wanshu...I'm sure you remember him Yoshida." With a twisted chuckle Genki looked me in the eye.

"Wanshu! That cannot be, I killed him and imprisoned his remains deep within Shokiji shrine on Koya Mountain where he came from the first time he set foot on this earth."

"So naïve samurai! You cannot just fully *destroy* a demon of such power and magnitude as Wanshu. His energies are far too much for anything in this world to diminish like the end of a simple candle. He has been waiting Yoshida, waiting for over five hundred years for his followers to conduct the ritual of awakening and bring him back into this world. And right now they are so close to performing it!

They have discovered the tools to bring him back. If he is able to return, the world will change into a hellish nightmare as demons will be brought forth en masse as the fabric of reality will wither and disappear between worlds. Mountains will crumble, the seas will become red with the blood of the living and boil like an unholy cauldron as the worlds of demon and man merge into one. Mankind and all other creatures will cease to be. This world will become nothing more than a deathly shell, unrecognisable from what it is now."

"Tools? What tools are these?" I asked

"In order to bring demon blood of his strength into this world you have to first give it life. So the Dai Oni needs a sacrifice, but not just anyone will suffice; you see that's the catch, there is one who will be unwillingly an energy storage of major proportions. The mythical *'Light of the Gods'* as it is called among my kind. Although they do not know it, they will not be able to see the energy they possess, in fact they will probably feel like normal. They will however be able to experience the connection with the demon world; they will see it both with their eyes and in their dreams. The demon world will haunt this person and they will be powerless to stop it. They will not be able to explain rationally what's happening to them and may resort to reasoning with it through comparisons to simple madness.

The host will carry with them also a special mark that signifies the light that burns unknowingly inside them. Word has it, my kind know who it is they seek and it is

351

only a matter of time until they will have her in their possession."

"Her?" I interjected, "This 'power conduit' is female." Then a sickening thought struck me, it was as if I had been hit by the means of enlightenment. So awful the thought that guilt hit me for not taking it into account sooner.

"Momoko!" I cried. How kind yet how cruel is karma making her the one to bring forth the next apocalypse. The girl who I cared for, perhaps even loved. The irony is so cruel and twisted. She was right under my nose this entire time, she was prime to be able to be put under my protection. Damn my stupidity!

"Ah yes! That's it! Momoko! Is it not fate that both you and her have crossed paths at this time. But that is not all that is required for this ritual. Her blood is the key yes, but, it needs a conductor to bring forth and flow the power it contains so that her energies can fill and awaken the Dai Oni." Genki looked like he was enjoying this little story telling. It was obvious that he could see in my eyes that I was hurting at the fact that Momoko was involved with this mess. It made sense, looking back, the Kappa had signalled her out of the pack of people when they assaulted the Budokan, separating her from the rest of the flock like a stray sheep. They *knew* even then that she was the one they needed. Genki continued;

"The conductor of energies is a weapon. A blade of hidden power, forged with the blood of an Oni and in ancient dragon's fire. It is a blade that contains the pure essence of ancient evil constrained by means long forgotten within its silvery edge. Even I don't know what this blade is…and that is the truth Yoshida! Though I can tell you that without it, they are not able to bring back Wanshu. I cant even tell you if they have the blade yet. Always remember that they require both tools in order to set free the Dai Oni and bring forth the destruction of man and the end of their rule in this domain."

"Is there anything else Genki? Anything that you can tell me that can help me? Is there a way to destroy or banish the demon if it is awakened?"

"There's nothing else that I can say, Yoshida. You've banished him before, I'm sure you of all people can do it again! That sword did a pretty good job of dispatching him last time you two faced one another. Though, if he is awakened by the Ritual then I don't know if it will have the same effect. He will become far more powerful than the last time he walked freely. Now…for this information that I have gracefully shared with you, please be generous enough to turn a blind eye to my recent 'straying' when it comes to satisfying my hunger." Standing, I returned the blade swiftly back at Genki's neck causing his eyes to widen horrifically as he feared for his life.

"If you are lying to me Genki, I will promise you that when I return whether it is now or in another five hundred years; I will take your head!"

"We will see samurai! We will see!" cackled Genki again, turning back to his soup.

Turning and barging out of the door, returning my sword to its sheath there was just the one thought on my mind; 'Momoko'. With haste I needed to get back to see her, at least then I can protect her. I can stop the Dai Oni from awakening and the world can remain safe. I wouldn't be able to live with myself if they already have taken her.

Running into the night, dodging skilfully through the trees, partly lit by the silvery light of the moon. Occasionally, a low branch would strike me in the face and I would curse it whenever it did but pushed on regardless. As I ran, the forest opened up swiftly as I entered a clearing. Stopping in its centre, breathing heavily as adrenaline rushed through me. This was not here before; was I going the wrong way?

Within the canopy of the trees surrounding me came the sharp whooshing sound of the sudden movement of the masses of leaves and the sudden movement of the branches. Then another one behind me, and another! Grabbing my sword and removing it from its sheath I steadied myself.

We are not alone, or so it seems…

Chapter 23 – Ambush of the Tengu

The whooshing sounds of the bustling leaves continued a few more times before through the shadows I spied a dark mass, almost camouflaged by the low light conditions of the night drop down to the floor. Two more shapeless dark masses dropped to join the first one in different places around me. It seemed that I was surrounded.

The masses stood up. From what I could see through the dimly lit night they were human. The way they moved, weight low as if stalking, would identify them as agents of the night; ninja. I had definitely seen way too many ninja films in my lifetime to stop me thinking they could be anything else.

"I am Yoshida Kintaro, swordsman of Imamoto dojo of Kakugawa. Step forth agents of the night and meet me in combat." My challenge rang out loudly in the night sky, allowing Yoshida to display himself as a warrior to the world once more. The warrior in front stepped forward, leaving the edge of the clearing and entering into the open space. His companions did the same. In the moonlight, their features were picked out delicately. They were not human.

It's face was that of an ugly crow's, oversized as was befitting the man-like proportions of its body, with a long viscous looking beak that was a sleek black as the night itself. It's eyes set to the sides like a birds, a deep yellow, like two orbs of bright morning sun. Even in the dark night time these orbs were visible, it was as if they lit themselves up in an attempt to instil fear within me. Jutting out from the black owagi worn body; instead of arms, there were wings, ashen grey-black feathers fanned out ending in a set of bird like hands containing long stick like fingers, nimbly holding sinister darts that were thin with a sharpened point.

"Tengu" said Yoshida. "We must be careful Jason-san, these creatures are dark agents of the demon world. They are like the ninja and follow similar sets of martial arts and methods of assassination, legend tells that it is the Tengu that taught the first ninja their deadly craft. The darts they carry are no doubt coated in some form of poison. If one of those cuts you deep, the wound would result in your imminent death and there is no chance of us getting any form of antidote in time."

Such comforting words, I thought sarcastically, watching the darts keenly with eagle eyes. The bird men poised, raising the dart high above their head and with lightning speed threw the darts at me. Dart after Dart whistled in the air as they flew towards me. Ducking, diving, swaying my body I dodged the aerial missiles that were launched most of which ended up striking trunks of trees or slowed by the leaves of bushes and other foliage. For those that were timed so that I could not move out the way they were dealt with effortlessly by being plucked out of the air by my sword creating a triumphant metallic clang as metal clashed with metal, dart against sword.

The Tengu leapt high in the air, gliding effortlessly with its long spanning wings. With a high piercing squawk it dived towards me, twisting in the air it drove itself in an attempt to crash into me. At the last moment, from gripping hard into the earth I did a dive of my own avoiding the diving birdman who landing with a precise roll before returning to its feet.

Turning to face him once more, I pointed the tip of my blade towards its throat. He stood before me, in the time it took for him to roll and stand he had drawn from a pocket unseen, a length of chain; the length of an arm and at its ends were octagonal shaped weights. A manriki-kusari, a weapon employed by the ninja because of its ease of being concealed and carried stealthily within clothing. Its weighted ends when used had the ability to crack open skulls and break bones with a surprising ease.

Twirling the chain in circular and figure eight patterns in front of him, swishing the air, the Tengu rocked himself forward and backwards. His weight shifting fluidly making it harder to judge the correct distance between him and me; more importantly, the distance between the sinister ends of his weapon and my skull.

Pulling back with my blade, readying to strike I stood poised trying my best to get into the rhythm of the Tengu's swings.

Now! I thought, as I swung my sword to cleave him straight down the middle. The Tengu swung the chain as I moved, striking the blade of my sword and shifting its line of attack off to the side, taking my balance with this unforeseen intervention to my strike. In one smooth motion he swung again; narrowly missing my head as the weight whistled past me and brushing my cheek with the wind that the weight produced. He returned to a fighting posture. He missed; that was a sure finishing blow! It seems that the Tengu wishes to have some fun first, he is merely toying with me.

Pushing myself away it dawned on me that my otherworldly opponent was highly skilled. This would not be so easy.

Striking again, this time in a horizontal arc, the Tengu jumped back, somersaulting effortlessly over my sword. Again and again I struck each attempt to kill him ended futilely as he was always just out of reach either moving or by use of his chain weapon. Then just as I thought I was about to end the miserable creatures life my sword was stopped still in its tracks. Instead of cutting through birdman it had hit the chain full on. In a blink of an eye, the Tengu had wrapped the chain around it and with a kick against my hands he disarmed me, casting aside the sword. It clattered and rustled the leaves that littered the ground and I shook my fingers as they were painful from the kick itself.

What do I do now? Do I run? No, that would be foolish! They would kill me quickly before I'd even reach the edge of the clearing. Watching the Tengu in front of me he walked over to my sword. Flicking it with his foot he lifted it up into the air, kicking it towards me allowing me to catch it easily and I was armed once more. It squawked loudly again with a series of cries; I guess it still intends to play. This time it will be the last time, either for him or for me.

Swinging the chain rhythmically once more it returned to its previous rocking and swaying. Now I knew what to do, I needed to disarm it, remove from it its weapons which he has had so much time to master. Steeling myself and with all my might I targeted the chain as it circled rhythmically. Hitting it as it swung in the air and with bright sparks the chain snapped into two sending the stray weighted end flying harmlessly away out of my sight. The Tengu watched it break away with complete disbelief, its beak opening slightly with sheer surprise.

By the time it returned its attention towards me it was too late for him. With a martial yell I had darted forward, slashing deeply, severing through the Tengu's neck. It dropped to its knees and as the body fell forward so too did its head as it tumbled away from the rest of him. Blood squirted like a fountain from the open vein in his neck.

The silence that followed hung for a mere agonising moment before the two Tengu that accompanied the fallen one at my feet burst out into action. Seeing that one of their own had been slain before their very eyes, especially as I believe that this one was perhaps the leader of the flock and thus the strongest and most deadly amongst them; they erupted into a hideously painful symphony of bird like noise. The sound was not unlike a choir of frightened songbirds who have been startled by a hungry predator.

Without hesitation they flew up into the trees and disappeared from both sight and hearing. Silence resumed, once I was happy that the Tengu had gone I relaxed. It was now safe and I returned my sword to its sheath.

'Momoko!' the purpose of my haste returned to me, I needed desperately to get back to her as I ran through the night. The only hope that was running through my mind was that I was not too late...

Chapter 24 – Rescue

D ashing from the train station to the hotel, my head was filled with the sheer dread of failing Momoko. If I was too late and thus she was kidnapped or worse, I would never be able to forgive myself. Darting through and past pedestrians there was no time to stop and to apologise, lives were at stake and the fate of the world.

Panting hard, I pressed onwards, my body was screaming at me in pain from all the running. I realised I had not stopped apart from the time that I had spent upon the train back to Himeji. Each minute upon the reliable transport was agonising, the thought of waiting like a thousand knives pressing into my skin. With the panic and sheer determination to return to Momoko's side it was hard to hide my thoughts and intentions from Yoshida.

"Please, Jason, you must calm yourself. If you are not centred with yourself then you will perish later and all will be lost."

Yoshida's constant attempt to calm me down was irritating and to me was more counter productive.

"Stop with the incessant worrying! It is not helping!" I snapped angrily, silencing Yoshida as I scrunched my face with anger. This did however help to numb the pain that was coursing through my legs.

Soon we will be back at the hotel, hopefully Momoko will still be there. Perhaps I was there in time.

Turning the corner, banging harshly into some poor pedestrian who was sent flying to the ground. The force of the impact almost knocked my sword and its covering out of my hand, luckily my grasp held steady and I did not have to waste time in sorting it out. Waving his fist he shouted angrily with curses as he struggled to get back on his feet. He was not my concern.

Scanning the scene, a heavy feeling fell on my heart. I was too late! Ambulances and police officers littered the scene, sectioning off the area with rolls of bright orange warning tape. The occupants of the hotel were arrayed themselves outside the front of the hotel. Some were wrapped up in towels, others were being attended to by the medical services. All of them however were locked with shock, screaming and moaning or wandering aimlessly to and fro in a desperate attempt to understand what had happened. It was like the aftermath of a bomb blast.

The one side of the hotel building itself had a massive hole blasted out of the side. There were no burn marks but the entire windows of a particular room had been blown away and shards of glass blanketed the street below. '1…2…3…' I counted the floors, the feeling I had sunk to a greater low as the revelation hit me. Momoko's floor. Momoko's room.

Rushing over to the crowd that had gathered I saw coach, white faced, sat on the edge of the pavement, a bright yellow blanket wrapped around him. He was still and statue like.

"Coach...what happened?...Where's Momoko?" still panicking, hoping to feel relieved by spying Momoko in the crowd but my heart said that she was not here.

"Jas...Jason...Where have you been?" Coach fluttered. He looked up at me with dead eyes.

"No time to explain Coach. Where's Momoko?" I was near to screaming at him. I was in no position to try and understand what he'd probably been through, nor did I care as there were more important matters at hand.

"Beasts...creatures came." Coach managed to say "Not like those at the Budokan. These were different, they were like giant birds. But man like" Coach stared down at the floor. Reminiscing on the terrible events. Damn Tengu got here before me!

"What did these beasts do?" I asked, trying to calm my voice so that Coach was able to speak freely in his shocked state.

"They stormed through the hotel, they killed some of those who tried to stop them." As he signalled to a lifeless body further down the hallway, a dart protruding from its chest. "I got knocked down in the corridor as they passed through. They knew where they were going. Straight for the Jap girl. That girl you like. They took her. Blasting away the windows and flying away. All you could hear was the screaming from that poor girl."

"How long ago were they here?" I asked, realising that there might still be a slim sliver of hope and a chance to catch them.

"About twenty minutes ago. But that's not all." Said Coach.

"What? What is it?" I asked, desperately seeking this piece of information.

"The bird men, they weren't alone."

I stared deep into the man's eyes with intent "Who was with them? Please tell me" I asked

"With them was a man. A Japanese man, but it was like he was not a man. His eyes glowed red as if they were on fire...In fact, they were on fire! I remember when I stared into them, for a split moment they burned. Tiny flames inside his eyes. It was horrible. It was a vision that will never leave me." Coach began to rock as the shock kicked in again. "One of the hotel staff went to grab him but he flung him through the lobby with the simple wave of his hand. He hardly touched him! But like a doll he flew as if made of paper." He continued rocking. "It wasn't...natural!"

This was an interesting development. A man? Who was this mystery man? Could it be that this man has something to do with all that had happened. I knew that soon this man will be revealed and it will become apparent his connection with this affair.

I noticed that some of the other competitors had spotted me and were staring, chattering amongst themselves in hushed tongues. I realised that to them my actions recently would be interpreted as being strange and peculiar but to have told them what was actually going on would probably result in them not believing anyways. It was best to make my exit as quickly and as quietly as possible.

"What shall we do Yoshida?" I asked, silently in my head.

"The demons have acquired the sacrifice, I only pray that they do not have the weapon they require to complete the ritual..."

"Do not speak of Momoko that way!" I snapped. Insulted by the total disregard he had in regards to Momoko as a person. She was, to our knowledge not confirmed dead and she had acquired a special place within me. She was not just a 'sacrifice' she was a human being and someone who I realised I cared for very much despite the fact that I barely knew her. It was one of those gut instinctual emotions you get.

"I am sorry Jason, I have the unfortunate habit of being too blunt. It is the warrior way within me. Sometimes I forget that in the manner of life and death, we have slightly different view points. But we still must not forget the matter at hand. We must realise that the demons are close to achieving their goal and I must stress to you the grave consequences that will occur to this world if they succeed."

Yoshida's word spoke truth, if the demon's did succeed then the end of the world as we knew it would be certain.

"It is I Yoshida, who should be sorry. Please forgive me for snapping at you so rudely. I am trying my best to not let myself become overwhelmed with emotions that could result in us failing."

"Do not be sorry Jason. All is fine. But we must be quick. The advantage that the demon's have over us is that we are blind to the knowledge of how close they are to their goal and to how long they have before it is completed." Yoshida carried urgency in his voice.

"Where will they take her Yoshida?" I asked

"To the place where it all began. Koya Mountain. To the temple close to its peak where I once slain the demon and entombed his body within. There are a few things that we must discuss before continuing Jason...."

"But time is not on our side. What is it that we need to discuss?" I said, the severity of our situation hit me fully.

"We need to discuss the enemy that we are about to face and in regards to Momoko herself"

"Well?" I asked

"The demon, 'Oni' is his species, he is one of the strongest of his kind. His body is strong and like iron against regularly forged swords. His eyes spark with the purest of evil and his claws are as sharp and as deadly as any katana that has been forged, even the bristly mane of its hair can lacerate the skin. You must be careful if we face him Jason. It was against this very same horror that I almost lost my life, it was my regret that Fujibayashi lost his. It is a pain of which even five hundred years could not lift and leave me with everlasting peace.

For it was my fault that he perished as I was too slow to react and kill the beast. I was...scared by the beast in front of me and such froze with fear, giving him the chance to kill my student, my friend. Only the anger and realisation of Fujibayashi dying did it drive me to act.

Because of his death, I believe is the reason as well as my original connection with the demon world is why I came back in you. It is the higher powers will to allow me to avenge his death again and by saving your woman, I can redeem my honour and put to rest my shame of allowing Fujibayashi to die.

However, if you can cut him with the Emperor Dragon, you will be able to kill him. I am sure of it. This sword is a very special sword, as you have seen, it has the ability to kill those creatures of the other world.

Be warned however, that not just any cut can kill him. You must either kill the black heart of the beast of sever its hideous head from the rest of its body. Only this will diminish the foul beasts light. To believe that a cut across its organs or a strike upon his arm will rupture its essence is foolhardy and will result in your death. This demon can withstand and survive a cut that could kill both man or the lesser of its kind.

Also, we need to also take into account the worst case scenario…If the demons have the sword *and* Momoko and they are able to complete the ritual before we arrive to stop it. That would mean that she has already been sacrificed. I can feel in your heart how connected you are with her. Try to avoid vexation taking over your heart and do not let it consume you like it did with me; remember you have tried your best to save her and if that has not been possible, then that is karma. Which is one thing we cannot change no matter how hard we try.

Use the sword with skill and with honour and it will serve your purpose well."

Although I found the story of Yoshida's initial encounter with Wanshu enlightening it was also reverent in how he let loose his feelings and shame on the matter that he considered to be a failure on his part. Something which I have noticed he was not one to do on a regular basis. It was humbling that he was able to release his feelings on me and it was also nerve-wracking when I considered that he was once scared by the beast. If he was scared then I'd hate to think what I would be like!

"Don't worry Yoshida, I wont fail you" I said, confidently.

"No Jason, we will not fail each other. I will do everything in my power for you to save Momoko and not experience the pain that I felt." Yoshida's words were comforting, it was if we were finally bonding as two warriors should. It filled me with hope, for I knew that together we will not fail.

"Where is Koya mountain?" I asked, returning to the haste to save Momoko.

"It is south of Osaka, in Koyasan" He answered. "It is not far. I believe if we take the intercity train, we will reach it quickly and hopefully intercept those damned Tengu. If the gods are on our side that is"

Yet another train journey. As soon as this is all over, or should I say if I survive this, I am looking forward to avoiding the trains as much as possible!

It seems that we were unable to beat the Tengu. Koya Mountain was not the peaceful vision of Japanese beauty it once was. From the once unbearable heat from the blasting sun up in the cloudless skies, now it had become dark, the skies blackened over the mountain with sinisterly foreboding clouds that spat dangerous forks of lightning that struck the ground with deep cracks of sound.

The streets have all stopped. Busy roads came to a halt as cars stood still with their drivers outside their vehicles staring wide mouthed at the maelstrom clouds that only covered the mountain.

Pedestrians talked and spoke in loud tones of muddled worry and intrigue. It was obvious that this sort of phenomenon didn't occur on a regular basis. Some pointed up at the mountain and from this distance, you could just pick out the temple where we needed to go. So small it was that if you didn't know it was there, you would simply miss it.

Pushing through the crowds, Using my hidden sword, still wrapped in its rich purple cloth, to separate groups in front of me as I made my way on foot to the mountain. Bystanders peered at me with inquisitive eyes as I was the only moving fish in a motionless sea of people.

Onwards I moved, trying my best to pick up the pace to pass those who had no intention of going anywhere. My efforts were thwarted as the closer I got to the mountain, the greater the volume of people that had gathered to watch the spectacle that was unfolding.

It was frustrating! If only these goggle eyed innocents knew the haste that I was in and the seriousness of my quest to get up that bloody mountain.

The dark clouds continue to speak doom and gloom on the mountain, the crackling lightning became more frequent and the boom of thunder, heaven's own artillery, was almost deafening. The air was rife with fear. Such a strange reaction human beings have when it comes to the frightening or the ominous of death. You would think that the smart mind will run away, in an effort of self preservation, to save oneself but no. Most would rather stand and observe their doom as it comes towards them not in an show of defiance but rather like the rabbit that stands frozen in the headlights of its death by the speeding car.

The road that leads to the path that runs to the heart of the temple was the busiest of all. A massed crowd was standing here, gathered and formed held back by a steady line of police. How quickly they had gathered to stem the crowds. You have to admire the efficiency of the Japanese in all manners of life.

Dressed in a mix of riot gear and regular beat dress they formed an almost impenetrable line as they stood steadfast, batons drawn and at the ready in case the mob tried to break through them.

The crowd ebbed forward but the police line acted like a rock and the wave just broke effortlessly upon it, one or two that got too close felt a sharp blow to their thighs and the batons that the police carried had the ability to drop them to the ground. These silly few then quickly crawled away so that they didn't feel any further moments of pain.

"Did you see those giant birds?" said one bystander to another as they engaged in conversation I was lucky enough to be within earshot and picked it out over the surrounding noise. Perhaps it were fate that meant that I had the opportunity to hear it.

"They flew up to the mountain and it wasn't long after that the clouds formed and all this madness started." He continued. "They were carrying someone, a girl I think, her screams were what caught my attention in the first place."

"A girl?" asked the other man "Nah, no bird could carry something that heavy" he shrugged off.

"No! I'm serious!" said the first man, almost offended that he wasn't believed. "They were as big as a man. I've never seen such a bird before. And it *was* a girl! It was hard to see from down here, but I wouldn't put her as any older as sixteen perhaps."

The second man added "Have you been on the sake today? You're speaking some crazy talk, you sure you're not drunk?"

"How long ago did you see her?" I barked, joining in their conversation in a desperate attempt to get some information.

"Oh…" said the man, shocked at my intervention. "I'd say it was probably more than an hour ago perhaps?" he offered. "Do you believe in what I'm saying?" he asked, hoping that I would give him some validity or belief.

"Yes...damned Tengu" I said, "How do I get up the mountain?"

"Tengu!" cried the second man. "Ha! Only the foreigners believe in your fairy stories! And Tengu!" the second man continued to laugh at the annoyance of the first. "If you want to get up that mountain the only path is up ahead, but you've got no chance of getting past the police. They have the entire area sectioned off. There's no way up and if you want to try and ask to get through be my guest! It'll be the most painful thing you ever ask for! Japanese police don't take any lip from foreigners, especially when they are all equipped for a riot."

"Thank you." I said, as I pushed through the crowd.

"Tengu! Ha!" came the exaggerated laughter of the second man as I walked away, the conversation drowning out of earshot.

After several minutes of pushing and shoving, to the dislike of several of the locals who looked at me in disgust as I moved through them; I managed to reach the front of the line. In front of me, behind barriers and other road blocks stood an army of police officers. Before me were the ones in the riot gear; covered in thick, plated body armour armed with a nasty looking baton with a small metal blob at its end. Black and sleek, I've seen before the concussive damage one of these extendable pieces of devastation can do when it strikes.

In his other hand was a large see through shield, made of a hardened reinforced plastic compound it had the ability to deflect and withstand some powerful blows. My road was blocked and I didn't want to shed innocent blood to reach my goal. It is seen as very bad karma to do so.

"Please let me past" I called.

"No sir, I cannot do that, now stay back" said the officer, lifting his hands and pushing away in an indication to move back from the barrier.

"I cannot do that. I need to get up to the temple!" I said, pointing up at the source of the trouble.

"Now's not the time to go up there and pray boy. Find some other temple to pray at. Move away!" he replied, his voice becoming ever more commanding. Now he shifted to adopt a more aggressive and threatening stance. The officers either side of him were now made aware of what was happening and looked over at me. They were ready to back up their fellow colleague at a moments notice.

"I need to get up that mountain! My friend is up there and something is going to happen that only I can prevent. You must let me pass! You are an innocent in all of this, I do not wish to harm an innocent to get there but I will if it means stopping a great evil occurring." I couldn't stress to him enough my need to pass.

"Back off!" he shouted as he reached for his baton. His companions now adopting similar stances and turning more aggressive towards me. This was not going to end well. If there was any other way I could sneak up the mountain I would but this was my path and the road was blocked.

Suddenly, there came a thunderous roar. One that echoed and reverberated loudly in the air and through the valley. It was not the roar of thunder, nor was it the roar of a mighty cannon; it was one more bloodcurdling and terrifying. It was a bestial roar, made by a mighty beast of great power. Such was this roar that the doom it created would ice over the hearts of most mighty warriors.

People around me flinched at such a sudden and horrific sound, panic began to spread like wildfire through the flock. Even the officer in front of me stopped and turned, his eyes were gripped with the fear it created. Where did it come from? From the temple at the top of the mountain. Please let the gods say I was not too late. Had the ritual been completed?

A moment of nothingness passed before from the mountain came another sound. A collection of animalistic snarls and high pitched chattering. It was the sound made by a multitude of creatures and from the sound it was clear that there were many.

From the path they swarmed, kappa, but not like those of the Budokan. These were lesser creatures, smaller and more nimble than the lumbering beasts before; like a subspecies. There faces had a long dog like snout, but no fur covered their bodies save for their backs where it was thick and matted like a great clump of hair. Their skin was a deep brown, leathery and tanned, their flesh covered in deep wrinkles like the hands of a gardener. Some of them carried in their clawed hands small rudimentary clubs, fashioned from wood or bone and although they were simple they would still be effective if wielded correctly.

They bounded and leapt and ran as they charged forwards towards the human mass before them. The crowd turning and running at the sight of the stampeding horde. Screaming loudly as they attempted to escape the demon pack that was coming for them. The sudden charge of the crowd had body after body falling and getting trampled as those behind them stepped and stamped on them. There was no doubt in my mind there would be several fatalities today from the crowd themselves alone. It could be that they were the lucky ones. For there was a fear that worse was to come.

Some of the heavily armed officers fired rounds into the swarm. The loud crack of the firearms sounding in the air. The squelch of the bullets hitting the beasts, penetrating their thick hides and sending torrents of blood spraying wildly. But it was not enough to stop them and they continued running.

The speed that they travelled at resulted in them covering the distance with ease and within what seemed like merely a heartbeat they were upon the police line. The officers battled with the beasts but they were too many and soon the was breaking.

Officers were pulled to the ground and swamped over by the pack of kappa. The screams of the fallen rang out as the Kappa clubbed them and feasted upon them. Biting and gnawing at their prey.

Time to get involved I thought as I pulled out the sword from its wrap. Tucking the sheath inside a basic belt that I had fastened from the wrap I charged into the turmoil.

Slashing and cutting, the sounds of the Kappa's death cries brayed out as they got cut down by my mighty blade. Swathing through the demon mass, leaving a bloody path in my wake I made my way through the demonic. It was as though I became a demon myself, the blood splattering against my clothes, staining it with its foulness. Soon the element of fear turned as the majority of the Kappa were made aware of my presence.

As I severed the head of the one, sending its lifeless skull into the air, one of the Kappa made a series of high pitched barking and squeaking noises. It was the command to retreat to the mountain and with a unified sweep they turned and retreated to its base. The motion was similar to a flock of starlings turning acrobatically in the air to change direction to avoid a predator, so perfect as if it had been rehearsed.

They moved, clearing the hundred metres or so until they reached the path and the surrounding high ground. Once they had reached this safe haven they reformed. Waving clubs and growling angrily, they became like an angry war like mob, an army insulting and enticing their opponents to meet them. Something I was happy to do.

On my side of the battlefield, the officers that were still alive went to help those in need. The injured lay groaning, blood poured from bite wounds, scratches and weapon wounds from the Neanderthal like clubs they faced. Those who were dead were left as the survivors turned attention to those that needed it.

Placing my sword out to the side, with a quick flick of the wrist, blood was sent splashing off its deadly surface to hit the ground with a splat. Defiantly I walked tall and made my way to the bustling army that presented itself. More blood was to be spilled today.

Closer and closer I got towards the swarm. When I reached close to the edge of the beastial pack, two of the more braver monsters charged headlong toward me. With two sweeps of my sword I severed the one in half and decapitated the other. Their bodies dropped to the ground, twitching violently with a death spasm. Leaving the twitching corpses and continuing my advance, more and more came at me but they died painfully by my sword before getting anywhere near to dangerously close.

Then suddenly they rushed towards me, deadly arcs did make my sword, cutting down body after body with every step I took. Carnage followed but at its centre was myself, creating a deadly dance with my age old sword; never retreating nor losing ground to the horde of demons.

One managed to jump on my back, trying to bite into my neck with grisly teeth. Using my sword arm to fight off those around me, my other slammed palm first into its face, breaking teeth and knocking the foul creature of my back and freeing me up once more.

Then there came a break, an opportunity, as one of my deadly cuts took out two of the monstrosities that were in front, making a gap in front of me. With a leap and a somersault I cleared out of the swamping pack. Now all the beasts were behind me, clambering over the dead they came at me again, almost undeterred that so many of their number had died by my hand. Such was their ferocity, I needed to become the same to overcome it, if not greater so. It was tiring and I was feeling the pressure build.

"Keep going!" said Yoshida, spurring me on to continue at the same pace. "you cannot give up Jason. We are too close to preventing disaster. Do not let these minions of the dark deter us from that goal. Think of Momoko. We must save her!" That was all that needed to be said, as soon as he finished those words did I became filled with a newfound determination. The motivation was near intoxicating. Yelling loudly I continued the chaos. So loud and terrifying was the yell that the Kappa in front of me were stunned, the last feeling they felt before they were killed by my blade.

Slashing my deadly dance with the encroaching horde, Kappa were dropping dead all around me, body parts, hands, legs, heads were severed and scattered all around my bloody path. More got killed as they continued their advance, a blood lust frenzy was all that they had to keep them going. One or two of them would get the odd attack through but it would be nothing more than a mere scratch that would prove to be nothing more than superficial. There were no serious cuts on my body but so many of them fell senselessly under my sword when all they had to do was flee to save their miserable lives. Were it not for the will of their evil master, I believe that their natural instincts for survival would kick in and they would flee without hesitation.

Then came another cry from one of the horde. Their numbers were now dwindled to a minimum and it was clear that they were unable to overcome me. With a scared series of calls they scattered, breaking away from the fight and disappearing into the surroundings. Until all that was left was me and the broken bodies of the Kappa.

Onwards to the temple. Onwards to save Momoko and the world as we know it.

Chapter 25 – Daku

A t the top of Koya mountain in Koyasan actually lies a small temple complex. The Okunoin temple is the birthplace of the Shingon sect of Buddhism and surrounding it lies Japan's largest and still active graveyard. It is here that the founder of this particular sect of Buddhism, the Kobo Daishi, is also buried. Such a spiritual place should not have been desecrated by the unholy demons and the fact that this is the case makes it most unfortunate. Although I was not a Buddhist, I did feel compelled to doing my best to eradicate the infliction that this special place was under.

However, it is not the Okunoin temple that was to be our focus, it was in the form of a small off shoot temple that is set into the mountainside. Although this stray temple is separate to the main Okunoin temple and was difficult to know whether or not it was older than the Okunoin, I would still have to traverse the vast expanse of the graveyard in order to reach it. This did not bode well with me, not simply because of the 'spookiness' factor that a graveyard naturally presents but the fact that the graveyard would be full of graves of different sizes and shapes that would be fairly packed together. If I was on the demon's side, I would definitely pick this spot as the perfect starting point for an ambush. The sea of graves provided the perfect cover for the ambushers to sneak around me and hide behind, the narrow pathways that would be there would help bottleneck me and limit my manoeuvrability. If I wasn't careful then maybe my body will become the next resident of this place. I gulped at the morbid thought that this produced.

I knew that some of the earlier kappa were still alive, but also there was a gut feeling that bit at me like the dull edge of a knife that there would be far worse horrors haunting and lurking in the grounds of the ancient graveyard.

Composing myself from the combat with the kappa, I approached the edge of the vast expanse of graves, the entrance jutting forth from the perimeter wall that was hiding most of what was to come beyond. There was no gate, as such, to this mighty entrance but there was a wooden arch that framed the way in.

The path that led into and through this entrance was a dull grey with lightly coloured cobblestone and as I began to approach, despite the wind and the thunder booming around me; an eerie mist descended onto the graveyard, as if it were by magic, making it more difficult to see the way. Was this part of the demon's doing? To try and hinder me with my advance.

Ever closer I got to the entrance way and my eye caught sight of something on the archway. The ever enclosing mist made it difficult to pick out what it was from a distance. Was it a bird? An eagle or a very large owl perhaps? Its size would indicate so.

But when it became close enough to distinguish, it was not a bird. More so, almost resembling a small bear, no larger than a child. It's body, disproportioned to the rest of his limbs, was covered in a thick and matted, brown fur. It's hairless pointed ears pinned right back as it levelled its equally pointy snout in my direction so that its large bulbous eyes could focus and stare at me as I made my way steadily towards it.

Instinctively, I reached for my sword, expecting worse to follow. As I did so, it raised one of its paws passively as if it were wishing to not allow things to escalate.

"Please! Please! There is no need for your sword young warrior!" it squeaked, the little goblin-bear's voice a high pitched, excited chatter. Much like how a hyena sounds when it laughs. "My name is Daku, the Otoroshi. I am guardian and caretaker for this holy place. I mean you no harm. No harm at all."

"Otoroshi?" I asked silently to Yoshida, hoping that he would be able to shed some light as to what this creature was and more importantly, if it was telling the truth and whether or not it could be trusted. If so, then it might be able to help guide me through the labyrinth of graves to where I needed to go.

"Yes Jason-san. Otoroshi are the mythical caretakers to the graves and the grounds of temples. This creature does resemble the description of such creatures and are said to be peaceful. They care more for the maintenance of the spiritual grounds that they reside in and do not hold any means for a effective offence. Though they are rarely seen by humans, I know I have never seen one." Said Yoshida.

The little creature ran its tiny paw over its head, brushing over its matted fur "So *you* are the young warrior sent to kill the evil one." It cackled "Let me take a quick look at you. Hmm, you carry the master sword of the ancient dragons. Very respectable. Yes, yes. You must be that warrior. You are the champion of man chosen by the gods themselves. In all their infinite wisdom...I must admit, they have interesting tastes." Its unique pitching tone was hard to read to see if there were any subtle undertones present.

"I am" I replied confidently, my head held high to the world, now I had accepted that this was my path that I was born to follow. All events in my life had directed me to arrive here at this very moment. Though the road ahead is far from foresight, it was just more footsteps along the same path.

"I see, I see! Be careful young warrior. For there is much *evil* buried within this mountain. Much evil indeed! And not just within the graves themselves. Mankind has been made quite unawares of its presence here as it lay in deep slumber. I fear they may know of it soon enough! Would be such a shame for this world to end. No more temples to attend to." He grinned wickedly. It made me doubt whether or not the Otoroshi was actually non threatening and if he was actually supporting my cause here.

"Ritual almost done. Very bad! The awakening of the Master has meant the spirits of the dead are no longer at peace. No, no. They have been disturbed from their slumber too by evil magic. Their peace disturbed. Such shame. They need to return to rest again."

The way that Daku was speaking, could it be that the demon has already been awakened? Is that what this little ugly bear was implying? If so, that would mean that Momoko would already be dead! Was I too late for her? Such thoughts and ideas were troubling. It was hard to shake them from my head, Yoshida was always trying to tell me to keep my mind clear and these thoughts could ultimately cost me my life. I would have no chance at all to help Momoko if I was dead. But it's harder than you think to just detach yourself from thought and emotion like Yoshida was able to do.

From the entrance to the graveyard, the air picked up the sounds of whispered voices. Unearthly moans and worried whispers that were practically indistinguishable as they amalgamated together, they wafted through the air. I could feel the hairs on my neck stand on end at the thought of the source of these ghostly whispers.

"He knows you are coming." Said Daku, his voice now more stern and sincere. "Him and his many dark followers. The dark one knows who you are! He is waiting, yes, waiting for you to meet him. Be careful though, for he wishes to play, he wishes to *test* you to see if you are worthy enough to face him once more. He has one of his most evil followers waiting for you."

"Is it the spirits of the dead that I should be worried about?" I asked, hoping for some further intelligence before progressing any further. Demons were one thing to combat, but how do you kill that which is already dead and has no physical substance to slice through with an ancient sword?

Daku laughed, ear piercingly high "Ah no! Not the dead, the dead should not trouble you here. Show respect to them and they should not hinder your path. All that are buried here are good people. Good people indeed. Once great warriors, priests, Lords of the past. They all reside here peacefully in my graveyard. I have seen them all come here. Many, many years I have spent taking care of these grounds. No, I think that there is something else that lurks in the mist. Very bad. Very bad indeed." Not exactly the words that I wanted to hear.

"Do you know what it is? Have you seen it?" I asked.

"Oh, that I don't know young warrior. All I know is that the spirits of this place are uneasy with its presence. There is an unholy fire that accompanies this dark creature. It is evil! Evil like the master! You must take great care young warrior. Or you may end up as one of my charges; denizen of my graveyard." Daku's eyes opened with terror, as if he himself has seen this creature and the very thought of it is harrowing to think of.

I bowed my head in respect of the knowledge that I have just received "Thank you Daku, that is most helpful."

He waddled across the archway, before bounding down onto the ground from the great height. He was like a little spring with his tiny hops, a bounding rabbit. "Go now, young warrior. Bring my patrons back to their eternal slumber. Yes, yes. I will see you soon. Good feeling I get from you, you will be glorious today."

With that he hopped out of sight and as I entered the archway and peered my head over to see where the little strange bear had gone to; he had vanished completely out of sight. He had become invisible and blended into the surroundings. Yoshida was right when he said that these little creatures were rarely seen. I can only imagine that they will only be seen if and when they wish you to see.

Thanking my fortune for meeting Daku I pressed forwards. Hand on sword, ready to draw against whatever evil creature that Daku had warned me about.

Chapter 26 - Abura-bō

Slowly I walked across the grey, cold cobblestones of the graveyard path. Flanking me on both sides were endless rows of gravestones. Each one was more different that it's neighbouring stones and I was made to walk in a constant state of alertness. The mist had come down quite heavy and it meant that I could only see about three or four rows deep into the sea of graves.

The only sounds that could be heard by my ears was the jumbled mess of voices that I had heard from the entrance. Even the boom of the thunder had stopped as soon as I entered. It was as if the graveyard itself was sealed in a soundproof bubble and that the outside noise did not effect this place. To say that it was spooky would be a complete understatement and the standing hairs on my neck were soon joined with the goose bumps on my arms as they all collaborated together to tell me that this was a very bad idea!

Yoshida broke the ambient noise around us "I think we are not alone." He said softly, his tone of voice adding

387

to the spookiness and not helping my nerves in the slightest.

"I agree Yoshida" I replied, scanning my eyes to the mist around us.

From out of the haze came the grey-blue silhouettes of what looked like people. Men, women, children, slowly they drifted towards me. They were the ghosts of the denizens of this graveyard, just like what Daku had told us. As ghosts they indeed had no substance; their details and contours of their bodies picked out simply as a bluish tinge, becoming quite translucent. Their mouths laid open as if gawping, only moving slightly as they tried their hardest to open and close properly but no sounds of substance was able to be produced. They were all dressed differently, most as simple peasantry. Though amongst the crowd of spirits there was the odd one or two that were dressed as armoured warriors, some were even dressed in the typical robes of a monk and those that were in this profession carried a suitable alms bowl in the one hand.

The voices became louder and louder as they glided at us. "What do I do now?" I hurried, not knowing how to handle this situation.

"I don't know" replied Yoshida "I have never faced Shiryō before!"

"It should be ok. Daku said that they will not harm us." I offered weakly, praying that the little bear was right.

The one ghost screamed like a banshee as it got close, flying itself towards and through me. I reacted by drawing my sword and cutting through the ghostly apparition. But my cut passed through the spectre as if it wasn't there at all, and true enough it wasn't. As futile as cutting through smoke.

When it flew through me, my body was hit with an icy cold shiver. It was as though the warmth and life had been temporarily stripped from my body. Possibly the most unpleasant and chilling experience that I have ever encountered before.

More and more of them became almost excitable, they flew wildly around me. They circled and passed through me. Every time one of them did so, I was hit by the terrible chill that followed in their wake. Each time was instilling an ever expanding feel of despair that was beginning to consume my thoughts. I needed to get out of this and soon.

Thinking back to Daku's advice, I remembered 'show the dead respect and they will not hinder your path.' It sparked a brainwave and I was quick to sheath my sword once more.

"What are you doing?" asked Yoshida. He did not feel complete in this sort of situation without his weapon in my hand.

I spoke calmly in reply "Trust me Yoshida. I have an idea. It is exactly what Daku told us to do."

Remembering back to the protocol in the temple that I had to do on our first night in Japan; I raised my hands in front of me and clapped three times sharply. Each clap echoed out as my palms came together and on the third clap I bowed my head.

Keeping my head bowed I spoke clear as crystal with reverence "I am sorry if I have disturbed you. Please let me pass so that I can rid you of the presence that has awakened you from your peacefully slumber."

Moments after saying my intentions to the Shiryō, the collection of voices faded out, the volume of the collective noise dying out to just simple whispers and taking a further moment to be sure it was safe to continue; I raised my head once more.

"Very good Jason-san! It's working" Came Yoshida. His voice raised with admiration for my educated, quick thinking.

The Shiryō slowly vanished and they had all disappeared bar one. In front of me stood the spirit of a monk, judging by his flowing robes that he wore. His bluish appearance resonated brighter and purer than those that had surrounded me. In his one hand was an alms bowl as was the customary apparel of the priesthood and in his other was a long staff with empty bells that dangled at the top of it.

His pleasant gaze looked into my own living eyes and he raised his staff hand up and bowed his head. Then he vanished from sight, fading out as if he had never been there.

"I believe we have been blessed from beyond the grave Jason-san" came a humbled Yoshida. Honoured by the blessing from the Shiryō of the deceased monk. It was pleasing to receive.

"Do you think that it was from the Kobo Daishi?" I asked, an eagerness to know who our blessing was from.

"I do not know Jason-san. But judging by his robes, he was a monk of high stature and regard. Except the blessing with both pride and humility Jason-san and do not dwell upon it for long, for we must press on with our quest to destroy the Master."

We had continued our on edge walk through the graveyard, the whispering was still emanating in the air as the ghosts still resided and the mist was still thick and hindered our sight significantly. More so than I would've liked and this put me further on edge. Yoshida was guiding my way along the path. We had to take a northerly route along the path and cut off down towards the West. Once reaching this point, the natural contours of the mountain would take us round to where we would find Wanshu's temple.

I cursed the mist that the Master no doubt placed to slowing us down. If it wasn't there, the time it would take for us to make this journey would've been cut down drastically and would buy us more time to rescue Momoko. I also cursed the Master for sending one of his dark minions to ambush us in this ghostly mist. It was not the best conditions for a fair fight to take place and it favoured the ambushing demon. Whatever it was.

"It's a bit quiet." I said "Apart from the Shiryō, I mean."

Yoshida hummed in acknowledgment "Yes Jason-san, it is quiet. Perhaps too quiet. I would've expected the demon that was sent for us to present itself by now." I scanned around, but everything appeared to be safe. "Do not allow it to lull into a false sense of security Jason-san. That is precisely the strategy that it is intending for us, as soon as we relax and forget it is out there that will be the time it will strike and we will be at a disadvantage. Remember, be on your guard at all times." Yoshida's words were serious and I nodded my head as they made perfect sense.

"I will not allow the demon to better me Yoshida." I offered weakly.

Still we continued our journey and still there was no sign of this hidden demon in the mist. The fact that it had not made itself known by any means was more irritating than anything else as I would prefer to face it quickly and get it over and done it. I was close to giving up all expectations of a demon actually waiting for us here.

"Perhaps Daku was wrong? Or misinformed? After all, the little creature did come across a little...strange. Maybe whatever is waiting for us has simply gone, or is maybe in a different part of the graveyard on the other side of the mountain? That's right, it might've thought we were going to arrive at a different entrance." It was a fair hypothesis, I thought. Maybe it was hoping we would take a different route through the graveyard. In that sense we had outsmarted the demon and we were in fact safe and now being overly cautious. By continuing at this pace we would more likely result in the demon conducting a search and eventually finding us that way when we could simply slip past him altogether.

I could feel the unimpressed look of Yoshida in my mind "Do not get complacent Jason-san! Have focus and do not give in to the temptations that the demon is trying to produce. Remember the demons are just as much cunning as they are dangerous. Keep your mind on the moment, for both our sakes and that of Momoko-san!"

I was forced to scorn myself for my lack of judgement and understood that Yoshida spoke from true battlefield experience and wisdom.

"You are right Yoshida-san. I am sorry for my lack of focus."

Ahead of us, through the dense and rolling mist came a shining reddish yellow light. Similar to that of a searchlight it haloed through the mist. I stopped to observe it, the warming haze grew bigger and bigger.

"What's tha…" My question was cut short as Yoshida screamed at me. "TAKE COVER!"

I dived quickly behind the nearest tombstone as an intense ball of flame shot passed me, crashing down some distance behind me on the cobblestone leaving a trail of burning and singeing debris of fallen leaves and sporadic foliage. Grabbing the handle of my sword I emerged from my hasty protection. Two more balls of flame flew at me and I dodged and swerved my body as they missed me by mere inches. The sheer heat of the flaming missiles scorched the air and I could feel how hot they were as they narrowly missed my cheeks. To be hit full on by one of this flaming missiles would result in my fatality of barbequed proportions.

Advancing forward, sword ready to be drawn, another light broke through the haze of the mist. It was larger than the previous balls of flame and as it flew towards me it laughed maniacally with a deep and sinister cackling. It was a giant ball of flame and inside it I could make out the image of what appeared to be a monk, blackened within the orb of fire.

It was flying towards me with great speed and again I was forced to dive for cover as the laughing, burning mass raced past me.

"What is that!" I shouted to Yoshida.

"That is the Abura-bō!" he shouted in response

"The what?!" I exclaimed

"It is the burning image of a once evil monk who's hate and spite for man while he was alive defies the Gods themselves in death and returns to earth as this fiery image so it can carry on hating. He now resides with the demons cause and has become one of their servants, allowing him to continue with the infliction of suffering on mankind! He was a twisted individual in life and now in death he continues to defile everything that is pure and good."

Returning to the path with confident strides, I turned to see that my enemy the Abura-bō had turned to face me once more. The monk within the inferno laughed heartily again. The very sound filled with the deepest malice that could be found hidden in the human soul.

"How do we destroy it?" I asked

"No one has been able to destroy the Abura-bō before." A sentiment from Yoshida that didn't exactly fill me with confidence "But it is believed that with one of the Eight Dragons. If we are able to pierce its black heart, we will be able to banish it!" Yoshida was uncertain, that was clear, but it was clear to see that this was the only thing we could rely on at this moment in time.

Sitting into a position ready for a quick dash I said "Ok Yoshida. Let's do this." With a yell I charged forward towards the hysterical monster. As I got within ten or so metres of him he narrowed his eyes at me and chanted in a strange language.

The amber glow around him switched to a sickly green as the edge of the flame burst forth, expanding in size like a balloon being blown up, seething over me with a blast of super hot air. The heat and pressure was more than I could stand and I was driven back into a retreat before I fell to this incredible heat wave.

"Argh!" I cursed, as the heat of the air had heated up the handle of the Emperor Dragon and burnt the palm of my hand slightly. "What are we going to do Yoshida? I cant get near him!"

"There has to be a way!" Said Yoshida, contemplating hard on the puzzle that was presented before us.

A barrage of multiple flaming missiles came forth to engulf us. Back peddling, spinning, turning, ducking and diving I avoided each of them. A single direct hit from any of them would've fried me instantly, leaving a charred corpse alone in this silent graveyard. The latest addition to its ever expanding collection of lifeless citizens.

It was hard to think on the move with so many fireballs coming at me, but in a slight break in the bombardment so the monster could advance on me I managed to say "I just cant get near him! If only we had a bow and arrow or something that could fire some sort of missile at him? We could attack him at distance!"

Yoshida exclaimed in revelation. An idea had come to him, inspired by what I had said, I only hoped it was a good one "I know what to do Jason. Please, trust me, allow me complete control of your body. We cannot allow this to go wrong. We only have *one* chance at this."

This worried me slightly. The complete and outright pressure that's put on you every time someone says the dreaded words 'we only have one chance.' The 'do or die' concept that was quite appropriate and held more meaning at a time like this.

"What are you going to do?" I asked sceptically

"I am going to turn the Emperor Dragon into our bow and arrow." His response sounded completely absurd! What on earth was he thinking!

"You what?!" I exclaimed, losing sense of decorum for a moment.

"Trust me Jason-san. Please be calm and give me control." With reluctance I switched off control of my functions from my own consciousness and handed the reigns over to Yoshida.

He turned my body so that I was partially side on to the demon. My legs were in a cross legged stance and allowed me to drop my weight lower than usual. The shift in weight loaded my leg muscles for whatever purpose that Yoshida had in mind and with a relaxed grace he raised the Emperor Dragon to a horizontal position to rest behind my head. With that, we waited motionless as if a statue. His focus was paramount and there was nothing that could distract him; we couldn't afford for him to be distracted even by the slightest of margins.

The Abura-bō continued with his relentless madman laugh and seeing the opportunity to storm over what appeared to be a sitting duck he raised himself up in the air so that his body hung suspended in the air about a foot from the ground by some unnatural means and he began to glide at me.

I could feel the heat steadily increasing with every spot of ground that the demon covered. It continued to rise, the demon getting nearer and nearer. Parts of my skin and clothing were beginning to singe with the heat. The tips of my ears and nose being the worst as they were the most sensitive. The air around us was hazy with the heat, 'What was Yoshida waiting for?' I said silently. If the Abura-bō got too close I would soon be burnt alive and reduced to a charred cadaver that was incinerated beyond recognition.

The demon screamed a joyous battle cry as he thought the end of my existence was at hand. Just as I thought that I was going to collapse from the burning heat my body exploded with action. Yoshida gripped and then pushed with my feet. Pushing from the ground he spun my body in a circular fashion, my arm swung out into an arc and at the perfect moment, released its grip on the Emperor Dragon. The swords own circular momentum took over from my own and it had powered my body into a complete circle.

The sword spun in the air with grace, cutting the air with a deep swoosh sound as it spun again and again at the Abura-bō. As it got closer, the edge of the blade could be seen to be heating up to a brightly coloured display of warm and vibrant reds and oranges. The Abura-bō's face changed dramatically, a horrified gaze as it realised what was happening. But all too late. Before, it had chance to alter its course out of the flight path of the incoming sword, it hit true. The sword penetrating its chest and plucking him helplessly out of the air as the invisible strings that held him aloft were suddenly cut.

He screamed as the flaming field around him extinguished in an instant and he landed with a skid on the cobble path. His blackened charred body halted and he clung desperately to the blade as it stick up from his chest. In his last moments he tried to pull out the ancient sword from him but to no avail, strength draining rapidly from its being, as he soon uttered his final, dying breath. Its head rocked back and his blackened mouth opened to expose irregular and equally blackened teeth.

With the Abura-bō now dead I was able to approach his remains and retrieve my sword. The first touch was a wary one and the handle was still quite hot. With a rip of my one sleeve I wrapped my palm to offer some buffering between my palm and the hot sword and on the second time, managed to pull it free.

"Thank you Yoshida." I said "That was a stroke of genius! Where did you learn that?"

Remembering an old story between himself and his pupil Fujibayashi, he replied heartily "Toda short sword style, secret technique." He paused before continuing "Sometimes even the master can learn from his pupil.

That technique we can thank Fujibayashi-san. May his soul rest in peace. Now we have a job to do!"

Pacing through the rest of the way through the graveyard to the forgotten shrine, we still advanced with caution. There was still no telling how many creatures or dangerous, mythical demons the Master had waiting for us here. There was no telling whether or not they would be as dangerous as the Abura-bō that we had faced; for we were actually lucky to have escaped the near fatal encounter practically intact, save for some slight singe and burn marks. If it hadn't have been for Yoshida's quick thinking on the puzzle we had, we would have surely perished and our quest would've been lost.

It shows the true meaning of knowledge and wisdom and how experience from those who have walked the path before is a valuable asset that should not be underestimated or overlooked. Yoshida in a sense was now my 'Sensei' which although commonly thought of to mean 'teacher' actually literally translates as 'one who has gone before'. His experience would come in handy again before this day is out.

My heart lifted as the exit of the deathly sea of stones finally came into sight. This was only for a quick glimpse as when I stepped through the archway that signalled the end of the graveyard we were confronted with the doom and gloom of the rapturous claps of thunder and the roaring wind that swept over the top of the mountain in complete contrast to the eerie silence of the graveyard.

The end of the journey was in sight

Chapter 27 – Disturbing Revelations

The wind howled violently, sending my hair flicking effortlessly under its formless power. Lightning continued to strike the ground around me. One bolt had struck a dried tree, its energies setting it easily on fire and sending up billows of blackened smoke that engulfed the entire tree in mere moments.

"We will be there soon Jason" said Yoshida, "This was how it was like before"

"You didn't tell me much about the first time this happened. It might help"

From within me, I heard Yoshida sigh disconcertingly as he was made to recall the first time.

"It was long ago, when myself and Fujibayashi was on the road fighting the demonic forces that plagued our land. At this time we had encountered many different monsters and fought them all. However, throughout the path we travelled, we both encountered references to a

'Master'. The identity of this was not a man but a beast, the leading representative of the demons on Earth."

"Wanshu." I interrupted,

"Through much interrogation with some captured and wounded beasts we tracked him down to his lair, which was here in Koya Mountain.

We were young and confident in our abilities that we went in to hunt the demon full on. With us we had two of the eight dragon swords, we were fully equipped to deal with any monster that we would've faced. Or so we thought.

The locals told of a creature that came down in the village in the night and took away hapless victims as they slept or wandered lonely the streets at night. They told of a disused temple up on the mountain top and they had stories that would frighten children and keep travellers away from investigation. They even said of foolish ronin who they would pay to rid the town of the beast. But all those who went up the mountain, never came back.

This once peaceful and spiritual place that was built upon Wanshu's lair had been defiled, for within the mountain itself, slept the demon and something unknown all that long ago woke him. Now they try to awaken him again."

Yoshida sounded as though his spirit was heavy. "We gave ourselves the quest to rid this world of this monster and so we came to the temple. As we entered, all around were the remains of its previous victims. Blood was everywhere. But these were scenes that we had encountered before in countless caves and forest groves by other monsters so it wasn't a sight that fazed us."

The temple, was it the same one as the one I saw in my dream when I first came to Japan? I asked myself.

"Then we entered its cave, its inner sanctum. The beast was unlike any that we had faced before. Its size and its ferocity was unmatchable. It was then..." Yoshida's voice fell heavy. "It was then that...that Fujibayashi..."

"It's alright Yoshida, I understand."

He continued "Then I killed him for what he had done. We fought long and hard, he had slashed me with his giant claws, causing me great pain but I drove my blade through its miserable heart. I burnt and buried the remains in its lair, sealing the entrance and carrying Fujibayashi back down the mountainside. We must not let him stir again, it was difficult enough for two Dragon Swords to subdue him last time. With only one, I fear the best way for victory is to ensure we kill whoever it is that is trying to wake him."

Cresting the top of the steps that led from the mountain route to the temple, we approached the edge of the temple grounds. My eyes widened in shock at what I saw. It was the same as the one from my dream. How can this be?

It was exactly how it was in my dream, the tiniest details were the same. From the broken entrance of the giant entrance and the holes in the windows to the feeling of loneliness and dread that came with it.

Yoshida warned me "Be on your guard Jason-san. We are about to go into the belly of the beast" His words made me slightly nervous. It made me think back to when I first landed in Japan. I came for a competition and a bit of a laugh and vacation. Now I was up a storm ridden mountain with a valley full of the bodies of dead beasts, armed with an ancient sword and a five hundred year old samurai's spirit guiding me throughout the way.

It's funny how things pan out!

The door creaked as I slid it open. The inside was not as horrific as it was in my dream. There was no signs of bodies strewn about as it was in my nightmare. A good sign as the demon was not yet about and feeding.

"Arrrrgh! Let me go!" came a high pitch feminine voice that came from nowhere. Momoko! My heart became filled with hope as this meant she was still alive and the fact that she was screaming so loudly meant that she was not seriously hurt in any way.

Where did it come from though? Remembering my dream I turned to face where the hole to the demon's domain should be. True enough it was there; the rubble that was previously the blockade to this entrance was scattered as if blown away by some mighty explosion.

"Through there" said Yoshida, "that's the inner sanctum. There is where we will save Momoko and hopefully the world"

Cautiously I stepped through the gap and steadied myself before descending down the steps. Moss covered and narrow, there was a fear of slipping and tumbling down.

The sounds of chanting and the struggling of Momoko began to hit my ears, the ritual was starting. It was now that I needed to intervene.

"Wait!" said Yoshida, "We still need to advance cautiously, we do not want to for prey to a trap. I believe that the enemy knows we are here."

"I understand" I said, angry at not being able to quickly save Momoko, worried that every moment that is spent moving cautiously would mean that I would miss the chance of saving Momoko.

As I entered the inner sanctum at the bottom of the stairs, It opened out into a vast expanse. At the far end of the cavern was a giant pool, braziers around the edge reflected upon its surface and the room was alive with the dancing flickering off its surface upon the roof of the cavern. Around the outside were suits of armour, ancient and antique in their own right, sat upon seats of stone. These empty dead suits had scary death masks that was lifeless and empty. By each of these was a weapon as old as the suit itself. They were varied, spears, halberds, swords. Old, yet surprisingly well maintained and devoid of rust.

In front of the pool was a giant table of marble; upon this lay Momoko, she was restrained by rope upon its cold surface, wriggling frantically she was trying to escape but her efforts were futile as her bonds were too strong.

Before her was a man, dressed in long ropes, marked with symbols that I did not understand. His head was covered by a tall hat, wide at the top. His back was to me, and his hands in front of his body, concealed from my view.

The chanting continued and as he chanted, his voice grew louder and louder, it crescendo up until it reached its highest peak. His frenzied voice sounded like it was speaking in tongues of three or four languages at the same time.

Without hesitation or break from his chanting he raised his hands up in the air above his head. In his grasp was a short sword that had the blade pointed downward at the victim beneath it.

"No!" I cried loudly. Lunging forward quickly I thrust my sword ready to spear this mysterious priest. "Stop! Wait!" screamed Yoshida as I acted rashly.

I should've heeded my charge, Yoshida was right, it was a trap as the priest was waiting for me. Spinning on the spot, his sword swept across parrying my blade and knocking me aside. Stepping back I readied for the next strike. He stood there laughing at me. Taking a good look his supposedly evil eyes were wide and as cheerful as if he had seen an old friend.

"By the gods" said Yoshida, it was as if he's seen a ghost...

"Fujibayashi!"

"Fujibayashi?" I asked, as surprised as he is. "How can this be?"

Fujibayashi spoke, his light tones were practically unnerving. "Hello Yoshida, or should I call you by your hosts name...Jason."

"Either is fine, we are one and the same." I said defiantly. Fujibayashi just laughed as if I had intentionally said something funny.

"How is it you're still alive?" I asked. Trying to make sense of it.

"Ah, Yoshida, but that is simple. I was never a man, I was always something else. You see, from the very beginning all those years ago when we first met, I've been preparing for this moment. For I wanted you to see the end of times when the demon Wanshu becomes unstoppable.

Have you not ever wandered why I was always so talented? Surely even you could've seen that my swordsmanship was beyond that of the ordinary man. But then again, I didn't realise until our time together that so was yours. So much skill and talent, I even wondered whether or not you could've been a demon just like I am and not know it, but then I would be reminded of your sickening sense of duty and your disgustingly righteous outlook to protecting the innocent; then it reminds me that you were always just a man. It was nice to travel with you back in the days, I've managed to learn so much from you. I thank you for those times…"

"But why Fujibayashi? Why not kill me when you had the chance, when I did not suspect you of being the vile monster that you are? Back then you surely would've had the chance to do so."

"Now, there's no need for insults Yoshida. Two reasons really, firstly, even back then your skill was just too good, although my talent was fuelled by my demon blood, yours was just natural, it was the reason why you were born. Back then I couldn't just kill you, it would've been a futile exercise. Secondly, if I'd have killed you, then life back then just wouldn't have been as fun really! Imagine all the adventure we would've missed out if I'd snubbed out your pitiful existence back then.

I've always been around you, guiding you now like you used to guide me back then." With that his appearance changed, his body shifted until it was not Fujibayashi. First, he changed to appear like the man we saw at the temple, then the waiter at the restaurant, the Jingasa salesman from when we went to see Genki, to the policeman at the foot of this mountain before returning to his original form. It was true, he had been with us all the while.

We began to circle slightly, keeping distance from one another, maintaining swords in deadly positions as we continued our *discussion*.

"But you killed your own kind? How were you able to live with that?" I asked cynically.

"Because what we faced were lesser creatures than me. You see, the demon world is more fickle than you realise. Their deaths were all part of the grand scheme of things and for them to die wouldn't have changed anything" He said theatrically. "Did you not ever wander how events panned out? Even back then, how we managed to get ourselves facing Wanshu in the first place. It was all orchestrated by me. Even that Kamaitachi you fought on the bridge in Kakogawa..." he paused as he drew my attention in fully. Yoshida went silent, for he never revealed much detail to Fujibayashi about that meeting.

"*I* am the Master." He cackled manically, laughing hysterically loudly in the reverberant cavern.

"No..." said Yoshida

"And you were under the impression that it was Wanshu! Ha! How short sighted and inept you actually are Yoshida. Supposed Dragon of the Shogun. I am the Master of the guiding the demon world on Earth. I am the Master of your very destiny. It is I who has pulled the strings and brought you back here, for you are merely my puppet!" He spat those last words with such viciousness.

"But why all this now? What is with this resurrection of old events? Couldn't you make Wanshu invincible back then, why all the charades until now?"

"That's a very good question...Let me enlighten you...Back then, us demons didn't have access to the very special sacrifice that's behind me. You see, she is a very special woman, there is only one of her kind every thousand years. Within her she possesses a light energy that is beyond measure. She is a human who has a direct connection with the demon world. A beacon of light and with this blade, she will spill this life into Wanshu and he will rise up to lead the world in a vision of pain and suffering." He ran his hand over Momoko's body, lightly touching the flowing contours. Momoko whimpered with a fearful yelp.

"Not if I have anything to do with it." I shouted, I was ready to kill him. Again.

Fujibayashi attacked first, swinging a variety of flowing strikes with his short sword. The culmination of his original short sword style and the techniques of Yoshida's school. With the length of my longer katana I managed to just hold his strikes at bay. Its length maintaining a safe distance between us, but some of his attacks were still quite close to doing me harm.

"I see you haven't slowed up Yoshida. Even in this boy's body! Still very impressive" Fujibayashi had overemphasised the word 'boy'. Impudent.

"It is this body that will finally put an end to your miserable existence, demon!" returning the favour, added a personal sting in the word demon.

Now it was my turn.

"The Dragon's Dance. Jason. I used it before to beat him, it's sure to work again. Allow me to flow through you, open your mind to me."

With that, I relaxed my body, letting my conscious mind relax with it, Yoshida took this opportunity to fully take over my body. Once there, I could only watch.

Adopting the stance to initiate the ancient technique, confidence filled me. This was where we will stop him and stop the ritual from completing.

Flowing back with a series of strikes of my own, high, low, circling and arcing the razor edge as it cut effortlessly through the air. Fujibayashi backpedalled, circled, jumped and ducked around it. Until it ended with myself dropping to one knee and spinning for the final horizontal cut of the Dance. Now with Fujibayashi behind me all I needed was the sound of the final drop as his miserable body hits the cold stone floor.

But no sound came. Fujibayashi should've died. No one has ever withstood the Dragon's Dance. It was always said to be an unbeatable series of techniques. Then came the cackle of Fujibayashi's psychotic laughter. He was still alive!

Rolling to avoid any sneaky attacks while he was behind me I turned, scornfully to see that he was still standing, pointing the tip of the Emperor Dragon at him.

"How?" thought Yoshida,

"Surprised?" said Fujibayashi "You see, I have had the last five hundred years to see through the weaknesses of your silly technique. Don't get me wrong Yoshida, it *was* a good technique, once, long ago. Now I have developed the secret to beating your 'Dance'!"

Looking round I saw that now Momoko was behind me and with a quick series of slashes backwards I cut her free from her restricting bonds. Throwing the remains of her restraints away she jumped to her feet and ran towards me. Clinging onto my body tightly, embracing me warmly making herself feel safe.

"Are you alright?" I asked bluntly "Are you hurt?" I said, without taking my eyes off Fujibayashi.

"No" she said, sobbing tears of relief into my arm.

"Step back" I said slowly, and she released me to take up position safely behind me.

Angrily Yoshida drove me to leap forward. Thrusting my sword in a determined fashion at Fujibayashi's throat.

He spun around the strike, latching on, grabbing and forcing me off balance, spinning me uncontrollably in a circle one way, then the other; my head kept itself low to maintain focus and the attempt to regain stability until...

Slash! A grisly, wet sound of the cutting through a mass of flesh. A sharp releasing groan of pain followed my cut. My eyes looked up to stare defiantly at Fujibayashi, but they soon dropped when it was not the evil face of Fujibayashi but the pale and beautiful face of Momoko.

Her hands shook as she gripped at the deep cut that had opened up her stomach. No! I thought. This cannot be happening! Dropping to her knees she feel, blood began to fall upon the stone floor like the initial droplets of a rain storm. Fujibayashi's laughter continued to ring out around the acoustically sound cavern as he moved away from us both. Allowing me to have the full impact of the situation consume me.

"Momoko!" I cried, dropping my sword to the ground, its chime mixing with Fujibayashi's incessant cackling. I lost focus on my enemy as he stepped away from us to let me have this 'moment'. Darting towards her I held her in my arms, her head pressing consolingly into my chest.

"I'm so sorry!" I said, as a tear accompanied my words, slowly falling down the contours of my check. "I'm so sorry!" I repeated.

"Don't...don't be sorry...Jason" said Momoko, pain wracking her as she struggled to speak.

"I was meant to save you, I was meant to take you away from this nightmare. But yet you're cut deep by my hand. This is all my fault. I'm sorry Momoko!"

"It's...it's not...your fault. You did your best Jason." She winced loudly. "It's...painful" she continued.

"Shush, don't say that; you'll be fine Momoko, I'll get you out of here." I said reassuringly, trying to reassure myself as much as her.

"It's ok Jason...I'm ready to die...I'm happy that you had the courage to come try and rescue me...just make sure you kill this monster."

She gagged and choked, blood was seeping from the cut in her open stomach. Then with a cough, blood entered her mouth as the haemorrhaging rose up through her. Bubbling through her like the rise of boiling water. It was obvious that she was dying, deep inside I knew that even if I did manage to kill what I was to face quickly, by the time she would've gotten to a doctor or an ambulance the amount of blood she's losing would mean it would be too late for her.

"I'm sorry...that we didn't...get the chance to know each...other better" she said, my heart filled with sadness. "I think...we would've gotten on...very well." She attempted a smile, blood trickled down from the edge of her mouth. Her eyes filled with a mix of sorrow and acceptance on the situation.

"I think we would've as well" I offered, trying to smile with her, but it was hard. Then came the voice of Fujibayashi, interrupting this moment.

"How touching Yoshida! It'll be all over for her soon." Looking down at her, her eyes began to flutter, as she tried to keep them open, but the life was seeping away from her too fast.

"No!" I shouted "Stay with me Momoko! You cant die!"

No matter how hard and forceful I willed her to hang on, it just wasn't enough. Her eyes continued to close and as they shut fully she let out a final breath and then it was over. Mourning controlled me, I began to cry, sobbing softly at first and then losing control of my emotions altogether.

The cavern shook itself violently, as if an earthquake had suddenly hit the mountain. Loose debris fell around the edge of the cave with a thunderous crash. Fujibayashi continued his initial chanting, matching the noise of the cave with his mysterious words. All the while, I couldn't take my eyes off Momoko's beautiful face. Bending my head down, I gave her a small kiss upon her forehead before laying her down upon the floor. Although the life had left her shell, she still appeared as if she was glowing with warmth. As if she was simply asleep.

Without warning the chanting and the shaking of the cave stopped together.

"Thank you Yoshida. It is done."

'Thank you?' I thought, how dare he.

"Thank you for completing the ritual of awakening and fulfilling your purpose in life...and soon death" he said, triumphant and arrogantly, he continued,

"You are truly inept, blind to the bigger picture. How I laugh at you! You pathetic excuse for the 'enlightened.'" I could hear his footsteps as he circled around. His pace as if he was doing a leisurely stroll. I could feel his eyes looking at me and I could feel the pleasure he was getting.

"It is your sword, not mine, the Emperor Dragon, that we, the demon world, needed to complete the ritual of awakening and purification." He said "Again I have been able to fool you and make you dance to my very whim. That sword you carry was what the Great Dragon used to bind Wanshu's true powers within before time and history began, during the immortal wars of man and beast. Long before the record of history began.

In order to release him, it needed to spill the light of the gods with the powerful essence of the great Dai Oni. Defiling the purity of its edge. And thanks to you that goal has been achieved!

Not only have you awoken my Master, but you have also killed the one that your host loved. Now he can feel the same pain and suffering that I'm sure you felt when you were unable to save me the first time round. The only difference is, is that she isn't able to come back!" Again he cackled as he taunted me, my sense of mourning was slowly being replaced with hatred. A vile mix of hate, anger and contempt; with every part of my soul I wanted to drive this sword through Fujibayashi's dark, cold, blackened heart.

"All you had to do was to stay away Yoshida. All you had to do was to stay quiet and leave this poor boy in peace. But no! You just weren't able to resist the temptation to return to the old life. How did it feel for you Yoshida? How did it feel to have another chance of killing the monsters that lurk in the dark? I bet it felt good! There's also that annoying sense of honour and duty that you have ruining your chances in life. All you wanted to do was to put yourself at peace with yourself for being unable to 'save' me. Have a look where that got you!" He threw his arms our wide, emphasising the futility of Yoshida's pride and his sense of duty. Yoshida remained deathly silent.

"You used him Yoshida! You used this poor boy just for your own means and now he's the one who's suffering. He'll continue to suffer now until the end of his days. He's just a boy, did you really think that he'll be able to handle himself against the might of the demon world? Against the might of Wanshu himself? Remember how difficult it was to kill him the first time round and that was with the two of us! You are nothing but foolish! Such stupidity!"

Anger now raged up inside me, it bubbled wildly like an unwatched pot over a burning fire. There was an area of me that listened to Fujibayashi's words, partly it rung true. I was just a pawn in all of this. Was Yoshida's intentions justified in the end? Right now, I didn't care, all that mattered to me now was being able to feel the bitter taste of revenge. Revenge for me, revenge for Yoshida but most of all, revenge for Momoko.

"It will be this boy that will kill you Fujibayashi." My words spoke with pure malice. "I will kill you for all those who you deceived and I'm gonna enjoy watching you die!" My head turned slowly. My eyes burned with the passion that comes with anger, I willed them to burn through Fujibayashi.

"Boy! You are nothing of a threat to the larger scheme of things. In fact, you could even join us! Why be on the losing side? You have potential, I can see that. We can banish Yoshida out of your head and you can become like a king! Serving the dark powers, everything can be yours. Join me as my master awakes and he will grant you amnesty as he lays waste to the pathetic world of man. I will show to him that it was *you* that brought the Emperor Dragon. He will see that you are a vital piece of the puzzle." He offered his hand gracefully in front of him. "Just take my hand Jason. Put down your sword and take my hand and become a king among the lands of men!"

"How about I take your hand with my blade before taking your head!" I yelled, rushing to my feet, grabbing the sword and charging wildly at him. A man possessed with anger there was no skill or technique in my attack. Only the sure burning will to kill Fujibayashi.

Through the red mist that consumed me I didn't know what happened next. Before I knew it, I found myself on the ground, my sword sliding with a metallic scrape across the floor out of my reach. Blood ran from my nose, luckily it wasn't broken.

Fujibayashi now loomed over me. His sword positioned against the back of my neck.

"I thought you would've taught him some of the old ways. Taught him the values of emotional restraint. Your lack of skill as a teacher has meant that you will lose today. No, I take that back, you were always a good teacher to me. But after all, we are both Japanese, this boy is nothing more than a foreigner, what does a gaijin know of the true essence of Budo. Your latest pupil is nothing more than a disgrace on the legacy that is Yoshida Kintaro, Shihan of Imamoto Dojo."

The cold steel was like ice on my neck, it feels strange when you know when your time is up. They say that your life flashes before your eyes. This isn't true, as mine didn't and neither did Yoshida's.

"Don't worry Yoshida, I will make this quick for you. Think of it because we were such good friends. You should've taken my hand boy. I would've made you great, everything you ever desired would've been yours. Your foolhardy feelings of love and subsequently revenge has led you to this. Remember that as you progress onto your next life. Now, with the most deepest regret, I must do what I have to do now."

As he finished, he brought the sword back. Allowing it to leave my neck he raised it as high as he could above me. Now was my moment.

With a quick spring I moved to my feet and grabbed him by the throat. With a quick grasp with my hand it resulted in him dropping his sword as I constricted his throat within my fingertips.

"You should learn to focus, Fujibayashi-san. I would've thought that over five hundred years you would've learnt the true value of silence. And the name is not 'boy', it's Jason Lazarus!"

Staring into his eyes, they became two orbs of burning flame. Futilely grabbing my arm, in an attempt to release the pressure he squirmed within my grasp. A worm within a birds beak. Tightening my fingertips, they penetrated the corrupt flesh of Fujibayashi and took hold of his windpipe. Tension came throughout my muscles as my feet gripped the floor. The muscles in my legs and buttocks tightened, my back and shoulders, right down through my arm. As if I was steadying myself to rip a great oak from the ground I pulled with all my might. Drawing from him his oesophagus in a bloody mess as his sticky blood sprayed into the air, throwing his wind pipe away like discarded rubbish.

I kept the contact between our eyes as he fell to the ground with a comforting thud. After five hundred years, he was now finally dead as he wept blood from his open throat that blanketed the stone around him.

"There were some techniques Fujibayashi, that not even you have had the chance to observe. That was one that I kept to myself." Said Yoshida through me, talking to the corpse of what he once considered to be an old friend and ally. But he had once thought that he had passed on before. There was only one way to be sure that he was gone for good.

Returning to my sword, I picked it up again and readied it in my hands. Walking back over to the body of the fallen Fujibayashi a quick vertical stab of its deadly bladed tore through his heart. There was now no argument, he was not coming back to haunt this world again.

Now Yoshida's heart can rest in peace for we exacted vengeance for Fujibayashi's vile betrayal, I took some comfort knowing this as Yoshida was growing to become more of a friend; even if at the beginning I almost believed him to be nothing more than imaginary.

Sheathing the sword with a triumphant scrape of the metal in its sheath, I ran over to Momoko, after all she's been through, it wouldn't be right for her to end up buried in this horrible place of evil. She was too pure and kind a person for that shame.

Picking her up, she was light in my arms. Blood had stained her clothing and her head drooped lifelessly as I held her. Such a heartbreaking sight. Turning with her body, I began to make my way over to the exit. It was time to leave this dreadful place, more of a tomb now than an inner sanctum of the mountain temple.

Slowly I walked with her, the pace set like a funeral parade. With sorrowful eyes I stared at her. Before, I couldn't quite know the same feeling that Yoshida had when he thought that he had failed Fujibayashi. It seems like I will have the same understanding as time goes on. Even now, it was almost unbearable, the thought of being the one responsible for the taking of her life.

She was innocent, beautiful, with her life ahead of her, but now; now she will not be able to live her life and it was my fault.

Reaching the open exit to freedom, before even touching the bottom step, I was stopped dead in my tracks. From the very deep of the mountain came a massive grumble, a groan and roar that rose up mightily.

It was not the mountain itself, it was not the echoes of an earthquake. No. Through my distraction with ensuring that Momoko was not going to spend the rest of eternity here, there was an important detail that left my mind...

It was the Oni, Wanshu, and he was now awake from his eternal slumber.

Chapter 28 – Wanshu the Oni.

M y feelings went as heavy like lead, sinking to new lows as the demon stirred. This was not going to be pleasant by any standards.

Gently placing Momoko down by the steps there was a moment where I silently promised her that she will not have died in vain. I will not allow whatever comes to leave this place and cause havoc on the world. Even if it costs me my life, like how Momoko needlessly sacrificed hers.

I stroked her hair, soft it was in my fingers. Such a waste it was.

After my brief moment, I went back to the main focus at hand. Slowly I turned around. The pool was now bubbling and splashing wildly, water was spilling everywhere on the cold stone. It changed colour, from a beautiful shimmering blue to a blood red. Now it resembled more along the lines of a molten pool of lava, as if with every second it was getting hotter and hotter.

From the thrashing pool emerged forth a beastly hand, the size of which being like that of an adult torso. Thrusting forth from its surface, gripping the air as it grasped for life, its deep red flesh touching air for the first time in over five hundred years. On the end of its five fingers was a large talon, jet black as obsidian and as sharp as any sword. The owner stretched them, flexing them to release the tension build in the powerful muscles from its age old hibernation.

Soon more of the beast appeared, bringing itself into view. Then the main bulk of the demon burst out of the pool, roaring loudly it shook his mane of blood red hair violently, shaking off the clinging water like a wet dog.

And there he stood. His mammoth mass loomed high in the cave as he towered at least three times my height. It was just like I saw him in my dream, it was his eyes however that disturbed me; a piercingly dirty yellow with slanted pupils that were as black as the darkest of nights. From here I could feel the purest of hatred and malice that were contained within their darkened pools. Where his heart would be, if indeed you could say that a demon of such evil has one, would've been black and lifeless; it bore had a scar on its chest from where Yoshida had pierced it so many years ago with the Emperor Dragon and banished him the first time round.

In its right hand he carried an axe of giant proportions to match his extended size. The long wooden handle that stretched from the floor to his shoulder was blackened as if it were charred in flame. The head of the axe too was made gigantic but unlike the charred effect of the handle it were joined onto, it was made of a cold steel that was polished to such an extent that its surface was as if it were a mirror. The long curving edge of the weapon appeared to be as razor sharp as a fine sword but there were chips along it that sort of spoilt the near perfect image of the axe head.

"Welcome Jason..." he growled coarsely "And welcome again Yoshida...old friend. I know you are here for it is written that our paths would cross once more. Jason, my name, is Wanshu the greater demon, master of all Oni, the devourer of man." Wanshu's voice was deep like a rolling thunder, his voice carrying with it the sting of death itself as he rattled off the numerous titles that he had bestowed upon him.

"I know who you are and what you are demon! And this time, I will be the one to end your existence in this world!" I screamed at him, it was because of him, because of his existence that Momoko had lost her life. I was determined to ensure that he will not leave this cave as long as I was still breathing. He will not feel the warmth of the sun on his flesh and that this cave, this underground temple will be his tomb once more.

Wanshu laughed, "You pitiful insect! A boy like you has no chance of killing me! I think you will find that you will not live past today." Wanshu lifted his monstrous leg high, as he stepped out of the pool which was his coffin for so long.

"This time, Yoshida, things are a little different. For I now possess the Light of the Gods within me. You have restored to me the power that I once had and more! Not even your special sword can help you now." Said Wanshu, willing me to admit defeat.

"In either case, I will do everything in my power to ensure you do not descend upon this world once more." I replied

Again, Wanshu laughed. "You have spirit boy and I can see the fires of passion in your chest, I see it burns like a furnace…admirable but often leads to foolishness." He looked over to Fujibayashi's lifeless body lying still upon the cold, damp stone of the cave. "You managed to kill Fujibayashi. Which I can tell you, is no easy feat. You could become an important and powerful asset to my cause…" Wanshu smiled, showing a mouth full of sharp, pointed, dirty teeth.

"But even I can see that it would be pointless to attempt to convert you to my quest. Fujibayashi was right, you would've been treated like a king, a GOD even, among your people! But you would rather throw that away to avenge the life of an insignificant human, this girl is merely a tool; an instrument of the gods themselves to set me free from the bondage of death. I think foolishness comes with that heart of yours. Allow me to show you the error of your mistakes."

"Please, I am in need to be taught a lesson…" I said, grabbing the handle of my sword, ready to draw it again. It's bloodshed would not quite be finished for the day and I required its lethal services one more time.

The beast swung the axe at me but I jumped back safely out of his reach. Although he was big and powerful, his attack with the heavy weapon was comparatively slow and cumbersome. With my speed and skill I would find it easy to outmanoeuvre him.

Again he swung it at me in a mighty double handed grip. This time I took the opportunity to relieve him of his weapon. I ducked under the blow and with a well timed strike I cut up at the thick wooden shaft of the axe. The Emperor Dragon surprisingly cut through it, almost perfectly save for a few minor splinters at the outer edge of the shaft and the heavy axe head was sent flying. With the intense might of the demon behind it, it soared through the air before crashing noisily with a tremendous bang and rumble into one of the displayed armour sets a the edge of the cave. The impact decimated the display with consummate ease and the noise that was made echoed thunderously with the acoustics of the cavern.

I couldn't help but smile triumphantly as I stepped back out of combative range. With a quick flick I returned the sword into its sheath ready for another draw and slash. Wanshu stared at the end of the shaft that he still kept hold of like a puzzled child over a broken toy before casting it aside with an outburst of rage. Discarding it with a clatter on the ground. He glared at me, angered at the loss of his weapon and frustrated that I was still alive and well with the upper hand.

I ran toward Wanshu, my steps quickened into a battlefield sprint, I moved towards him like an arrow, ready to pierce his cruel heart. As I got within striking distance of the demon I pulled my sword out, drawing and slashing in a singular motion. My strike bounced off its thick hide leaving no cut or visible wound. Again and again I tried to cut and slash the demon. Every time I hit him, I was greeted with the same disappointment of my sword bouncing and gliding harmlessly off his hide.

My heart was sinking as I saw the tide of this battle change direction. The feeling of hope was leaving me as my efforts were being shot down at every strike. In a last act of desperation I lunged forward at him, putting every ounce of strength, every last thought of willpower that I had, hoping to find a weak spot that I could penetrate. With a sudden jolt I was halted as Wanshu caught and grabbed my sword in its behemoth hand.

Pulling hard and frustratingly I couldn't budge it from his grasp. The blade wasn't cutting into his palms either and it was stuck steadfastly within its iron grip. With a quick twist of Wanshu's wrist, his herculean strength snapped the blade clean in half and with its other arm he threw me back across the cavern with a powerful backhanded swipe, to hit hard against the cavern wall. The impact was such that ribs broke and blood vessels ruptured as I fell to the ground with a painful thud.

Blood filled my mouth and I spat out its salty essence upon the floor in random spatter. Peering at the small collection of bloody spots, it seemed hopeless and was as though I knew what the outcome of our encounter would be before it had ended.

"You see! Now I am more powerful than before! Not even your blade has the power to even cut my flesh, let alone kill me. Give up Jason, you are just no match for me now."

My temper rose up, driven by the pain of my ribs I tried to stand. A shoot of pain made my senses go white as I collapsed with a short yelp again to my knees. Wanshu rumbled a terrible laugh at my pain.

"How pathetic your human body is. So fragile. See how it breaks easily under my might. I gave you the chance to join me at my side. You had the opportunity to become someone great that your fellow man would bow down at your feet. You would only have answered to me and no one else. But now look at you! Nothing more than a failure, you have failed yourself, your woman and now your world is doomed."

Looking down to Momoko who was laid near me, her body was cold and still like a sad picture. Regret washed over me, I was failing her again and shamefully. I now didn't possess my weapon, my body was broken and worse of all my heart was now empty of anything that resembled positive feelings.

My body was crumbling on the inside. Several places inside of me were now suffering from internal bleeding. My eyes closed, the light around me faded into darkness as everything became blurry and I slowly slumped onto the ground. It was coming close to my time to die, my time for my life to be extinguished and myself and Yoshida can rejoin the great continuum that was the afterlife. Perhaps I too would become reborn in some other poor soul and damn them to continue in the life and path of a demon killer. Maybe my new host will be more compliant sooner than I was. I hope so for their sake. That was my problem, I should've listened to Yoshida; I should've accepted what was going to happen so that I could've prepared myself better. Maybe then I might've been able to protect Momoko.

The world was turning white. A high pitched choir of silvery high notes was all that could be heard. The sound entered my body and nothing it seems could've drowned it out. I was at the brink of death itself.

But wait, this can't be the end. This wasn't how everything was supposed to end up. I was supposed to walk away from this the hero! It is supposed to be Wanshu that is lying lifeless on the cold stone floor. The shame of the thought is just too much.

Momoko. The name repeated itself, as if echoing in my head.

No. I cannot let her down. She must not have died in vain. I will not fail her!

A powerful warmth exuded from my core as if my soul had become fully nourished and enriched with a sense of well being. A new found energy flourished inside, it seemed to numb the pain that would've been overpowering to anyone else that would have felt it. It was a spiritual anaesthetic, the thought of her brought me back from the abyss of death and returned me to the material world. Returned me to the cave and back in the presence of the demon, her murderer.

Anger and adrenaline mixed together in a powerful cocktail, my pain receptors shut themselves down, the pain disappearing completely and I was able to come to my feet. My body, now felt as though it was fresh and alive, it felt new. It felt strong, and this energy was accompanied with a pleasing warmth. Even Yoshida's voice fell silent within me whether he chose to be so or that I had somehow unconsciously blocked him it remained unclear.

Clearing my mind, focusing purely on Wanshu, my face changed to that of one of pure, malicious hatred. Hatred for him, what he was and everything indecent that he stood for and represented. Good was going to triumph over evil here, the age old battle between these two cosmic imbalances was to continue with us.

My eyebrows furrowed to a point, the edges of my mouth turned up into a sadistic smile. I was preparing myself to really hurt the demon, I was going to destroy him and his very essence. I could only imagine that it would appear quite disturbing for anyone to witness it.

A voice entered my mind. I did not know it and without being able to speak to Yoshida I could not get any clarification from him to see if it was familiar. It spoke, saying;

"The bearer of the Emperor Dragon, will become such that even he would not have to use it. The sheer essence of the bearer will overpower the darkness."

Such a message I was not given much chance to decrypt as Wanshu had quickly noticed that I had not passed from this world into the next and was soon upon me. Dodging my head I moved out of the path of Wanshu's fist that came flying with such force. It crashed into the wall behind me, sending debris flying around me and bouncing off me harmlessly.

With another forceful swing he swung at me, this time I dived gracefully out of its path, rolling fluidly and standing back to my feet with ease.

Wanshu turned angrily, full of frustrated hate and struck again. His gigantic fist shuttling at speed and would surely drive me into the ground.

Confidence in myself consumed me, as soon as I had returned to my feet I felt somewhat different; as if no longer 'Jason Lazarus'. With a solid thrust I stepped forward and struck my palm against the incoming fist filling it with the purest of contempt, a bitter hatred for his very existence and the will to stop this dark monstrosity.

A solid thunderous crack and a flash of white light that was blinding erupted as my overshadowed palm and his gargantuan fist collided. I stood strong while the lumbering Wanshu was surprisingly staggering back with a painful growl.

"H...How?" he stammered, before composing himself again and releasing a tirade of blows. Each was blocked by my hands and arms which came out unscathed where they should've been annihilated. The last strike from the demon I blocked him, my defence aimed at one of his sinisterly cruel talons, shattering the boney claw with ease in a bath of light. Splintered bone came off in all directions, the light illuminating each individual splinter, that as they burst forth looked like an exploding firework.

Wanshu moved away in stunned silence, clutching hard at his hand with the shattered talon; as a demon, I was sure that he's seen some unexplainable things in his time but not even he could fathom a reasoning for what was occurring. I was sorry to say that not even I could enlighten him, it was a mystery to me! But I wasn't complaining, oh no, for now I was in the perfect position to avenge Momoko. She was my driving force for destroying this hideous creature.

"The tide has turned demon" I said, coldly and calculative and indeed they have.

"I don't know what manner of sorcery you've employed human but it will not be enough. Now I will destroy you!"

He lifted his arm ready to hammer down on me. As he did so I jumped in the air, the distance I covered was unnatural and I slammed my fist into its chest. A rupture of light and sound sent shockwaves that rippled through the dense cave. Wanshu screwed his face up with a tremendous pain as he hurtled backwards against the far wall.

"Rarrrrr!" he roared, pain stricken. "This is not possible!" he cried painfully "With the Light of the Gods I should be unstoppable! That is what is written!"

"Your end is nigh beast, enjoy these final moments in this world. They will be the last, you will not live long enough to have the light of the pure sun warm your diseased hide."

With another quick jump I dived at him again. As he was slumped on his knees he did not have the agility to move out of the way. Making another fist I sent the bottom part of it hammering down upon his skull.

"Noooooooo!" he cried,

A blast of warm light bathed us as Wanshu's death cry was soon followed by the horrific crack as his skull collapsed under the sheer power. His mangled body fell from my fist as I landed.

The cave resumed silence again, I was now the only living thing left standing. From Wanshu little spotlights shone from sections of his body. Like a disco ball came the little white lights that grew bigger and bigger, they widened until they met with their neighbours. Soon his whole body was just a source of white light.

Boom! The body of Wanshu exploded, the shockwave was large, the air that was blasted blew my clothing and hair back as if in a gale. Still I remained like a living mountain, the air flowing around me dynamically. The flesh of Wanshu catapulted out, varying from large chunks to smaller specks before burning out of existence like ash.

The cave shook again, like it did before, but this time much more violently, rock and rubble fell dangerously from the ceiling. The shockwave had unsettled the cavern and it was coming down around me. One falling stone had crushed one of the armour suits that were on display, such a waste of an antique Yoroi that would've been priceless to any collector or museum. Stone stalactites threatened to skewer me as they crashed noisily to the ground. Cracks appeared along the cave floor, harmless at first before opening up into great precipices. The watery pool broke open and water drained quickly upon the cavern floor.

I needed to get out of here before this place became *my* tomb! Running over to the entrance, I stopped momentarily to pick up Momoko and I held her in my arms. Pushing my way up the stairs, back into the temple topside. Wall hangings had already fallen haphazardly and littered the floor.

A bulky, wooden ceiling support fell in front of me, blocking my way. Clambering over the blockade, more and more of the building was collapsing around me. Run! I thought.

Bolting out of the door, I only just made it in time before the temple fully fell into a heap of ruin. Dust and fine debris blasted out of the doorway as it finally collapsed and then became very still.

Panting slightly, I took a quick breather. Momoko still in my arms. I was gladdened slightly by being able to bring her out of that dark hole. Though this lifted me slightly, it was only slight as it didn't replace the sadness and the shame that I bore for being responsible for her death.

"I am sorry for your loss." Said Yoshida, it was the first time he had spoken since the fight with Wanshu. It felt reassuring hearing his voice again. That I wasn't alone once more on the mountain top.

"You do not need to feel sorry Yoshida. It was my fault, my responsibility for me to bear." I said, slightly stung with myself.

"No Jason. You do not need to bear the whole of it yourself. I once felt what you are feeling. Mourn for her loss yes, but do not let it consume you like I once did." Yoshida was trying his best to provide me with some comfort. However, I wasn't in the right frame of mind to accept any words from anyone. It was too soon to hear words of this nature.

"Now is not that time. You have had your retribution today Yoshida, now I must hope that I can find mine someday." My tone was solemn. It was normally not of my own, once cheerful nature.

Picking up Momoko once more, I peered up at the sky above. With the sun replacing the dark clouds that once circled the summit I took a prayer to the gods, asking them to grant forgiveness upon me and with small and shuffling, exhausted steps, we began our descent down the mountainside.

To whatever awaits us.

Epilogue

Every step down the dreaded mountain side riddled my body with essence of pain. Physically, from the confrontation as the adrenaline had began to die down and as such return to me the activity that my pain receptors had been going through all along. Also emotionally, as with every step I peered down at the beautiful face of Momoko and the thought of her passing stabbed deep within myslef, as if several knifes were poking their way around my insides. On both accounts it was reassuring to feel it for it reminded me that I was still alive and out of the nightmare.

The sun glistened beautifully upon her, reflecting delicately off the fine contours and the elegant shape of her face. How could I have let this happen?

The leaves rustled and crunched underneath the weight of my feet as I descended the hallow slope. Around me, in the trees, the birds had returned to song; now the mountain side was safe and all was well. Their songs however did not interest me in the slightest as I was already starting a state of mourning for the loss of Momoko. A loss that I knew deep down I could've prevented.

My thoughts drifted to the short time that we had spent together, flashing back and forth from the time that we first met at the welcoming dinner on the first few days of arriving in Japan; to the time that I watched her asleep after sending her back off to sleep from her heavily interrupted slumber of nightmares.

I should've picked up on it all then; I should've seen the connection that night but I didn't. Fujibayashi was right, I was blind to the bigger picture, such a connection was blatantly obvious. I wasn't able to protect her back then and I wasn't able to protect her when it really mattered.

"Jason-san. It was not your fault that Momoko-san lost her life today. Always remember that it was Fujibayashi's treachery and cunning that deceived us all, myself included in that. You were not to know that she was the chosen host of the fabled light of the gods. You and I both knew that if you had known sooner, then you would've stayed at her side and allow no harm to come to her." Yoshida's comforting words were not having the desired effect. "Mourn for her passing, but do not let it control your life like it once did to me. Take comfort in the fact that you were able to avenge her death and save the rest of mankind from its impending doom."

"But if I was able to save her, then there would've been no need to avenge her death. Or even save the world for that monster as it would not have been able to have been brought back to life." I spat angrily at Yoshida.

"You have retained your honour Yoshida-san. You can be at peace now, it seems that I now have to carry the burden of her death. This is the way of your concept of Karma. Do not try to deny me of that task nor of the blame; it is my fault she is dead."

I stopped briefly and placed Momoko's body on the ground. It was clear to me that my body needed some rest as the pain had reached almost unbearable limits and I was close to collapsing. A cool breeze stole the harshness of the bright sun away and it allowed me time to gather my thoughts together.

I was interrupted by a strange male voice that came from the tree line "I am sorry for your loss Jason-san. The death of such an innocent girl should not have to be on anyone's conscious."

My head darted quickly from side to side to discover the source of this intrusion. "Who said that?" I called out, still unable to locate where it originated from as I glanced around at ground level.

"My name is Sango." He said, as he spoke my ears picked up the source and my head turned sharply to target it. Crouched on a thick branch of one of the surrounding trees there indeed was a man. Dressed head to toe in black and cream robes, save for his face that was only half covered by a silk head scarf across his nose and mouth, he perched on this branch like a bird. Sticking out on a sheath on his back I could see was the handle of a sword.

Springing up to my feet, I stood in a defensive stance ready to receive him if I must. He raised one hand in a friendly gesture. "Please, Jason-san *and* Yoshida-san, I mean you both no harm." Sango spoke gently and passively.

"Are you not a demon?" I asked, still inquisitive as to the actual nature of this stranger who somehow knows my name and no doubt my purpose at this dreadful place. It was difficult now to distinguish between man and beast as I knew now that the demon can take human form very easily.

"No." he chuckled. "I am not a demon...I am a shinobi of the clan of Koga ninja. I am one of the last traditionally practicing members of my family's style. I am a friend." He offered.

"How do you know both my name and Yoshida's? If you are not a demon there is no way that you would know who lies within me."

"I know a lot more about you both than you may think. My profession is based around the gathering and collating of information. In the picture of the infinite cosmos, you two are very special and there are other ways of finding out your identities."

Still, I eyed him with suspicion; for I did not know what was real and who to trust anymore. His explanation also, was not entirely satisfactory. Everything I had experienced tends to tear away at one's sense of reality "What do you want?" I barked.

"I have been sent by my masters to investigate the status of the beast Wanshu, as we heard the news that the ceremony of awakening was taking place here at this time. Your exploits are no secret to our organisation

Jason and also, to see if you have survived such an encounter with the Dai-Oni; which I am happy to say you have.

If you hadn't, then it was to be my mission to do everything in my power to ensure that he was not able to experience the light of day once again. Even if said actions cost me my life." He nodded his head with light admiration that I was able to perform such a feat and perhaps relieved that he didn't have to. "It is a sad thing to see that the light of the gods was contained in such an innocent girl and her death is truly a sad affair. The gods themselves can have the tendency to play little games like this as a test to the strength of mans will."

What right did he have to talk about Momoko? He doesn't have to cope with her death and her blood on his hands as I did. He couldn't comprehend how deeply this has cut into me, how deeply this would scar me once the dust has settled and the word of the events that happened here died away to mere whispers.

"It seems however, that with the slaying of both the demon Fujibayashi and the Dai Oni Wanshu, that I am able to report good news back to my masters." Sango spoke with joy in his voice. Perhaps he is trustworthy, though I didn't want to take a chance at it as it could still be an elaborate ruse.

"Who are your masters? I thought you said you were the last of your clan?" I asked. With all the recent talk of 'masters' I was becoming quite sceptical whenever I heard the word mentioned and if I didn't hear that word for the rest of my lifetime, I would be quite happy.

"I am one of the last. But my masters are not fellow Koga, more so, they are members of a heavenly council of mankind that operate for the sole purpose of ridding this world of the demon and its kin. It's name I am unable to disclose to you now, perhaps I have already told you too much but you are not like the average man. You have seen the demon with your own eyes and have fought it with your own hands and shed your own blood to eradicate it. There is something about me that says that you could be one of the foretold Heaven's Reborn, if so then you are either a blessing or a curse."

"But I have destroyed the Oni. The world is now safe...Isn't it?" I said, hoping that he would simply reply with 'yes' but I knew in my heart that he probably wouldn't.

"The world is never completely safe." Replied Sango. "There are more than just the Dai-Oni Wanshu that exist. The council that I am a member of, deal with the demon on a global scale. Do not be naïve to think that demons only reside on the island of Japan. With your experience and skills, you could become a valuable asset to their struggle to protect mankind." Sango raised an eyebrow, trying to gauge whether his offer had interested me. It had not.

"No Sango. I do not wish to do any more of this. An innocent girl has lost her life because of me where she could've easily been saved. Her death is on my mind and mine alone and it would be disrespectful to her name if I continued this pursuit and possibly put more innocent lives in jeopardy." I expected Yoshida to interject and try to persuade me otherwise, as he was prone to do but he surprised me by staying silent.

"That is a shame that you think in such a way Jason-san. Please realise and understand that the world we live in is always in constant danger and attack by the creatures of the dark realms. One day, the council of the Brotherhood will summon you because of your unique talents and purely on the level of exposure that you have been given to the demonic. You will hopefully see the importance of this action and you will join the ranks of the Brotherhood in order to fight them. You may not like it, but then again, when you are faced with adversity you either stand up or crawl on your knees...I think I know which one your spirit will agree is the right one." Sango eyed me up and down, a look of puzzlement followed as if something were amiss. "May I ask you. What has happened to the Emperor Dragon Sword? I know you entered the shrine with it, but yet you do not have it on your person now."

I stared up at him in his lofty perch. "The Emperor Dragon Sword is lost. It has been snapped into two parts and its blade is now useless." Sango's eyes widened with shock at this, to him, the destruction of such a sacred sword is practically incomprehensive for him to imagine.

"But how was it that you killed the Oni?" he asked

"The sword was useless after the demon harnessed the power of the gods. So I used my bare hands" I replied coldly.

"How can that be? An Oni is very difficult to kill even with one of the Dragon blades. But especially when it has been instilled with the light of the gods! That's simply impossible!" he raised his voice with disbelief.

"It is true Sango. I do not know how and I do not wish to even offer to you an attempted explanation. Nothing is clear to me anymore; I only want to put this behind me now."

Sango rubbed and scratched at his chin with the purpose of trying to make it easier to think. "Most interesting. It is something that I will need to include in my report." He continued to scratch at his covered chin. "At this moment you do not wish to be a part of this anymore. But one day you will receive a calling and I guarantee that you will respond. Until we meet again Jason-san"

With that Sango leapt up into the canopy of the trees and soon became out of sight.

"I do not think we will see each other again mysterious Sango" I muttered quietly underneath my breath. Realising that Yoshida was still silent I spoke to him softly. "Why didn't you say anything back then? I would've thought that you of all people would've mentioned something when I said that I wasn't interested in his offer."

"Jason-san. You have been through a terrible ordeal that has had some depressing results from it. It would be unfair of me now to try and persuade you otherwise when it comes to your own personal views with what to do with your life from this point. I will always be here with you Jason-san and I believe that Sango is right; one day will come when you will decide to take up his offer and on that day I will still be there with you when it comes to making your decision."

The modesty and compassion held in his words almost brought a tear, but I was able to hold it back. "Thank you for your understanding Yoshida-san. I know that my decision countermands your own personal indoctrination of the ways of Budo, that I too am beginning to experience and comprehend myself. But this is something that I have to do in order for me to even begin to get over the grieving that I will no doubt endure. Thank you again."

"Your welcome Jason-san. It has been an honour to serve with you." He responded, proudly.

With my break over and Sango vanished out of sight, I picked up Momoko once more and continued on my journey down to civilisation once again. From my high vantage point I could see the bustle of the crowd that had gathered again at the base of the hillside. Once more, the police held back the mob of people as paramedics were tending to the injured from the first stampede of the kappa.

I would try to get past the lines of people who no doubt wanted to see what had occurred. Though I'm sure that the were not familiar with the whole truth.

A sudden thought hit me, it was to do with something that Sango had said. He mentioned something obscure about the 'Heaven's Reborn'. At the time I wasn't too intrigued by what it meant or what significance it held as I was too busy voicing my objections. Too much had happened for me to take notice of it. But now that he had gone and my head has had some time to catch up it did hit a nerve, like a bell ringing inside my head.

"Yoshida? What do you think he meant by 'Heaven's Reborn?'" I asked.

"Hmm. I don't know Jason. It is something that I'm not familiar with." He replied honestly. "There is something about it that makes me think we will find out one way or another…"

I cut him off short.

"No! I am not going through all this again! I have killed Wanshu and that is the last of it. The world is safe, I've done *your* duty and it is the last time that I am going to go through this nightmare." Then followed a deathly silence as I shot the subject and even the notion of returning to this path that I had originally had thrust upon dead in its tracks. I was reluctant to do it when I first had it laid upon me and now that the opportunity to step back and away from it was now open to me I was more than happy to attempt to forget the dark underbelly that lurks in the dark recesses of the world.

My life and its path is now in the hands of what tomorrow may bring. All I wanted now however is to be just left in peace.